NINE
MILES
NORTH

NINE MILES NORTH

a novel

Katherine Ann Meyer

EPIGRAPH BOOKS
RHINEBECK, NEW YORK

Paperback ISBN: 978-1-948796-21-7
Hardcover ISBN: 978-1-948796-22-4
eBook ISBN: 978-1-948796-23-1

Library of Congress Control Number: 2018945284

Book design by Colin Rolfe.

Epigraph Books
22 East Market St., Suite 304
Rhinebeck, NY 12572
(845) 876-4861
www.epigraphps.com

NINE MILES NORTH

a novel

Katherine Ann Meyer

EPIGRAPH BOOKS
RHINEBECK, NEW YORK

Paperback ISBN: 978-1-948796-21-7
Hardcover ISBN: 978-1-948796-22-4
eBook ISBN: 978-1-948796-23-1

Library of Congress Control Number: 2018945284

Book design by Colin Rolfe.

Epigraph Books
22 East Market St., Suite 304
Rhinebeck, NY 12572
(845) 876-4861
www.epigraphps.com

to Brian

PART I

The Garret

Pennsylvania, 1776

I T IS IMPOSSIBLE TO OVERLOOK blood on snow . . . even when the snow is neither deeply drifted nor newly fallen and covers a February landscape that has already wearied of winter's starkness.

But while the snow was not fresh, the blood assuredly was.

Constance's heart skipped a beat, increasing its pulsation with rapidity as she sighted the bright crimson anomaly in her father's field. Yet while this gave her pause, what she next spotted near the blemished snow produced an audible, startled gasp. For there, where the barren snowscape gave way to overgrown reeds and tall grasses lining the creek bed, there protruded an arm, as still as death, clothed in brown wool and discernible to the elbow, the rest of it obscured by the dense, lifeless vegetation.

As Constance's hand moved instinctively to cover her mouth, the hem of her skirt tumbled to the snow and was promptly as damp as the edges of her cloak.

After a moment, she regained mastery of her senses, though she never removed her eyes from the unsettling sight before her, and, grasping her skirt once more, she gingerly made her way to the edge of the creek's bank, carefully stepping past the red snow.

Bracing herself for further distress, she peered cautiously past the tall reeds and saw that the grass behind the outermost edge no longer stood tall, but was flattened beneath the weight of a body — the body of a man whose outstretched arm had only a moment ago brought her to a startled standstill.

Although men had been fighting a war for nearly a year now, and though her own colony had seen its share of the conflict, Constance herself had been spared the sight of any violence, and neither had she ever so abruptly encountered bloodshed.

She stood there, transfixed and petrified, uncertain as to what course duty and compassion demanded. She saw no movement, no sign of life, and yet — she could not be certain. The blood had looked so fresh . . .

She took a step nearer the body. Despite the blood on the snow, there was really very little sign of any trauma. One side of the man's upper ribcage appeared to be wet and reddened by a patch of blood, and his right leg was bent into such an unnatural position that Constance knew at a glance it was broken. The man was lying on his back, and Constance found herself scrutinizing his chest, searching for any sign of movement that would indicate life. It was futile, though, from such a distance, as his woolen coat concealed any discernible respiration.

Constance tentatively approached the body, glancing for the first time at the man's face as she crouched beside him. Although his eyes were closed, Constance could see that he was quite a young man, perhaps twenty-five years of age — only a few years older than herself. This revelation somehow increased both her sympathy and her anxiety, for she truly feared that he may be beyond any help which human hands could provide.

She gave no thought to the hem of her frock, which was fully immersed in the shallow snow, as she knelt beside the man, reaching down to unfasten his coat, that she might be better able to feel a beating heart where she could see no evidence of such. But she had barely put a finger to the clasp when she felt a sudden, forceful grip upon her wrist, causing her to cry aloud in terror. It was the man's own hand that had seized her.

Yet, even as his sudden grip had so alarmed Constance, it seemed that her cry had likewise startled him, for at the sound of it, he loosened his grasp. Clearly, he had not supposed the person bending over him to be a lady, and even in his present state of semi-consciousness did he manage to lift his eyelids for the first time. Where he had partially raised up his head and one shoulder in seizing her, he now fell back again into the snow, breathing heavily, his face contorted in pain, his momentary vigor given out.

And yet, when he spoke, his voice betrayed remnants of the deter-mined strength that had allowed him to clasp her wrist so surely. His straightforward words — emanating low between gasping breaths — were as defiant as the gleam in his eye.

"I'll hang before I talk to the Redcoats."

Enough said. Constance's brown eyes lit up in comprehension and dismay.

She glanced back at the red-spotted snow on the other side of the tall grass. She noted horses' hoof prints all around it, and she had no doubts now that the riders had been the same scarlet-coated men who had arrived at her father's house only an hour before, and with whom her father had jovially departed shortly thereafter, none of them ever speaking a word in her presence about this man who had been left in the snow.

Constance spoke to him in a gentle tone, but her quavering voice revealed her inward anxiety. "I — I must fetch someone to help you."

She felt his grip on her wrist tighten once more.

"Not one of *them*," he growled.

Constance hesitated before she spoke again. "You are in Loyalist country here. There are none who share your political views. But there are many who will show compassion to a wounded man and who can render you aid—"

"And then turn me over to their bloodyback tribunal!"

"What does it matter, so long as you are alive?"

Despite the rising urgency in Constance's voice, the man gave her no response, his labored breathing the only sound in the frostily tranquil meadow. Constance was aware that his hand still encircled her wrist, though only loosely now.

She spoke again. "Sir, you need help . . . tending to your wounds . . . and shelter. It will not snow again, but it will turn bitterly cold once darkness falls in only a short while. If you are left here, you will either bleed to death or freeze. There is so little time . . ." And she could not help glancing anxiously toward the already-darkening horizon.

The man lifted his eyelids again and looked squarely into Constance's troubled eyes.

"Then you'd best leave me here to die in peace."

Constance was astonished at this man's persistent audacity in the face of his own demise. Why should he be willing to forfeit his life rather than face the British tribunal? And she was equally confounded by her own reluctance to disregard his willfulness. She knew she ought to have run off long ago to seek the aid he so desperately and so immediately required, regardless of his own irrational objections. And yet, she found her mind racing to try to think of someone — anyone — who might render him aid without the consequence he so adamantly opposed. She could think of only one place, though, where he could evade the fate he was determined to avoid.

During the fractional second that these thoughts passed through Constance's mind, the young man kept his focus trained upon her . . . his eyes defying her to turn him over to his adversaries.

But her next words must have disarmed him somewhat, for she saw the bold gleam in his eye waver. She spoke quietly, but resolutely. "I will take you to a safe place."

And the man allowed Constance to carefully remove his hand from her wrist as she thoughtfully shifted her focus from his face down the length of his body. He was well-built: tall and broad-shouldered, with a strength that would attest to an able-bodied fitness. Constance knew it would be well beyond her capability to convey such a man anywhere on her own. She must think quickly . . .

The blood from the wound above his ribcage had by that time completely saturated the wool of his coat, and Constance knew she had not the luxury of time for contemplation. Her brow furrowed into an apprehensive frown as her gaze lingered on his awkwardly-twisted leg.

Softly touching the man's shoulder, she tried to sound reassuring, although once again her tremulous voice seemed to reverberate with her pulsing heartbeat. "I am going to fetch someone to assist me." Before the man could protest, she added hurriedly— "Someone whom you can trust. I will be back as quickly as I can."

And before the man could voice either affirmation or objection, Constance rose and hastened away, trying to outpace the trembling which overtook her . . . though whether such trembling was due to fear for the man's life or the burgeoning realization of her own impending predicament, she could not say.

❦

Navigating between sleep and wakefulness, Ethan was at first only vaguely aware of a cold sensation on the left side of his chest. Bitingly cold it was . . . as if his skin there had somehow been laid bare to the snow for a length of time.

But when he managed, with great effort, to force his eyelids open, the sight he beheld was so unexpected that it further hastened the revival of his senses, even before his vision had become fully focused. For the blurred hue he immediately perceived was not the anticipated grey of the Pennsylvania sky far above his head, but rather a conspicuous brown, and much nearer than his eye had been prepared to fix upon.

He heard a rustle nearby, and, turning his head slightly, he glimpsed a large dark shape disappearing into the shadows.

Ethan frowned and returned his gaze once again toward the brownness directly above him. As his vision regained its proper focus and perspective, he saw that what he had expected to be dismal sky was actually a long wooden beam. There were many of them . . . dark brown wooden beams running the length of the ceiling in a low-raftered room where he was lying.

Before he could reach further comprehension of his surroundings, Ethan became painfully aware of the coldness above his ribcage once more. Stinging, pricking coldness; it overshadowed every other sensation before he realized that it wasn't coldness at all, but heat . . . heat throbbing with such intensity that it had momentarily distorted his perceptions of fire and ice. The burning sensation brought a grimace to his face, though he made no utterance, and after what seemed an interminable lapse of time, the pain subsided into a somewhat duller throbbing . . . not pleasant, but bearable for the time being.

There was a grey woolen blanket covering him, and, using his right arm, he pushed the blanket away from his chest in order to examine the source of the pain. There was little to see of any wound, for much of his chest had been bandaged — and very properly — but he could see where the bandages were discolored near his ribcage, where the blood was seeping underneath, although it had not soaked through.

The smallest of movements — turning his head, pushing away the blanket — had taken tremendous effort, for Ethan felt stiff and inordinately weak. He sensed that it would be beyond his present capabilities to sit up or even raise his head. It was an entirely foreign feeling to Ethan, this weakness; he disliked it immensely, and he frowned in fierce determination as he endeavored to muster the strength to sit up. It was then that he felt the other pain — this one as piercing as a dagger as it shot up the length of his right leg.

Cursing and gasping for breath, he fell back upon the pillow, yanking the blanket completely off so that he might see his legs. It took but a glance for him to comprehend the reason for such racking pain. While his upper body had been stripped completely bare, save for the bandages, his lower limbs were enveloped in more than the usual trappings. His familiar breeches had been rolled up above the knee, and below them, his right leg was encased in a rather poorly-bandaged splint.

And then he began to remember . . . a frightened horse, a gunshot, the shallow snow.

But where was he now? Ethan turned his head upon the pillow and surveyed his surroundings.

Although the room was low-raftered, it was spacious and full of various articles, many of them medical in nature. A physician's anatomy chart stood against one wall, and beside it, some narrow shelves filled with what appeared to be small dispensing jars, dust-covered and empty of any contents. He himself seemed to be lying upon a narrow-framed cot, such as might be found in an infirmary, and a tall stool had been placed beside it, apparently to function as a makeshift bedside table, for occupying its small circumference was a roll of bandages, a pair of scissors, and a bottle of brandy.

Whatever sort of infirmary this was, there was nothing to distinguish it as either British or Continental, yet Ethan knew that his chances for survival — or escape — depended on that distinction. He wondered what had become of his pistol . . .

He tensed instinctively as he heard the unmistakable tread of approaching footsteps, soft though they were. Turning his head in the direction of the sound, he realized that the gaping shadow into which the blurry dark mass had earlier disappeared was in fact an opening leading to a descending stairway.

Ethan braced himself for the worst — a glimpse of scarlet emerging from the darkness — but was met instead with another wholly unexpected sight.

Two figures emerged from the stairwell. The first was a young lady — a girl, really, whose years could scarcely number more than twenty. Her slender, graceful figure was arrayed in a tasteful floral-accented gown, and a dainty lace-trimmed cap sat prettily atop her light brown hair. But it was her eyes — large and serious — that Ethan noted. He had the vague impression that he had seen this girl before.

Following her was a woman whose physical appearance stood in stark contrast to the young lady's, for the woman was neither young nor slender nor stylishly attired. Where the young lady's complexion was bloomingly fair, the woman's was darker than the brown wooden beams above them, and splotched with purplish freckles. Her age was reflected by the grey wisps of hair poking out from her head-kerchief, and her garments were nondescript and functional — the common attire of a household slave. Her shape was what made her remarkable, though, for she was nearly as broad as she was tall. Yet she was not winded from her ascent, and one could see at a glance that her ample girth had naught to do with idleness, for the formidable arms emerging from the rolled-up coarse-wool sleeves looked as if they could just as capably lift a barrel as turn a spinning wheel. Ethan guessed that this woman was the blurry dark shape that had rustled away upon his waking.

The young lady approached Ethan, but stopped several feet away from his cot as her eye fell upon the blanket on the floor. There was a gentle reproach in her voice as she spoke.

"You ought not to have removed the blanket. The last thing you need now is to catch a chill."

Her words were hardly enlightening, and Ethan was not particularly inclined to entertain proprieties in his present state. He could not suppress the wryness in the tone of his response: "Yes, well, perhaps you'd be so good as to replace it for me, Miss? I'm a bit out of sorts today, if you hadn't noticed."

The girl remained unperturbed by his brashness and merely nodded serenely, but her thoughtful brown eyes were intelligent, and Ethan was certain that his sarcasm had not been lost upon her. As she stepped lightly toward his cot and picked up the blanket from the floor beside him, he felt a tinge of remorse for his impertinence, and he managed to mutter a civil "I thank you" when she placed the blanket over him.

But he still had no answers . . . no knowledge of his whereabouts. Was this girl friend or foe? And more importantly, was he in the custody of the enemy or his allies?

The girl did not seem to feel a pressing need to provide him with any explanations, although her next statement, unassuming as it was, provided him with more insight than he had henceforth gleaned.

"I . . . I am Constance Jameson."

Ethan's eyes narrowed. "Jameson? A relation of *Doctor* Jameson?"

Constance nodded. "He is my father. You are in his house now."

Her words immediately clarified the situation for Ethan, and how unfortunately. He scowled.

Constance herself seemed somewhat perplexed. "Are you acquainted with my father?"

There was no use in mincing words now. Ethan was not about to endear himself to an adversary. "Matthew Jameson bears no love for the cause of independence. He is well-known to be an ally of the Redcoats in this colony." He was already casting his eye about the room, wondering again where his pistol was.

Constance replied quietly and evenly. "Aye, my father is a supporter of the king's men. And he has no knowledge of your presence here, though you be but two floors above him."

Ethan looked directly into her eyes — his suspicion and disbelief apparent, his newly-formed perceptions suddenly incongruous and disintegrating.

But she met his gaze steadily and said simply, "I told you I would bring you to a safe place. This garret is safe . . . for now." She had hesitated before voicing the last two words, and a fleeting cloud of troubled uncertainty passed over her face.

As for Ethan, this unanticipated revelation raised a thousand new questions in his mind, but before he could give voice to any of them, the girl spoke again. She seemed to have suddenly remembered the presence of the dark woman standing in the shadow behind her.

"This is Jenny." Constance gave a nod toward the stout slave, who said nothing, but only looked at Ethan with a mixture of suspicion and curiosity. Constance went on: "You can trust her. She does not speak, but she understands very well. She helped me bring you here yesterday. She's quite strong for her age."

Ethan didn't doubt that. The woman had the build of an ox in its prime.

Constance's wariness must have been dissolving, for there had begun to be a gentle warmth in her tone and in her eye as she continued speaking. "Jenny put you up on the horse. I tried to help, but 'twas no easy task, as you had lost consciousness by then. I was so afraid that you were . . . you had lost so much blood . . ."

Ethan was not unmoved by the tender concern reflected in the girl's tone as she lowered her eyes, lost for a moment in reflection. When she lifted them again, she spoke tentatively, though her sincere conviction was evident in her entreating look.

"My father could help you, if you'd let him. He is a practiced physician — the best there is."

Even from his pillow, Ethan set his gaze firmly upon her, and, despite the escalating pain above his ribcage, he spoke in a low, even tone.

"Your father would undoubtedly receive a handsome reward for my capture, so if it is profit you seek, run and fetch him now. But I doubt he would deem it necessary to render any sort of medical attention to one whom he expects to see swinging at the end of a hangman's noose."

He caught only a glimpse of the dismay upon her face before the sudden stabbing pain reverberated throughout his body, causing him to wince and clench his teeth, his frame rigidly taught as he clutched at the bandaged wound upon his chest. He could feel the sweat pouring over his face as the lacerating pain gripped his body. He was vaguely aware of a startled gasp beside him, followed by a breathless "Jenny!"

Then . . . something cool and damp upon his perspiring brow.

The searing pain subsided again after a few minutes, but it left him straining for breath, his chest heaving as he attempted to draw air back into his lungs. Even with his eyes closed, he felt as if the room was spinning, and, succumbing once more to the lightheaded weakness of blood loss, his senses plummeted again into an endless black oblivion.

ETHAN AWOKE TO ONE QUESTION dominating his thoughts: *Where were the papers?*

Though it was only the second time he had opened his eyes beneath the long wooden beams of the garret, the appearance and proximity of the rafters no longer disconcerted him. Indeed, he was already agitated before he had fully wakened, for as he regained consciousness, his thoughts had been instilled with the urgency of the present moment, with a vivid reminder of where his priorities lie. *The papers*. Where were they?

Realizing he was quite alone in the room, his immediate inclination was to rise and search for the papers, but one impulsive attempt to shift his leg off the cot sent a jarringly painful reminder of the reason he was thus abed. He glared at his splintered leg — fractured at best, possibly even broken. Then, too, there was the wound above his ribcage, where he had felt the blistering heat of a lead ball tearing through his skin. He frowned as he glanced about the garret. How was he going to escape? It would likely be weeks before he would be able to put any sort of meaningful weight upon his injured leg.

He was strong, though, and no stranger to risk or boldness. But even if he could somehow escape from the garret . . . what then? He knew the location of Jameson's house . . . in the heart of the countryside, miles from the nearest town, and every farm in the vicinity adamantly Loyalist. Ethan knew that the region's allegiance to the Crown had been the reason the British garrison had considered it a prime spot to set up camp not two miles away . . . and why there was so much danger in his own presence.

And what of the girl who claimed he was safe under the roof of the enemy? Was she now in possession of his papers? Of his pistol?

So many questions, and no answers.

From where he lay, he surveyed the room. It was commodiously spacious, and Ethan guessed that it ran the entire length of the house. He could see only one very small window set into the far wall, underneath the space where the two sides of the sloping roof met. From the garret's height, which he knew to be three floors above the ground, nothing except the cloudless sky was visible through the window's glass. The daylight seemed to be fading, though, and as there was no candle, the austere space began to be cast in shadows.

His cot was set against one of the long walls, and though he scanned the remaining perimeter of the room, he could see no evidence of his personal belongings or effects. Reaching below the cot, he felt along the floorboard beneath the space where he lay and was quite gratified when his fingers encountered an object that felt of familiar leather. Straining to pull it out from beneath the cot — for the object was set back near the wall and at a rather awkward angle — he managed at last to extract it and beheld in his grasp one of his own boots. Dropping it onto the floor, he reached again underneath the cot, but even as he rolled a bit onto his side — ignoring the increasing pressure such movement placed upon his bandaged chest — he could not locate the boot's mate, though he was certain it must be under there, beyond his grasp. He wondered if his other belongings were under there as well. If only he could ascertain as to the whereabouts of those papers . . . or if they were even still in existence. He would have preferred to learn that they had been destroyed rather than discover that they had fallen into the wrong hands.

His sharp ears perceived the very first footfall upon the stairs. He turned his eye expectantly toward the stairwell and determined before the ascending figure came into view that the footsteps were not light enough to be the young lady's, and was therefore not surprised to see a dark, kerchiefed head emerge from the shadowy passage.

Jenny. As the slave came fully into view, Ethan was once again struck by the woman's formidable size. She was remarkably nimble, though, for one of her age and proportion, for she was carrying a wooden bucket which might well have been empty, so easily did she bear it up the steps, yet Ethan could clearly see water swirling within it, nearly to the brim.

What had the girl said about this slave woman?

"She does not speak."

It was an unusual thing to have said, yet there had been no disdain in the girl's voice when the words were spoken. And the slave woman did not need to speak in order for Ethan to comprehend the look of suspicion upon her face when she saw his black leather boot lying beside the cot. A morose frown creased her countenance.

As was typical of such a servant, she did not look directly at Ethan, but set about her task — pouring some of the water first into a basin which was propped up in one corner, then filling the pewter tankard which had been placed upon the makeshift table.

As she set the tankard within Ethan's reach, his eye fell upon her earrings; they were not the commonly drab hoops that slave women often wore, but rather dangling ellipses, gleaming so brightly that they looked to be genuine gold. Despite her impaired tongue, Jenny must have been well-favored to own such precious objects.

After completing her task, Jenny set the bucket against the far wall and settled herself upon a stool near the stairway, keeping her eyes doggedly fixed upon the floor.

As the woman remained motionless and her mistress did not appear, Ethan fell back into his previous mode of contemplation.

He generally considered himself to be quite resourceful — indeed, his profession demanded it — and though he had many times extricated himself from perilous situations, he had never before been at such a physical disadvantage as to be forcibly, compulsorily bedridden for any length of time. He knew that until his leg healed enough for him to be able to walk or ride a considerable distance, it would be impossible for him to make his way out of this Loyalist-infiltrated corner of the colony. But was he necessarily even safe within the garret? Could he trust the word of a young lady whose father so ardently supported the ideals of the enemy? In his present condition, it seemed to Ethan that he had little choice. But he must remain wary and watchful. It brought him some small measure of encouragement, at least, to discover that the wound above his ribcage did not throb quite as painfully as it had the previous day, nor did he feel as inordinately weak, although he knew that strength is not soon restored after profound blood loss.

The shadows deepened across the garret as late afternoon turned to dusk, and the very stillness of the space increased Ethan's awareness of sounds in distant regions of the house. None were discernably perceptible; certainly, much of the household activity took place on the ground floor, well below him. But he could periodically hear doors close, an occasional murmur of voices, and once, a resounding clatter, as some unfortunate soul was doubtlessly overly-careless in clearing away the dinner plates.

Then, once again, Ethan was immediately conscious of a footfall upon the stairs — this one so light and graceful, it was assuredly Jenny's young mistress. She was preceded by a soft illumination which, upon her appearance at the top of the steps, was revealed to be a flickering candle, its amiable light casting a warm glow around her. Unlike her indifferent servant, Constance paused when she observed Ethan's vigilant eye upon her.

"Ah, you are awake," she murmured. She crossed toward his cot and set the candle in its base upon the tall stool, beside the pewter tankard. "Jenny will go out and get you some food from the kitchen once we have rebandaged your wound. She must wait until the cook leaves."

This girl truly puzzled Ethan. She had such a gentle, unassuming manner about her — as if it was nothing out of the ordinary that she should be harboring a fallen fugitive in her father's garret — and she carried herself with a natural poise that reflected a degree of quiet self-possession. Even so, as she stepped nearer to where Ethan lay, he saw something else in her thoughtful brown eyes . . . a certain softness . . . a very feminine vulnerability. He had seen it before, in the snow, though only fragments of that memory remained with him. It had caused her to hesitate then, and it did again now, for she glanced into his eyes before moving close enough to be able to examine his bandaged chest.

It was, perhaps, because of that glance and that vulnerability that Ethan's question to her was not issued with the sharpness of tongue that would have reflected his state of mind when he had first wakened with the thought upon his lips: "What has become of my possessions?"

The question was very direct, despite Ethan's deliberate restraint, but if the girl seemed momentarily disconcerted, it was only due to the question's abruptness, for there was no guile or artifice in the tone of her response.

"Your possessions? We had to cut your shirt from you, and the blood had seeped all the way through your coat. Jenny took them both out to the rubbish pile and burned them. Your boots are under your bed." Even as she said this, her eye fell upon the one boot beside the cot, but though she looked a bit perplexed, she showed none of the suspicious contempt that her servant had upon seeing it there. Constance absently pushed it back under the cot.

Ethan scowled to himself. The young lady had once again succeeded — however unintentionally — in providing him with a completely unsatisfactory response. Whether or not this girl was trustworthy, he had at least attributed to her a fair amount of intelligence. Now, his patience fell a bit to the wayside.

"I had some other things . . . personal effects. Were those burned as well?"

And he knew immediately by her reaction that he had not been wrong in his initial assessment of her. This girl was neither foolish nor senseless. She met his level scrutiny with a guileless, comprehending eye, and she spoke with simple, forthright unpretentiousness.

"I should not think that your personal effects would be of much use to you here. But you must not worry. They are quite safe, and whenever you choose to leave from here, I will gladly return them to you."

And Ethan felt as if a knot tightened within his abdomen. It occurred to him that if this girl had indeed been speaking the truth, then he would most certainly have proved himself to be an ungrateful louse. For the second time in this young lady's presence, he felt a twinge of shame. It was a feeling he was not accustomed to, and it rather unsettled him.

Even so, she still had not given him the information he sought. Were the personal effects that were now in her keeping the ones he needed? She had never mentioned the papers, and he could not ask about them outright as long as there was a chance that she had not discovered them. But she must have found his pistol . . .

The girl herself, oblivious to Ethan's restless meditations, had once more shifted her focus to the task at hand. Bending her head to examine the outer bandages encircling his chest, she gingerly put a finger to the bandage, keeping well away from the spot of blood-browned seepage above his ribcage.

"I think we must change the dressing today."

Ethan was not sure if this musing was directed toward anyone in particular, but it was followed by a murmured "Jenny", and he glanced up to see the slave woman — who had risen from her post at the top of the stairs — give a light tug upon one of her dangling earrings and hasten forward to assist her mistress. Or, perhaps it would be more accurate to say that it was the young mistress who assisted, for Jenny did the actual unbandaging, dressing, and rebandaging, while Constance assisted by cutting the bandages and arranging the pillow so that Ethan was propped in an upright position during the procedure. He was exceedingly glad to be able to muster the strength to pull himself upright against the pillow, for it would have been an impossible task the day before. A less able-bodied man would have quelled under the pain, but Ethan took it in stride, for he was not about to suffer the indignity of having the glowering slave prop him up like a rag doll.

However surly Jenny's attitude, though, Ethan could not help but be impressed with her bandaging skills. Her strong dark hands were rough, but worked deftly and quickly, and when she was finished, her young mistress gave a pleased nod to the handiwork. The slave woman apparently reserved her sour-faced glares for Ethan alone, as she acknowledged her pretty mistress's compliment with a smile and another tug upon her earring.

Ethan himself had little chance to voice appreciation, for supporting himself in an upright position over such a prolonged period of time had taken a toll upon his stamina, and the pain was beginning to throb again, not only in his chest, but in his leg as well. He felt perspiration running down his neck. As he closed his eyes, he slid back down to a horizontal position. Then, he felt the touch of a cool, soft hand upon his brow — a welcome contrast to the coarsened ones that had rebandaged his wound.

When he opened his eyes several minutes later, the girl was still beside him, re-rolling the excess bandages. The slave woman was nowhere in sight, having apparently departed back down the stairs.

Despite his momentary relapse, Ethan was not inclined to sleep. Constance must have sensed this, for when she saw his eyes upon her, she fetched a low stool from against the wall and, setting it beside the cot, she perched upon it, still rolling bandages, and began to talk to him in her unaffectedly amiable — but sensibly quiet — voice.

"Jenny went to fetch you something to eat. I'm afraid you will have to make do with whatever she is able to smuggle under her apron. Although, I did happened to glance in one of my father's books today—," and here she reddened slightly; apparently, covert glimpses into the doctor's medical books were outside the sphere of propriety expected of such a young lady, "—and it stated that wounded persons ought to be kept to a vegetable diet, so I'm hoping that she can procure something other than what remains of the trout served at dinner."

"I rather think she does not like me, your Jenny," Ethan pointed out.

Constance gave a rueful smile. "I daresay she fears for my well-being, should your presence be discovered. Jenny is very devoted." She grew more reflective. "You see, Father never paid for her. He acquired her as part of a transaction with her former master. This house and land have always belonged to my mother's family . . . my mother inherited it all, as there were no direct male heirs, and my father left the city to bring her back here, for she preferred the country life. My elder sister was still an infant at the time. I gather that my mother would have liked Father to give up practicing medicine and take up the life of a gentleman farmer, but he would have none of that. He is far too fond of his profession and has no patience for idle ways," and Constance smiled, thinking on her father's habits. "Besides, he saw a need for a country doctor here. Of course, they inherited the slaves as well as the land, but Father determined that the workers were overtaxed by the amount of labor put upon them, and so he set about procuring two more men to work in the fields.

Jenny came with them as part of the bargain; her former master did not think she was worth keeping . . . not even worth living . . . as she could not talk." Constance shook her head, a troubled frown creasing her brow, and she spoke in almost a whisper. "I fear he was very cruel to her. He called her 'Jenny', for he said he was 'generous' to let her live at all as she was no use to anyone without a tongue. She had been put out in the fields to work with the men at the hardest labor. Her master made an agreement with my father: if my father would buy three field hands instead of just two, Jenny would be included in the bargain at no cost." Constance shuddered. "I think the man would have killed her otherwise . . . she bears scars up and down her body . . . surely not a reflection of undue insubordination on her part. When she came here, my mother would not hear of her being put to her former labors . . . my mother never thought a woman should be working out in the fields, not even a slave. She knew that Jenny was smarter than her former master credited her, so she taught Jenny domestic skills — to assist the cook and work in the scullery or laundry and even inside the house. Mother believed in treating even the lowliest servants with kindness. Jenny loved my mother for it and was terribly devoted to her. Of course . . . that all happened before I was born, and I only know what my father has told me. But as Jenny has always been a part of the household I've known, I cannot imagine how we ever would have managed without her."

Constance was caught up in distant reflections as she related this lengthy tale and was paying little heed to Ethan's attentiveness . . . but he was ever mindful of her, and well-attentive to the warmhearted sincerity of her narration. There was no pretense, no trace of artifice in her manner. In a moment of brash impulsivity, he determined to trust his instincts and concede the risk implied.

"Miss Jameson . . ."

Constance glanced up, summoned out of her reverie.

Ethan scrutinized her face intently as he carefully chose his words. "Before I was brought down, I had on my person some papers . . . they are sure to be among my personal effects now in your keeping."

The girl was either a brilliant actress or else genuinely perplexed. She shook her head. "I have no papers."

Ethan persisted. "They were folded, inside my coat."

But Constance remained nonplussed. "I am sorry. I did not think to retrieve anything from inside your coat before sending it to the rubbish pile. We had to work very quickly, to bring you here unseen, and I — I — could only think to attend to your leg and to stop the bleeding. You are fortunate," she added, her voice becoming hushed as she glanced down at his fresh bandage. "The ball did not lodge in your ribcage. If it had, you'd likely have awakened to find my father standing over you," and she gave him a conciliatory smile, "for I certainly have not the courage to attempt surgery."

Ethan was only half-listening to her. A torrent of new thoughts were coursing through his mind as he processed the ramification of her earlier words. If she was telling the truth, *the papers had been destroyed*. Nothing but ashes now, atop the rubbish heap.

A surge of relief washed over him. At least no lives would be endangered on his account, except perhaps his own; and as he was accustomed to improvising in that regard, the thought of any immediate threat to his own survival did not dampen his relief. Even the splintered leg and throbbing pain seemed inconsequential, though he did appreciate the soothing coolness of the damp cloth placed upon his brow by the doctor's daughter before she took up her candle and, assuring him that Jenny would soon return with some food, disappeared down the shadowy stairwell.

WHEN ETHAN OPENED HIS EYES the next morning, the low-raftered room was illuminated by a single band of very bright sunlight streaming in through the small window. The light did little to alleviate his agitated thoughts, though, which were once again flooding his brain with doubts and misgivings — the contented relief of the previous night erased by new insights invading restless slumber. Now that the pain was receding and he'd taken some sustenance, he had a better grasp upon his situation and could think with his former clarity, even if his body could not yet function with its former vigor.

His immediate thoughts dwelt upon the young lady . . . Constance Jameson. She continued to puzzle him. Ethan could not trust any person who resided in this homogenously Loyalist territory, least of all the daughter of Matthew Jameson. He had been prepared that she should betray him . . . prepared to discover that everything she said was a lie and that at any moment he would hear the tramp of heavy boots upon the stairs as Colonel Lyndhurst, or one of his red-coated henchmen, came to take him into the custody of the king's tribunal.

And yet, three days had passed since he had been brought into the garret, and despite his persistently wary skepticism, he had been given no cause to mistrust the girl. He had been convinced that she had spoken the truth the previous evening, when he had asked her about the papers' whereabouts. He was in possession of nothing else the British would want, except his own life, and attempting to take that would hardly require trickery on their part, considering his present condition.

But why, then, had she rescued him at all? And why should she be willing to maintain the secrecy of his presence for such a length of time as it would surely take him to recover? It could be no small undertaking for such a lady, even with the assistance of an able-bodied servant. She must necessarily be placing herself into a situation where her customary levels of comfort and well-being were unequivocally compromised; not to mention certain chastisement should her father ever learn of her endeavors.

If Constance Jameson was not deceiving him, why should she take such a risk? Ethan strove to conceive of an explanation. Was she secretly a supporter of the Patriots' cause, against her father's wishes? Or did she somehow stand to gain personally from this endeavor? Ethan frowned at that suggestion. Although he could not say why, somehow he knew that he was doing her character a grave disservice to even allow that thought to cross his mind. She had never asked him any questions — not even his name — nor attempted to pry any information from him.

Ethan had plenty of time to ruminate over these various points of uncertainty, as the garret was quite deserted and no one appeared for the greater duration of the day. Upon waking, he had discovered upon the makeshift table a bundled cloth containing some biscuits, and the tankard had been replaced with a small jug of fresh water. Although he had taken some sustenance the evening before, it had been scant; he found he was hungry again, and he ate the biscuits, wishing there was a bit of meat or cheese to accompany them.

He heard once again the various distant sounds of activity on the floors below, much the same as he had earlier noted, and all typical of such a country household — faint, indiscernible voices; doors closing; footsteps; and once, a merry peal of girlish laughter, the tone of which was much too exuberantly vivacious to be his demure young guardian.

It was not until late in the afternoon that Jenny appeared, toting a fresh bucket of water, from which she filled the jug, before she set about re-dressing Ethan's wound. She frowned all the while, and though she performed her silent task as capably as she had the previous day, Ethan was certain that her strong, mottled hands would have applied a much gentler touch had it been her mistress she was tending instead of him.

Constance appeared at the top of the steps just as the slave woman pulled the last bandage across Ethan's chest. Jenny had not propped up the pillow as her mistress had done the day before, so Ethan was relying solely on his abdominal strength to support himself during the re-bandaging process. Fortunately, he had recovered considerable strength after his intake of some nutrition and days of rest, and he was gratified to observe that his muscles were starting to once again respond with the athletic competence to which he was accustomed.

Constance set a delicate-looking bundled handkerchief upon the tall stool and then cast a glance at Ethan's freshly-bandaged torso. She addressed herself first to Jenny.

"Oh, you've finished already! I ought to have been here sooner to help you with the bandages, but I see you've done it very well on your own."

And Jenny's round, darkly-freckled face glowed with genuine pride at the praise. She gathered the saturated bandages from the floor and held them aloft with an inquiring glance toward her mistress. Constance gave her a nod, to which Jenny responded with a light tug upon her earring and proceeded down the steps, carrying the blood-stained bandages with her.

Constance turned her attention to her patient, who was still supporting himself upright upon the cot.

"Would you like to sit up for a bit?" she asked, reaching for the pillow which Jenny had not bothered to touch.

Ethan eyed the bundled handkerchief.

Constance smiled. "You must be hungry," she said, propping up the pillow behind his back, then taking up the bundle. "I am sorry that we cannot bring you anything at regular intervals." She unwrapped the handkerchief to reveal some wedges of hard cheese and some sippets, doubtlessly left over from tea. "This was the best I could obtain, without being noticed," she added, her tone apologetic.

Any sustenance looked delectable to Ethan, for the morning biscuits seemed like aeons ago, and he gave her a nod and a "thank you" before falling upon the cheese and sippets with voracity. But his attention was not entirely focused upon the food before him, and he continued to watch Constance intently as she tidied up the makeshift table then went to fetch her low stool from its place against the wall.

Not until she turned back toward the cot, stool in hand, did she realize she was under such scrutiny. She paused in her step, the color rising self-consciously upon her cheek as she met his gaze, then averted her eyes and proceeded toward Ethan's bedside. Once perched upon her stool, she fixed her attention upon the makeshift table, where her unbundled handkerchief, now emptied of its contents, was laden only with crumbs.

"Tomorrow I shall attempt to bring you a slice of pork pie, if you think your stomach would tolerate it." There was shyness in her smile, but her voice was warmly bright.

Ethan shook his head, frowning in perplexity. "I cannot under-stand you, Miss Jameson. You are your father's daughter, and it is nat-ural enough that your sympathies should lie with the Loyalists. Yet in consideration of your actions, I cannot help but wonder if you instead support our cause for independence." He leaned slightly forward. "Miss Jameson . . . are you a Patriot, however clandestine?"

Again he watched closely for her reaction, and again her face be-trayed no sign of discomposure. She met his unwavering scrutiny with a clear, guileless eye. She did not answer immediately, but Ethan sensed no uncertainty in her pause, only perhaps a moment taken for her to frame her thoughts.

"I am only a physician's daughter . . . a young lady of no conse-quence," she responded unaffectedly, "and therefore am not obligated to choose sides or even express an opinion in political matters."

But Ethan did not believe that she was wholly disinterested; he was going to hold her accountable for the intelligence behind those soft brown eyes.

"Even so," he persisted, "you are plainly aware of the divisions incited by recent events in these colonies. You must have some thoughts on such significant issues."

Constance again took a long moment to reflect before she replied, and when she at last spoke, Ethan sensed that her words were chosen with care.

"I have lived all my life in this colony. And while many would say that twenty-one years is not enough to draw conclusions of any merit, all I know is that I have never been discontented or unhappy while living here under the rule and protection of England. My father, who is a man of wisdom and integrity, has many valid, legitimate reasons as to why he believes we are better off remaining under the protection and leadership of our mother country. And yet . . . ," she looked across to Ethan, "I can also understand where some of the colonists feel they have been victims of certain injustices on the part of the British parliament and king. I have no doubt that in their minds and motivations, your Patriots feel that their cause is noble . . . and anyone — Patriot or Loyalist — who stands up for what he truly believes to be honorable must be commended." Constance sighed and rose from her seat, almost restlessly. She crossed to the window, looking absently out as she continued speaking. "This war has been very difficult for my family. Sides are not always as clearly defined as you and my father would have them be. These divisions you speak of exist on a very personal level for us. My elder sister's husband is a Patriot."

Ethan raised his eyebrows incredulously. "I am amazed that your father would have permitted such a union."

"They were married long ago, before men ever thought to divide themselves between Loyalist or Patriot allegiances. You see, my sister is seven years older than I. There were three brothers born after her, whom I never knew — all died in infancy. They are buried out there . . . beside my mother." Her gaze drifted to a distant point beyond the window's glass, which Ethan could not see.

Constance stood at the window for a moment before turning back toward Ethan and resuming her explanation. "Father could not have foreseen that my sister's husband would ally himself with the rebels' cause. Of course, my sister must stand beside her husband and his beliefs. Father understands that and would never disown her for it, but her husband is not welcome in this house, nor does Father ever mention his name. Naturally, it has put something of a strain on relations between our household and theirs, though the love between my sister and us is well understood. But it has all been very hard on Father." The tone of her voice had grown even quieter than usual, and her last words had been spoken reflectively, almost to herself.

But when she looked up at Ethan again, she addressed him directly, with spirit. "I am sure you cannot conceive of my father having such a tender heart that he should be pained by these domestic complexities. You think of him only as an ally of your enemies, a threat to your cause for independence. But he is more than just a Loyalist . . . he is a man who has worked diligently — has made sacrifices — in order to rise to the top of his profession. He treats everyone with courtesy, justice, and respect, be they gentlefolk, farmer, or slave. He loves dearly his daughters, just as he loved his wife, and in everything he does, his only thought is for the well-being of his family. You would not understand these qualities about him, knowing only his name and his political bent."

As Constance concluded this defense of her father, there was an incandescent fervor shining in her luminous eyes, which Ethan found intriguing. It was unexpected, coming from such a gentle young maiden. Nevertheless, his response was steadfast and firm:

"When men are at war, it is best not to think too deeply on the personal virtues of the adversary. There may come a day when one must place the safeguarding of the higher cause above the preservation of the individual and his virtues."

Ethan regretted his words as soon as they were issued, for the effect upon the young lady was immediate. In the space of a breath, her entire countenance changed. As she stood there, stricken and bewildered, tears clouded her eyes as she stared at Ethan in stunned disbelief. Once again, and overwhelmingly, shame washed over every fiber of Ethan's valiant, fearless, reckless soul. He was confounded by it — that this girl could so disconcert him with one look. Even if the words he spoke were true, they had been carelessly uttered, and, in retrospect, they must have sounded excessively callous to such a lady. He cursed himself for hurting her.

He sought at once to redress his thoughtlessness, and the contrition in his tone was genuine.

"Miss Jameson . . . I am sorry. I spoke without thought, and I assure you that it was not my intent to intimate that I would — that your father—," he faltered, uncharacteristically. What was it about this girl's wide-eyed gaze that robbed him of his usual assurance? Frustrated, Ethan averted his eyes as he collected his thoughts, and when he turned his focus upon her again, he spoke levelly. "I am truly the most ungrateful wretch on the earth. You have been kind enough to take me in and attend to me when you might have easily — and understandably — left me for dead. There was no call for me to speak so brazenly. I . . . pray you will forgive such carelessness."

After the innumerable hours he had spent debating the credibility of this young lady's trustworthiness . . . he could never have conceived that he would be thus humbled before her. It was in complete opposition to his characteristic audacity, and he was fortunate to have such a gracious young attendant, who did not seek to exploit his newly-humbled demeanor.

Constance drew closer to Ethan's bedside and spoke with a quiet solemnity. "Your attitude toward your enemy is undoubtedly common amongst men on both sides of this conflict, and I am very grateful not to be one, for I am sure that I could never affect such a stance. However, I can see where it would be a matter of self-preservation for those who must fight and literally face their opponents."

Ethan saw in her eyes the flicker of a question . . . a question Ethan prayed she would not ask, though she had every right to an answer. But while she looked as if she would like to put such a question to him, Constance did not speak further, but sat down once more upon her little stool and fell into a thoughtful silence.

Ethan reached for the handkerchief on the makeshift table beside him, and, wishing he had one of his own to offer, he shook the crumbs off of it and held it out to her.

"Here," he said, "I believe this belongs to you and not to Jenny."

She took it with a forgiving smile.

"Aye," she said, dabbing at her moistened eyes. "How did you know?"

And for the first time, Ethan grinned at her, his comely features enhanced by his beaming visage. "'Twas the first lavender-scented cheese I ever ate."

And Constance laughed — a charming, musical little laugh — as a sparkle brightened her eyes. She presented such an engaging picture that Ethan was momentarily distracted from the pain in his splintered leg, which had been exacerbated because he kept shifting about restlessly.

But in spite of all that Constance had told him, Ethan still could not satisfactorily account for his presence in Dr. Jameson's garret. He knew that his mind would not be at ease until he had further insight into his circumstance, and as he looked at Constance sitting beside him, still smiling softly to herself, he felt certain that she had been ever truthful with him, and that she would be so now.

He leaned toward her, his eyes searching hers.

"Miss Jameson . . . you profess no allegiance to our Patriots' cause, but if that be true, then why are you sheltering me here?"

As Constance looked at him, the smile faded from her lips, and her eyes became serious and thoughtful once more.

She spoke with candid simplicity. "I cannot bear to see anything die."

Upon hearing this simple explanation, Ethan could not help but think about her standing at the window, gazing out upon the distant gravestones, and he wondered how much she had seen of death. But though it was certainly the noblest of explanations, and fittingly feminine in its sentiment, it did not entirely satisfy Ethan.

"You might have turned me over to your father for treatment, or to the British soldiers, and spared yourself the trouble of such a situation as you have taken upon yourself."

Constance gave a little shrug, as if those options had been easily laid aside. "You indicated that your life would be forfeit if the British had you in their custody. It would have been the same result."

Ethan leaned back upon the pillow, turning her words over in his mind, feeling his own merits to be suddenly remarkably insignificant.

And while he was thus pondering, Constance rose, folded her dainty handkerchief, and bid Ethan good evening before heading toward the stairwell. But just as she reached the top step, Ethan stirred from his contemplation.

"Miss Jameson!"

Constance turned back toward him.

Ethan paused before speaking again, knowing well the implication of his words.

"It's Shaye."

Constance tilted her head inquisitively.

Ethan elucidated. "My name . . . Ethan Shaye."

And Constance's warm smile conveyed her deeper understanding of this impartation. With a gracious inclination of her head, she said, "Good night, Mr. Shaye," then turned and disappeared down the narrow steps.

CONSTANCE WAS TRUE TO HER word, and better, for the next day she brought to Ethan not only a slice of pork pie, but a small jug of cider as well. She and Jenny appeared together quite early — the slave woman toting her usual bucket of water, and Miss Constance carrying a basket over one arm.

Ethan was already sitting upright upon his cot when they entered, for he was regaining more strength each day, and although his bandaged wound and splintered leg would take their natural course of time to heal, he was restless of lying abed and ready to resume any small measure of physical exertion that could be undertaken, even if it was only supporting the weight of his abdomen by sitting up.

His mouth fairly watered as Constance laid the contents of her basket upon the tall stool, but he was not to have the gratification of immediately satisfying his appetite, for her basket was not yet empty. She next produced from it an object with which Ethan was well familiar, though he could scarcely have expected to see it in Constance's delicate grasp.

"Father and Polly are away from the house today, so I managed to slip this out of Father's bedchamber," she explained, setting a wood-handled razor beside the cider jug. "It is a good day for us to borrow it, as he shall be gone a long while, and we can put it back in its proper place long before he returns home. I could not help but notice yesterday that your face is starting to get a bit bristly," she added, glancing at Ethan's face with a mildly critical eye.

Ethan could not help but be amused. In the midst of a war in which he had been shot, laden with a fractured leg, and was now being harbored as a fugitive — Constance yet considered the maintenance of his personal appearance to be a matter of utmost importance. But he was willing enough to let her have her way, until a few moments later when she clarified her own role in the process.

"I daren't trust myself with such a task, of course," she mentioned conversationally, as she unpacked the remaining shaving paraphernalia. "Goodness knows I've never handled a blade of any kind, and I know well enough 'tis not the sort of undertaking you'd want attempted by an untried hand. Jenny has some experience, though, and can do it well enough, until you're able to do it yourself again."

One glance at the swarthy servant's glowering stare, and Ethan was not at all certain that he wouldn't prefer the younger woman's untried — but undoubtedly better-intentioned — hand to be wielding the blade. However, as the young lady seemed content to be a mere observer, Ethan resigned himself to the slave woman's unsympathetic manner. As with the bandaging, Jenny's large hands moved skillfully — despite the sour grimace upon her face — although Ethan was not entirely convinced that the razor would have been handled with such precision were the young mistress not looking on. Nevertheless, when the process was finished, Ethan had to admit that there was some satisfaction in being back to his usual clean-shaven state, even if there was none to appreciate it except himself and his amiable guardian.

After shaving him, Jenny proceeded to re-dress Ethan's wound, though Constance remarked that it appeared to be healing nicely and may no longer require daily rebandaging. Ethan never heard her formally dismiss the slave woman, but as he finally set about consuming the pork pie and cider, he observed Constance give Jenny a little nod, which Jenny seemed to understand, for she touched her shining earring, gathered up the soiled bandages, water bucket, and chamber pot, and proceeded down the stairs — no longer sour-faced, but placidly contented.

Although Ethan could see that Jenny served her mistress well, he was not sorry to see the slave woman depart; it was as if a dark, sullen cloud overhanging the garret had evaporated, lightening the atmosphere of the entire room and allowing him to speak freely to Constance.

Despite the attention Constance would give to such practical domes-
ticities as shaving and bandaging, Ethan's own thoughts ever returned to
the world outside and to that cause from which he had been so abruptly
exiled, but to which he longed to return. He hungered especially for information regarding those who were his closest compatriots.

He did not wait for Constance to finish gathering the shaving articles back into her basket, but questioned her straightaway.

"What news do you hear about the war?" he demanded. "Has there
been any fighting in recent days?"

Constance glanced at him over her shoulder, then continued her ti-
dying with a shake of her head. "I can tell you nothing. My father, of
course, keeps up with the current situation, but he is unlikely to bring
up such topics of discussion before his daughters. The news I come by is
generally overheard in his discourse with guests or upon excursions into
the city, but I have been a party to neither lately." She turned back to
Ethan and added, with an apologetic smile, "I'm afraid the only news I
could impart would hardly interest you . . . it has only to do with a neigh-
bor's new baby or the thaw that has begun to set in."

This thought seemed to jog a memory within her, for she paused and
turned her head toward the window as her gaze became distantly distracted. When she turned back to Ethan, he saw it again . . . that glimmer of an unanswered question in her eye. He had seen it only yesterday
and knew it was inevitable that the thought would come to her again, but
he'd hoped it would be longer delayed.

"I still do not know why you were in the snow," she murmured, stepping nearer to the cot where Ethan sat upright, his watchful eye upon
her. Constance stood beside him, and there was earnestness in her own
eye, although her voice was shyly hesitant. "You must forgive my curiosity, but I . . . I have been puzzling over you." She looked self-consciously
down at her hands, toying with a silver ring about her finger. "I suppose
it is none of my concern, but I cannot help wondering who you are." She
glanced back up at Ethan with that shyly inquisitive look which he found
quite appealing despite his burgeoning apprehension.

He was bound to be merciless, though, for the issue was too critical for him to speak hastily, and as he gave no immediate response,
Constance continued speaking, her hesitant tone gaining warmth and
momentum as she gave voice to her inner reflections.

"I have tried to reason it all out . . . who you are, why you should be
lying in the snow. I've tried to recall things you've said . . . but I can make
no sense of it. All I can seem to do is determine whom you must *not* be.
You are strong and well-built—," and here a soft crimson blush rose upon
her cheek as she inadvertently glanced at his bare chest, "—not someone
who idly sits behind a clerk's desk all day; and your face is tanned, as
one who is assuredly out-of-doors a great deal. Yet I cannot think that
you are a farmer or a laborer, for you speak as one who is well-bred." She
paused in her ruminations, her brow knit in puzzlement. Then, "I think
you must have some connection with the Continental military — why
else would you be wary of the British tribunal? And it is certain your
allegiance lies with the Patriots' cause. Yet, your coat was not that of a
soldier, nor did it bear any military insignia. In truth, I know only what
you have told me . . . that your name is Ethan Shaye . . . and nothing
else." She sighed. "Father always speaks of the virtue of reason, and I'm
afraid he would be very disappointed in my attempts at reasoning here."
Finding herself under Ethan's silent, uncompromising gaze, the color
rose in her cheeks once more. "I . . . I am sorry. You must forgive the
ramblings of such a senseless girl as I. I have no cause to voice such que-
ries. You never asked to be brought here — indeed, you tried to prevent
my intervention — and you undoubtedly have valid misgivings."

In truth, Ethan's furrowed brow and grave countenance signified not
disapproval, as the young lady suspected, but rather only a reflection of
the fierce deliberation transpiring inside his mind. He had readily anticipated that she should touch upon the subject of his identity at some
point — it was natural enough that she should — and during the past
week he had spent many of his long, solitary hours pondering how he
should respond to such questioning. Simple evasion was generally his
tactic of choice, but this situation was extraordinarily different from any

other he had encountered, and he was not at all certain that evasion was appropriate or wise. He might devise some fabrication — some plausible scenario which this young lady would readily believe. But he had not yet fully conceived of such a scenario, and now, as he looked at her — her soft, solemn eyes trained upon him — all notions of fabricated tales evaporated, and he knew he could tell her only the truth. Indeed, her apprehensive countenance did not sit well with him, and he tried to speak reassuringly, even as his manner was forthright.

"Miss Jameson, I assure you, there is no one in this colony who has a more justified claim upon this information than yourself. And you are well within the bounds of propriety — if there can be such a thing in this situation — to question me thus. I ought to have imparted such information to you long ago, as it has bearing on your own circumstance." He had successfully eased the self-reproach in her demeanor, and it was now with an air of attentive curiosity that she tipped her head slightly to one side in that inquisitively fetching manner. Seeing her anxiety thus diminished, Ethan's own tautness slackened a bit, and he leaned his back against the pillow as he continued speaking. "You are too critical of your own reasoning abilities, for you are correct in guessing that my profession is associated with the military. Although I hail from North Carolina, I am currently serving with a Massachusetts regiment, under the command of Colonel Naismith. My rank is Lieutenant." He saw her eyes widen, but he continued on, anticipating the question she would likely have voiced. "The reason I was not wearing a smart blue regimental coat when you found me is because I cannot have anybody in these parts — especially the British regulars — recognize me as a member of the Continental Army, or as any kind of Patriot."

He stopped his narrative there, for no other reason than to put her intelligence to the test. And indeed, she did recognize the weightiness of his words, for her wrinkled brow, perplexed frown, and averted gaze showed plainly that she was pondering their meaning. And Ethan did not interrupt her contemplation . . . there was too much at stake in the words that would need to be uttered by one or the other of them.

Still lost in thought, Constance sat down absently upon her little stool; it had been drawn up directly to Ethan's bedside, and as the stool's height was slightly lower than the cot's, her head was now at his shoulder, near enough that he could hear her quiet breathing as she ruminated.

When she turned her focus back upon him, there was still uncertainty in her expression. "Do you mean to say that you are some kind of . . . explorer? No—," she immediately corrected herself, knowing she had chosen the wrong word. "I mean a . . . a scout?"

Ethan gave a slight shake of his head. "Not exactly; although I have done my share of scouting . . . and fighting." He chose his next words carefully and without haste. "In recent months I have served General Washington in a different capacity. I . . . seek to obtain tactical information from our opponents."

Constance comprehended immediately, and her eyes widened again. "You're a *spy?*" Her disapproving frown suggested that she did not think highly of the role. "It does not seem a very honorable way to fight a war," she objected, "using deceit and trickery."

Ethan had little patience for this sort of impractical feminine analysis. "Wars have been won and lost due to the efforts of military intelligence since ancient times. Your Redcoats have an extremely sophisticated division of intelligence, and the king's treasury to back it."

Constance still did not appear convinced of the merits of the profession, but she fell back to pondering once more, and when she spoke again, it was evident her thoughts had progressed to other aspects.

"And so . . . the British soldiers were after you because . . . because they discovered you were a spy?"

Ethan's eyes narrowed darkly as he shifted his focus away from her. His tone took on an undisguised bitterness. "Aye; 'twas that turncoat Larson. He was bound to recognize me on sight. I've thrashed that coward's hide before, and I would have done so again if his bloodyback cohorts had not been mounted and charging like the devil—"

Startled to feel a soft touch upon his arm, Ethan glanced back over at Constance, whose troubled eyes were fixed upon him and whose hand had unwittingly crept up to settle lightly upon his arm. Conscious once more of her presence, Ethan took a deep breath and gave a reassuring pat to her hand (which she hastily withdrew, blushing gracefully).

Restlessly repositioning himself against the pillow, Ethan continued his tale in a somewhat lighter tone. "At any rate, only two of them took off after me. My horse was faster, though, and I gave them a good chase. Those fools could barely stay astride their mounts, let alone fire with accuracy, which was fortunate for me; otherwise, this—," he gingerly touched the bandage above his ribcage, "—could have been much worse than it is." He did not elaborate upon that point, but from the way Constance stared somberly at the bandage, he knew she well–comprehended the inevitable consequence had the musket-ball veered half an inch to the left. Ethan continued on: "They may have hit my horse as well, for as soon as I felt the heat of the lead ball in my chest, the horse reared suddenly, throwing me to the ground." His eyes narrowed again as he strove to remember. "I — tried to raise myself up, but it was impossible. As soon as I moved, I felt such a shooting pain in my leg, I knew I could do nothing. I — think I tried to drag myself a ways . . . but I must have blacked out." He shrugged. "And then, I suppose you must have come along and found me."

Constance nodded absently, and there was silence for a long while as they both sat lost in thought. But when Ethan stirred, his countenance was grave, and he leaned forward, looking directly into Constance's eyes, and spoke slowly, with level deliberation.

"Miss Jameson, you must understand the consequences should the British inadvertently learn of my presence here. A captured spy is no ordinary prisoner of war. He is assured execution, almost certainly by hanging. And those who harbor a spy will not be easily reprieved."

Although Ethan knew that she understood well enough the implication of his words, she showed no sign of trepidation, but only looked away, apparently ruminating over the ramifications of such profound consequences. When she spoke, it was with candid surety.

"I do not think you need worry on my behalf, for who could discover my doings except for my father? And he would certainly not turn me over to any other authority, even though he should be dreadfully displeased with me."

Ethan knew this was true, but somehow he had felt it important for her to be aware of the gravity of the situation in which she had placed herself. And despite the severity of it all, he could not help but be somewhat pleased at her unfaltering commitment to a cause whose worth she considered to be greater than her own security. *She could not bear to see anything die* . . . He wondered if she had inherited such an aversion from her father, whose profession entailed saving lives, but who undoubtedly saw many lost.

Constance spoke again, as if some new thought had just occurred to her.

"I do not know what became of your horse," she said with regret. "They must have taken it away with them."

Ethan cleared his throat. "Ah, yes, well . . . I may have referred to it as 'my horse', but truly," — he grinned unapologetically — "I stole it from them."

And Constance's attempt to look reproachful failed completely, for Ethan's roguish grin was so infectious, she laughed in spite of herself.

ETHAN WAS WAKENED QUITE EARLY, not by the natural end to slumber, nor even by the usual sound of Jenny's begrudging entry with her water-pail, but by the glaringly bright light streaming through the narrow window, its path falling right across his cot. It was nearly blinding to one whose eyes were first opened after a fitful sleep, but it was very welcome, for it meant the days were lengthening. Even from the confines of his garret-infirmary, Ethan could sense that the world outside had changed during the night; there was in the air a freshness and a mildness which signaled that the thaw had begun in earnest, ending winter's frigid hold upon the earth.

The earth's new-found vitality seemed to permeate Ethan's limbs as well, for he was restless and unsettled, and the day seemed to pass even slower than usual. Indeed, it had been several weeks since he had first been brought into the garret, and the sedentary confinement had begun to be a genuine trial for him whose customary lifestyle was characterized by physical activity and cognitive assertion. And even though Miss Constance appeared in the afternoon — earlier than her usual hour — accompanied by Jenny, Ethan still felt as if a dozen hours had passed since the sunlight had first wakened him.

The lightness outside must have enlivened Constance as well, for there was a spring in her step and a becoming bloom upon her cheek. Her pretty straw hat was tied with a ribbon beneath her chin, and she brought into the room with her the refreshing, invigorating scent of the outdoors, which only stirred more Ethan's longing to partake of that world outside.

She gave him not a glance, but hastened straightaway to the window, exclaiming, "It is so heavenly outside today!" as she lifted the latch and pushed the sash outward, allowing the clean, crisp air to fill the room with its freshness.

But as she turned back toward Ethan, she stopped rather abruptly, and her bright smile faded as she set her attention upon him, for though he had not moved since her entrance, she only now noticed an unanticipated change; rather than sitting or lying upon the cot with his legs outstretched upon it as his circumstance and condition had prescribed, Ethan now sat upon the cot as if it were a bench or a sofa, with both feet upon the floor — his uninjured leg bent at the knee, with the foot flatly grounded; and the splintered leg stretched straight, with his heel resting upon the floorboard.

Constance untied the ribbon from beneath her chin and removed her hat as she approached him with a more moderately-paced step.

"You know you cannot hurry a bone's healing," she scolded lightly. "If you are impatient, you will likely injure it again and only prolong the healing process." She set the hat down beside her basket and, in the absence of a comb, ran her fingers through her long, brown hair, indifferently pushing some wavy locks back behind her dainty cap.

"I have not put any weight upon it," Ethan asserted defensively, "— yet", he added under his breath, though Constance could plainly hear.

She raised her eyebrows, but could not suppress an understanding smile. "It must be quite difficult for you to be so confined," she said sympathetically. Her expression became thoughtful. "I must think of some sort of diversion for you, so that you might pass the time in a more fruitful — or at least pleasurable — manner."

She bent down to her basket and pulled out what appeared to be a white cloth. "I did bring you something today, though nothing amusing; nor is it even immediately useful, but I thought it might be worthwhile once your wound is better healed."

She unfolded the white cloth, which turned out to be in actuality a man's linen shirt. "Father gave it over to be mended so long ago, I do not think he would miss it soon if he has not already." Holding it aloft, her expression turned to doubt. "Of course, Father has an entirely different build . . . ." She glanced scrutinizingly at Ethan, then back at the shirt. "He is not as tall nor as broad-shouldered as you . . . and his belly is decidedly rounder." And she sighed dejectedly, looking at the shirt with contrite disappointment.

Ethan could not help but laugh good-naturedly. "Here now," he said soothingly, reaching for the shirt, "you mustn't fret . . . 'twas a fine idea to bring it. I can put it to good use in other ways." He glanced slyly at the large slave woman, who had situated herself subordinately beside the water basin. "I'll use it as a banner and wave it at Jenny next time she glares at me; then she shall know I've surrendered. She shall have won whatever battle is between us, for I cannot hope to overcome such persistently antagonistic looks as she bestows upon me."

Constance could not conceal the sparkle of amusement in her eye, though she did her best to suppress it by adopting a lofty tone. "Don't you pay him any heed, Jenny," she said. "He is far too brazen to deserve any concession on your part."

Ethan rather hoped that Jenny would not exact any sort of immediate disgruntled vengeance, as he next found himself at the mercy of her rough-hewn hands for a re-dressing of his wound. But she displayed only the usual sour-faced animosity and customary indelicate touch, of which her mistress took no notice — and rightly so, for Jenny looked upon that young lady with a mild, doting regard, as a ewe-sheep might look upon her precious lamb.

Constance watched intently as Jenny removed the old bandage and dressing. "Is it still seeping?" she asked.

Jenny shook her head.

Constance seemed pleased. "Ah, that is good." She continued addressing the slave woman. "Then I think we do not need to change it out every day. Would you say twice per week would be enough?"

Jenny frowned and shook her head.

"Thrice?"

Jenny nodded and gave a tug upon her gleaming earring.

Constance smiled. "Very well."

Ethan found this whole interchange interesting, as it was not customary for a mistress to consult her slave on any matter, but he supposed the faithful servant had more experience in the practice of treating wounds than had the young lady, even should that young lady be the daughter of a physician.

Once the bandaging was done and Jenny had gathered up the wrappings, Constance handed her the small cider jug, which had sat empty for several days, although the water supply was always ample.

"See if you are able to refill this," Constance instructed the servant. "I know it is not an easy task, with Uriah presiding over the storehouse . . . but in the next day or so, see if you can manage it." And she gave the dark woman an encouraging smile, to which Jenny nodded and touched her finger to her earring.

Jenny then departed down the steps, cider jug in hand.

Ethan looked after the stalwart slave with a quizzical frown. "That woman," he said pointedly, "is constantly fingering her earrings. Aren't they quite ostentatious for a servant?"

Constance let her own gaze stray to the dark stairwell, where Jenny had just disappeared. She smiled fondly. "Ah, you have noticed her little gesture. Aye, her pretty earrings are a source of great pride for her. They belonged to my mother. She left them to Jenny when she died. It does seem rather unorthodox, but Mother always treated her with kindness, and—," Constance looked thoughtful, "—I rather suspect she and Jenny had some sort of understanding . . . that Jenny would look after us when Mother had gone." She shrugged somewhat sheepishly. "Of course, Mother could not have known beforehand . . . when her time would come. She had survived several childbirths already, but with Polly . . . ," Constance's eyes were as softly tender as her voice, ". . . well, she died when my younger sister Polly was born. I was but four years old at the time." She slipped into silence, her eyes not seeing Ethan, nor the garret, nor the sun-lit window, but only seeing some long-past tableau playing out in her memory.

Ethan called her benignly back into the present; his low, resonant voice subdued. "Do you remember her?"

Constance sighed. "Sometimes I seem to remember her very clearly . . . how she would smile upon me so kindly and hold onto my hand when we walked beside the brook. But other times, I wonder if my memories are real, or if they are only images fabricated from stories people have told me about her." She sat down upon her stool beside Ethan's cot. "I do know that my memories of her seem to fade more with each passing year," she said wistfully. "I suppose it is natural enough — it has been seventeen years since she died. Father has a miniature portrait of her that sits atop his bedside table. I like to look at it sometimes, just to impress again her image upon my mind, though the portrait was painted long before I was born, and she could never have looked so young when I knew her. Of course, Father will never part with it while he lives, and afterwards it shall go to my elder sister. That is as it should be, for she certainly knew our mother best and has the truest memories, having been nearly eleven years old when Mother died."

There was sadness in Constance's voice, and Ethan could tell that, in spite of her noble words, she wished that she, too, could have had eleven years' worth of memories of her mother.

She almost immediately cast her eyes downward, however, as if ashamed of the thoughts she had voiced. "'Tis selfish of me to bemoan the few memories I have, though, for at least I have some. Poor Polly has none at all. She never knew our mother."

She was surely sentimental, but Ethan could not think less of her for it, for there was no artifice to her sentiment.

When she glanced back up at him and saw his eyes upon her, she seemed to recall the purpose of her tale, and the sadness that had clouded her face dissolved as she refocused her thoughts. "I have digressed terribly; I am sorry." She gave him a remorseful smile. "You are very good and patient today."

Ethan did not feel compelled to point out that he was a captive audience. And truly, though there may have been a time when he would have had little interest in listening to such emotive recitations, he found Constance's narrative neither trying nor insipid. Perhaps it was due to the very circumstance of his confinement — any diversion was welcome — or, perhaps it was the way she had unconsciously bent her head closer to his own as she had wistfully lamented her mother's passing.

Regardless, she now lifted her head, brightened her visage, and resumed upon the original course of her narrative. "The way Jenny tugs upon her earring . . . it is habit, no doubt, but also has a purpose and a history, with ties to my mother as well. When I was a very small child and knew little of the world, much less of the subtleties and complexities of communication, I did not understand why Jenny would not speak to me. She helped Mother care for me and my sisters, but she did not answer questions, nor bid me good morning, nor even respond when I spoke to her. The idea that she *could not* speak was beyond my comprehension, and I would get so frustrated and upset that I would cry and cry. I think that in my simple child's mind, I thought that Jenny was somehow angry with me or disliked me, and I would run to my mother in tears because Jenny would not respond when I spoke to her. My mother was very wise in the ways of children, and she knew that, at only three years old, I could not be held accountable to formulating only questions which might be answered by Jenny with a nod or shake of the head, so she devised the touch to the earring as a way for Jenny to communicate with me. It was a clever trick, for even the smallest child is bound to be enchanted with a special method of communication . . . it was as if I was privy to a secret language, which only Jenny and Mother would share with me. Of course, Jenny did not have Mother's earrings then — only simple hoops, I think — but she did not discontinue her little signal after Mother died, and as you have seen, she continues even now communicating with me in that way, though I am sure it is now just a perfunctory gesture for her."

Ethan was perplexed by this explanation. "And yet . . . what does it mean?" he asked. "Does this gesture translate as simply 'yes'?"

Constance raised her delicate shoulders in a tranquil shrug. "It means whatever she needs it to mean," she said placidly. "It is, I suppose, a sort of . . . acknowledgement that she understands what I have put to her. She is extremely perceptive and always knows what I require."

Ethan nodded thoughtfully, recalling how Jenny had not waited for Constance to dismiss her, but had known quite intuitively that her mistress had granted silent permission, and the tug on the earring had acknowledged as much. Jenny was indeed perceptive . . . perceptive enough to realize that the fugitive's situation put her young mistress at risk, in more ways than one; such perception on Jenny's part was evidenced by her continued animosity toward him.

Before Ethan had further opportunity to dwell upon the slave woman's unique method of communication, his attention was distracted by a sudden, soft melody which seemed to be drifting in through the half-opened window. The musical sound was unmistakably that of a spinet, though Ethan could hardly suppose that its player was actually out-of-doors.

Constance heard it, too, and smiled with some affection. "That is timely," she remarked. "'Tis Polly at her spinet."

Seeing Ethan's quizzical look, Constance rose from her stool and crossed to the window, pushing it open further and leaning out slightly, as if searching for the source of the music. "She must have the parlor windows open," she noted to Ethan. "It does sound as if it is originating outside the window, doesn't it? The parlor is directly beneath us, although two floors below." She pulled the window nearly shut again as she murmured, "I only hope our voices do not carry so clearly."

"And are you as musically inclined as your sister?" inquired Ethan, as Constance crossed back toward the cot.

She shook her head modestly. "I do not play half as well, nor with as much enjoyment as does Polly. She is a lively girl, but is remarkably focused when sitting at the spinet. She has a natural ability. Father dearly loves music and saw to it that all three of his daughters received instruction. I much prefer singing to playing, though I have no such talent as Polly . . . and not before an audience," she added self-consciously, as if fearing Ethan might demand an impromptu performance there in the garret.

He was looking upon her with curiosity, though, as she drew her stool up to his bedside once more. "With a lively sister, a discerning father, and a handful of servants on the premises, how do you keep them from discovering me up here?"

"That is easy enough," said Constance, daintily arranging her skirt as she sat down upon the stool. "As my elder sister is married and resides elsewhere, the household keys have been put to my keeping. I just take care that the door at the bottom of the steps is locked at all times — though you are not confined here," she hastily assured him, "for the door can be unlatched from this side without the key. Access to the door is through a seldom-used room, thank goodness. . . . it used to be a sewing-room before the addition was built onto the house. Now it is only utilized for storage."

"Even so," Ethan contended, "they must surely take note of the fact that for the past few weeks you have been absent for a period of time each day. How do you explain your regular forays into the garret?"

Upon hearing this question, Constance looked decidedly uncomfortable. She reached for a loose strand of hair, which she proceeded to twist around her finger in a distracted manner. "That is not so simple," she confessed, the color rising in her face. "I . . . I told them that I have undertaken to make a very special gift — for my father's birthday — and that I require the garret's privacy and space to work on it."

While Ethan was impressed with the plausible practicality of her explanation, he could see that she herself was ill-at-ease with such deception. He did not doubt that it was probably the first instance in her life where she had resorted to any type of fabrication.

As if reading his thoughts, Constance was quick to defend herself. "I *shall* make him a gift," she declared. "I — I just have not yet thought of what it could be," she added forlornly.

"Oh, come now," said Ethan cheerfully, "you are a very accomplished young lady. Surely you will think of something. When is his birthday?"

Constance flushed a deeper crimson. "August," she murmured despondently.

Ethan raised his eyebrows. "August? That is yet a long while. I see your dilemma — they will expect something rather impressive after so many months. Perhaps you could make him a new shirt?" he suggested jocularly, with a nod toward the one sitting at the foot of his cot.

Constance was not appreciative of his lighthearted suggestion. "It is easy enough for you to be cavalier," she admonished, "as you are not faced with such a dilemma."

In spite of his natural inclination to remind her that her dilemma was, in fact, fairly inconsequential compared with his own perilous situation, Ethan held his tongue, for he could see that she was genuinely downcast over her predicament, and it was, after all, on his behalf that she had entangled herself into such a quandary.

He attempted to soothe her with reason. "Well, I shall certainly not be here for the duration of all those months, and as it will no longer be necessary for you to sojourn into the garret once I am gone, you need only explain to your family at that time that you have finished with the gift."

"Aye, 'tis true," Constance admitted, though she still looked doubtful. "Yet even a span of only two or three months is more than what would be required to embroider some handkerchiefs, which would be the usual sort of handiwork I'd turn out for him. Although . . . ," as she paused, her countenance became thoughtful, "I do have some talent for needlework. Perhaps something a bit more elaborate . . . ."

That was all she said, but it seemed she had formed some new idea which appeared to satisfy her for the moment, and she rose, still turning over her newly-formed thoughts within her mind. "I shall have to go to town," she murmured, mainly to herself. "Perhaps even tomorrow, if Uriah is going to get some supplies. Dougherty's has the finest selection of threads, I think."

Still caught up in her planning, she bent to pick up her hat and her basket. As she reached for the basket, however, she gasped quite suddenly, halted, and then straightened again with an "Oh!". She turned back to look at Ethan, and he wondered if she was unwell, so much of the color had drained from her face. But before he could attempt to raise himself from the cot on the weight of his uninjured leg, Constance spoke:

"I — I had nearly forgotten." She did not immediately elaborate, but only cast her eye back toward where the basket sat upon the floor. She stared at it for a few moments, and when she finally looked up at Ethan again, her countenance was very serious and her manner very hesitant. "I . . . brought you some other things." She spoke quietly, tentatively . . . as if she was nervous. She turned slowly back to the basket and, reaching down, pulled out another bundled cloth — quite bulky and sizable and perhaps even heavy, for she carried it enfolded in both arms to where Ethan sat. She set the bundle down on the cot carefully, gingerly even, but Ethan scarcely look at it, for he saw when she was beside him that she was trembling slightly, and he glanced up into her face, fearing again that she was not well. But though she was still pale and hesitant, she straightened herself up, with her eye focused upon the bundle, and spoke very softly, yet resolutely, through lips that were visibly quivering.

"These . . . these are yours, Lieutenant Shaye."

And she took a step backward, as if to distance herself from both Ethan and the mysterious parcel.

Ethan did not attend to it immediately, but, frowning, kept his eye upon her, for he did not like the change in her demeanor — the hesitance, the trembling, the distance. But she made no further attempt to explain, and in keeping her attention resolutely set upon the bundle, she seemed intent that he should open it, so that once he had reassured himself of her well-being, Ethan turned to look at the parcel beside him.

The sense of foreboding was palpable, and Ethan could feel his own heartbeat accelerate as he reached toward the bundled cloth. He did not lift the parcel, but unwrapped it where it lay, revealing its contents laid out openly upon the cot.

And instantly he understood.

And instantly everything changed.

There were three objects wrapped within the cloth, all very familiar to Ethan: a wooden canteen engraved with the military seal of his regiment; a small leather pouch as is used to carry powder and shot; and . . . a wood-handled pistol.

His pistol. He picked it up, his fingers instinctively conforming to the smooth wood. It was still loaded.

He set it back down upon the cloth, his thoughts racing in a torrent of confusion and comprehension, the only sound in his ears the thudding of his heartbeat within his sturdy chest.

He finally brought himself to look up at Constance, who had not moved but whose eyes met his own — her vulnerability never more apparent than in that moment. Neither spoke, but only stared at one another for a long, long time. And in the silence, their eyes communicated plainly what each knew to be true.

The wary watchfulness which had existed between them from the first, which had gradually been diminished over the course of time, now dissolved completely. There could be no more uncertainty, no more wondering; for, by the agent of a pistol, their roles were now reversed.

Never again could Ethan question her trustworthiness. It was now Constance who must trust. It was now she whose life was susceptible . . . laid squarely in Ethan's hands.

The roles were surely more fitting now — it would seem natural enough that the strong young man should hold dominion over the gentle maiden. But Ethan's mind did not harbor such thoughts as he looked upon Constance; for though Constance's delicate female body may be physically vulnerable, she had by her actions demonstrated a strength of integrity which was to be revered. And every bit of her gentleness and vulnerability — which could easily be liabilities instead of virtues in such a circumstance — she was entrusting to Ethan's keeping. Such a bequest would testify to either the girl's naiveté, or else to her unassailable faith in the honor of a Patriot spy.

The significance of the relinquishment was not lost upon either one of them, as was evidenced by the prolonged silence. And despite his pensive frown and her wide-eyed wariness, there was no awkwardness between them as they looked at one another. There was only a new and unspoken understanding.

Ethan was the first to break the silence, although his words were strangely halting for one usually so fearlessly self-assured. He merely gave a nod toward the young lady and rendered a gruff, "Thank you, Miss Jameson."

He turned his attention again to the objects beside him and, gathering them into the cloth once more, placed the entire parcel beneath his cot, beside his boots. "I shall keep these articles here." He addressed Constance very deliberately, ensuring that she would see that the pistol would be kept in plain sight of them both.

And although Constance did not voice a response, her countenance reflected her appreciative comprehension, and she gave him an acknowledging nod. Then, with her hat still in hand, she picked up her basket and hastened to the stairwell — taking, it seemed, much of the day's brightness with her as she departed.

A DAILY ROUTINE HAD BEEN established from the beginning of Ethan's concealment in the Jamesons' garret. Every morning, very early, Jenny would climb the garret steps, toting her wooden bucket, and refill the water basin. She would appear again later in the day — usually in the early evening — to replenish Ethan's drinking water (or cider, if he was fortunate) and change out his bandages if necessary. She usually brought something to eat as well, and he was given a shave whenever Dr. Jameson's razor could be safely smuggled away for a few hours, which was fairly frequently as the doctor often rode out for hours at a time to attend to patients across the countryside. Jenny never tarried longer than was necessary, but performed her duties quickly and efficiently — and always with a disgruntled grimace, so that Ethan should never suppose her to be in any way softening in her dislike of him.

Jenny's pretty young mistress came up to the garret but once each day, often accompanying Jenny in the early evening, but she always stayed after the slave woman's departure, for she knew that Ethan would be in want of diversion by the end of the day, and she gave him as much of her time as she could manage without raising suspicion amongst the other members of the household.

It could never be long enough to satisfy Ethan, though, for once the initial period of physical weakness and constant pain had passed, he found the duration of the long, empty days to be insufferable. The isolation and lack of mental stimulation were trying enough, but even those factors did not vex him half as much as the restricted mobility. He longed to jump up from the cot to which he was confined and exercise his restless limbs, for he *felt* alert and energetic, but he knew that he must curb his impatient impulses and heed the words of the young mistress, for to exert himself before he was even marginally healed would be a grave mistake, and he must content himself for the time being with shifting only between sitting upright and lying down. And so it was that he found himself in purposeful anticipation of Miss Jameson's daily visits, for they provided the only variation in the course of the monotonous days.

Constance was ever true to her word, and she assembled an assortment of objects meant to offer some diversion to Ethan during his hours of solitude. Gathering such effects proved to be a difficult task for the well-meaning young lady, for with her father and sister the only family members residing in the household, and without access to most of her father's possessions, Constance was hard-pressed to provide anything that would suit such a man as Ethan Shaye. As it was, the collection she presented to him was not large, but surely well-intended. It consisted of a case of playing cards, a domino box, some loose sheets of paper and a pencil, and three books. ("We have many books," Constance had explained, "but I did not want to draw attention, lest too many should have disappeared from Father's shelves.").

Constance herself had no trouble keeping well-occupied during the hours she spent in the garret. She had indeed thought of a fine gift to present to her father for his birthday, and shortly after her conversation with Ethan upon the subject, she had ascended the garret steps laden with an assortment of packages from her excursion into town — mostly spools of thread in a variety of bright, rich hues.

"I shall make over his brown waistcoat," she had declared, her soft eyes shining with enthusiasm as she produced the waistcoat from among her parcels. "It is very old, I think, and seldom worn, so it will be quite magnificent when I've embroidered it."

And so Miss Constance never sat idle during her visits to Ethan, but would draw up her stool beside his cot and work diligently upon her needlework as they conversed.

Ethan would often, in these hours, endeavor to enlighten her as to the ideals and principles behind the Patriots' cause. He would relate incidents of injustices enacted by the British king and parliament and even of the red-coated soldiers stationed in the colonies. He told her of the earliest Patriot leaders — how they had tried every means possible to alleviate the situation peaceably; how they had attempted to persuade the king to treat his colonists fairly in order to avoid the necessity of war; and how their words had only provoked the British government to impose further restrictions upon the colonies. And he recounted to her tales of the heroic deeds rendered by his fellow Patriots, for he had seen much — in battle, as well as in scouting and spying endeavors — which attested to the bravery and loyalty of his allies in pursuit of liberty. And while Constance listened placidly to these accounts, her head bent industriously over her needlework, she readily discerned in Ethan's tone the earnest fervor of his convictions.

As for the assortment of articles meant for Ethan's diversion, in truth they did little to help the time pass during the solitary hours of each day, though he knew Constance meant well in her provision of them. Playing cards and dominoes could scarcely provide amusement without a partner (or a wager), and while he did peruse the books, they were hardly enticing — an illustrated volume of botanical species native to the Northern Colonies, a history of Aquitaine, and a well-worn copy of

Descartes' *Meditationes de Prima Philosophia* written in the original Latin script, with which Ethan was already familiar, having studied it during his school days.

And so it was only the sheets of paper and the pencil which might afford him some few hours of occupation, and these he did put to use, notating thoughts and observations pertaining to his recent military objective; for in those long hours it was truly where he found his thoughts ever digressing . . . back to that adventurous life and to that cause that was dearest to him. He could not help but think upon his last endeavor; it was the first time in his career that he had failed to complete such a mission.

The matter weighed more and more upon his mind. It was the urgency of time which drove his thoughts thus, for while more than a month had passed, and events may well have transpired which would render his acquired information now obsolete, there was still a chance that it was not too late. He yet remembered the crucial details contained within the documents that had been inadvertently destroyed, and it was in cataloguing those details that he put to use the paper and pencil provided by Matthew Jameson's daughter.

His thoughts often turned to that young lady . . . Miss Constance Jameson. She had never voiced support toward the ideals of independence for the colonies, but neither had she ever outrightly aligned herself to her father's Loyalist convictions, even while alluding to her contentment with living under the king's regime. To Ethan's mind it was one of the most incomprehensibly frustrating characteristics of Miss Jameson — this persistent unwillingness to show any interest in the current tide of political or military affairs. At the same time, it did not wholly surprise Ethan, even as it frustrated him, for as Miss Constance herself had observed, such affairs were generally outside the realm of feminine interest.

One thing was certain: If he was going to put her loyalties to the test, he must do so immediately. The information he had gleaned from the British encampment had benefited no one in the many weeks since his near-capture, and he must search out every avenue possible to put the information into the hands of his compatriots, who may yet use it to their advantage, ere it would be rendered forever useless and his endeavors all in vain.

Ethan did not devote time to the formulation of words or plans, but rather put the issue to Miss Jameson directly one afternoon.

She was perched upon her stool, as usual, her nimble fingers at work upon her embroidery, the colored threads an admirable companion to the cheerful hues in her graceful spring gown. But Ethan was far too intent upon his purpose to take note of her attire or the way the late-afternoon sunlight — streaming through the open window, making patterns on the floorboards — cast a soft shine upon her light brown hair.

He leaned slightly toward her, speaking with purpose, even as he maintained a certain deliberate nonchalance in his tone. "Miss Jameson, I should very much like to send word to the commander of my regiment. Do you know of any means to convey such a message?"

Constance glanced up from her sewing. She comprehended at once the implication of the question and shook her head. "Nay."

Ethan yet persisted. "There is no way, then, to send any kind of communication?"

Constance knew that Ethan had well understood the meaning of her initial response, and she gave him a befittingly reproachful look. "Even if there was a way, I would have no part in it."

Ethan scowled. Her response was not unexpected, but the quickness of it irritated him. She had not even considered it, had not so much as hesitated in her objection. And then there was that feeling again — that inexplicable guilt — which perhaps nettled him more than her swift refutation and which made him feel like a cur for asking such a thing of her. He would not confront that feeling, though, nor seek to explain its source, but only glowered all the more fiercely.

Constance saw his scowl, and, sighing, she set her sewing down upon her lap and attempted to elucidate. "You must not suppose that my willingness to attend to you — to your recovery — has aught to do with any desire to aid your cause for the colonies' independence. You know I harbor

59

no allegiances there. My loyalties lie only with my father and my family."
Ever tranquil in her resolve, she picked up her needlework once more.

But Ethan could not be so placid. He never could. And her last
words had touched off a new stream of troubled thoughts toward which
his mind digressed. For truly, though Constance remained steadfast in
her allegiance to her father, would her father be appreciative of such loyalty if he discovered that she was harboring a Patriot fugitive under their
garret roof? She herself had admitted that her father would be "dreadfully displeased" should he discover her furtive deed. How would such
disapproval be manifested? Ethan wondered if Dr. Jameson would ever
raise his hand to such a gentle-natured daughter. The idea displeased
Ethan greatly, and he frowned just thinking about its possibility.

When he glanced over at Constance, he found her eyes already upon
him, studying his face, noting his frown.

She shook her head sympathetically. "Such black looks today." Her
accusation was very gentle, the momentary reproach already forgotten. "I
fear you are determined that nothing shall please you."

Her soothing compassion only unsettled Ethan more. He would not
allow himself to be placated, and he shifted restlessly on the cot, his
brow still furrowed darkly as he addressed her. "My presence here is a
constant threat to your well-being. What would be the repercussions for
yourself should your father discover what you have been about?"

Although Constance did not immediately respond, she neither
seemed taken aback by the question, and Ethan sensed it was not the
first time she had contemplated the subject.

Lowering her eyes, she picked up her needlework again. "I do not
know," she murmured.

However unsatisfactory this statement, Ethan detected no evasion on
her part. It was undoubtedly true . . . it was very likely that Constance's
father had never been given cause to chasten his daughter, and certainly
not for an infraction as significant as this.

"I daresay you've never known the brunt of your father's anger,"
Ethan suggested sullenly.

Constance paused again in her sewing, looking thoughtful, and Ethan could not help but wonder when he observed after only a few moments the hint of a smile playing about her lips.

"There was one instance . . . ," she mused aloud, ". . . though I have not thought upon it these many years." She paused, apparently still reflecting, but there was an undeniable warmth to her expression, as one who is thinking back with fond affection. "I was only a child," she related, seeing Ethan's questioning expression, "surely not older than eight years old. My Aunt Sybil had come to live with us after my mother's death, to help with our upbringing and manage household matters. My elder sister had reached the age where she was to attend her first ball in town, and my aunt was going to introduce her, for my aunt was from Philadelphia and well-established in society. I was, of course, much too young to attend such an affair, so I was relegated to the role of mere bystander to the elaborate preparations — looking on as my sister was fussed over for weeks ahead of the event. I was envious, of course, of all the attention she received . . . the gown fittings, the shopping expeditions, the exquisite dancing slippers ordered from Philadelphia." Constance smiled ruefully. "Even at such a tender age, I was fond of pretty things."

In spite of his sullenness, Ethan could not help but smile at this, for he knew that Constance had not outgrown her love of "pretty things"; while her attire was always befittingly tasteful, it was the little touches — the graceful floral accents of her pastel-hued gowns, the delicate lace trim adorning her dainty white caps — which attested to her partiality toward such aesthetically pleasing details.

"Naturally, my sister was very excited," she continued, "to be attending her first real affair of society, to show off her figure and her newly-mastered dancing skills. She talked of nothing else for weeks; the entire household seemed to be focused upon the upcoming event, or so it seemed to me. I was dreadfully jealous." And here Constance smiled again, amused by the childish notions of her younger self. "I never said a word to anyone, but I was determined that I would go to the ball. To an eight-year-old girl, I suppose reason and logic were non-existent, and

I formulated a wonderful plan . . . so I thought. After my sister and aunt were dressed and on their way, I told Polly — who was only about four years old at the time — that we were going to the ball, and we crept upstairs and put on our best white Sunday gowns, then—," she interrupted herself with a delightful little laugh at the endearing senselessness of the schemes of an eight year old, "—we somehow managed to slip out of the house — I'm sure I don't know how we got past Jenny's watchful eye — and set out on foot for the ball. The fact that I had no idea how far away the town was, nor even in which direction, did not hinder me, and Polly and I confidently made our way to the high road, trudging along in our best gowns. Needless to say, our adventure did not last long. We had only just made it to the bridge at Parson's Brook when we began to feel drops of rain. I will never forget the feeling of dismay when I looked down and saw that my favorite white gown was becoming spotted with raindrops. As we crossed the bridge, the rain began to fall in torrents. I think it was the truest soaking I've ever had in my life. We were just as quickly apprehended by Father's manservant, who promptly marched us back down the road and to the house and unsympathetically presented us to Father. What a sight we must have been! Two small girls . . . shamefaced, bedraggled, muddied, and soaked through to the skin, in our Sunday gowns."

Ethan grinned as Constance laughed affectionately at her own misadventure, for it was amusing to think of this demure young lady caught up in the imaginatively lively joys and mishaps of childhood.

He scrutinized her with interest, for she had not yet touched upon the subject which had first prompted her anecdote. "And did your father reprimand you?" he asked.

"Oh yes!" Her smile gave way to meditative reflection once more. "I was sent up to bed without any supper. But it was the scolding my father gave me beforehand that was the more severe punishment. I cannot forget, even to this day, the stern look upon his face when we were brought before him. I had never seen him angry, and I fairly shook with fear. Polly was sent out of the room — she was so young, my father could not hold her accountable; the misadventure and the fear of reproach had been punishment enough for her — but he bid me to remain, and I confessed most tearfully to every detail. He then expressed his disappointment in me, not only because I had run off and spoiled my gown in the process, but because I had endangered my small sister, who looked to me as a model of proper conduct and whom I had led astray. When I was sent up to my bedchamber, I think I was truly more miserable knowing that my dear father was disappointed in me than if he had raised his voice or his hand to me, which he never did. I cried myself to sleep, but all was mended the next day, for Father knew that I had learned my lesson well, and he smiled at me kindly first thing in the morning, so that I would know he was not angry with me."

And Constance herself was smiling affectionately as she thought upon her father's wise and loving upbringing of his daughters, and when she took her leave of Ethan shortly thereafter, she felt contented, for her patient's sullenness seemed to have dissipated. Yet, in truth, Ethan could take little solace from the insight into Dr. Jameson's temperate application of justice. For while Constance's father had had the wisdom to know that being sentenced to bed without supper would suffice as punishment enough for a conscientious child, Ethan doubted that her father would now — a dozen years later — apply such a mild reprimand to his grown daughter's breach of conduct should Constance's transgression be discovered. The thought weighed heavily upon Ethan's mind and only reinforced his determination that he must depart from the garret's refuge at the earliest possible moment.

As THE DAYS WORE ON and Ethan's strength continued to improve, he found new devices with which to occupy himself during the long, solitary hours. As soon as he had been able to sit up with his feet upon the floor, he had begun to devise a series of physical exercises which could be done from his upright position, which served to maintain his body's strength and agility as well as relieve some of the restlessness of his constrained limbs. Eventually, he was able to rise from the cot and stand for some length of time, taking care to put all of his weight on his uninjured leg. He did have one instance of impetuous over-eagerness, when he put the slightest bit of pressure on his splintered leg and immediately regretted it, for the sharp pain which traveled from the leg all the way up his spine (or so it seemed) was a definitive reminder that such premature efforts were not only physically painful, but detrimental to the overall healing of the bone, and only served to delay his return to the outside world. As trying as it was to his patience and his pride, he knew he must still wait until he was further healed before venturing to put weight on the splintered leg again.

The cause of the Patriots was still his foremost concern, however, and not a day went by that he did not question Constance about the progress of the war. She told him what little she could and made a concerted effort to give heed whenever her father discussed such matters with gentlemen guests, though he seldom did so in her presence. As little as she was able to impart to Ethan, however, it was enough that he could discern apparent trends; namely, that agitation was mounting in all of the colonies, but the largest contingents of British and Continental troops were assembling to the north, in New York. Even so, there was no word of any specific battles or even skirmishes, and Ethan felt certain that there were great gaps in the information Constance was able to provide. He longed to break free of his confines and learn of the war's progress firsthand by again partaking in the events that were shaping the destiny of his country.

ETHAN KNEW BY THE SOUND of the footfall upon the stairs that something was perceptively different. The light step was familiar enough, but its hurried pace was unusual, and as the hour was quite late for Constance to be ascending, Ethan was already anticipating some sort of anomalous circumstance to have arisen. And indeed, when Miss Constance emerged from the stairwell, it was not only the quickness of her step which seemed to substantiate Ethan's conjecture, but her very appearance; for she was wearing an elegant gown of rose-colored silk, exquisitely fitted, trimmed with ribbon across the bodice and lace cascading from the sleeves. And though she never pinned her hair up, on this night her brown locks were entwined with a silk ribbon rather than offset by a dainty cap, and a string of iridescent pearls encircled her graceful throat.

The lithe swiftness with which she had ascended the stairs conformed to the air of brisk agitation about her as she hastened across the room toward the cot.

Ethan, for his part, did not let her brisk gait disconcert him, but, noting her attire, raised his eyebrows questioningly. "Running away to the ball, Miss Jameson?"

Constance, coming to a rather breathless halt before him, laughed at his quick-witted astuteness. "No, no . . . though 'twould be a fine night for it. There is no sign of any rain, not even a cloud in the sky."

Now that she was nearer, Ethan could see that her hastiness was accompanied by an animated vibrance which reflected a state of mirthful gladness.

"We have guests dining with us below — Widow Bennett and her family. Her two sons have just returned from studying in England,

and Father is hosting a splendid dinner to welcome them home." It was evident by her enthusiasm that she thought it a very fine occasion, and her words poured out with eager rapidity. "I cannot stay long — a few minutes only. After all, I could hardly excuse myself from their company on the pretext that I needed to work upon my father's gift! Daniel Bennett has brought his violin and is going to play for us later . . . he's very accomplished, or so says his mother. Polly's just at the spinet now." And indeed, a distant melody could be faintly discerned drifting up from the nether regions of the house. Constance continued, catching her breath in her eagerness, "I only excused myself momentarily — saying that I needed to fetch my fan from upstairs. It *is* rather warm downstairs with so many people gathered in the parlor. There are six other guests besides ourselves, you know." Constance paused in her recitation and peered more closely at Ethan. Her tone somewhat subdued, she murmured, "Oh, you look warm as well. 'Tis no wonder, being confined to these upper regions of the house, where the air is most apt to be oppressive."

She laid her fan upon the tall stool and flitted over to the wash basin, returning with a dampened cloth (wrung out at arm's length over the basin so as not to splash her gown) and was about to dab it upon Ethan's perspiring brow, but then, remembering his improved condition — for he was sitting upright, with his feet on the floor — she glanced at him apologetically and held the cloth out to him. Ethan took it from her accordingly and mopped his face and brow, grateful to feel the refreshing dampness against his perspiring skin.

Constance was about to seat herself upon her stool, as was her custom, but she paused quite abruptly and straightened again, as if she had suddenly remembered something of importance.

Ethan glanced at her as he set the cloth aside. "You will not even sit for a moment?"

Constance flushed rather sheepishly. "Oh, 'tis just that I — well, 'tis easy enough to wash a day-gown whose hem has been resting upon the floorboards, but this gown—," she fingered the elegant rose-colored silk of her skirt, "'twould not be well for me to dirty it."

Ethan gave a nod. "I see." He continued, "I would stand and allow you to sit here, but somehow I suspect you will not have me up on my feet." He did not mention to her that he often stood during the hours she was not there; he was not certain she would approve, even though he placed no exertion upon the splintered leg. "However," he went on, "you are very welcome to sit beside me, if the cot's height would suit you better than the stool."

Constance made plain her objection to this suggestion with a prim shake of her head and a look of mild reproof, which only served to aggravate Ethan. It *had* been a rather brazen suggestion on his part, and under ordinary circumstances he would not have deigned to put forth such an idea, but these were hardly ordinary circumstances, and he said as much, struggling against his irritation to maintain a tone that was very deliberately even.

"Miss Jameson, whether you sit or stand is no concern of mine, but if it is only your ideals of propriety which prevent you from putting us both at ease — for I confess, my own sense of propriety is affronted when a lady stands while I am seated — then you are needlessly depriving yourself of a very reasonable measure of comfort. You may think of this as a kind of 'bed', but in actuality it is only a 'cot', and in its present mode of use it is really more of a 'bench', so I hardly think you would be compromising your respectability should you choose to sit here. And—," he continued on before she could protest, for his impatience was mounting over the absurdity of the situation, "—if it is my present state of being only half-clothed that gives you hesitation, I might point out that you have looked upon me every day for more than two months, and the fact that I have never donned a shirt in that entire period of time — for the most practical of reasons — has never brought so much as a blush to your cheek, nor has it ever prevented you from sitting in close proximity to me," —indicating the little stool only six inches from his bedside— "even though my upper half be clad in nothing except a bandage across my chest!"

Constance looked only mildly shocked, which bespoke of her sensibility, for she doubtlessly recognized the truth in his words despite his increasingly acerbic manner of delivery.

Ethan, for his part, having vented his frustration (and privately cursed the senselessness of the entire female race), collected himself, and, leaning back against the wall, fixed his gaze upon Miss Jameson, addressing her in a tone that was markedly subdued, though still assured: "If, however, it is my very person whom you dislike or fear . . . then you are wise to maintain your stance under the semblance of propriety."

There was neither challenge nor intimation in his tone or his countenance; it was simply a straightforward conjecture, and it seemed to give Constance pause as she met his eye.

After a moment, a wisp of a smile graced her lips.

"I can truly only stay for a moment," she maintained, even as she took her seat beside Ethan, leaving just enough space to appease her proprieties, yet near enough that he could detect the scent of a light floral fragrance about her . . . a treasured perfume for the occasion, no doubt, and one that suited her perfectly: subtle, sweet, delicate.

Awareness of this may have roused Ethan's senses, but it did not assuage his state of mind, for despite his jocular greeting and offhand manner, he was really rather unsettled by Constance's appearance. Whether it was the alteration in her attire, the lateness of the hour, or something else which nettled him, he could not say; but as he looked at her sitting beside him, his brooding manner was more telling than words.

"What is it that puts that bloom upon your cheek tonight?" he murmured moodily. "One of the widow's sons, no doubt. I daresay she is in high anticipation that one of them should marry you."

Constance smiled knowingly. "If there is a change in my complexion, it is only due to the excitement of partaking in such a fine occasion, for we seldom host gatherings these days. As to the question of marriage . . . ," her eyes sparkled at Ethan, "while it is possible that one of

Widow Bennett's sons may have some notions in that regard, I rather think it is the widow herself who harbors some motive in her own right. My sisters and I have long suspected that her regard for our father transcends mere neighborly esteem."

"Well, if she has two sons and your father has two unmarried daughters, it would seem there could be more than one alliance made," Ethan observed.

Constance only smiled again, but did not pursue the subject further; instead, she turned the focus of the conversation upon Ethan himself, glancing at him sideways. "You seldom show interest in topics of such a domestic nature. Have you never given thought to an alliance for yourself?"

Ethan's scornful frown made plain his opinion of the matter. "Marriage is a liability for any soldier, and even more so for a spy. In my profession, such a commitment would only be a hindrance and a distraction. I have no time — or patience — for a wife. And I need hardly mention," he added, "that it would be the worst kind of match for any woman. The wife of a soldier rarely sees her husband, and should her husband be a spy, then her burden of isolation would only be compounded, for she must always know that he faces certain danger every day and that his life could be forfeit at any moment. There is naught good that can come of a soldier taking a wife," he concluded, shaking his head with conviction.

Constance considered his words for a moment. "And yet . . .," she mused thoughtfully, "many women *are* the wives of soldiers, and even now — at this moment — tending their hearths alone, wondering when their husbands shall return . . . or even if they shall return at all," she added softly.

Ethan made no reply, but Constance's gentle tone had alleviated his moodiness, while she herself seemed to have temporarily forgotten her hurry to return to the guests below.

She soon came out of her reverie and smiled warmly at him. "Well, Lieutenant Shaye, in spite of your contempt, I suspect you left behind more than a few broken hearts in North Carolina; for you are very handsome," she pointed out with unflattering matter-of-factness, "and," she continued with a twinkle in her eye, "you can even be quite pleasant when you choose to be."

Ethan glanced over at her. She was looking at him expectantly, patiently awaiting his response, undoubtedly anticipating a tale of tragic romance or youthful love unrequited.

Heaving a resigned sigh, Ethan indulged her, and — knowing she would not be impressed by a soldier's dalliances — racked his brain to recall any lady who had ever occupied more than an hour of his thoughts or attention.

"There was one young lady . . .," he began slowly, frowning in his attempt to recall details, ". . . her father was the clergyman at the church my family attended back in North Carolina. This was, of course, before I was sent away to school in the North, so I was hardly more than a boy at the time. I remember she used to bring me plum-cakes and wait for me under the hawthorn tree at the end of the lane near my school-master's house, so that she could walk part of the way home with me each day. I wouldn't allow her to wait at the school-master's gate, for fear my fellow schoolmates would see her." He chuckled at the memory, though Constance tried to look indignant at his merciless treatment of the young lady.

"Oh, you were very cruel to be ashamed of her before your friends!" she remonstrated, smiling nevertheless, for it was apparent that even in his schooldays Ethan had been audacious and self-assured. "And then what befell?" Constance prompted, eager to hear the climax of this youthful romance.

But Ethan was not so enchanted with the subject and put little effort into further recollection. "Oh . . . I went off to my studies in the northern colonies," he said disinterestedly. "She might have harbored a notion that we had some kind of understanding — that I was going to go back and marry her someday once I had finished my education. She was very weepy when I left, and even gave me a lock of her hair."

Constance wrinkled her pretty forehead . . . she had begun to suspect that this tale was not going to have the endearing elements she'd anticipated. What's more, Ethan seemed satisfied that the tale was ended and needed further prompting to continue.

"Is there no more to tell?" Constance asked rather plaintively. "What became of your young lady? Did you never go back to your home in North Carolina?"

Ethan looked at her with a rather cavalier sparkle to his own eye, for he knew well enough this was not the course Constance hoped the tale to take. "I completed my studies to please my mother, but it had always been my ambition to follow in my father's footsteps. He led a regiment in the Seven Years' War, which is how he acquired his land in North Carolina; it was part of his pension from the British government." His voice gained warmth and momentum. "Nothing thrilled me more as a lad than listening to his tales of battle and adventure. But, of course, by the time I'd finished my education, the recognition of the colonies' mistreatment by the Crown had become the prominent issue in the North, so I aligned myself with their cause and committed my services to the defense of the colonies. Once the war began, I found my abilities well-suited to the life of a soldier and spy. I was given a Lieutenant's commission . . . and never thought more of returning to North Carolina."

Though Ethan plainly felt there was no more to tell, Constance was hardly contented with the tale's resolution.

"But . . . the young lady . . . she had given you a lock of hair to remember her by. What became of that?"

Ethan shrugged carelessly. "I could not say. Lost sometime during my schooling, no doubt."

Constance sighed, resigned to disappointment. "What an unromantic conclusion. Are all men so unsympathetic to a lady's affection? I only hope she has since found herself a worthy gentleman and is not still pining after you."

Ethan laughed at this admonishment. "Considering that I was not more than seventeen when last I saw her, and I am now five-and-twenty, I rather think she has moved beyond such a childhood fancy. And I should hardly expect you to berate me for callousness — not five minutes ago you were sighing over the plight of women whose husbands must be absent during these times of war. How should it be for any woman who was so unfortunate as to be bound to me? She would not know what had become of me these past months. Likely she would think me dead. She could not know that —," he paused abruptly as he glanced at Constance, "— that I was being so well-cared for," he concluded in a tone that was suddenly subdued.

And Constance felt the color rise in her face, for she realized that the modest distance at which she had so carefully situated herself had inexplicably narrowed during the course of their conversation. The two of them were, in fact, sitting quite together upon the cot, but the course of this circumstance could not be attributed to any purposeful design on the part of one or the other, but rather seemed to have come about quite inadvertently, as might naturally occur whenever there is familiar discourse between two who are quite at ease with one another.

Ethan saw her blush and became aware of a permeating intensity bestirring within his own veins. This girl alone possessed the ability to evoke such internal agitation, and it never failed to unsettle him. Yet, how unwilling was he to surrender her back to the world below — a world she seemed to have forgotten for the moment.

Nevertheless, he knew he must not detain her longer, and as he inclined his head toward hers, he gave her a reluctant smile and quietly conceded, "It sounds as if someone is playing upon a violin downstairs."

Constance's demeanor changed at once. "Oh no!" Her dismay was apparent as she hastily scrambled to her feet, her thoughts once more attuned to that world beyond the garret. "The violin — I did so want to hear it!" she exclaimed, hurrying toward the stairwell, then stopped short as she realized the more pressing concern. "Oh, they will be wondering what has become of me — gone to fetch my fan! They will surely have sent someone after me by now!"

In her agitated haste, she very nearly made it to the stairwell before Ethan's voice called her to a halt. "Miss Jameson!"

Constance looked back over her shoulder.

"I think your story might be more plausible if you took this with you." And Ethan held out the fan toward her.

Constance gasped. "Oh! Yes, indeed!" She scurried back to the cot and gratefully took the fan from him. Then she paused, her purpose momentarily diverted, and as she bent her head closer to Ethan's, he saw that her eyes once again glimmered with the excitement of the occasion. "I meant to tell you . . .," she intoned happily, "our cook has turned out the most marvelous steamed pudding for the evening's finale. I shall see that Jenny gets a bit of it up to you . . . somehow."

And with a warm-hearted smile, she turned and hastened back to the stairwell and descended down toward the strains of the distant violin.

DESPITE CONSTANCE'S ASSERTION THAT IT would not rain that evening, her words were perhaps too quickly spoken, for during the night, while the household slept, grey clouds thickened over the countryside, and by the time the earliest risers stirred, the rain had commenced — not just intermittent droplets, but an unrelenting downpour. And as is so often the case in the midst of springtime, once the rains begin, they do not abate. Over the course of the next few weeks, the sun rarely showed itself, and even during the daytime a murky dimness enveloped the garret, as what little natural light penetrated the window was as cheerless as the grey world outside. And as the precipitation mingled with the warmth rising from the verdant earth, a sultry humidity encased everything, adding a level of discomfort to the garret's austerity.

Such inclement conditions took a toll upon the disposition of the fugitive, for in those seemingly endless grey days, Ethan was restless and irritable. His impatience won out over reason, and he began to spend more and more time on his feet, silently limping across the floorboards in his hours of solitude, undoubtedly slowing his leg's healing, but preserving his soundness of mind, for he had no doubt that prolonged immobility would have driven him to madness. Still, he was relatively careful not to overextend himself so that the bone would continue to heal, and as the days wore on, the splint was removed and the limp became gradually less pronounced.

He was able to maintain his strength and fitness by engaging in the physical exercises he had devised for himself, but though he devoted a good many hours to those endeavors, he still must spend the greatest proportion of his time sitting or lying upon the cot, and the confinement became nearly unbearable. His moody sullenness was reflected in a persistent scowl which rivaled even Jenny's antagonistic frown and which troubled Jenny's tenderhearted young mistress. Constance did her best to allay Ethan's restlessness, and she met with a fair measure of success, for he could not long be discontented while she was there. But once she departed from the garret each evening, Ethan's sullenness would set in once more, so that by morning he would again be glowering.

Constance sought new diversions for the restless fugitive, for she knew that his situation would be more tolerable if his mind was occupied during his long hours of seclusion. She made it a point to look out for newspapers, which her father would sometimes bring back from town. While Dr. Jameson may have raised an eyebrow at his daughter's sudden interest in current events, he did not object to her request that she might look at the newspapers before they were relegated to the burn-pile, and so she was able to occasionally procure one for Ethan.

Ethan was much gratified by this small favor and poured voraciously over every column, for though the printed news was never recent, it provided a long-awaited link to the outside world. He paid special heed to anything pertaining to the war, of course, yet he could find little encouragement in the printed reports, for there was no word of any victories for General Washington or the Patriot soldiers, although confrontations with British legions seemed to be escalating in number and intensity.

While access to these publications alleviated Ethan's craving for information, it only served to increase his frustration at being unable to reunite with his associates and take an active role in the events unfolding in the colonies. He spoke of little else to Constance, who listened with a great deal of patience and sympathy; and, indeed, her gentleness invariably soothed his agitation.

After what seemed an interminable duration of greyness and precipitation, there came at last a break in the showers and finally a night where Ethan slept without the incessant patter of raindrops echoing through his slumber. It thus seemed unnaturally quiet when he awoke the next morning, and he guessed that it was the unaccustomed silence which had caused him to oversleep, for a plate of biscuits upon the tall stool indicated that Jenny had already come and gone, though he had heard not a sound.

But as the day progressed, he wondered if something was amiss, for he realized that the encompassing silence was not entirely due to the absence of falling raindrops, but also to an inordinate stillness within the household below. He detected only intermittent sounds throughout the day — only a few muffled voices and soft footsteps — and he took extra caution in his own movements, hardly venturing more than a few steps from the cot, lest any activity should be heard in the quiescence below, though this self-imposed restriction of movement made the day seem even longer than usual.

Neither Jenny nor her mistress came at the customary hour, which only reinforced the duration of solitude and the conspicuousness of the silence. As the long day at last gave way to nightfall, Ethan became increasingly mindful of every slight sound, always expecting to hear the creak of the door or a tread upon the steps, which would signal Jenny ascending with a jug of fresh water. He heard nothing so familiar, though. The only sounds were distant and infrequent, from the floors below.

The garret had grown uncomfortably warm throughout the day, exacerbated by the dampness which hung in the air after the cessation of the rain, and the sultriness did not abate once the sun set. The ensuing darkness brought no relief to Ethan, who could feel the sweat clinging to his brow and running down the back of his neck. He had never wished more to see Jenny's robust figure, if only for the cooling water she would surely convey, but it seemed his anticipation would be in vain, for the dour slave woman did not appear.

Resigned that there would be neither relief nor company that night, there seemed nothing to do except sleep, and as Ethan lay back upon his pillow in the darkness, he attempted to situate himself as comfortably as possible despite the oppressive heat. His eyelids had barely closed, however, when he heard a sound — very soft — upon the steps.

He was alert at once, eyes opened and head turned toward the stair-passage, where a hazy light could be seen growing brighter and brighter as it neared the top step. He knew well enough that such a soft footfall must only belong to Miss Constance, and he sat up as she appeared out of the darkness, carrying a chamberstick to light her way.

Although Ethan had suspected an aberrance in the household routine, there seemed nothing out of the ordinary in Constance's manner, except that, as she drew nearer, he thought he discerned some weariness in her thoughtful brown eyes, and though she smiled in her usual gentle way, when she spoke, her tone was so hushed it was almost a whisper.

"I am sorry to come at such a late hour. I hope I am not disturbing your— Oh!" she interrupted herself, her voice yet low, as she set her chamberstick upon the tall stool. "Jenny has not been here," she murmured reflectively, seeing the empty biscuit plate. "I do not know if she will come tonight." She looked toward Ethan apologetically.

He made no response, only beheld her silently, unwilling to admit even to himself how empty the day had seemed without her amiable presence.

"Jenny has been needed below all day," Constance continued. "She has had much to do, tending to my father. He was taken ill last night — this thick dampness in the air has given the fever to many whom he has attended throughout the countryside, until he himself fell prey to it. He will be well, though. His fever has now turned, and my sister will sit with him for a while." Her relief was evident in her tone and her visage. "Still," she added, "I am sure you understand that I could not ask Jenny

76

to forsake her attentions to my father, although . . .," her forehead wrinkled in some concern as she glimpsed the water jug lying empty on its side near the cot, "I had hoped she might have spared a moment to bring you some fresh water." Her soft eyes grew anxious as she noticed the sweat glistening upon Ethan's brow, visible even in the dim candlelight. Her voice — already subdued — dropped to a whisper. "I will find a way to bring you something cool to drink." As she stepped closer, her eye fell upon his bandage, and she frowned, for it was soaked through and beginning to unravel. "That needs rebandaging," she murmured. "Jenny would certainly have attended to that." She stood in the semi-darkness, contemplating, while Ethan kept his silent gaze fixed upon her.

When Constance came out of her reverie, she spoke with solemn resolution. "I shall attend to it. It will not do to wait until the morrow — it will likely be quite undone by then, and 'tis a simple enough task."

Knowing that Ethan might voice objection to this idea, Constance deliberately averted her gaze and immediately set about her preparations before he could dissent. But he remained quite silent, as he had been from the first.

The candle's soft light illuminated only a small sphere of space near the cot, and Constance slipped into the garret's shadowy darkness for a moment, returning with the water basin, which she set carefully on the floor next to the tall stool.

While she stood there beside the cot preparing a fresh bandage, Ethan took it upon himself to remove the old one. It was not difficult — his wound had nearly healed — and there was little substance to the bandage of late. But it was wet and ragged with perspiration, and though Constance had voiced no reluctance, Ethan would not have her delicate fingers touch such grittiness, so he removed it himself, noiselessly and adeptly.

A hush had fallen over everything . . . not just the darkened garret, but seemingly the entire household, for not a sound emanated from below, nor from the night beyond the window. Neither did they speak — the maiden nor the fugitive — for in the silence was found their understanding.

The permeating darkness may mask many elements, but so, too, can it give rise to heightened sensation, and both girl and soldier were well conscious of these faculties; for in such an austere setting, in the light of but a single candle, what may appear to be only a dim, obscure corner of the garret became for them now an intimate haven of warmth, beyond the reach of the peripheral shadows encircling them.

The darkness, the sultry heat, and the silence together conspired — not only to heighten senses, but to alter inhibitions as well, and where once Constance had hesitated merely to sit alongside Ethan, she now found purpose in it, even though he was less respectably situated, for he had been reclining, preparing to sleep; and though he now sat upright, his legs were still stretched out upon the cot before him. He was near enough to the wall that there was just space at the cot's edge for Constance to perch there, facing him, in such close proximity that when she bent to pick up the cloth from the basin, her hair brushed against his arm . . . a sensation of which he was keenly aware, though the young lady herself was not. But once Constance had wrung out her cloth and sat upright again, she, too, seemed to sense that something unprecedentedly solemn was transpiring, for she hesitated before lifting her eyes, at once aware of the darkness and the nearness of Ethan . . . aware of the warmth of his body . . . of his sturdy arm . . . his broad shoulder . . . his chest laid bare . . . so near that she could feel the heat of his body disseminating across her own. And for all the previous times she had looked upon him, here were suddenly new inhibitions rising where there had been none, for her cognizance of his nearness stirred feelings which had hitherto been only vague impressions held in check, but which now manifested themselves in bated breath, a stirring within her breast.

Suddenly shy, yet mindful of her task, Constance began by bathing his chest and shoulders with the dampened cloth. And though her face was only inches from his, she took great care that her eye should not meet his, keeping her head bent and her eye trained fastidiously upon the cloth's movement as she gently and silently drew it across his chest — where beads of perspiration gleamed in the flickering candle-light — and then along his shoulders and arms, where she could feel his muscles tense instinctively in tandem with the cloth's progress.

Yet even as her dampened cloth cleansed and cooled the fugitive, Constance felt a feverish warmth rising within her own body. It was an overarching, persistent sensation which took no relief from the droplets of water that splashed her hand as she dropped the cloth back into the basin on the floor.

Neither was she to find assuagement in her next endeavor. Still avoiding Ethan's eye, she picked up the fresh bandage and repositioned herself with one leg tucked underneath her on the cot, so as to be able to reach across and around him. She sat there for a long while — her face deliberately turned away from him, and therefore away from what little light there was — feigning to examine the bandage in her hands, though she could barely discern it in the darkness. In truth, the unfamiliar sensations which had stirred within her bewildered and disconcerted her, and she hesitated to begin a task where there would be no protective boundary of cloth separating her hand from his skin.

As she tentatively turned her head back toward the light, she un-wittingly glanced up into his face, only to find his brooding eyes trained upon her. Without averting his gaze or speaking a word, he took the bandage from her hand and held its edge in place against his chest.

Conscious once more of the heat rising both within and without, Constance lowered her eyes and began to unroll the bandage, pulling it slowly across Ethan's chest, taking care that her fingers should not en-counter his skin. Such deliberate caution proved incompatible, though, with the requisite procedure, and as she leaned across him to bring the bandage around his ribcage, she very nearly toppled, but she felt his arm about her waist, steadying her.

Trying to ignore the surging fluctuation within her breast, Constance quickly placed one hand upon his shoulder so that she might steady her-self, and Ethan duly relinquished his hold upon her.

But his sturdy arm had been reassuring, and Constance set to work once more, her stability ensured with her hand resting softly against his shoulder.

And from the first touch there was a transcendence — a wordless understanding, primordial and sublime; for they were not strangers . . . a deeper unity had long been cultivated between them, and now the darkness would become their sanctuary, enfolding them in its hallowed empyrean.

And in the flickering shadows, under the spell of the candle's soft glow, Constance moved as if in a dream — immersing herself in her endeavor, slowly pulling the bandage taut across Ethan's front. Filled with a sense of reverence, both wondrous and fearful, she allowed her sense of touch to guide her hands. As she gently smoothed the bandage, she could feel the rise and fall of his chest beneath her fingers, and when she leaned across him, she felt his warm breath upon her cheek. She closed her eyes for a fleeting moment, mindful of the nearness, conscious of the rapid acceleration of her heartbeat.

The only sound was the quiet rustle of Constance's petticoat as she carefully lengthened the bandage across his back, around to the front, and then repeated the circle again. Her delicate fingers were soft and soothing against his perspiring skin, and though neither Constance nor Ethan attempted to speak, there was an implicit understanding between them . . . an awareness with every touch. Notions of time and place were suspended. Logic and reason had flown. The simple procedure had been transformed into a rite, ethereal and sacred. There was a revelation with every breath, with every touch, and behind the silence was a suppressed tension that in the darkness was almost palpable. They were alive only to the existing moment . . . only to each other . . . to every subtle movement, every visceral awakening.

Constance found the unfamiliar rise of sensation and emotion to be both enthralling and unsettling, so it was that as she finally fastened the bandage in place, she felt a measure of alleviation, yet did not hastily remove her hand, but instead allowed her fingers to remain for a moment, gently pressing the bandage's seam against his chest.

She could not avoid his eye any longer, and as she slowly pulled her hand away, she hesitantly lifted her gaze . . . shyly, uncertainly . . . only to have it arrested — held fast under Ethan's own pensive contemplation. His brow was knit and his countenance broodingly absorbed as he looked at her. The ardor reflected in his eyes caused Constance to blush, and though she prayed that the tremulous fluttering within her breast was not manifested outwardly, she could not look away.

Even in the waning candlelight, Constance was near enough to Ethan that she could clearly see the word form upon his lips, though his face was half-concealed in shadows; a word slowly drawn out upon a breath; a whisper so hushed that it hardly broke the silence; just one word . . .

"Constance."

It was but a single word, yet its intimation was conveyed as much by his penetrating gaze as by his solemn, fervent whisper.

And still Constance could not look away. Her countenance reflected profound tenderness . . . uncertainty . . . awe.

Aware only of one another, they could not know that the world outside persisted in its course of indifferent banality. So it was that they were both startled to hear a blunt "thud", which abruptly shattered their hushed idyll.

Constance started with a gasp, and both turned their heads to see Jenny standing just inside the room, the water jug beside her on the floor where she had set it with such unceremonious bluntness.

Constance was immediately on her feet and hastened to distance herself from the cot. "Jenny! I — I did not think — that is, I did not know if you would come. I — I have already attended to the rebandaging, so, if you'll just see to Lieutenant Shaye's . . . other needs . . . ." Her words came tumbling out in a manner as flustered and disconcerted as her emotions, and as she sailed past Jenny toward the stair passage, she caught a glimpse of such a severe grimace upon the slave's dark face that she knew Ethan's observations about Jenny had not been ill-founded.

The swarthy slave woman's austere, accusing glare was plainly directed at Ethan, though, and it was very begrudgingly that she carried the water jug to his cot after her mistress's swift departure.

Ethan, for his part, swiftly recovered his mental assurance, and though his heaving chest bore lingering physical testimony to the intensity of his recent fervor, he met Jenny's dark looks with a steadfast eye as he leaned back against the pillow.

DESPITE HIS SEEMINGLY SWIFT RECOVERY of self-possession, Ethan was not indifferent to what had taken place, nor was he unconcerned. Once his faculties of reason had regained authority over instinctual inclinations, he was greatly troubled and spent a sleepless night upon the cot, unable to quiet his mind in the silence of the garret. His thoughts dwelt upon not only what had transpired between Constance Jameson and himself, but also upon the origins of that communion. For he knew that what had existed between them in the shadowy candlelight was not merely a fleeting moment of unrestraint, but was the product of something that had been kindled long ago and inadvertently nurtured across subsequent days and weeks and even months. In all that time, Ethan had never permitted his thoughts to venture into that perilous realm of affectivity. He had purposely pushed such thoughts aside, and he was determined that he would not now entertain any such deliberations. Yet, it seemed that the more resolved he was to deflect such sentiments, the more agitated his mind became, and he slept only fitfully, spending most of the night lying upon his back, frowning into the empty blackness.

That night seemed to stretch as long as the isolated days, and the longer he lay there, the more convinced Ethan became of one prevailing certainty: he needed to be back in the company of fighting men; back where his instincts and impulses could be trusted; back where blood and sweat were as much a part of existence as muscle and flesh; where strength and boldness meant survival; and above all, where that moment-to-moment survival left no time to confront unwarranted complexities within.

Reaching down beneath the cot, he silently grasped onto his pistol — the tangible connection to that world he would reclaim. The familiarity of its weight and contour strengthened his resolve as he fingered it meditatively in the darkness.

As the sun rose the following morning, it became apparent to Ethan that the days of predictability had run out insofar as any sort of routine beneath the garret's rafters. No one could have climbed the stairs without his cognizance — so tenuous was his state of slumber that he was alert to every sound, even during the earliest morning hours, and he would certainly have heard Jenny's prominent footfall, even had she appeared as early as she had the previous day. Yet, when Ethan's usual hour of waking had long passed, still Jenny did not appear, nor did she as the morning progressed.

Ethan had other matters to contemplate, however, and despite his lack of sleep or sustenance, he arose from his cot quite early and began silently pacing about the room, noting with satisfaction that he was able to put almost his full weight upon the injured leg, though any physician would undoubtedly maintain that it still required a duration of time before it could be considered completely healed.

It was late in the morning when Ethan finally heard a footfall upon the stair. He was standing as close as he dared to the window, but when he heard the footfall, he turned toward the stair passage, his brow furrowed, for it was not Jenny's tread at all, but that of her young mistress.

Ethan had not expected to see Constance so soon. Yet no amount of readiness could have prepared him to confront the girl who emerged from the stairwell, so altered was her demeanor. She paused for only the briefest moment at the top of the steps, but even in that instant, Ethan knew that something was very wrong.

Constance's face was ashen and taut, her eyes distant and grave. The features of her countenance were stricken with bleak affliction, made all the more apparent as she stepped into the dim light of the garret. In one hand she held a cloth parcel, conveying it with uncharacteristic carelessness, utterly inattentive to the fact that one end had come undone, allowing a dusting of crumbs to fall to the floor as she crossed toward the cot and laid the parcel on the stool with a trembling hand.

Ethan's misgivings turned to concern, and any cautions upon which he had resolved were at once forgotten when he saw her afflicted state.

He moved toward her, but she did not wait for him to reach her side. Neither did she look at him, but only shook her head disconsolately and spoke in a tremulous, quivering voice. "It is so horrible to think of it. That she should be unjustly blamed! And the fault is only mine. They beat her!" She turned toward Ethan, looking directly into his eyes, her own eyes clouded with sadness, her voice choked as she repeated, "They beat her!" And suddenly overcome, she covered her face with her hands and sank down despairingly upon her little stool.

Ethan frowned, worried and perplexed, as he sat upon the cot near Constance. "What do you mean? Someone was beaten? Jenny?" he conjectured.

Constance nodded and looked up sorrowfully. "She was getting a bit of food for you out of the storehouse — as she does every morning when our manservant Uriah is taking supplies over to the kitchen. But today — I do not know why — Uriah returned early and caught her with the gingerbread. He accused her of stealing it, and—," her voice broke off again as tears welled in her eyes, "—oh, it was none of her fault! She should not have been beaten! I did not know until it was too late. I ran out there as soon as I heard . . . but he had already tethered her to the post outside the smokehouse and put the switch to her." A sob escaped as she continued, "I told him to stop at once — that Jenny had done nothing wrong, and that 'twas I who told her to take the gingerbread. But I could see that he did not believe me. He asked why I should have wanted her to take it and at such an early hour, and I — I—," her voice faltered in her anxiety, "—I could give no explanation. I could not reveal the true purpose, and I — I could not think. I just stood there as if frozen . . . as silent as Jenny. I could think of nothing to say — my very silence incriminating her! He did not beat her more, but . . . 'twas not the beating that was the worst of it. It was seeing Jenny there like that — the look upon her face. Oh, Ethan—," Constance fixed her anguished gaze upon him, "—if you could have seen her — the way she looked at me! Such shame and sadness in her eyes. In all the years she's been here, she has never committed any offense which merited punishment. Even after my mother died, Jenny has always served faithfully and obediently. She prides herself upon it. And now . . . my father will surely hear of this and will think less of her — she knows that. That was the shame I saw in her eyes." Constance shook her head in heavyhearted misery. "She has done nothing wrong . . . she was only acting upon my bidding, as she has ever done. I am to blame, and yet I go unpunished! Is there to be no justice for her?" This grief-stricken outpouring had taken its toll upon Constance's strength, and she slumped down, burying her face in her hands again, and sorrowfully lamenting, "If you had seen the look upon her face . . . ."

Ethan frowned in concern at Constance's state of grief. He shook his head. "You must not blame yourself. You have done nothing wrong, nor has Jenny. It was an unfortunate occurrence, nothing else. If you must assign guilt, then cast it upon me, for it is my presence here which compelled her actions. Jenny knows that you are not to blame. The incident will soon enough be forgotten, and everything shall be right again."

But Constance would not be consoled. Distraught, she rose from her stool. "No, you are wrong. Things cannot be so easily righted." Looking utterly forlorn, she turned away and murmured, "Everything seems tangled of late."

Ethan knew that it was more than just Jenny's plight that had contributed to Constance's muddled emotions. Still frowning, he rose and crossed to where she was standing.

Hearing his footsteps behind her, Constance turned her head.

Ethan reached for her hand. "Constance . . ."

But Constance shrank back. Her soft eyes were suddenly beseeching, her lips quivering. "Don't — oh, I beg of you, don't!" she breathed tremulously. "Do not touch me . . . please do not touch me!"

Deeply troubled by her imploring anxiety, Ethan withdrew his outstretched hand, that Constance's distress might be allayed.

But it was too late. With one last anguished glance, Constance turned and fled down the stairs.

FOR THE SECOND CONSECUTIVE NIGHT, Constance found no peace in slumber. Although she was awake long before the sun rose, she continued to lie abed, well-aware of the early hour, yet still struggling to grasp some remnant of the rest which eluded her disconcerted mind.

Because she was mindful of the dawn's tranquility, she was all the more startled when the door to her bedchamber burst open with forceful intensity, and Jenny was suddenly at her bedside. The slave woman's large bosom heaved in urgent respiration as she grasped at Constance's shoulder, attempting to shake her from slumber.

Constance, being already awake, sat up at once, much panicked by Jenny's ominous expression.

"Jenny! What is it?"

It was not customary for a slave to wake any member of the household unless there was urgent necessity, and Constance's first thought was for her father — fearing that his recovery might have taken an unforeseen turn for the worse.

But the young mistress and her servant had a longstanding ability to comprehend one another, and it took but an instant for Constance to realize that Jenny's vigorous earring-tugging had naught to do with the master, for the dark woman's round eyes were focused upward.

"The garret? Is there something the matter with Lieutenant Shaye?"

Constance did not need to wait for Jenny's emphatic nod to know that she had guessed correctly.

Rising hastily from her bed, Constance hurriedly donned a shawl over her night-shift, and, taking the chamberstick from Jenny, scurried past the slave woman out into the dark, deserted corridor.

Jenny did not follow her mistress down the silent passage nor up the narrow wooden steps behind the door in the store-room. Constance took no notice of her solitary state, though, as she ascended through the darkness, her lithe, bare-footed swiftness giving way to a more cautious pace as she neared the top, for she was suddenly aware of a foreboding — a sort of inexplicable dread for which she could not account, but which compelled her to pause before setting foot upon the garret's floorboards, conscious of her heart's pounding.

Her presentiment was substantiated almost immediately, for though she held her chamberstick aloft, daybreak was already penetrating the garret's small window, casting a grey morning light throughout the room, and she did not require a taper to see that the cot against the wall was unoccupied, nor that the window was unlatched. Assuredly, the stillness was more telling than any observation.

The room was deserted.

Ethan was gone.

Constance did not move for a very long time. She just stood there, at the spot where she had emerged from the stairwell, in her night-shift and cap and bare feet, clutching her chamberstick . . . trying to come to terms with the emptiness of the room; trying to ignore the desolate pang she felt inside of her, in a region just below her pulsating heart.

Even from where she stood, she could see that all of Ethan's belongings were gone as well — his boots, his canteen, his pistol, even the ill-fitting shirt borrowed from the mending-pile. But when Constance finally ventured to step closer to the cot, she saw that he had left one thing behind. In the center of the cot, just beside the pillow, lay a single sheet of paper, folded in half. Her name — "Constance Jameson" — was plainly penciled across the front.

Setting her chamberstick upon the stool, Constance slowly picked up the paper and sank down upon the cot's edge. After staring at the paper for a few moments — unable to yet fully grasp that Ethan was gone — she at last carefully unfolded it with trembling fingers and, upon turning it over, found it to be a letter, written in Ethan's terse, masculine hand.

June 3, 1776

Dear Miss Jameson,

I must apologize for imparting this farewell to you in writing rather than in person. It is a reflection of my own weakness of character that I could not convey it any other way.

I realize that you might view my departure as inordinately abrupt — as my leg is not completely healed — but I assure you that I have considered the matter over the course of days with thorough deliberation, and my decision was not made in reckless haste. I am confident in my ability to undertake the journey to safer grounds, and it is undoubtedly to the benefit of us all that I should take my leave at this time.

Miss Jameson, you must not think me lacking in sincere gratitude for all that you have done for me. I owe my very life to you, and I hope you know that I would not hesitate to repay that debt in kind, though I pray such adversity may never befall you. As it is, the escalating strife between the colonies and the Crown suggests that there will yet be many long battles fought upon this soil, but should I emerge from this war with my life intact, I will seek to honorably repay the debt I owe.

Again, I ask that you forgive the nature of this communication, and be well-assured that there is nothing impersonal in the sentiment of gratitude it conveys.

God keep you, Miss Jameson. I know you will understand why I must leave before you wake. I remain

Your grateful servant,
Ethan Shaye

Constance's eye lingered for a long while on the last sentence: *I know you will understand why I must leave before you wake.*

She knew that those words conveyed a deeper meaning, and she could not longer hold back the tears — gentle tears which flowed from the depths of her tender heart and which left silent, poignant traces upon the paper where they fell.

And yet, even in the midst of her quiet tears, Constance's eye alighted upon a postscript at the bottom of the page, hastily scrawled underneath the signature; and as she read this after-thought, she could not help but smile affectionately through her tears, for the words so plainly evoked Ethan's indomitable audaciousness:

P.S. I would be greatly appreciative if you could hold off until mid-morning reporting the horse missing from your father's stable. I will leave it somewhere on the other side of Durbin's Creek.

Yours, E.S.

PART II
The Military Encampment

July 23, 1776

COLONEL NAISMITH LOOKED REFLECTIVELY AT the paper on the table before him. He leaned back in his chair, contemplating the general's orders. Even though it was the hottest part of the day, in the hottest month of the year, he'd drawn closed the flaps over the tent's entrance, sealing in the heat, yet ensuring privacy. This meeting would require secrecy, and the participants would have to sacrifice the luxury of ventilation for the necessity of security.

The grey-haired colonel absently drummed his fingers upon the tabletop as he deliberated. There was no decision to be made — the general's orders were plain enough and were not entirely unexpected, knowing, as the colonel did, the recent difficulties encountered by the Patriot army. Yet still he pondered, for the general's orders were complex and must be carried out with precision and caution, as the tide of the entire war could well turn upon the success or failure of the enterprise.

His reverie was interrupted as the tent flaps parted and the lieutenant entered, hat in hand — his dark blue coat and white breeches still dirt-smudged from the morning's battle, but his stance in conformity with military regulations as he stood before the colonel.

"You wished to speak with me, sir?"

Colonel Naismith nodded. "Yes, Lieutenant Shaye. I must speak with you regarding a matter of the gravest importance and which demands a level of discretion that I know you to be well-capable of preserving."

Ethan gave a nod in acknowledgement of this confidence.

Colonel Naismith continued: "It has been well over a month since your return to this regiment — a return which, I need hardly say, we perceived to be somewhat miraculous, considering you had been missing for several months and were presumed dead. A great deal has occurred since then, and you have done an admirable — I might even say outstanding — job of resuming your military duties . . . fighting, riding, scouting as we moved our encampment into Delaware, leading the men boldly into hostile territory and into battles and skirmishes. The men respect you and look to you as an exemplar of bravery and discipline." The colonel looked at Ethan with a hint of a sage twinkle in his eye. "You may have them fooled as far as the discipline goes — for I know you to be stubbornly self-willed at times — but I do concede that your inherent instinct for survival has served you well in your capacity as both soldier and spy." The colonel's expression turned serious once more as he continued: "Which brings me to the purpose of this conference . . . ." He paused, leaned back in his chair again, and looked fixedly at Ethan. "Lieutenant Shaye, I am certain that I do not need to point out to you the fact that, although the wounds you sustained in your absence have healed, you have not been assigned any further duties pertaining to spying or intelligence-gathering. But, I have received today a communication from General Washington which indicates that you shall forthwith be given the opportunity to resume such endeavors." His acute grey eyes narrowed perceptively as he studied Ethan's countenance. "I see that pleases you," the colonel observed, nodding judiciously. "Yes, I know you've been impatient to set out upon such a mission again. I confess, it is my own reservations which have kept you from it, though such reservations in no way reflect upon my perception of your abilities, for I know you to be highly-skilled in that regard." Colonel Naismith smiled rather contritely. "Your father was one of the finest military officers on this continent, and I consider myself privileged to have been his friend and colleague. I cannot conjecture as to what sort of advice he would give to you were he alive, but I do not think he would be happy with *me* — considering that I have permitted you to undertake every death-defying mission that came your way and to risk your life at every opportunity. Your continued success as a spy swayed me into indulging your eagerness to take on the most dangerous of ventures time and again . . . but when that success was abruptly ended, and when we thought your life to be forfeited . . . ." He did not complete his sentence, but his severe look across the table at Ethan made plain his unwillingness to compromise his better judgment again. "You are far too valuable an asset to our cause for me to hastily give consent to another such enterprise. However —," his tone became briskly resolute as he rose from his seat, the general's orders in hand, "there are higher powers who would override my personal hesitations, and General Washington has commanded me to dispatch you — and no one else — upon a covert mission." He paused and gave Ethan a sternly critical look, though there was nothing of censure in his tone. "The general seems to be of the opinion that you are the best spy in the Patriot army . . . and also that you are anxious to undertake another such commission."

The colonel's last words were rather pointedly accusatory, and a trace of a rueful grin played about Ethan's mouth.

"Ah yes," Ethan conceded. "I . . . may have said something to that effect when he visited our camp earlier this month."

Colonel Naismith nodded knowingly. "Aye, I suppose you would have . . . and after I'd been telling him over and again in our correspondence that you were not yet ready to take on another such assignment." He sighed heavily. "At any rate, he is convinced that you are the only man suited to a task of this importance."

Ethan was impatient to hear the details of the commission. "I will readily take up whatever the general commands of me, just as I have ever followed your orders, sir," he asserted.

The colonel's eyes narrowed perceptively. "You'd best hear out the requirements of the assignment before you become overly-pleased about it, for this task is unlike any other you've set out upon." He glanced down at the paper in his hand, quickly reviewing the contents. When he looked up again, his expression was very somber, and he addressed Ethan with unambiguous gravity. "I cannot stress enough to you the urgency of this situation and of the direct effect your efforts will have upon the future of our cause."

Ethan was befittingly subdued upon hearing this austere prologue.

Colonel Naismith continued: "I know that you are well-aware of the tribulations facing our compatriots to the north and west. The bulk of our troops, under the direct command of General Washington, have been trying to secure a strategic advantage over the British in New York and Canada for many months now. I need not add that this initiative has failed to result in any notable successes for our men, nor that the situation has been detrimentally exacerbated by the British blockade of all our northern seaports, thereby cutting off our soldiers from necessary supplies and weapons. Much of New York is Loyalist country, so General Washington's men are not able to procure a great deal of help from the civilians of the region. The shortage of sufficient weapons and provisions is starting to take its toll upon our troops, and General Washington is particularly concerned about being able to procure adequate food and medical supplies if they are forced to remain there into the winter months . . . which he seems to indicate may well be required of them, even though it is only now mid-summer." He looked intently at Ethan. "Our numbers are already declining — numbers that have never been commensurate with the number of Redcoats, but which are now diminishing at an alarming rate. Our men are cut off from their main supply sources and outfitted with inadequate weapons. We cannot hope to hold out if we continue to lose so many of our own number, and it will be worse if the men lack food and medical provisions. Although some blockade-runners have made their way through the barricade of ships, the scant resources they have been able to provide are not nearly adequate. We have relied upon a different method over the past few months — a method which has proved successful until recently. Provisions are received at ports and waterways in the South, then transported by land north into New York. Of course, the main obstacle is the British road blockade set up at the Maryland border, which has effectively hemmed in the northern territories, even though New York is the only region which may be said to be completely under British control at this time. Our operation has been effective in maintaining a somewhat sufficient level of provisions to the troops in New York, who rely upon our allies in the South and overseas. But —," Colonel Naismith leaned forward, "—this crucial supply line seems to have lately been sabotaged. Five of the last six provision transports have not made it through the British road blockade. This is where General Washington requires your services. We have no other realistic means of getting weapons and supplies to his men . . . we must counter this sabotage and restore our ability to utilize the resources available from the South."

Ethan frowned, perplexed. "Would it not be feasible to forcibly remove the road blockade?"

Colonel Naismith shook his head. "Be assured, my boy, the Redcoats are not going to easily abandon this stranglehold on our troops. The road blockade is set at a strategic position, well-fortified and well-defended. Should it come under fire, they would defend in force, thereby requiring our contingent to divide in order to meet them, and we could never withstand such a weakening division amongst our number. Not now. No, the only way to ensure subsistence for the general's men is to secure our overland supply line. Someone is informing the British guard of our covert actions, and it shall be up to you to discover the identity of that informant."

Ethan's brow knit. "Do you suspect it is one of our own who is betraying us?"

Colonel Naismith again shook his head. "It is difficult to say. There are many individuals and many steps involved in this enterprise, and as it is all clandestine, none of the persons involved will openly provide you with information, for they will not know you to be a military ally. There is a place in northern Virginia called Merrilltown, on the banks of the Rappahannock River. There, the provisions are received and organized under the direction of Mr. Joshua Porter, a well-respected merchant and longtime supporter of the Patriots' cause. The supplies are loaded into wagons and concealed in a variety of ways — under bales of hay, inside barrels and hogsheads, even sewn inside bolts of fabric — any means that would evade detection at the road blockade. Naturally, though, the

British maintain strict measures of security. Every traveler must present a pass — signed by a British official — to be allowed through. And that is the point at which our enterprise has broken down of late. Mr. Porter sends each wagon-driver with a pass — forged, of course, but immaculately so; and the British guards at the barricade have always accepted the authenticity of the passes and permitted our drivers to cross into Maryland . . . until recently. As I mentioned, five of our last six wagons have been turned away at sight, the most recent only days ago, on the sixteenth of July."

"Perhaps the forger has grown careless," suggested Ethan.

But the Colonel once more gave a shake of his head. "The signatures are meticulous, and they are varied, so as to appear inconspicuous. Moreover, we have successfully sent through wagons that were not covertly transporting supplies, as well as witnessed other wagons — holding genuine passes — granted swift permission to continue northward. It would seem that the guards are somehow alerted to the identity of our specific provision transports, even though the provisions themselves are well-concealed and well-protected from thorough searching."

It was a lengthy narrative for a hot day, and the colonel took a drink from the flask on the table as Ethan pondered his words.

"Is Mr. Porter himself beyond suspicion?" Ethan queried.

Colonel Naismith recorked the flask. "One would suppose so," he said. "He is a merchant of some prominence and was a public supporter of our cause even before the war began. He is also a personal friend of our ardent advocate, Mr. George Clymer, which would, of course, seem to be an excellent validation of the man's character. And yet, as you yourself have easily surmised, Mr. Porter is certainly the man most readily knowledgeable about every detail of the shipments, and General Washington indicates that he is not to be held above suspicion, for in times of war, loyalties can be tested and can sometimes shift. Mr. Porter himself proclaims to be utterly bewildered by such deliberate betrayal and certainly appears to be most disconcerted by the continuation of the sabotage."

"Does he forge the signatures himself?" inquired Ethan.

Colonel Naismith shrugged. "I do not know. That would certainly be worth your while to discover." The colonel seemed to hesitate a moment before continuing. "There is one thing which I have neglected to tell you, Lieutenant Shaye. When I mentioned that five of six wagons have not succeeded in passing through the blockade . . . that was somewhat misleading. In actuality, six of the last seven wagons have been unsuccessful. Five of them were turned away by the British guards, but one of them was attacked on the high road between Merrilltown and the blockade. The driver was killed — shot in broad daylight — but it was no work of bandits, for the wagon and its contents were left upon the road untouched. Clearly, the aim was to prevent the wagon from ever reaching the blockade. Only one fact is evident: whomever is the perpetrator . . . he will go to extraordinary means to prevent our supplies from reaching the general's men. There may well be several people involved, for it is not a simple endeavor — to uncover our plans and then effect their sabotage. The incident upon the high road demonstrates the inherent danger in store for anyone who attempts to intervene on behalf of the Patriots' cause, for our adversary has already committed murder." Colonel Naismith looked squarely at Ethan. "The general is convinced that you are the man who can put a stop to this treachery. I confess, I am not as convinced as he is. I know well enough that the threat of danger will not trouble you. But the nature of the assignment is a broad departure from the role you are used to assuming as a spy. You are to go to Merrilltown and present yourself to Mr. Joshua Porter with a letter of introduction, which Mr. Clymer has kindly agreed to provide. You will be there under the pretext of surveying an extensive piece of property located a short distance from the town. We have, in fact, acquired a sizable bit of acreage about nine miles north of Merrilltown, fronting onto the high road. There is a house of some sort on the property, and it is there that your collaborator will be stationed. General Washington did not specify any particular man for that duty, so I have selected Sergeant Dowling to serve as your cohort."

Ethan could not help but be pleased at that, for Sergeant Henry Dowling was a familiar and trusted friend.

Colonel Naismith continued: "Sergeant Dowling's primary duty will be to serve as a liaison between you and myself. The property where he is to be stationed is approximately halfway between Merrilltown and the area where I shall be encamped with a small contingent of men, awaiting word from you and prepared to assist, if necessary, in the capture of the saboteurs. It is imperative that you do not communicate with me directly. All communication must go through Sergeant Dowling. It will be simple enough for you to journey the nine miles to his location, under the guise of carrying out your surveying duties for Mr. Clymer. Dowling's other responsibility will be to keep his eye out for the supply wagons that pass upon the high road. If you can discover when a shipment of provisions is to be sent out, you must alert Dowling, so that he can watch for it or watch to see what becomes of it if there is another attack upon the road. If you are unable to alert him, then I, at least, will be able to send him word afterward as to the success or failure of the wagon to traverse the blockade. It may take a considerable span of time before we are able to successfully coordinate communication, and undoubtedly even longer before you are able to obtain the information we seek. And that, Lieutenant Shaye, is the one aspect of this mission that most concerns me, insofar as your purpose. I am not certain that your instinct for survival will serve you in this situation, where you must deal not with soldiers, but with civilians. You must bide your time and be patient . . . you must gain the trust and friendship of Mr. Porter, and thereby gain access to his routines and acquaintances. It is possible that he himself is betraying us, or that he is an accomplice to treason — for such subterfuge would be considered treasonous; but that shall be for you to determine — whether it be Porter, or another individual who is somehow gaining access to his information. Either way, it will take time on your part. Therein lies the biggest challenge, I fear. You have proven yourself time and again to be a valorous fighter and a capable spy. But this will require a different set of skills: patience, watchfulness, reason. *Patience.*" He stressed again that essential quality and observed as Ethan shifted rather uneasily. "I can see by the look in your eyes that you do not relish such an assignment," the colonel noted. "You prefer the physical nature of battle or the thrill of slipping behind enemy lines. But in winning the general's respect with such feats, you have perhaps inadvertently recommended yourself for this commission, which will likely force you into circumstances less appealing to your inclinations. Do not forget, though, that there will be many lives — perhaps even an entire war — depending upon your success."

They were daunting words, to be sure, and while Ethan well-comprehended their implication, he did not dwell long upon them, but turned his mind instead to practical matters. "You have mentioned more than once that I am to maintain a facade — that of a civilian surveyor. I have donned civilian's attire whenever I've gone amongst the enemy, but in the course of spying I've scarcely ever been required to interact with those whom I am targeting. I . . . do not think I would be adept at playing a 'role', so to speak."

Colonel Naismith nodded approvingly, for it was an intelligent point. "Aye," he agreed, "this mission will undoubtedly require a great deal of interaction, for you will not be amongst the enemy, but amongst allies — or at least amongst those who profess to be allies — and naturally you will need to utilize some measure of discretion in your discourse. But you may be at ease, for you are not required to adopt any sort of fabricated presentation. I know well enough that such artificiality would not suit your temperament. So long as no one suspects your military connection or the true purpose of your presence in Merrilltown, you need not be concerned about revealing anything of a personal nature. As a matter of fact, so long as you are certain that you have no connections in Merrilltown, you are to utilize your own name — without your Lieutenant's title of course. In the unlikely event that you are required to enforce martial authority, it is essential that your name be in recognizable conformity with that on your official papers. As for the surveying—," here the colonel unwittingly drew himself up with an air of self-satisfied pride, "—that was my own idea. I know your father did a bit of surveying, and it seemed a plausible facade for this situation. It is a respectable profession to suit your breeding and at the same time could credibly justify your sun-tanned features . . . and give you a reasonable alibi for spending some hours outside the town each week. Are you hesitant to take up the profession for a time?"

Ethan thought back to the numerous surveying expeditions upon which he had accompanied his father. Surveying was tedious, methodical work, which he detested. Still, he was willing enough to endure it for the greater cause. He shook his head, smiling wryly. "It must be the paramount sacrifice for our cause, I suppose — that I take up a profession which so sorely tries my patience."

The colonel indulged him with a curt smile. "General Washington will undoubtedly be appreciative of your extraordinary efforts." He rose and briskly began to put his papers back in order. "You shall depart for Merrilltown three days hence. That should give you adequate time to make preparations and acclimate your mind to the task. We will arrange for your lodgings, but the exact course of your work I shall leave up to you and your intuition. And now, if you will send Sergeant Dowling in, I will inform him of his assignment and give him instructions as to his duties." The colonel paused in his activity and looked up at Ethan, who had already donned his hat and was about to take his leave. "Lieutenant Shaye—," the colonel came around the table and stood directly before Ethan, "I shall not attempt to impart any advice to you — as you would undoubtedly ignore it and do just as you please — but I would ask you to be watchful. This assignment may seem innocuous enough to you, but exercise some caution nonetheless. Remember, this person — or persons — has killed once, and may not hesitate to do so again."

HAVING BUILT A SMALL FIRE at the edge of the encampment, Lieutenant Shaye and Sergeant Dowling sat apart from the other soldiers, that they might be able to discuss the details of the general's assignment.

Henry Dowling was a wiry young Irishman whose parents had mi-grated to the colonies when Henry was still a babe in arms. Orphaned at a young age, he had scavenged and begged his way through childhood and youth and at the age of twenty-three had presented himself to the Patriots' army with nothing but the clothes on his back and a dagger at his side. The dagger was Henry's only possession of value . . . the only possession left him by his father, who had been a poor sailor, but who had brought to the New World not only his dreams of a better life for his family but also the only article of worth acquired from his voyages to distant lands. The blade itself was unremarkable — a small, brass-hilted hunting dagger — but it was the scabbard that set it apart; crafted from fine dark leather with brass fittings at the throat and tip, the scabbard's embossed throat was inlaid with a rare embellishment: a single dazzling blue stone which, though Henry could not identify the name, was as-suredly by its beauty and brilliance of great value. It was the object's sentimental associations, though, which endeared it to Henry, for he had treasured it and guarded it throughout his rough-hewn existence, keep-ing it always at his side, though he did not hesitate to put the blade to good use, whether it be to cut rope or skin an animal.

Lacking Ethan's familial prestige and educational advantages, Henry had worked his way up to a non-commissioned officer's rank through energetic diligence and eager tenacity. And though he possessed neither Ethan's athletic prowess nor his easy confidence, Henry's cheerful good humor and willingness to work hard had won him the esteem of both the officers and regulars within the ranks.

Now, sitting before the small fire opposite Ethan, Henry fingered the dagger absently, pulling it in and out of the scabbard. He seemed uncharacteristically distracted and stared unseeing into the fire's grey-tinged embers. Ethan, being occupied with cleaning and oiling his pis-tol, attempted only intermittent discourse and paid little heed to his friend's withdrawn demeanor until Henry at last spoke.

"I hope the colonel has given proper thought to his decision . . . in-sofar as choosing me to partake in this assignment."

Ethan looked up from his task. He had detected the nervous edge in his friend's tone, and he comprehended Henry's uncertainty. He knew that Henry had only once before been given a personal commission, and that enterprise had not gone well, for Henry had faltered and been captured, then faltered again, placing in jeopardy the position of their entire regiment and necessitating a hasty relocation as well as a perilous rescue — which Ethan himself had led — in order to extricate Henry from the Redcoats' clutches. More than a year had since passed, but Sergeant Dowling had never again been dispatched out on his own.

Ethan had realized from the first that Henry's role in the Merrilltown operation was relatively simple, and he guessed that Colonel Naismith had selected Henry more out of benevolence than any conviction that the young sergeant was especially suited to the task. But Ethan knew also how his friend desperately longed to prove himself worthy of being entrusted with such important enterprises as Ethan was regularly assigned.

In an effort to bolster Henry's confidence, Ethan affected an air of unconcern and went back to cleaning his weapon. "I would not doubt the colonel's wisdom if I were you," Ethan said. "He is seldom amiss in his decisions. He evidently feels that you are the best man for the endeavor."

But Sergeant Dowling was not convinced. "I've scarcely been given any opportunities which required me to act alone. I only hope I shall make decisions in accordance with his expectations."

Ethan shook his head. "You are hardly likely to be called upon in that capacity. As I understand it, your task is to keep an eye out for the supply wagons on the high road, or to look out for any other suspicious activity that may occur there, and to await word from Colonel Naismith or myself, then pass the communication from one to the other. You will have no difficulties carrying out your duties. If you want to worry about anything," Ethan continued, grinning at his friend, "best save it for when we set out for Virginia. It sounds like you shall have more than ample time during this assignment — sitting in solitude in a country house along the high road, waiting for passers-by. I do not envy you your task . . . too much inactivity for me."

Henry grinned back. "Aye, I shall undoubtedly set about improving my gardening skills to pass the time. Won't it make me appreciate the action of the battlefront when the mission is completed!"

Ethan nodded in concurrence, heartened to see his friend cheerful once more. "Aye . . . you'll be longing to dodge bullets before a fortnight is passed. In all likelihood you'll be spending your time on your knees — praying that I might soon ferret out the traitor and so put an end to your boredom."

"Ah, then perhaps the colonel ought to have given my role to you instead," Henry suggested slyly, his blue eyes sparkling with their usual good humor. "'Tis you more than I who needs a lesson in the virtues of patience and prayer."

PART III

The Town

Ethan Shaye arrived in Merrilltown on a day that was pleasantly agreeable in an unremarkable sort of way . . . words that could well summarize the character of the entire town. The town sat on the banks of a pleasant river, the streets were lined with agreeable residences and shops, and it was populated by citizens who appeared to be agreeably pleasant and altogether unremarkable. Yet, Ethan could see from the first why Merrilltown, Virginia, would be considered a favorable base for gathering and transporting the Patriots' supplies. In appearance, it resembled any number of other such towns across the South. Running parallel to the river, the town's main thoroughfare — bearing the uninspired name of "Hay Street" — could be easily traversed from one end to the other in a leisurely ten-minute stroll. The businesses and homes along this street were sensibly trim and well-kept, and passers-by could glimpse attractive, low-fenced gardens and orderly stable-yards to the rear of these unpretentious establishments. The merchants and tradesmen themselves seemed to maintain a steadfast — if unhurried — clientele, and the district bore an overall air of modest prosperity. A number of streets branched off from Hay Street, and there the businesses were quieter and the houses slightly larger and more generously spaced, with leafy green branches hanging over the lanes. Eventually, at some distance from the town center, small pastures and orchards separated the residences. The further the distance from the main thoroughfare, the further apart, fewer in number, and larger the houses, with the most substantial homes sitting beside the peaceful river.

Ethan had taken up lodgings near the center of town at a respectable tavern called Lethbridge's, where the public-room's lively atmosphere attested to its popularity with the local citizens and where the accommodations were comfortable enough, if somewhat austere in their simplicity.

Upon arrival, Ethan immediately dispatched to Mr. Joshua Porter the letter of introduction from Mr. Clymer, then, having put his horse in livery, set out on foot to examine the environs of Merrilltown.

It did not take him long to appraise his new surroundings. The layout of the community was well-familiar to one who had himself been brought up in the South. At the center of town, alongside the high street, lay a sizable Green, suitable for market days or musters and undoubtedly the site of occasional proclamations or performances by traveling players. To the west of town lay the white-steepled church, as old as the settlement itself and surrounded by gravestones in the churchyard — crumbling grey testimonials to the generations who had once worshipped on that sacred ground and starkly forthright reminders to the present generation of the fleeting nature of their own mortality. To the east rose a series of sloping wooded hills, where atop the highest stood an imposing brick manor house — the seat of the requisite provincial gentry — overlooking both town and river, adding an element of picturesque grandeur to the cheerfully unassuming setting.

Having thus acquainted himself with the general vicinity, Ethan returned to Lethbridge's, but he had scarcely crossed the threshold of the establishment when he was approached by the proprietor, who informed him that a gentleman was waiting to speak to him in the public room. As Ethan had been absent only an hour, he was surprised to learn that the caller was none other than the merchant Mr. Joshua Porter, who had received the letter of introduction and had promptly hastened over to the tavern to greet Mr. Shaye and ensure that the accommodations were adequate.

Despite the fact that Mr. Porter was in charge of assembling the army's provision transports — and therefore one on whom Ethan's suspicions must naturally fall — it was impossible to be unimpressed with the merchant's hospitable manner. Mr. Porter was a tall, spare man of fifty, whose blue eyes were kindly and shrewd. He had greeted Ethan with warm cordiality, and he seemed genuinely delighted that a friend of Mr. Clymer's should be temporarily residing in the neighborhood.

Mr. Porter's visit was but brief — after introducing himself and ascertaining that Mr. Lethbridge had given Ethan satisfactory quarters to the rear of the building, away from the bustle and noise of the street, the merchant departed with apologies for such haste ("Business takes no respite"), but not before extending to Ethan an invitation to visit him at his home the following day. This precisely suited Ethan's purpose, and he wholeheartedly accepted Mr. Porter's invitation, knowing well that such an opportunity could prove significant to the furtherance of his objective.

MR. PORTER HAD INDICATED THAT he could best receive visitors during the morning hours, before the day's business must consume his attention, so it was quite early when Ethan presented himself at the merchant's house the following day.

The house itself was handsome and respectable in appearance, set on a sizable piece of property that sloped gradually down to the river, where, in the distance, Ethan could see a mid-sized vessel moored alongside the embankment.

A cheerful young slave girl with a wide, toothy smile opened the door in response to Ethan's knock. After admitting him into the house and learning his name, she promptly went off in search of her master, leaving Ethan to wait in the central hallway — a high-ceilinged space which ran the length of the house and off of which opened several doors. At the rear of the hall, a bannistered staircase led to the upper floors. The furnishings and appointments in the room were tasteful and refined, but unostentatious. Mr. Joshua Porter was apparently a man of moderate prosperity.

Ethan did not wait long before the smiling housegirl returned and informed him that Mr. Porter would be yet delayed some minutes, but that Mrs. Porter would receive him directly.

Ethan gave a nod and, clutching his hat, followed the girl through a wide door on the right-hand side of the entrance hall. He was shown into a spacious, comfortably-furnished parlor, where he was received by Mrs. Joshua Porter.

Mrs. Porter, who appeared to be considerably younger than her husband, was a fashionably-attired woman whose very fine figure offset her very ordinary face; her unremarkable eyes were presently alight with the interest and anticipation of receiving such a guest.

"Mr. Shaye —," she greeted him, rising from her seat at the little round table where breakfast had been laid out, "—my husband informed me that you were expected today. You are most welcome here."

Ethan gave a slight bow in her direction. "I thank you, Madam, for your kind hospitality."

Mrs. Porter seemed pleased by his easy, off-hand politeness. "Do sit down," she chirped, motioning to a chair at the table as she took her own seat once more. "Mr. Porter will be here momentarily, and the breakfast has only just been set out — there is some rather nice herring, and the butter is fresh."

Perhaps it was the lilting trill of her voice, or the simper of her smile, or the excessively ornate breakfast cap — or the combination thereof — that gave Ethan the immediate impression that Mrs. Joshua Porter had not a thought in her head weightier than a feather. And as he sat down, thus appraising her, he could not help but think that she might prove to be a valuable — and accessible — source of information regarding her husband's covert activities, for Ethan knew that he must not look upon any visit to Mr. Porter's house as a mere social call.

The promise of such an effortless resource was at once called into question, however, as Mrs. Porter prattled on: "I must apologize for my husband's delay. I do not understand why he insists upon conducting business at such an early hour. I am only grateful that he attends to it in his study, for I cannot abide to hear business discussed over the breakfast table — so insipidly tiresome! I cannot follow such matters, nor should I care to. You must not think too badly of him, though, for I am certain that he did intend to greet you this morning. Something or other came up unexpectedly, as is often the case, but Mr. Porter has been notified of your arrival, and I expect that he and Monsieur Brisonneau are even now concluding their discussion."

Ethan had not the slightest idea who Monsieur Brisonneau was, but anyone conducting business with Joshua Porter at such an early hour must be noted.

Mrs. Porter, however, in her eagerness to provide excellent hospitality, afforded her guest little chance for contemplation. "Won't you have some chocolate, Mr. Shaye?" she inquired, shooing away the toothy servant girl who was hovering with the jam-pot. "Or would you prefer coffee? I myself cannot bear to take chocolate at breakfast anymore; after all these months of drinking nothing else at tea-time . . . I have had quite enough of it."

Her tone was slightly resentful, but Ethan knew well that many households had abstained from drinking tea during the boycott of the British import, and there were undoubtedly a multitude of wives who were likewise reluctant participants in their husbands' patriotic stand against the commodity that was such an integral part of social custom.

Ethan stated his preference for coffee and was efficiently served a cup while Mrs. Porter turned the course of conversation:

"We are so happy to be able to entertain a friend of Mr. George Clymer," she declared, then added, "Not that I am personally acquainted with that gentleman, of course, but my husband has spoken very highly of him on many occasions, and I am well-aware of Mr. Clymer's excellent reputation in the northern colonies. Do you think that he himself will be journeying to Merrilltown at any time while you are here?" There was an unmistakable hint of eagerness in her tone at the prospect of hosting such a prestigious guest.

Ethan shook his head. "It is very unlikely. The work for which he has commissioned me does not require any oversight on his part."

It was the first time since his arrival in Merrilltown that Ethan had been required to mention his supposed reason for being there. While he could easily fabricate details about the surveying, he hoped that Mrs. Porter was not going to pursue the subject of Mr. George Clymer — a man Ethan had never met — for though he could smoothly enough engage in necessary deception, he knew that he trod precarious ground when the subject was an actual acquaintance of the lady's husband.

Fortunately, Ethan's response had deflected Mrs. Porter's attention to the less-precarious aspect of his guise.

"Ah yes," she intoned rather airily. "I'd forgotten you were here to work. You must remind me — what is your profession? I know Mr. Clymer mentioned it in his letter, but I cannot recall."

"Mr. Clymer has commissioned me to do some surveying for him."

Mrs. Porter's face fell a bit. "Oh, indeed. Surveying. Something to do with measuring land, isn't it?" Her indifferent vagueness made it plain that this topic held as much appeal as discussing business at the breakfast table, and she quickly pressed on to more compelling subjects. "Well, I hope that your work will not occupy all of your time while you are here. You must allow us to include you in our little gatherings and introduce you to our acquaintances. I daresay Merrilltown seems quite provincial in comparison to the cities you have seen in the North, but we do have a very respectable set here, and I am confident you will find adequate diversion."

Ethan made no reply; he was, in truth, growing a bit impatient with the inanity of Mrs. Porter's discourse, and he hoped that Mr. Porter would appear soon. Yet he knew that it was crucial to make a favorable impression and so kept his unrest in check, acknowledged the lady's statement with a half-hearted smile, and occupied himself with spreading butter on a slice of toast as Mrs. Porter continued along in her discourse, oblivious to her guest's disinterest:

"'Tis quite a pity that you couldn't have arrived a few days earlier. Judge Merrill hosted a lovely dinner up at the Hall, to which I'm sure you could have secured an invitation — being a particular friend of our family. Judge Merrill is our local magistrate, you know, and is rightfully admired for his genial nature and great generosity. No doubt you've caught a glimpse of his family's residence, Merrill Hall — the large house up on the hill. It is a beautiful estate." By the way her eyes shone and her voice warmly resonated, it was evident that Mrs. Porter thought very highly of the town's patron and sought to impress her guest with such distinguished social connections.

Ethan cared nothing about the local gentry, but managed a polite nod toward his hostess. "I'm sure he is a very worthy gentleman."

"Oh yes, indeed!" Mrs. Porter uttered with enthusiasm. "The Merrills are a very old and prominent family in these parts, and Judge Merrill has been so good as to extend his friendship to his neighbors. Mr. Porter and I have been invited to the Hall on several occasions and have each time been received most graciously." Even in the midst of this self-important commendation, Mrs. Porter's mind seemed to be working ahead of her, for no sooner had she uttered the last word than her face brightened as if with a new and sudden thought. "Do you know —," she intoned, leaning forward, "— when we were at Judge Merrill's gathering on Tuesday, I could not help but note that Mr. Denton and his wife were in attendance with their daughter. She is their only offspring and likely to come into a respectable—"

To Ethan's great relief, Mrs. Porter was interrupted before she could suggest a match for her newly-arrived visitor, as a door opened at the far end of the room, and two gentlemen entered. The first man Ethan recognized to be Mr. Joshua Porter, who strode toward the breakfast table, smiling affably, as Ethan rose to his feet.

"Ah, good morning, Mr. Shaye!" the merchant greeted Ethan jovially. "'Tis a pleasure to see you again!"

"Good morning, sir. I thank you for inviting me to your home."

"I am sorry I was detained, but I trust that my good wife has adequately seen to your comfort?" And Mr. Porter patted his wife affectionately on the shoulder as he positioned himself behind her chair. Seeing them together for the first time, Ethan noted more acutely the marked contrast in age between Mr. Porter and his wife.

"Indeed, she has been most considerate in her hospitality," Ethan replied.

Mrs. Porter beamed as her husband gave a satisfied nod and made his way around the table, speaking as he moved:

"Mr. Shaye, I should like to introduce Monsieur Brisonneau, a business associate of mine who is visiting us from France."

Ethan turned toward the gentleman who had followed Joshua Porter into the room and who had thus far remained silent. The man bowed quite formally, as was perhaps the custom in his country, and addressed Ethan in a thick French accent:

"It is a plaisir to make your acquaintance, Mr. Shaye."

Never one to be bothered by such things as discrepant formalities, Ethan responded with the customary practice of his own countrymen — namely, a civil nod of the head accompanied by a conventional "Your servant, sir."

Although he harbored no prejudices against foreigners in general, Ethan almost immediately formed a negative opinion of Monsieur Brisonneau, for the Frenchman's outward manner was condescendingly aloof. As the three men took their seats at the table, Ethan noted the way that Monsieur Brisonneau discreetly ogled Mr. Porter's wife.

Mr. Porter and Monsieur Brisonneau each took but little sustenance at the breakfast table — dry toast and chocolate for Monsieur Brisonneau and only coffee for Mr. Porter — and neither man seemed completely at ease. Ethan had the impression that, despite their outward display of politeness, the two business associates had more pressing matters to attend to.

In spite of such slightly unsettled mien, however, Joshua Porter did not neglect his duties as host. He seemed genuinely interested in the welfare of his newest guest, as was evidenced by his uncontrived discourse: "So, Mr. Shaye, you have been in the North, I gather?" he began. "You must recount to us the latest news. I'm sure you can understand how difficult it is to obtain current information, being situated, as we are, in such a peripheral region. Tell us, what news do you hear of the war's progress?"

Ethan did not answer immediately, deliberately tarrying over his coffee as he considered his response. He knew that Joshua Porter must assuredly be well-apprised of the war's progress and had only put forth the question because it seemed conventionally requisite. Neither did Ethan wish to overtly reveal his own ample knowledge of the subject, and so he answered cautiously. "I have been much in transit, and most of what I hear has been picked up in village taverns or wayside inns — venues where facts are often intermingled with hearsay. And in truth, what little I have learned is much the same news as has been forthcoming for the past few months . . . namely that the British continue to have the upper hand, although there are some small victories for our own troops." Ethan leaned back in his chair and spoke his next words nonchalantly, even while keeping his eye fixed on Mr. Porter. "I understand that General Washington's men are beginning to suffer a shortage of provisions due to the British blockade."

If there was a momentary flicker in Mr. Porter's eye, it was impossible to tell whether it was a reflection of patriotic indignation or well-concealed culpability. Only one thing was telling: whatever his immediate thoughts, the mild-mannered host made no attempt to evade the subject. "It is a hardship indeed," he remarked gravely, "and I fear it may be a costly misfortune for our side if the situation is not soon remedied. It will be autumn soon enough, and then the cold will set in across the northern colonies. I like not to think what will befall our soldiers if the blockades remain intact."

"Come now!" Mrs. Porter interrupted plaintively. "Let us not have such talk of war and hardship. It is as bad as business and twice as dispiriting."

Mr. Porter conceded with an indulgent smile for his wife. "Very well, my dear. We shall defer such discussion until there is no lady present."

Mrs. Porter seemed satisfied and had no trouble broaching a more agreeable subject. She turned toward her newest acquaintance and spoke with some enthusiasm. "Mr. Shaye, do you know that Monsieur Brisonneau is teaching me to speak some French?"

Ethan glanced at Monsieur Brisonneau, who was alert at the sound of his name. Mrs. Porter went on without pause: "Of course, it really would have been unthinkable before all of this, but my husband says that our Patriots are determined to form an alliance with France, and it should be quite acceptable to learn some of the language. It is quite difficult, but Monsieur Brisonneau is wonderfully patient with me, and I am making progress, though the words don't sound half as pretty when I say them as when he does." She looked to her tutor. "Eh bien, Monsieur?"

Monsieur Brisonneau nodded, but his smile lacked warmth — neither was it deferential — and Ethan suspected that the Frenchman thought more of the lady's figure than of her linguistic abilities.

Mrs. Porter leaned confidingly toward Ethan. "You must be very nice to Monsieur Brisonneau," she charged him, well-pleased with her own advice, "and perhaps he will teach you some phrases as well!"

Ethan had no intention of ingratiating himself to the Frenchman, and the only thing he wished to learn while in Merrilltown was the identity of the saboteur. He was, however, once again spared the awkwardness of a tepid response; before he could even acknowledge Mrs. Porter's suggestion, there was heard in the hallway the sudden patter of scampering feet, accompanied by a child's high-pitched voice crying out "Mama! Mama!".

All at the table turned their heads toward the sound as the door to the room burst open and a small golden-haired boy of six years old bolted into their midst. He gave no pause, but ran straight toward the lady of the house and climbed up on her knee, shrilly crying out his displeasure:

"Mama! Rachel is being horrid and will not let me wear my Patriot cockade!" And he pointed resentfully at a young slave woman who had followed him into the room carrying a small cocked hat and looking vexed herself.

"Now, now, love," Mrs. Porter cooed soothingly, attempting to smooth the child's flaxen hair. "Rachel is quite right. You must not wear it today."

But the boy would not be pacified, and his blue eyes reflected his discontent. "'Tis not fair!" he protested loudly. "You said I could wear my Patriot cockade on special days, and today I am reciting for Mr. Merrill!"

The boy's angelic looks were apparently only a facade, for there was nothing celestial about his disagreeable manner.

Mr. Porter was frowning across the table. "For heaven's sake, Anne," he admonished his wife, "do hush that child, and remember our guests."

"Aye, your father speaks the truth," Anne Porter clucked to the boy on her knee, although her tone was hardly reproachful. "You must show your best manners and bid our new visitor a proper 'Good morning'."

Still distempered, the child eyed Ethan sulkily.

Mrs. Porter continued placidly: "Caleb, this is Mr. Shaye. He will be visiting here in Merrilltown for a time, and you will likely see him often at our house, so be a good boy and give him a proper greeting."

The child Caleb mumbled an indifferent "How-do-you-do," which seemed to satisfy his doting mama, for she turned her attention to another topic, though her focus remained fixed on her son:

"Are you ready for your recitation today, dearest?" she asked the boy somewhat anxiously. "You mustn't disappoint Mr. Merrill."

The child's face brightened. "Aye, Mama. I spoke my piece before Rachel this morning and didn't miss one word! Shall I recite it for the visitors?"

"Aye, if your father says you may."

Caleb looked eagerly toward Mr. Porter, who was still frowning but gave an impatient nod. "Be quick about it, lad. You have already taken a great deal of our guests' time."

Mrs. Porter set the child back on his feet. "There now, my clever boy," she intoned with an encouraging smile. "Speak exactly as you will before Mr. Merrill."

And the *enfant terrible* was transformed, his countenance suddenly becoming as innocently angelic as his golden looks would suggest. His blue eyes were clear and solemn as he piped:

"I will sing of mercy and judgment unto thee, O Lord, will I sing. I will behave myself wisely in a perfect way. O when wilt thou come unto me? I will walk within my house with a perfect heart."

The child's mother — oblivious to the incongruity between the psalm's virtuous words and the young speaker's unpleasant disposition — was clearly enchanted by the boy's flawless recitation, and as soon as he returned to her embrace, she kissed him, exclaiming, "That was perfect, my darling! You must say it in exactly that way for Mr. Merrill, and he is sure to give you a commendation!"

Even at six years old, the boy's smile was smug as his mother gave him a final pat.

"Now run along," she bade him fondly. "You mustn't be late for school today. You shall wear your cockade soon enough, I promise."

And so the child departed, dashing out of the room (but not before giving the much-maligned Rachel a furtive kick to the ankle as he snatched the offensively unadorned hat from her hand.)

After the door had closed behind the boy and the servant, Anne Porter turned back toward Ethan, still smiling over her child's accomplishments. "Caleb is such a clever boy," she mused proudly. "You mustn't mind his little fretting over his hat. He puts us through that at least once per week. He adores his 'Patriot's cockade', as he calls it — just an ordinary black cockade, really, but it does resemble those worn by the Continental soldiers. He is only permitted to wear it on special occasions."

Ethan was rather astonished that she should so lightly dismiss the boy's "little fretting". He felt certain that in any other household, such appalling behavior on the part of a child would have been met with stern retribution.

"Have you any other children?" he inquired somewhat warily of his hosts.

Joshua Porter smiled benignly, evidently appreciative of the opportunity to turn the conversation in a different direction. "Aye," he said, nodding. "I have another son, who is yet upgrown. He has recently turned eighteen years of age and has joined up with our Virginia militia. They are encamped nearby, and you will undoubtedly see him, for he is frequently here with us."

The wording of the response, as well as the age of Mr. Porter's elder son, made it plain that the elder son was not the offspring of the lady presently sitting at the table — who must herself be only a decade older than eighteen and who was apparently Mr. Porter's second wife.

The current Mrs. Porter was not content to let the focus stray from her own son, however. "Caleb has only recently begun his schooling," she confided proudly to Ethan. "Mr. Merrill has endowed a small school for the citizens of the town, and he has graciously allowed Caleb to enroll at only six years old, for the child is exceptionally bright."

Ethan had no wish to return to the topic of young Caleb Porter, and so he adroitly focused his response upon a different aspect of the subject at hand. "Your Judge Merrill sounds like a very broad-minded and philanthropic magistrate."

Mrs. Porter stared blankly at Ethan. "Judge Merrill?" Then her face brightened with sudden comprehension. "Oh, no, Mr. Shaye — I was referring to Mr. Zachary Merrill, who is the grandson of Judge Merrill and who lives with his grandfather at Merrill Hall. It is Mr. Zachary Merrill who established the school and oversees its direction. But yes, you are correct — he is a fine gentleman and a renowned advocate of education."

Joshua Porter nodded in agreement. "It is true. I have heard Zachary Merrill say on many occasions that education is the key to building stronger communities and that every boy in Merrilltown ought to receive schooling. He has even had a few of his slaves receive instruction in reading and writing."

"Although not alongside the boys of the town, of course," Mrs. Porter was quick to add. "You will, I am certain, become acquainted with Mr. Merrill before long. He is in town very often — much more so than his grandfather — and even dines with us now and again."

Ethan responded to this disclosure with a brief nod, even as he silently wondered if the lady was ever going to retire from the breakfast table, that the men might converse upon more substantial topics. Yet, as it turned out, this silent query was answered almost immediately — and not to Ethan's advantage.

Mr. Porter had long ago finished his coffee, and — evidently feeling he could no longer afford to tarry on a business-day — pushed his chair back from the table and announced, "Well, Mr. Shaye, I'm afraid I must be off to my day's work," as he rose to his feet.

Monsieur Brisonneau instantly did the same. The Frenchman had not uttered a word during the entire breakfast, though Ethan did not know if that was due to a language barrier or if it was merely his natural inclination to remain aloof. At any rate, he now appeared to be quite ready to take his leave.

Joshua Porter, on the other hand, was more cordial upon the necessity of departing. As Ethan rose to his feet, his host gave him a hearty shake of the hand across the table and mentioned good-naturedly, "You must come back when we can sit down and talk at leisure, without such distractions as were present today." And the merchant's eyes sparkled at his wife, who responded with an unapologetic smile. "I want to hear how Mr. Clymer is faring in Philadelphia," Mr. Porter continued to Ethan, "as well as hear more details about your work. I cannot help but think that I have set a poor example of hospitality — always having to rush off to deal with affairs of business. I've had a dreadful time with a ship that arrived early in the week — it's kept me occupied from sun-up to sundown. But it's due to finally set sail tomorrow morning, so perhaps you could call again the following afternoon, if you are able."

Ethan nodded. He would be certain to avail himself of such an opportunity to speak in-depth with the merchant. "That will be fine," he assured his host.

"I am sorry we cannot offer you accommodations here with us while you are in town," Joshua Porter said. "In addition to Monsieur Brisonneau here, we have had a regular influx of relations descend upon us throughout the summer, and more expected within the fortnight. But you must count yourself amongst our regular dinner guests, and I hope that you will not hesitate to make use of the house's amenities as if it were your own."

Ethan gave a slight bow. "Thank you, sir. That is very kind of you."

Mr. Porter nodded, then turned to his business associate. "Well, Brisonneau . . . shall we be off then?"

The Frenchman gave a polite bow in Mrs. Porter's direction. "Good day to you, Madame."

Ethan noted that the Frenchman's eyes lingered for a moment on the lady's physique before he turned to Ethan.

"I am honored to have met you, Mr. Shaye."

Ethan felt less honored, but gave a courteous nod nonetheless.

So it was that the merchant and the Frenchman took their leave, consigning Ethan to endure for another hour the lively, depthless chatter of his enthusiastic hostess.

⌘

ONCE HE HAD EXTRACTED HIMSELF from Mrs. Porter's well-intentioned hospitality, Ethan did not immediately return his horse to livery, but instead — craving exercise and fresh air — rode out into the countryside. He thought about riding the nine miles to Henry Dowling's outpost, but, having been instructed to communicate with his colleague only when necessary so as not to draw attention, Ethan instead turned his horse in the opposite direction and headed past the churchyard and across the open meadows south of town where his steed could run freely.

Once Ethan had adequately revived his senses, he slowed his horse to an easy canter and allowed the creature to maintain a comfortable gait for the duration of the excursion.

As he rode, Ethan reflected on his visit to the home of Joshua Porter.

He had gained nothing in terms of information or evidence regarding the merchant's participation in the Patriot's supply transport, much less insight into any violations committed in connection with that operation. As for Mr. Porter's character — Ethan had not spent sufficient time in the merchant's presence to form an accurate opinion, but upon first impression, it was difficult to find fault or flaw in the man's bearing, or indeed, any indication that the merchant would be a party to treasonous misconduct. And yet, Ethan knew that such mannerisms as are regularly adopted upon first introduction can scarcely be relied upon to reflect a person's true nature. So, too, did he know that he must not place inordinate faith in hasty appraisals of character, however much Mr. Porter's hospitality appeared sincere.

In truth, Ethan was much more inclined to distrust Monsieur Brisonneau, if only for the Frenchman's contemptible manner and aloof temperament.

The more Ethan reflected on the situation, the more he disliked the commission with which he had been entrusted, the commission which seemed so ill-suited to his natural abilities. And yet, while he preferred to rely on instinct over ponderous deliberation, and swift action over moderation, he knew that he must persevere — and willingly, no matter how trying the pace of progress — in order to best serve the cause to which he was wholeheartedly committed. He would draw on skills that had served him well during previous missions. Now was the time to be resourceful — to be vigilant. He could be watchful for as long as his patience held out. For now, he must maintain perspective and remember that he had already accomplished an incremental, but crucial, achievement: he had gained the confidence of the person most directly involved with the provision transports; and in relation to that, he had secured the prospect of future visits to the house wherein was surely contained the information he needed in order to ensure the survival of the general's men.

DURING THE COURSE OF HIS first days in Merrilltown, Ethan took to making his few necessary purchases at Reid's Dry Goods Store, which was located only a short distance from his quarters at Lethbridge's Tavern. So when he discovered on the day following his visit to the Porters' house that he had lost a button off of his coat, he set out on foot in the direction of that tidy little shop.

On his way there, he passed by the silversmith's establishment, where he could not help but notice the ornate, enclosed carriage drawn up before the door. Although the carriage's interior appeared to be unoccupied, a liveried coachman sat dutifully atop, minding the horses — a superior, broad-flanked team — and a dark-skinned man stood in attendance near the compartment door. The slave was outfitted in respectably dignified footman's attire and stood with his head held high, his demeanor confident.

As Ethan passed, the slave looked him in the eye and bid him a courteous "Good day, sir."

This salutation was unexpected, for it was not at all customary that a slave should speak out so boldly. Yet there was nothing impudent in the dark man's tone or attitude. As Ethan continued across the street to the door of Reid's shop, he wondered if the dark man was perhaps not a slave, but rather a freedman, although such status was uncommon in the South.

The small dry-goods store was devoid of customers when Ethan entered, but the shop's proprietress, Widow Reid, greeted him with convivial familiarity.

Widow Reid was a cheerful, plump woman whose generous amplitude seemed to fill nearly all the space behind her narrow counter. She took an avid interest in the lives of all the townsfolk, and especially any visitors, so it was that when she had first made Ethan's acquaintance several days earlier, she had seemed well-pleased to learn that he was planning an extended stay in town. She was no doubt eager to have a new ear — and subject — for her friendly gossip.

And now, upon hearing Ethan's request to purchase a button for his coat, she not only provided him with a choice from her finest selection of brass buttons, but she insisted that he give over his coat to her, that she might attach the new button in its proper place.

"For I know how it goes with young men," she clucked, wagging her head with maternal sagacity. "My own son is just your age — five-and-twenty — and likewise without a wife to tend to his needs, and I've seen often enough how carelessly he undertakes such tasks. I have to reattach half of his buttons whenever he visits — and that is to say nothing of mending his seams!" And she scrutinized with narrowed eyes the coat presently in her grasp, as if it might be analogously guilty of sporting neglected seam-lines. It was quite a nicely-tailored coat, though, and — other than the button — she could find nothing which would necessitate the intervention of her needlework skills.

As Ethan awaited the button's repair, he leaned up against the counter, where he had a clear view through the large front window of the elegant carriage still stationed across the way.

"'Tis a fine carriage there," he remarked, with a nod toward the silversmith's shop.

Mistress Reid paused in her stitching and glanced out the window. "Aye, that it is," she agreed with a wide, cognizant smile. "And it belongs to a fine gentleman — Mr. Zachary Merrill. I saw him alight nearly thirty minutes ago. He must be on a lengthy errand, though he is likely extending it by way of pleasant conversation, for he is a good-natured gentleman and a great patron of Mr. Quinn, the smith."

Ethan recalled Mrs. Porter's adulatory description of Mr. Zachary Merrill. She and Widow Reid had both characterized the grandson of the town's magistrate as "a fine gentleman". Ethan could not help but wonder if the elder Merrill was as esteemed as his grandson amongst the populace.

Widow Reid was yet conjecturing about the proceedings at the silversmith's shop. "Mr. Merrill must be about ordering something new from Mr. Quinn," she surmised, her eyes back upon her needlework, "else he'd likely just send Thaddeus in to fetch the finished piece."

"Thaddeus?" Ethan's eye shifted to the scrupulously-attired footman standing beside the carriage.

Mistress Reid confirmed his speculation with a nod. "Aye, Mr. Merrill's manservant. That's him — the Negro standing out in the street next to the coach."

"He is a freedman then?" Ethan conjectured.

Mistress Reid chortled, her round comical face crinkling drolly. "Lord, no! You're not likely to find a freedman in this region — and you'd best be suspicious of any Negro who says he is one. Nay, Thaddeus is a slave — and a valuable one, I daresay, for his efficiency and manner are nearly in line with a proper English footman. Indeed, I should be surprised if Mr. Merrill has ever been given cause to raise the whip to Thaddeus, for I have never seen a Negro so capable in his work. Of course," she conceded, "Judge Merrill sees that all of his slaves are baptized, but Mr. Zachary has gone even so far as to allow Thaddeus some instruction in reading."

Ethan found this circumstance rather curious, as he himself had been raised in the South and had never encountered in the region anyone who advocated literacy for slaves. He remembered, however, that Joshua Porter had referenced Mr. Zachary Merrill's broad views on education.

"Are all of Mr. Merrill's slaves given to literacy then?" he inquired.

Widow Reid shook her head. "Nay. Only Thaddeus and a few other house servants, I think. And their abilities are only minimal, as I understand." She smiled mindfully. "While it may be true that Thaddeus can read a few words — such as may be useful in his service to Mr. Merrill — and he is undoubtedly brighter than most of his kind, he knows his place well enough, and despite such little liberties as Mr. Merrill allows him, Thaddeus will not overstep his boundaries. He is often the emissary of Mr. Merrill's goodwill and is therefore quite a favorite with the townsfolk. —There now!" Mistress Reid stood abruptly, looking well-pleased with herself, and held out the coat toward Ethan. "'Tis as good as new, and I secured that button with extra stitches, so as to be sure it withstands whatever you put to it, for I can see you are a young man who regularly engages in riding and hunting and all manner of pursuits which would put wear upon your garments. Well, you just bring them to me, and I'll sew on your buttons or patch your breeches, for you'll likely need some looking-after while you're here."

Ethan thanked the widow, smiling good-naturedly at her earnest benevolence, and, donning his coat, he exited the little shop.

As he began to walk back toward Lethbridge's, Ethan's attention was diverted by the sound of voices across the street, and he glanced in the direction of the silversmith's shop just in time to see the slave Thaddeus closing the door to the compartment of the carriage that was yet drawn up before that establishment. The slave then proceeded to climb up to his post, as the silversmith called out blithely from his doorway, "Good day to you, Mr. Merrill, and thank you, sir!" And the carriage pulled away with a clattering of horses' hooves as the coachman urged the team on in the direction of Merrill Hall. It was a rather dramatic departure, and several onlookers stared in reverential awe as the distinguished equipage passed them by.

Ethan, however, was not one to be impressed by ostentatious displays, and the carriage and its occupants were soon forgotten as his thoughts turned to the morrow, when he planned to return to the Porter house.

GOOD FORTUNE WAS ASSUREDLY ON Ethan's side. His second visit to the Porter house began most auspiciously, as he was shown immediately into Mr. Porter's study, and the cheerful housegirl informed him that Mr. Porter would see him directly, but that Mrs. Porter was not at home, having gone into town to make some purchases. This suited Ethan's purpose in every way, for as cordial as the lady of the house had been, Ethan wished to have an earnest talk with Joshua Porter, unhindered by the light-minded chatter of the merchant's wife.

Once the housegirl had retreated, Ethan found himself momentarily sequestered in the room where, upon his previous visit, Mr. Porter and Monsieur Brisonneau had been conducting business prior to their entrance into the parlor. While the two business associates had, upon that occasion, entered the parlor directly from the study, Ethan was admitted into the study through a different door, one which opened off of the central hall. Yet, the fact that the study was accorded two portals was hardly a testament to the room's dimensions, for the two doors occupied nearly the entirety of the adjacent walls in which they were situated. Indeed, the room's scant width held little more than a desk and two chairs. Well-stacked bookcases lined the other two narrow walls. Ethan had the impression that the room had been built as something of an afterthought; such a contrast was it to the spacious rooms surrounding it.

He wasted not a moment of his seclusion. If there was to be any tangible evidence of Joshua Porter's involvement with the Patriot supply transports — honorable or otherwise — it would likely be contained in this room. And though the servant girl had indicated that her master would be in straightaway, Ethan was never one to hesitate when confronted with an opportunity to advance his objective, and he stepped quickly around to the other side of Mr. Porter's desk. Examining the shelves against the back wall, he pulled out a random leather-bound book, of which there were many. Opening the front cover, he found it to be a shipping log, dated several years earlier. He silently flipped through the pages, but found nothing out of the ordinary, and so slid it back into its place upon the shelf. Hastily glancing at some other volumes, he found them all to be similarly typical records common to a merchant's office: ledgers, almanacs, shipping logs. There were dozens of them, and it was impossible to discern from the binding which might pertain to recent or variant activities.

Knowing that his host might appear at any moment, but knowing, too, that he might not easily secure another such opportunity, Ethan turned back to the desk and dexterously pulled open the drawer. Before he could examine the contents, though, his eye fell upon something sitting atop a stack of ledgers on the desk: a thin, leather-bound volume, not unlike the other shipping logs lining the shelves behind him. Although it seemed improbable that the information he sought should be so readily accessible, Ethan yet picked up the book. As he opened the cover and glanced at the first page, his heartbeat quickened, and he abandoned all interest in the desk drawer, noiselessly pushing it closed as he focused his attention on the contents of the open book.

It was indeed a log of sorts, written in the same hand as the shipping logs upon the shelves, though this book contained no mention of ships or tariffs.

Ethan quickly surveyed the uncomplicated layout of the first page. It was as a ledger, but divided into only four columns. The first column was labeled "Date Dispatched", and there were listed dates ranging from February 10, 1776 at the top of the page, to May 11, 1776 at the bottom. Beside each date were printed two names in a column labeled "Emissary", the first set reading "T. Hitchens/Major Bentley". The other pairs of names in the column were similar: always an initial and a surname followed by a military ranked name, several of which Ethan recognized to be British officers. The third column was labeled "Itemization" and contained lists of goods and quantities, such as "20 barrels of flour, 17 kegs of rum, 48 pairs of stockings, 7 barrels of powder, 40 lbs. of shot", which was recorded in the first row. The other rows beneath that column contained similar inventory listings. The fourth and final column was labeled "Date of Receipt" and there, like the first column, was written a range of dates, each date of receipt generally being two to three weeks after the correlating date dispatched.

It took but a matter of seconds for Ethan to appraise the information and determine that this must assuredly be a record of the supplies sent out to General Washington's troops under the direction of Joshua Porter.

Ethan turned over the first page and found that the next pages were merely a continuation of the chronological documentation, which ended a quarter of the way down the third page. The last few entries on that page were notable for the easily-distinguished discrepancy in their last column. Instead of a specific date recorded under "Date of Receipt", there was instead written a single, stark word for each entry: *"Intercepted"*. One was marked *"Intercepted, casualty"*. The final entry under "Date Dispatched" was recorded as July 16, 1776 — the date Colonel Naismith had mentioned as being the most recent instance of the transport's failure to traverse the British blockade.

There could be no doubt in Ethan's mind now as to the purpose of the logbook. He cursorily thumbed through the remaining pages, but found them all to be blank. His thoughts were racing as he closed the book and laid it back atop the stack of ledgers. If this was indeed evidence of Joshua Porter's role in the Patriot supply line, why would it be sitting out in plain sight atop his desk? Was it merely carelessness? Surely it was not due to ignorance, for Mr. Porter was unquestionably a man of intelligence and would not have been chosen for such a pivotal role in the military provision enterprise were he lacking in judgment.

And yet . . . Ethan had to remind himself that he was not in enemy territory and that Porter was not engaging in any unscrupulous activity — at least not overtly. There was really no cause for the merchant to conceal the logbook. But even if Porter was innocent of sabotage, he must know that someone in the vicinity was conspiring against the Patriots. He must know that the information contained in the logbook should be kept closely guarded against the would-be saboteur . . . .

Ethan's pondering was abruptly diverted as he heard a footstep in the hall outside the door. With the swift, silent step of one who is practiced in covert tactics, he reached the opposite side of the desk just as the hall door opened and Joshua Porter himself strode into the room.

"Good day to you, Mr. Shaye!" the merchant greeted Ethan, extending his hand in friendly salutation.

"Good day, Mr. Porter," Ethan returned, grasping his host's extended hand. "I hope I am not calling too early?"

"Not at all!" Mr. Porter maintained, motioning for Ethan to have a seat in the chair facing the desk. "I am quite pleased to say that I have finished my obligations of work for the day and so can at last act the proper host." He made his way round to the opposite side of the desk — where Ethan had been standing only moments before — and proceeded to pour out some sherry from a decanter at the side. "I thought we could better converse in here," Mr. Porter continued, setting a glass before each of them. "Though the front rooms are more comfortable, we are less likely to be interrupted should my wife return within the hour." He shook his head with a good-humored smile. "Anne is a fine woman and a wonderful wife, but it is difficult sometimes to discuss anything of consequence in her presence."

Ethan wholeheartedly agreed, though of course he did not say so aloud, but instead remarked upon a different topic. "I gather, then, that the ship which had given you so much trouble has by now pushed off successfully?"

Mr. Porter nodded, sitting down in the chair behind the desk. "Aye, though I thought it never would! 'Tis one thing I can say in praise of England — perhaps the only thing — her ships were regulated with some measure of efficiency. At least I could have a general notion of when they were due to arrive, how long they would stay in port, and what inventory they should carry. These foreigners are so inconsistent; they always arrive unpredictably and bring with them issues that ought to have been resolved in their country of origin, forcing them to tarry here in our ports for long spells of time while they get everything sorted out."

"If they are forced to circumnavigate or run the blockades, that would surely account for their erratic dates of arrival, would it not?" Ethan suggested.

Mr. Porter shook his head. "I cannot say for certain. That is why Monsieur Brisonneau has journeyed here from France. He contends that when his ships leave the harbor there, everything is in order. I myself can barely communicate with captain or crew, as none ever speaks but three words of English, so I can receive no explanation for the difficulties en route. Brisonneau must sort things out, or I shall be forced to look else-where for my cargo carriers. Although —," he added with some regret, "I shall be hard-pressed to find another so willing to run the blockades."

So Ethan was given some understanding of the disagreeable Frenchman's role in Joshua Porter's shipping trade. He would have liked to know more about Brisonneau's purported business dealings, but he did not want to seem overly-inquisitive at such an early stage, where trust must still be fostered. Yet, he felt that it was crucial to establish the log-book's accessibility to one such as Monsieur Brisonneau, who was lodg-ing within the Porter house, and so he proceeded to inquire, in the most nonchalant manner: "Do you have an office down by the wharf then? Or do you conduct all of your business here at the house?"

Mr. Porter smiled broadly. "Ah, you must take care never to put forth such a question before my wife. She shall claim your very mention of the subject as evidence in support of her intent. She has been goading me to no end about building an office away from the house, so as not to have 'seafarers constantly lounging about the front hall', as she put it. Which is, by the way, entirely an exaggeration on her part. There is seldom the necessity for any but the ship's captain to meet with me here in my study, and then only for the briefest duration of time. No, her rationalization is but a tenuous pretext; I know her to have an ulterior motive — for I overheard her after church one Sunday discussing with Mistress Lindley what a delightful china closet this little study will make." He laughed with good-natured indulgence at his wife's harmless little scheme. "Well, I may just give in to her on that matter," he conceded, "though she must not be told as of yet. In truth, though, that very subject calls to mind something I wished to discuss with you, Mr. Shaye." The amusement faded from the merchant's eyes, to be replaced by earnestness. He leaned forward across the desk and spoke to Ethan in a frank manner. "I have recently purchased some additional property — a nice piece, directly across the river. I'm thinking of clearing some of it and putting it to use; it would make an ideal location for an office and perhaps another warehouse. I have a warehouse now, near the wharf, but could easily utilize some additional storage."

This rather piqued Ethan's interest, as it could pertain to the requirement of storing supplies for the Patriot army; but how it should pertain to anything which Joshua Porter might wish to discuss with him, Ethan did not know, and so he continued to listen attentively — although with increasing misgiving — as Mr. Porter elaborated:

"I have not done anything with the land as of yet — have not even had anyone out to look at it or to appraise the practicality of my plans. It requires a complete survey. I was going to send to Williamsburg for a surveyor, but seeing as you are stopping in the neighborhood for a time — with skills highly recommended by Mr. Clymer — I was hoping you'd consider undertaking the task yourself."

Ethan silently cursed Mr. Clymer. What business had the man to make such a recommendation in a letter whose purpose was simply introduction? Ethan now wished he'd read the letter himself before dispatching it. He was well-practiced in repairing broken seals.

Mr. Porter must have noted his guest's hesitation, for he hastened to add, "You shall, of course, be duly compensated, and I know that your work for Mr. Clymer must be your priority. There is no hurry in order for this survey." He smiled benignly.

Ethan knew that Mr. Porter's offer of a commission was intended as a gesture of goodwill, and to outrightly refuse such an honorable gesture would not only be discourteous, but could well jeopardize his status of privilege within the Porters' realm of hospitality. Still, he knew that his surveying abilities were not credible enough to compare with a genuine professional in the field.

As Ethan had still given no response, Mr. Porter continued to address the context of the idea: "I know that your work requires you to be out-of-doors a great deal, but when it comes to laying out the measurements on paper, or completing correspondence, or recording . . . well, whatever it is a surveyor records — I myself not being practiced in the profession am not certain of exactly what is entailed — but in any case, you are very welcome to utilize this room and avail yourself of any supplies herein — paper, ink, and the like — for I know that the thin walls of a public lodging house are hardly conducive to concentration." Mr. Porter must have noticed the flicker of attentiveness which had momentarily enlivened Ethan's countenance, for the merchant continued with further enthusiasm: "I assure you, Mr. Shaye, it would be no imposition. I am generally in here during the morning and early afternoon — which I presume are the hours you would most likely be out upon the land, taking your measurements. By the time you are ready to take up your pen each day, the study would be vacated and at your disposal. It is a very tidy arrangement," Mr. Porter concluded, "if you should find such terms acceptable."

Ethan could not have conceived of a more auspicious opportunity, and he was not about to let such a chance pass when it was so handily proffered. All traces of hesitancy had vanished as he made reply. "Thank you, Mr. Porter," he affirmed with conviction. "I should be very pleased indeed to make a survey of your land, and I appreciate your confidence in my abilities." He could work out the practicalities later.

Joshua Porter seemed well-contented with Ethan's acceptance of the premise, and Ethan turned the discussion back to the subject of the merchant's trade:

"The river seems very quiet," he remarked. "Is there a great deal of shipping commerce in this region?"

Mr. Porter shook his head. "Nay, very little. The Merrills maintain some piers along the river and its tributary; Judge Merrill owns several plantations and utilizes some mid-sized craft in transporting tobacco and other goods, but the river narrows after passing Merrilltown, so my wharf is the only destination for any ships which might traverse this far. I have a warehouse alongside the wharf, where we store the cargo that is brought off of the ships. Eventually the cargo is loaded onto smaller vessels to send upriver for distribution throughout the South. We can walk down to the landing, if you'd like to take a closer look. There are no ships moored there now — only a light barque — but you'll often enough see larger vessels when you're about the place. You could also get a glimpse from the riverbank of the new land I've purchased. It's too late today to sojourn across the river, but we'll row across another day and inspect it further. You will find a rowboat tied to the quay below, which you may freely utilize once you begin your survey, as you'll need to make frequent crossings then." Mr. Porter pushed back his chair and stood. "Shall we proceed to the wharf, then? It is no great distance from the house."

And so Ethan accompanied his host down to the riverbank, where the merchant showed him about the wharf and warehouse, pointed out the newly-acquired property on the opposite bank, and apprised Ethan of the day-to-day operations and methods of the shipping trade.

Ethan only half-listened to this discourse. A myriad of thoughts were whirling within his brain. To be given such unprecedented access to the household wherein lay the answers he sought was prodigious fortuity. Such a gesture on the part of Joshua Porter would seem to squarely indicate the merchant's innocence in the matter of treason. And yet, as much as Ethan was inclined to trust the integrity of Mr. Porter, such patness did not sit well with him. Suppose Mr. Porter had been given cause to suspect Ethan's motives? Was it not possible, then, that the merchant's benign hospitality was merely a guise meant to establish his credibility?

Admittedly, Ethan thought this premise unlikely, as there was no one nearer the vicinity than Henry Dowling who knew of the mission to uncover the saboteurs.

Then, too, there was the matter of the logbook. To so easily come across tangible evidence of Mr. Porter's involvement with the Patriot's cause was surely significant, although there was nothing to the logbook that would implicate Joshua Porter in any treasonous activities. Indeed, the logbook's contents seemed only to reinforce that the merchant was doing exactly what he was supposed to be doing — directing the covert transport of goods north to General Washington. Still, Ethan decided to send word of the logbook's existence and whereabouts to Colonel Naismith. The Colonel might have some further insight which may — Ethan prayed — hasten the resolution of the issue, and therefore hasten his resumption of bolder endeavors.

IT WAS NEARING NIGHTFALL SEVERAL days later when Ethan received a message, delivered to Lethbridge's by a youthful slave in patched breeches.

Returning to his room with the missive, Ethan glanced at the seal — marked quite prominently with a "JP" — before breaking it open and examining the contents of the message. Despite the initials set into the seal, the script upon the page was not that of Joshua Porter, but was instead written in a lighter, daintier hand. It read:

"We were just discussing the latest word from Philadelphia — and you're likely more current on it than we are — that our peers in Congress there have approved some sort of letter to the king, pronouncing the colonies free from the Crown's rule. Has Mr. Clymer mentioned aught of this to you?"

"Ah, you are Mr. Clymer's young friend!" exclaimed one of the other men, standing at Mr. Porter's right. "I have heard Mr. Porter speak of your arrival and of your acquaintance with George Clymer."

"Forgive me," Joshua Porter intoned to all present, "I should have introduced Mr. Shaye. He is indeed here on a commission from Mr. George Clymer — going to survey some property Mr. Clymer has acquired near Merrilltown. He has also agreed to do some surveying for me." He turned again to the gentleman on his right and added, "You are aware, I am sure, that I purchased that tract of land across the river." Then he turned back toward Ethan. "Mr. Shaye, I have the privilege of introducing you to one of the pre-eminent citizens of our community—," and he indicated the gentleman to his right, "Mr. Zachary Merrill. Mr. Merrill . . . Mr. Ethan Shaye."

And so, as Ethan nodded in acknowledgement, he took a closer look at the man standing beside their host.

Zachary Merrill was a stocky, round-faced, impeccably-attired man of about thirty years old. His eyes were of such a light blue that one would be tempted to describe them as "cool" if it wasn't for the fact that they shone with convivial brightness. He shook Ethan's hand affably.

"It is an honor to make your acquaintance, sir," Mr. Merrill declared with hearty goodwill. "I hope you will find an opportunity while you are in the region to come up to Merrill Hall and meet my grandfather. He does not get into town as much as he would like, but he is always eager to receive visitors. There have not been many travelers passing through of late, since the war's inception, and I know he would welcome the diversion of a guest with news from the northern colonies. Even in his advanced years, you will find him to be as ardent a Patriot as the best of us."

"I am sure I shall," Ethan replied. "And I thank you for your hospitable invitation."

Mr. Porter then introduced the other men, noting their professions, and the dialogue recommenced, Mr. Merrill's reference to his grandfather's patriotism having set the topic of discussion back upon its original course.

In truth, Ethan was somewhat surprised by Mr. Zachary Merrill's relaxed affability. The much-revered grandson of the town's magistrate did not at all conform to Ethan's expectations. After hearing so much adulation heaped upon Zachary Merrill, Ethan had envisioned him to be something of a patronizing dandy who accumulated indebtedness from the townsfolk by bestowing meager favors upon them while smirking behind their backs. Yet, while Mr. Merrill's fashionably-tailored coat and ruffled shirt may have conformed to the notion of a dandy, there was nothing condescending in his manner, and indeed, he seemed to think nothing of standing and conversing with the gentlemen presently gathered, though his birthright and station would assuredly place him in a loftier circle.

After a time, as the discussion amongst the men progressed, Ethan was again asked as to whether he had received from Mr. Clymer any verification of the rumor pertaining to the colonies declaring their independence from the Crown.

The notion did not entirely surprise Ethan, for he had heard such reports circulating in the military encampment, but he felt it wise to distance himself from any subject upon which he might be asked to remark at length, and so he answered with a safely noncommittal, "Alas, I cannot say that Mr. Clymer has taken me into his confidence on the matter. We have lately spoken only of the task for which he has commissioned me. However," he added, "should such reports of independence prove to be true, I shall be among the first to voice my 'huzzah!'"

This declaration was met with approving nods and concurrences from the other men, and Joshua Porter brought the discussion to a close with the suggestion that they ought to adjourn to the parlor before Mrs. Porter should grow agitated by their absence.

The other gentlemen concurred good-naturedly and filed out of the drawing room, still conversing amongst themselves.

Ethan paused to take a cursory glance at a scale-model miniature ship displayed in a cabinet just inside the door to the room, and thus was he the last to make his way across the hall toward the parlor.

He was met at the parlor door by Monsieur Brisonneau, who had just crossed from the staircase at the far end of the hall.

"Ah, good afternoon, Monsieur Shaye," the Frenchman greeted Ethan with a bow.

Ethan did not reciprocate the formality, and merely gave a nod and a tepid "Monsieur Brisonneau." He had not softened in his initial dislike for the French emissary.

Brisonneau either did not detect this coolness or chose to ignore it, as he continued addressing Ethan in a manner which was characteristically polite, though hardly congenial. "I believe Madame Porter was inquiring after you earlier. She will be pleased to learn that you have arrived. I had just gone to fetch my pocket-watch." (And here the Frenchman opened his palm to reveal an ornate gold-and-ivory watch case.) "It is from Paris. Madame Porter thought some of the guests may be interested in seeing the ivory inlay."

Considering that Monsieur Brisonneau had uttered hardly three words upon their first meeting, this unheralded — albeit restrained — disclosure was unexpected, and Ethan surmised that the foreigner's previous reticence could not be attributed in any great part to a deficiency in speaking or comprehending the English language. This insight hardly elevated the man in Ethan's esteem, however, and as Brisonneau went forth into the parlor, Ethan tarried a moment in the hall, thus preventing the necessity of further conversation with the Frenchman. Despite the fact that Ethan knew he must learn all he could about Brisonneau's dealings with Joshua Porter, he felt no inclination nor made any effort to establish a more congenial rapport with the Porters' houseguest.

After allowing a sufficient interval for Brisonneau to assimilate amongst the other guests, Ethan himself crossed the threshold into the parlor . . . an innocuous step resulting in a consequence he never could have foreseen.

Indeed, when one enters a room crowded with people, it is often the case — whether by chance or design — that one's eye should immediately and inadvertently be drawn to someone of familiarity, should there happen to be such a recognizable figure in the room. Such was the case with Ethan as he entered the parlor. Yet, considering that there were only a very few faces he could have recognized within the room, how swiftly and dramatically was he altered by the one his eye alighted upon . . . one whose own eye chanced to meet his at the same instant.

Ethan halted just inside the doorway, his gaze at once arrested.

And assuredly, a span of months was bridged there in one moment, with one look.

There was no uncertainty, no unwavering doubt . . . he could never forget those solemn brown eyes. Though he had doggedly put them out of his thoughts during waking hours, they had persistently and unmercifully haunted his dreams at night. And here they were now — staring at him from across the room with . . . what? What sentiment was reflected in those soft eyes? If he had been in possession of his senses, Ethan would undoubtedly have recognized the sentiments, for they mirrored his own and bespoke of emotions beyond mere recognition: astonishment, bewilderment, wonder.

Certainly not dismay.

For Ethan, apprehensiveness set in only after he had returned to his senses, realizing that his situation was at once imperiled by the presence of a girl who could so readily identify his true profession.

This thought had only just taken root and was nowhere near directing any sort of action, other than increasing the acceleration of his heartbeat, when he was quite abruptly distracted by a voice beside him.

"Mr. Shaye! I am so glad that you have come!"

Ethan only reluctantly took his eyes off the girl and turned to acknowledge Anne Porter's greeting. He murmured something absently, and Mrs. Porter — taking no notice of his distractedness — sociably slipped her arm through his, asking:

"Have you met some of the other guests?"

Ethan glanced back toward the girl again. She had averted her own gaze and a slight frown creased her brow.

"Aye," Ethan replied, yet distracted. "I have met Mr. Merrill and some of the other gentlemen."

"Excellent!" Mrs. Porter looked very pleased. "Then I must introduce you to our visitors. Come!" And releasing his arm, she started toward the opposite side of the room.

She had not taken more than three steps, however, before realizing that Ethan was not following her. Indeed, when she turned back toward him, he seemed quite rooted to the spot and none too willing to follow her.

Mrs. Porter smiled and, returning to where he stood, took his arm once more. "Come!" she repeated encouragingly. "This won't take but a moment, I promise, and then you can return to the gentlemen."

And so it was that Ethan was led to Constance Jameson.

Glancing up, Constance saw them approaching. She did not take her eyes off of Ethan as he neared, and though Ethan could not bring himself to look away, he was conscious of his heart pounding within his chest as his mind raced in a torrent of consternated thoughts: Why was she here? Would she divulge his profession? What was that look in her eyes — what was she thinking?

Did she remember what he could not forget?

Before he could even begin to sort out these thoughts, he found himself standing directly before Constance and heard Anne Porter's bright voice beside him:

"Mr. Shaye, may I present to you my younger sister, Miss Constance Jameson?"

Her sister! Ethan could barely comprehend, but managed a polite bow nonetheless.

Mrs. Porter completed the introduction: "Constance, this is Mr. Ethan Shaye. He is visiting Merrilltown on some business." She leaned in toward Constance and added with a note of importance, "Doing some surveying for Mr. George Clymer of Philadelphia."

Ethan stiffened in anticipation that Constance's response might prove to be his undoing.

But Constance did not move — only looked up searchingly into Ethan's face, her luminous eyes bewildered. She did not understand.

Of course she could not understand. How Ethan wished he could draw her aside and explain! It was impossible, though. The room was crowded with people, and Mrs. Porter was at hand.

That lady was quite dismayed at her sister's prolonged silence. "Constance — whatever is the matter with you?" she chided. "Remember your manners and give Mr. Shaye a proper greeting."

Constance flushed and lowered her eyes, as Mrs. Porter turned to Ethan.

"You must forgive my sister," she contended. "She is not usually so neglectful of her manners. She has endured some difficulties of late, which I'm sure must have some bearing on her present state."

Ethan was still looking at Constance — though Constance's eyes remained averted — and he frowned upon hearing Mrs. Porter's words.

"I am sorry indeed to hear that she has been put through any sort of tribulation." Although he was ostensibly speaking in response to Mrs. Porter, his focus was still upon Miss Constance, and his tone so gentle that she looked up at him again. Ethan immediately turned toward Mrs. Porter, for he could not look into Constance's eyes without awakening sensations that were better left in check. "I . . . truly hope that her adversity is now overcome," he continued in a more solid voice, "but should I be able to render any aid in the matter, I pray that she would not hesitate to ask my assistance, as such would be gladly given."

Anne Porter smiled. "That is very kind of you, Mr. Shaye, though I hardly think you would be able to alleviate my sister's situation." Mrs. Porter lifted her fan to her lips and whispered to Ethan from behind it: "I will tell you about it later. No need to bring up such troubles here. But— oh!" she interrupted herself, lowering her fan and speaking aloud once again. "Here's Polly now!" A young lady who was passing by turned

her head, and Mrs. Porter drew her into their little group. "Mr. Shaye —
may I present to you our youngest sister, Miss Polly Jameson. Polly —
this is Mr. Ethan Shaye, who is also a visitor to Merrilltown."

Still somewhat disconcerted, Ethan turned toward the youngest Jameson sister and bowed, murmuring an inconsequential greeting
which the youngest sister returned in a manner nearly as indifferent.

Polly Jameson. Ethan well-remembered hearing the strains of Polly's
spinet drifting upward from her father's parlor below.

Although Polly was but seventeen years old, she held herself with
confident poise and self-assurance. Her countenance, however, reflected
some state of agitation. Releasing herself from Mrs. Porter's grasp, she
moved to Constance and took hold of her arm. "Do step out into the
garden with me, Con," Polly implored. "It is quite stuffy in here, and I've
had such an ordeal trying to converse with that Monsieur Brisonneau.
He is really terribly difficult to understand . . . and not altogether agreeable, I must say," she added somewhat disdainfully.

Anne Porter frowned with some severity. "Polly, you must not make
such a judgment before others," she admonished, "and after only just
making Monsieur Brisonneau's acquaintance!"

Polly merely shrugged, apparently indifferent to her eldest sister's
scolding, and turned her attention back to Constance. "Do come with
me, then," Polly urged. "You are looking quite flushed yourself and could
do with some fresh air." And with a quick curtsey in Ethan's direction,
Miss Polly took her leave, her arm still entwined through Constance's
and thus propelling that young lady's departure as well.

Constance — still silent, though perhaps regaining some composure — had time for only a quick nod toward Ethan and Mrs. Porter
before being led away toward the door.

Ethan was still looking after them when Mr. Zachary Merrill approached and addressed Anne Porter.

"Mrs. Porter," Mr. Merrill greeted that lady with a bow, "I must
compliment you on the tasteful arrangement of your parlor. That chaise
is new, is it not?"

Mrs. Porter fluttered her fan, beaming at such a compliment. "Why thank you, Mr. Merrill. It is indeed a new addition to the room, although it is not of itself new to this house. We have only just moved it from the drawing room to make a place for the spinet, which was graciously spared to us and sent down from Pennsylvania."

To Ethan, this seemed a rather puzzling statement, but he could scarcely dwell upon it, so disconcerted were his thoughts already. He paid little heed to the remainder of the conversation between Mrs. Porter and Mr. Merrill and offered only perfunctory responses and rhetorical interjections.

What was he to do?

He considered the possibility that he should leave — right now, without delay. Leave Merrilltown and lay aside any possibility that he should compromise the success of his mission or the survival of General Washington's men.

But then . . . Constance would never know. She would never understand why he had been there — she would only know for certain that it had been under the pretext of deception, and her memories of him would be forever tarnished.

No . . . he could not do that. He must see her again, speak to her in private. He would find an opportunity . . .

Mrs. Porter was eventually called away by her husband, and though she seemed reluctant to depart — for she had been engaged in conversation with the distinguished Mr. Merrill — she promised to return as soon as she attended to the comfort of some recently arrived guests.

Just as Mrs. Porter stepped away, Constance and Polly Jameson re-entered through the door at the far end of the room. Ethan was not the only one to notice.

"They are amiable young ladies, are they not?" remarked Mr. Merrill, with an eye upon the two ladies in question. He shook his head gravely. "It is a shame what they have been put to — surely they are the least deserving of such circumstances."

Ethan frowned. "I am not familiar with their circumstance," he asserted. "I know only that they are the younger sisters of our hostess."

"Indeed," Mr. Merrill nodded. He cautiously lowered his voice. "They have suffered some misfortune due to the loyalties of their father — a supporter of the Crown. When our own troops gained control of the eastern counties of Pennsylvania, the Jamesons' property was seized, along with that of other Loyalists in the region. Their father was apparently quite a prominent leader amongst the Loyalists there, and he fled to New York City, which, as you undoubtedly know, is under British martial authority. He sent his daughters here to stay with their elder sister until he is able to send for them." Mr. Merrill's countenance was yet grave as he added, "I do not, of course, begrudge our good cause, but it is a shame when such innocents must suffer the humiliations of war."

Ethan nodded, appreciative of the explanation, yet troubled, for his gaze was still upon Miss Constance, and she looked none too well.

Constance glanced across the room toward Ethan, then looked quickly away when she saw his eye already upon her. Though she still stood at the side of her sister Polly and amidst a circle of other guests, Constance did not appear to be partaking of the conversation, but seemed absorbed in her own thoughts.

Ethan watched as Anne Porter approached Constance and whispered something into her ear. Constance shook her head slightly and put her fingers to her temple, as if indicating that her head ached. Anne frowned in concern, then said something, motioning toward the door to the hall. Constance glanced at the door and nodded. Without tarrying further, Constance curtsied briefly to the surrounding company and departed from their circle, making her way toward the door.

Ethan did not hesitate in his own objective. He was hardly even cognizant of the excuse he made to Mr. Merrill, but he extracted himself from that gentleman's company and hastened toward the door through which Constance had just exited the room.

He stepped into the central hall and found it quite deserted except for a slight figure just setting foot upon the stairs at the far end. Ethan made his way swiftly and silently toward the staircase, and spoke softly, but urgently, just as Constance was halfway up her ascent:

"Miss Jameson!"

Constance was halted at once, glancing back down over her shoulder. Ethan took a step closer and put one hand upon the bannister as Constance slowly turned to face him. She looked at him for a moment before beginning a measured descent back toward the landing. She never took her eyes off of Ethan as she moved, nor even when she came to a stop several steps up from the ground, where she stood at a level only slightly above him, though the bannister separated them. She held his gaze, but did not speak, and yet Ethan thought nothing of it, for he, too, was wholly absorbed.

Standing motionless, looking into those thoughtful brown eyes, Ethan was transported . . . no longer standing in the spacious, elegant hall, but instead, lying under the low-beamed rafters of a dim and austere garret, and remembering the soothing touch of a gentle hand upon his brow.

Even when Ethan at last found his tongue, his voice was hushed, as if he still needed to take care that his words were not heard by those below. "Miss Jameson . . . I . . . thank you for your discretion in there."

How familiar was Constance's gentle smile! She replied softly: "Well . . . 'twould be no simple matter to explain our . . . prior acquaintance."

Her tone was full of warmth, and Ethan unwittingly moved his hand a bit further up the bannister, nearer to hers.

They fell into another silence. But where their voices lapsed, their eyes were very much engaged. Indeed, neither seemed willing to sever that connection, nor to look away for even one moment.

Ethan could scarcely fathom the reality that Constance was here before him, so displaced from the only context in which he had ever known her.

That she should be the sister of Joshua Porter's wife . . .

That he should see those serious eyes trained upon him, here, at this unexpected juncture . . .

It was Constance who finally broke the silence, and though her words were simple, there was eloquent tenderness in their expression:

"You look well."

Her soft smile conveyed the sincerity of the sentiment behind the words.

And Ethan's response was not a mere formality. He spoke in a hushed, awed tone:

"You are . . . unchanged."

Constance blushed and modestly lowered her eyes. While a stranger may have thought Ethan's words lacking in expected decorum, Constance understood well enough the ardent warmth in his eyes.

But even as Constance averted her gaze, Ethan was yet studying her face, and he added: "Yet there is about you a wistfulness that was not there before. I . . . am sorry . . . about your situation."

There was some necessary awkwardness in his last statement, which Constance surely comprehended, knowing where Ethan's loyalties lay in opposition to her father's. She lifted her eyes once more — no longer blushing and shy, but puzzled. She tilted her head slightly in that fetching, inquisitive way of hers, and spoke with evident perplexity:

"My sister said that you were doing . . . surveying work. She called you Mr. Shaye. *Mr.* Shaye. Have you given up your rank and your military affiliation then? Given up a cause that you were willing to die for?" She shook her head. "I cannot believe that you have."

Her words broke the spell and brought Ethan back to the reality of his own present situation. He inadvertently stiffened, and a slight scowl creased his brow.

"No," he replied curtly. "I am . . . still employed in the same manner of profession."

It was an obscure response, and Constance yet stared at Ethan questioningly, but Ethan remained sullenly silent.

"You would not have them know your rank or profession," Constance ventured, keeping her voice low. "But why are you here under this pretext? Why should such covertness be required? You are among your own kind — there are no Loyalists here."

Ethan turned his head, frowning absently at the white-painted knob at the bannister's end. He would not deceive Constance, but he chose his next words carefully. "There is treachery in this town. My success in rooting it out depends upon a measure of secrecy." His tone took on a purposeful firmness. "Secrecy which must not be compromised . . . under any circumstance."

Constance flushed, understanding well enough the implication of his words. "I see," she murmured, her manner at once altered. She straightened and held her head erect, though she could not conceal the affliction in her dark eyes, nor prevent her voice from quivering a bit as she spoke. "Do not be alarmed on account of my presence here," she said with measured constraint. "Your personal agenda is no concern of mine, and you can be assured that I shall not reveal anything about you or your profession. And now, if you will excuse me, I am not feeling well today and must rest."

And before Ethan could so much as acknowledge her departure, Constance turned and hastened up the stairs.

Ethan remained with one hand still upon the bannister, looking after her. He wanted to utter her name, to call her back, to convince her that she had misconstrued the meaning of his words. Yet he knew that she had not — that the meaning she had understood was indeed the truth. He must not call her back. He must suppress the feelings of guilt and remorse which now crept up inside of him. He must suppress the inclination to right the grievance he had wrought. He must put distance between himself and the girl who could prevent the success of his mission. He must think of the higher cause.

Still, he lingered at the foot of the stairs, looking up into the emptiness of the corridor above, where Constance had disappeared into the grey dimness.

When Ethan at last turned away from the staircase, determined to quit the premises straightaway, he was startled to find that he was not alone in the hall. A dark shape rustled in the shadow near the back door, and Ethan did not need but an instant before recognizing the formidable figure glaring at him with such familiar severity.

Ethan maintained an outward appearance of composure, despite the unexpectedness of the encounter. "Ah, Jenny," he greeted her in his most offhand manner, though he wondered how long she had been standing there. "How delightful to see you again, and in such fine spirits."

His breezy sarcasm was apparently lost on the swarthy slave woman, whose continuous glower suggested that she had indeed witnessed Ethan's conversation with the young mistress.

Ethan merely gave Jenny an affable nod and sauntered past her out the door, his apparent insouciance concealing the turbulent maelstrom whirling within his mind.

ETHAN AVOIDED THE PORTER HOUSE for the next few days. After informing the landlord at Lethbridge's that he expected to be very pre-occupied with his work for a time, Ethan rode the nine miles to Henry Dowling's outpost, determined to put Merrilltown and its inhabitants out of his mind, at least for the interim. He tarried there in the country-side despite the fact that he had little information to convey to Sergeant Dowling, and despite the fact that such tarrying was in opposition to Colonel Naismith's instructions. Ethan did not care. In the company of his comrade, amidst discussion of battles and regiments and military en-terprises, he was able to forget his latest tribulations and reconnect with that part of his life that he had temporarily — and reluctantly — relin-quished. When he set back out to town, his spirits were much restored.

But the respite was bound to be short-lived. Ethan knew that he must not impede the progress of his commission. He knew as well that advancing that purpose would necessitate a return to the home of Joshua Porter.

Mr. Porter himself initiated such a return. Just over a week had passed since Ethan had attended the gathering at the Porters' house, when he received a note from Mr. Porter indicating that Tuesday afternoon would be an opportune time to come and make use of the study, as the merchant himself would be occupied with the customs officials at that time and would not be utilizing the room for the greater part of the day.

Ethan, of course, could not disregard such a forthright opportunity to proceed with his assignment, so he set out once again toward Joshua Porter's house on the appointed day.

The smiling servant girl seemed to be expecting him this time, for she led him directly into Mr. Porter's small study without any attempt to present him to either master or mistress.

Although Ethan had known that Mr. Porter would not be at home, he was greatly relieved by the general quietude within the household, which would seem to indicate that Mrs. Porter and her sisters were likewise absent. As Ethan followed the housegirl through the central hall toward the study, he somewhat furtively surveyed the environs, half expecting to see Jenny's sour visage grimacing at him from a corner; but the lower level of the house appeared to be quite deserted.

Ethan carried with him some measurements of "Mr. Clymer's" property, which he had obtained while visiting Henry Dowling, for he knew that, once situated in the study, he must carry out some true measure of his purported occupation. However, once the housegirl had lighted the sconces and table candle — providing adequate illumination to the small, windowless room — and subsequently departed, Ethan was hardly inclined to immediately set about copying land measurements.

Instead, he appraised the state of the compact room. The desktop had been cleared — likely in anticipation of his own utilization — save for the inkstand and a stack of paper, evidently also provided for his benefit. The slender little logbook was nowhere to be seen, but Ethan lost no time in searching for it. He was certain that Mr. Porter would not be put to any trouble in concealing it, as it bore no condemning evidence to the casual eye.

He pulled open the desk drawer, but quickly determined that the leather-bound book was not contained therein. Turning his back to the desk, Ethan surveyed the bookshelf against the wall. Scanning the volumes, his perceptive eye almost immediately fell upon the object of his search, wedged quite carelessly and even conspicuously between two thick shipping logs. It appeared that Joshua Porter had hastily slipped the logbook into an available space in order to accommodate Ethan's work at the desk.

The master of the house could have spared himself the trouble.

Turning back toward the light of the candle on the desk, Ethan set about to peruse the logbook's pages, but found that the book readily opened to the same page he had last inspected upon his previous visit. The reason for this was at once apparent: A folded piece of paper was lodged there between the pages, thus facilitating the immediate location of the logbook's most recent entry. Ethan removed the paper and glanced at the logbook's columns. There was only one further line recorded upon the page since he had last examined the entries, and it was incomplete at that. The entry neither was dated, nor was there recorded a date of receipt in the final column. But the two center columns contained written information, similar to those preceding it. There were two names: G. Marten/Colonel Adderly, followed by a list of inventory — mostly medical supplies and sundry dry goods, though Ethan noted the inclusion of "one case Dutch infantry muskets".

Ethan appraised the concise entry quickly, then, setting the book down, he turned his attention to the folded sheet of paper which had marked the logbook's page. Stepping closer to the candle's illumination, he unfolded the paper, and as he did so, a smaller scrap fell to the floor. Ethan gave it a cursory glance but determined to first inspect the paper in his grasp, as it appeared to be a note, written in a solid, resolute hand. It did not take but a moment for him to scan the contents of the brief missive:

Mr. George Marten of Virginia is hereby granted permission to enter the colony of Maryland and shall be allowed free access to the roads in that colony and in the territories held under British command. This privilege of passage is to be revoked and confiscated upon return to the Virginia border.

Colonel John Adderly

As he finished reading the message, Ethan continued to stare at the paper for a few seconds more, ruminating over the substance of the words.

It was unmistakably a blockade pass for the Patriot supply wagon . . . but when was it to be utilized? The message was signed, but not dated.

Ethan eyed the scrap that had fallen to the floor. Setting the pass upon the desk, he bent to retrieve the smaller bit of paper, and upon straightening, held it directly beneath the candle's light. The scrap seemed to have been torn from a larger page, for its edges were ragged, and upon it was written a signature: *Col. John Adderly, 46th British Reg.*

Ethan set it beside the blockade pass upon the desktop. The hand-writing was identical. He glanced again at the open logbook sitting near the center of the desk. Taking up the blockade pass in one hand, he reached for the logbook with the other and examined them both closely, his brow furrowed in concentration as he compared the writing on the paper with that of the logbook's entries.

If Joshua Porter was the forger, he was a master, for the scripts bore not the slightest resemblance. If he was not . . . then someone else in the vicinity was given open access to Joshua Porter's information regarding the Patriot supply shipments and was, in fact, Mr. Porter's collaborator.

But who?

There were numerous persons who seemed to frequent the Porters' residence — both business colleagues and Merrilltown neighbors. To whom would Joshua Porter entrust his confidence in matters of such gravity?

And yet — the simplest explanation would surely find Porter himself to be both organizer and forger, and therefore in sole possession of the information. Such a scenario would, of course, also cast singular suspicion upon Porter, however genial his character or overt his professions of loyalty to the Patriots' cause, for it was plain that the saboteur — whether one man or more — was privy to the information recorded in the logbook . . . or to the source of that information.

Suddenly aware of footsteps in the hall — although undoubtedly just the passage of servants — Ethan was recalled to the precariousness of his prying, and hastily, noiselessly, refolded the pass — inserting the small scrap of paper as he did so — and closed it back between the pages of the logbook, which he subsequently slid back into its place on the shelf.

He knew he must have something to show for his time, but though he sat at the desk with the surveying papers spread before him, pencil in hand, he did little more than frown into the abyss for the next half hour, a torrent of uncertainties streaming through his mind.

He tried to piece together the implications of the pass found in the logbook. Who had penned it? When was it to be utilized? Would it earn its bearer passage through the blockade? Was Joshua Porter apprehensive about dispatching another supply shipment? Or was he confident in the success — however it be defined — of the enterprise?

Yet even these intriguing complexities could not sustain Ethan's concentration for any length of time, for his ruminations were invariably punctured by intruding thoughts whose substance had unrelentingly laid siege to his reasoning during the course of the last several days. He had stifled such thoughts with deliberate tenacity, but it seemed that now, in the quiet confines of the small study, in the house which harbored the source of his disconcertion, he could not further vanquish them.

Every thought reflected the name and image of Constance Jameson. And the thoughts filled him with restless discontent.

But what — or whom — could be the source of such discontent? Surely Miss Jameson herself must be the perpetrator of this internal discord, for whom else could it be? Her appearance in Merrilltown — so unexpected and so ill-timed — placing in jeopardy Ethan's every circumstance and complicating his carefully-constructed plans.

He scowled deeper into the void as these reflections consumed his consciousness. Aye, it was surely she who was the cause of the unsettling agitation which had taken root within him and given him no peace since her appearance in Merrilltown.

Yet, somehow . . . the unsettled restlessness was familiar . . .

But no, he would not dwell upon that. He must not. He would not seek further explanation for the permeating knot which had twisted itself into the pit of his abdomen these recent days, the sensation of which even now deepened the crease of his frown.

And yet . . . even in the present dimness he could see the image of her face over the bannister — her expression transformed in one moment from tender affection to dismayed affliction. It was not the first time he had seen her countenance altered at his doing . . . but it was the first time he had not rectified it.

And there it was again, that hollow pang gnawing at his insides.

Surely it could not be his own doing . . .

His conclusions were far from satisfactory, and he well knew it, but he would not permit himself to seek another cause for this inward conflict, nor even to reflect upon it further. For resentment toward himself was a path Ethan Shaye liked not to tread.

And so he put a stop to his deliberations and forced the reawakening of his alertness. He realized that his palms were sweating as he clutched his pencil, and his whole body was tense. He took a deep breath and rose from his chair, still frowning to himself, but determined to depart the premises immediately, though he had naught to show for his time.

After gathering his belongings, he cast a last look at the shelf where the logbook protruded only slightly from between the thicker shipping logs. Mindful of the need to completely conceal his activities, he reached out to push the slender volume fully back into its proper position, but just as his fingers touched the binding, the door to the hall suddenly opened.

Ethan quickly withdrew his hand and turned toward the door, where the figure of a man was silhouetted in the open doorway.

As his eyes adjusted to the light emanating from the hall, Ethan found himself facing a young man whom he did not recognize and who had himself stopped short upon sighting Ethan.

Neither spoke for a moment, but only eyed one another suspiciously, until the stranger took a step further into the room and addressed Ethan curtly:

"Who are you?"

Ethan's sharp eye had quickly appraised the stranger and determined that the young man was, in fact, hardly more than a boy; certainly not older than eighteen, though he had put his question to Ethan very directly and maintained his suspicious frown.

Ethan did not feel compelled to give a hasty account of himself and met the question with self-assured coolness:

"Ethan Shaye."

He offered no elaboration, but he saw a glimmer of faint recognition in the youth's eye, replacing a fair measure of the suspicion there.

"I have heard your name," the youth acknowledged, then added, "I am Tristan Porter."

Of course. Ethan should have guessed that this was Joshua Porter's elder son —with his hair as yellow as his half-brother's and his natural suspicion at discerning a stranger in his father's study.

Ethan conceded that some explanation was in order.

"Your father has permitted me to make use of his study while I am in Merrilltown. I have been doing some work for a mutual acquaintance of ours."

"Aye." Tristan nodded, apparently already apprised of the situation. He seemed not inclined to converse, though, nor did he seem entirely convinced of Ethan's purpose there.

Despite the fact that each had recognized the other's name, there remained a wariness between them.

Ethan silently questioned what Tristan had witnessed upon opening the study door. Had he seen Ethan's hand reaching for the slender logbook? There was no way of knowing for certain, and this doubt made

Ethan uneasy. Outwardly, though, he gave no indication of concern, for he knew he must win the trust of Joshua Porter's elder son, and if Tristan knew aught of his father's covert aid to the Patriots' cause, he would need to be thoroughly convinced that Ethan knew naught of it. Indeed, Ethan must take every precaution in not casting suspicion upon himself. Colonel Naismith had assured him that he need not play a role nor adopt any artificial attitude in his endeavors, but Ethan knew he must attempt to placate any doubts in Tristan's mind, and so — detesting more and more this assignment — he racked his brain for words that would sound natural and unassuming in this most unnatural of situations.

"Your father said you had joined the colony's militia," was what he settled upon in an attempt at casual discourse, coming round to the front of the desk as he spoke.

Tristan nodded again. "Aye. We have a camp downriver. I have been two months enrolled."

It was the closest thing to conversation Tristan had uttered, and Ethan feigned protracted interest in the topic, though his tone of voice still reflected cautious composure: "Do you intend to enlist with the Continentals then?" He noted a slight gleam brighten Tristan's eye.

"Perhaps," Tristan replied. "But I think I should better serve in the Patriots' navy. There shall be eight warships put to sea before the year is out, and ample opportunity for sailors and officers." Tristan could not conceal the edge of enthusiasm in his voice, but his momentary animation was just as quickly dampened, as he added, "Though my father would have me stay closer to home."

Ethan's response was carefully worded: "Yet surely your father knows better than most the necessity of able seamen protecting our waterways and harbors. His own shipping trade has been affected by the war."

Although Ethan watched closely, Tristan's sullen expression did not change.

Tristan merely shrugged, saying, "I have grown up watching the ships upon the river and observing my father's trade, but watching and observing do not make me an able seaman." And he said nothing more, having given Ethan absolutely no insight into his knowledge of his father's activities nor revealing any suspicions toward Ethan himself.

And for his part, Ethan had had enough of the conversation's stilted manner and the overall contrived nature of the situation. His patience was spent, and he abruptly terminated the encounter. "I am sure you do your father credit in your endeavors on behalf of the Patriots' cause. And now, I must be about my business and return to my lodgings. Good day," he concluded with a brusque nod, which Tristan returned in kind.

"Your servant, Mr. Shaye."

The sound of several voices in the corridor — along with the fact that Tristan was still standing before the hall doorway — prompted Ethan to make his exit through the parlor door. He hastened across the deserted parlor toward the opening to the central hall, but it seemed his further delay was inevitable, for there he very nearly collided with Anne Porter, who was just entering the room with Mr. Zachary Merrill. Following close behind were Mrs. Porter's sisters and Monsieur Brisonneau.

"I beg your pardon, Mrs. Porter," Ethan apologized rather shortly. He involuntarily glanced at Miss Constance, who quickly looked away, her countenance flushed and disconcerted. Ethan hastily reverted his attention back to Mrs. Porter, who had not been at all discomposed by the unexpected meeting and would detain Ethan further.

"Why, Mr. Shaye!" Mrs. Porter smiled brightly at him. "This is a happy coincidence! We were just bemoaning the fact that we had not one more person for our card game — for you know it is impossible to play with only three, and Constance and Polly are being very obstinate in refusing to take part, though perhaps you may have better success than we have in persuading them. We could then have three sets for piquet."

The youngest sister, Polly, wrinkled her brow and shook her head. "We shall not be persuaded," she protested determinedly. "After riding about the countryside in an open carriage all afternoon, we are mussed and tired and wish to refresh ourselves. Moreover, as Constance remarked earlier, it seems very early in the day to play at cards."

Although Mrs. Porter had a ready response to her sister's objections, Ethan paid little heed to the repartee which continued between the youngest and eldest siblings for several minutes.

Throughout it all, and in spite of his impatience to depart, Ethan was keenly aware of Constance's presence, though he very deliberately avoided looking in her direction, instead keeping his eye purposefully fixed upon her sisters. And without looking upon her, he could not know her thoughts, for she remained silent. Yet, however gratified Ethan would have been to gain a moment's insight into her thoughts — to take in her features and demeanor for only one brief instant — he determinedly resisted the impulse, though it required the full measure of his resolve.

This internal strife further fueled his agitation, so that his restlessness would have been quite apparent to any observer, had the situation not been dominated by the ongoing card-game discussion between Mrs. Porter, Miss Polly, and Mr. Zachary Merrill, who had joined in after a time in an attempt to reasonably placate both sisters.

"If you have your heart set on whist," Mr. Merrill was saying to Mrs. Porter, "and Miss Polly wishes to entertain us with her music, there is no reason you cannot both have your way, for if Mr. Shaye would take the fourth hand, then—"

But here Ethan's forbearance gave out. "I am sorry," he interposed rather brashly. "I am unable to stay longer." He turned to Mrs. Porter. "Perhaps you can induce your husband's son to join you."

Mrs. Porter, still slightly flustered over Ethan's blatant interruption of her most distinguished guest, was only mildly attentive to his words. "Oh, is Tristan here?" she asked distractedly, peering past Ethan as if expecting to see her stepson sitting in the parlor.

"I've only just left him in the study," Ethan elucidated, then went on briskly before his hostess could interject a response, "—and as I have a great deal of work to do yet today, I must bid you all good afternoon." And with a nod to Mrs. Porter and another in the general direction of the rest of the party, he hurried past them into the hall and out the front door, without so much as a word or acknowledgement toward Miss

Constance. He could not bring himself to even cast a glance in her direction, lest he should find those luminous dark eyes trained upon him — solemn and questioning . . . or worse, reproachful. Then, there would be no peace for him.

ETHAN'S ATTEMPT AT SELF-PRESERVATION proved entirely futile. All that he had seen, heard, witnessed, discovered — and not seen — at the Porters' house that afternoon flooded his brain for the remainder of the day and well into the night, even unto his slumber. He was afforded no repose. He could neither order nor assimilate his thoughts with any measure of reason, nor even determine where to direct his concentration. All the uncertainties he had grappled with in the study seemed to be magnified in their complexity as he veered from reflection to deliberation to speculation: the logbook, the signed pass, the intrusion of Tristan Porter, the signature on the scrap of paper, . . . and Constance. Always Constance. Somehow his stream of thought always returned to her, though she had naught to do with his commission. But she surely had everything to do with the unrest which had taken hold of him in recent days and which now manifested itself so conspicuously upon his senses.

All of these disparate, fragmented thoughts turbulently revolved within his brain for the duration of the night, with the consequence that he dwelt upon not any subject long enough to come to any rational conclusion or resolution.

BY MORNING'S LIGHT, ETHAN FELT not at all rested, and instead of facing the day with spirits renewed, he was only ill-tempered and tense. Determined to shake off the tautness which gripped both his body and his disposition, he set out on foot from his lodging-house quite early, seeking to dispel his unrest with exercise.

He headed east out of Merrilltown toward the forest-covered hills which had beckoned to him nearly since his arrival, with their promise of shady seclusion and potential for exploration.

At first, he followed the road, for its initial course led in the direction of the hills, and thus he walked a fair distance from the town before he found himself at the foot of the nearest and tallest hill, which marked the beginning of the Merrill estate and upon which stood Merrill Hall, the elegant seat of Judge Merrill. Here — just as the dirt road branched into two, with one path continuing up the hill to the property's impressive wrought-iron gate, and the other angling north and gradually veering away from the hills — stood a small clapboard building surrounded by a wooden picket fence. Ethan paused a moment as he passed the structure, for there was some activity in the small yard, where a dozen boys clamored and ran about with cheerful shouts of youthful exuberance.

Ethan determined that this must be the school which Mr. Zachary Merrill had endowed for the town, and it was only fitting that it should be established at the foot of his grandfather's estate.

As Ethan stood observing the lively schoolyard, he recognized amongst the boys young Caleb Porter, who, while the smallest pupil in the school, was presently at the center of attention, standing in the midst of an admiring group of onlookers, his closed fist held aloft. Although the boy was at the far end of the yard, his piping voice carried to the road as Ethan heard him proclaim:

"See what my brother has brought me? Real musket balls!" And the child opened up his hand to reveal his treasure, as the other boys crowded in closer to better view Caleb's prized acquisitions.

Ethan noted that the small tri-cornered hat sitting atop Caleb's yellow hair sported a black cockade to one side, and it seemed that the coveted embellishment, along with his brother's gift, had afforded Caleb a blissfully auspicious start to his day, judging by the exultant gleam in his eye and the way his pearly little teeth flashed in the midst of his childishly proud smile. Despite being the youngest boy in school, he showed no bashfulness in addressing his fellow schoolmates and clearly relished the attention of his encircled admirers. This fact did not surprise Ethan, as it seemed to be in accord with the shamelessly impudent manner demonstrated by the boy upon Ethan's first visit to the Porter house.

He heard Caleb's voice pipe up again amidst the onlookers' barrage of questions. "These are the only musket balls my brother had left," Caleb boasted, "'cause he used up all th'others shooting Redcoats dead. He's killed thirty or forty by now."

This wholly implausible fabrication was met with derision on the part of some of the other boys, for even in their state of youth, they were aware that the colony of Virginia had seen but little in terms of battle or even skirmishes.

Caleb's face reddened, not due to any embarrassment at being caught exaggerating, but rather due to outright indignation at being thus disbelieved. His proud smile turned to ire, and he would undoubtedly have responded to the older boys' scoffs with a childish retort if the schoolmaster had not at that moment opened the door of the schoolhouse and summoned the young scholars inside.

As Caleb Porter pocketed his musket balls and sulkily tramped after the other boys toward the schoolhouse, Ethan turned away and continued his journey toward the more distant hills, leaving behind him the road as it veered back to civilization and instead following a narrow and almost imperceptible footpath through the tall grass.

His thoughts having been successfully diverted by the scene in the schoolyard, Ethan continued reflecting upon that little tableau as he walked.

Caleb Porter had boasted about getting the musket balls from his brother — a reference to Tristan Porter, who was in actuality the child's half-brother.

Ethan frowned to himself, for the name of Joshua Porter's elder son must invariably conjure up in his mind the recollection of Tristan Porter's unexpected entrance into the study at the moment when Ethan's hand was incriminatingly placed upon the logbook. And yet . . . if Tristan found suspicion in that circumstance, would that not point to the fact that he himself must have knowledge of the logbook's contents and importance? Ethan slowed his gait as he pondered this. It was not inconceivable that Tristan was the Patriots' betrayer, or an ally of the traitor. Under ostensible pretext of making frequent visits to his father's house from the militia's encampment, he would be in the unique position of having ready access to both the Porter home and the world beyond Merrilltown. He would have no trouble examining the logbook's entries at regular intervals and conveying the information there gleaned to—

To whom?

Surely Tristan could not himself ride all the way to the Redcoats' border blockade without raising suspicion. It was too great a distance and in the opposite direction of the militia encampment. If Tristan Porter was involved in sabotaging the Patriots' supply wagons, he must have an accomplice.

But even with Tristan's ability to freely access the information, Ethan could not convince himself that he was the saboteur. In the first place, there was the issue of the boy's age. A lad of only eighteen years would hardly have the expertise or reliability to be entrusted with carrying out such critical work for the British. And — even should he prove to be inordinately capable — what would be his motive for such treachery? Ethan could not conceive of any.

While all of these speculations passed through his mind, Ethan had continued along the course he had set out upon. He had long since begun his ascent into the hills behind the Merrill estate, and as he forged deeper into the forested wilderness, his thoughts became diverted by his surroundings.

When he first approached the hills, he had seen that they were not gentle slopes at all, but jagged inclines of craggy precipice, which had doubtlessly been hewn of rock by the river's coursing tributary long ago. They bore no resemblance to the lofty hill nearest the town — where stood Merrill Hall — which had been conquered by human engineering, with its lush green landscaping and ornamental gate. No, the other hills were rugged, wild, and covered with dark green pine forests.

The footpath dissolved only a few meters into the wooded incline, but Ethan was more than happy to let his senses guide him as he made his way through the forest gradient. The trees were well-spaced at first, with little undergrowth, which made for fairly easy maneuvering between them despite the forest's indistinguishable vastness and pathless uniformity.

As he climbed higher, Ethan noted that the forest grew denser, and thus cooler, as the overhanging branches blocked out most of the sunlight. It was a welcome coolness and helped to further alleviate the tension that had built up inside of him since the previous day.

He basked in the stillness, in the silence broken only by the occasional chirping of birds and by the light tread of his own feet upon the earth. The ground was uneven in many places, leading Ethan to make his way around or over numerous ridges and rocky knolls which jutted out at unexpected intervals. And as he neared the hill's summit, his sharp ears detected the unmistakable sound of distant water. Immediately and instinctively altering his course in the direction of the sound, he soon noticed that the trees before him thinned, and the ground beneath him became rockier. In only a few moments, he sighted the forest's perimeter, and he found himself standing at the periphery of a ledge — a steep bluff which was the culmination of a nearly vertical wall of sheer and ancient rock. Looking downward over the edge, Ethan saw that it was a very deep and narrow ravine which cut right through the center of the rugged hills. Though he could not see the bottom, he heard with clarity the trickle of running water emanating from the ravine's depths.

With no way to cross, Ethan turned back toward the wood and continued upon his original course. Having reached the hill's summit, he found that the opposite descent was much gentler, as the hill gradually sloped downward until the incline gave way to level ground once more, and he found himself standing upon the mossy bank of a peaceful grey river. Pausing there upon the bank, he surveyed the landscape on either side. He could not see the river's source, but his keen sense of direction and skillful awareness of nature's contours told him that this was the

Rappahannock's tributary. It was a very placid river, its stillness marred only by the occasional watery concentricity of a fish coming to feed at the top. Willow trees lined the opposite bank, their branches creating mist-like curtains where they skimmed the river's surface.

A dilapidated pier extended into the water only a few yards from where Ethan stood, and he observed another further down the river. There was an overgrown path running along the bank between the two piers and continuing past the second pier to a low, crumbling wooden building which probably at one time served as a warehouse.

Ethan guessed that this spot must have once been the main wa-ter landing upon the Merrills' property — before the Merrill ancestors had built up their worldly affluence, no doubt, and before the grand Hall had been constructed upon the manicured hill overlooking the Rappahannock proper, where the barges from Judge Merrill's downriver plantations now unloaded their cargo at an impressive port below the main house.

Ethan made his way down the embankment to the water's edge and stepped gingerly onto the decaying pier, which — despite its deterio-rating appearance — proved sturdy enough beneath him, and with its length afforded him a better view of his surroundings.

And yet, in looking upriver and down, there was nothing to behold but wilderness and solitude. If it were not for the aging pier and neglect-ed warehouse, one could almost imagine that humankind had not yet discovered the secluded haven.

The day was heating fast, however, and having left behind the cool shade of the forest, the lure of the water proved irresistible. Giving free reign to his impulses, Ethan shed his outer clothing and dived off of the pier into the river. He was at once invigorated, for his body was most content when actively engaged, and the hike across the hilly terrain had merely whetted his appetite for physical exertion.

He did not surface until he had nearly reached the far pier, but the moderate chill of the water had already begun to refresh both his heated body and his unsettled mind. As he filled his lungs with air, he noted a sweet fragrance whose headiness somehow seemed at odds with the river's unadulterated briskness, but he gave only a cursory glance toward the vegetation growing along the river's edge, then dove once more beneath the surface, for it was the water that rejuvenated his spirit.

He spent the next hour swimming the tributary's tranquil waters, plunging and diving to his heart's content, until every remnant of tension had been washed away by the diversion of exercise and the reconnection with the natural world. As the old landing had apparently fallen into disuse, so too was the tributary now devoid of any traffic, and Ethan was left quite undisturbed.

At last, with his senses thoroughly revitalized, he swam back to shore and stretched out upon the riverbank, where he lay for another quarter of an hour, contentedly basking in the sun's drowsy warmth.

His natural penchant for adventure was not yet quelled, however, and when he finally rose and dressed, he determined to return to town by a different route, that he might further explore the surrounding environs.

So it was that, instead of retracing his steps back into the forest, he followed the river southward for quite a way — a direction he knew would eventually lead him to the tributary's source. He had no doubt that all of the territory in the vicinity, however wild, was held by the Merrills; indeed, he had tread a broad arc around the distant hill which was the seat of their estate. As he had no wish to encroach upon that inhabited property, he kept to the river's course until he was certain that he had bypassed any possibility of crossing onto the magistrate's estate. Then, leaving the tributary behind him, Ethan began an ascent up another forested incline — an incline which seemed to form a wedge between the two rivers.

The hill itself was as craggy and unpredictable as the one which had led him to the old river landing, but now, when he had climbed to the top and made his way to the forest's edge, he was met with an entirely different sight than that which he had beheld earlier in the day. For here was no treacherous cliff-bordered ravine separating him from a neighboring hill, but instead, a vista quite splendid to behold. For the bluff gave way to an open view over the Rappahannock River, the proud source of the tranquil tributary at his back. From his position, Ethan was afforded an impressive perspective encompassing the Merrills' bustling new wharf directly below him, all the way to the riverside houses at the outskirts of Merrilltown. The hill sloped down quite steeply toward the river, but unlike the vertical wall of rock atop which he had stood that morning, this descent could be viably undertaken. Ethan noted, however, that if he descended toward the Merrills' new landing, he would still be required to walk a fair distance to town in the open, sunlit heat. He decided, therefore, to maintain his hilltop course a measure further until he reached a point nearer his destination, at which time he would forge his way downward.

So he turned back toward the wood, and, as he could not circumvent the trees, he made his way amidst them, relying as before on his sense of direction to guide him, and when he perceived that he had gone an adequate distance, he once more headed to the edge of the forest, where he might gain a clearer view of his position on the hill. His intuition had not failed him, for he was indeed at an advantageous point to descend as near to the town as this hill would bring him.

Moreover, the ridge on which he now stood overlooked none other than the Porters' river landing.

Ethan did not descend, but stood where he was, for he was well-positioned to observe the activity at the Porters' dock, and surveying the scene below him at once brought his mind back to the purpose of his duties and the cause to which he had dedicated himself.

He watched with interest for a long while. A sizable merchant vessel was moored upon the river near the pier. Industrious slaves diligently unloaded wooden chests and barrels from the ship's hold onto smaller boats, which were then rowed to the landing.

Ethan recognized Joshua Porter standing near the pier, along with another man, apparently overseeing the activity as the cargo was brought ashore.

It was upon this dockside enterprise that Ethan focused his attention, following closely the movements of the laborers at the pier as they shouldered the heavy crates and transported them to the landing. Once ashore, the cargo was systematically divided and allocated to its temporary holding-place: some was carried to Porter's warehouse beside the river, some was placed onto a river barge that was docked at the opposite side of the pier, and the rest was loaded directly into wagons to be taken overland.

Ethan occupied a truly auspicious vantage point for observing without himself being observed, and not one detail of the proceedings below escaped his keen eye, for upon sighting the ship moored at the Porters' landing, he had immediately called to mind the blockade pass lodged between the pages of the logbook in Joshua Porter's study; he had discovered it there only the previous day. And now, as he watched a portion of the cargo being loaded into wagons, Ethan wondered if one of the wagons was bound for the Maryland border.

It was impossible to know, for while he might attempt to follow the path of one wagon, he could not track them all. And there was certainly nothing extraordinary to observe in the activity below which would indicate an anomalous course for one of the wagons. Indeed, the unloading and distribution of the cargo appeared to be quite routine, and similar procedures could undoubtedly be observed at every merchant's dock in the colony.

Perhaps, if he could make his way down to the landing before the wagons departed, he might overhear the names of the drivers, for he remembered the name on the pass was Marten. He pondered what excuse he might give if he was to be spotted at the landing . . .

In the midst of this contemplation, Ethan's attention was distracted by some movement on the periphery of the scene before him. A short distance from the dock, a small party had just emerged from the Porters' garden gate and was strolling along the path which led to the river. Ethan at once recognized it to be nearly the same group he had encountered in the Porters' parlor the day before: Anne Porter, Constance and Polly Jameson, and Mr. Zachary Merrill. Monsieur Brisonneau had been replaced by young Tristan Porter, who now walked beside Polly Jameson at the front of the party. The other three followed a few paces behind.

But Ethan had eyes for only one. In beholding Constance, every-thing else was forgotten, and he stood as one transfixed, as the knot in his abdomen — which he had spent the better part of the day unloos-ing — took hold once more, its remorseless pull extending upward into the cavity of his chest.

Without averting his gaze, he absently stepped closer to the tree be-side him, as if to further conceal himself from view, although in truth there was no danger that Constance should see him, so well-shielded was he by the ridge's height and abundant foliage.

And so, from his hidden promontory could he at last look upon her without constraint. And indeed, as he beheld her, his eyes betrayed him in the eloquent honesty of their expression, for unguardedly seeing her thus, the bold and daring soldier could not remain unmoved.

He paid no heed to the others in her company . . . indeed, why should he? For him, there was no face sweeter than the one upon which his gaze lingered. How well he knew every feature of her countenance! Yet . . . he observed in her countenance a trace of sadness as she looked wistfully across the water, for she had paused at the river's edge, even as the others continued along toward the landing. They did not seem to notice that she had remained behind, and Constance made no attempt to follow them. She appeared to be lost in thought as she gazed absently toward the opposite bank.

And Ethan frowned slightly, for the sadness in Constance's expres-sion troubled him, though he sought to dispel emotion with reason: After all, was it not natural enough that a young lady in her circum-stance should be somewhat heavyhearted? Having lost her home, been separated from her father, and had her life's certainties jeopardized — some measure of dejection was surely to be expected, was it not? Ethan did his best to convince himself that no measure of her sorrow could be attributed to him. Yet, as he stood there, this unsubstantial self-defense gave way to other thoughts, by which his frown gradually dissolved, and he became pensive once more.

How strange it was to see her there — in the vastness of the out-side world, in the bright light of day, among other people. He had been accustomed to having her nearly to himself, within the confines of the garret, her little stool drawn up beside his cot — so near that he could have reached over and touched her without any effort.

What he would not give to touch her now!

But it was impossible. There was too much at stake. There were too many barriers.

He had made no attempt to see her or communicate with her since their abruptly-terminated conversation at the staircase in the Porters' hall nearly a fortnight ago. He knew well enough that that occasion's sudden — and unpleasant — ending had been his own doing. He had stubbornly resisted the impulse to immediately soothe hurt feelings or to make explanation to her. How could he have done otherwise? There were higher obligations which surely demanded his loyalty at all costs. And yet . . . such adherence to duty had never before caused him so much unrest nor given rise to so many doubts.

Since that day, he had very deliberately avoided her, though he had been less successful in putting her from his mind. But now! Having en-countered her again yesterday on his way out of the Porters' house . . . he had disregarded her with a callousness that was not true to either his character or his feelings for her. And therein lay the contradiction — that discrepancy between his feelings and his actions — which was the source of the relentless knot in his stomach, the strife in his mind.

And what must she think? What would Ethan have seen in her soft brown eyes had he dared to look into them before hastening away from her presence yesterday? He ought to have looked, for since that hour, the state of not knowing had gnawed at his conscience in a manner more unsettling than the harshest castigation.

And indeed, in beholding her now, solitary and forlorn beside the river's bank, he knew that every thought of her which had arisen in his mind of late had been unjust. He never had — nor ever could

PART III: THE TOWN

have — resented her. The discord which had been fomenting inside of him for a fortnight was, in truth, resentment against himself.

And Ethan frowned again, deeper than before — not in a troubled way, as when he had perceived Constance's wistful despondency — but with the much darker glower of self-loathing, for he could blame no one except himself for the barriers which now existed between them . . . and within him. Indeed, while he had time and again fearlessly and willingly taken on the adversary upon the battlefield, his most formidable foe was surely the one sequestered deep within himself. It was the only one he could not vanquish.

Even as Ethan grappled with these inner demons, it appeared that Miss Constance was to be offered some solace. Mr. Zachary Merrill had noticed her absence from their coterie and had gallantly gone back to attend to her. Ethan watched as Mr. Merrill approached Constance and spoke to her. They were too far away, of course, for Ethan to hear what was said, but he could clearly discern their features and expressions, and it was plain that Mr. Merrill was expressing some chivalrous concern as to her welfare.

They stood there for several minutes, talking together and looking out over the river, but while Constance's thoughts may have been successfully diverted by the magistrate's grandson, Ethan's black mood only intensified. Neither was his self-condemnation alleviated when he saw Constance take Zachary Merrill's arm, which that gentleman had proffered in coaxing her to turn away from the river and resume their course upon the path toward the landing.

Constance rewarded Mr. Merrill's consideration with a polite smile, but it was not the smile Ethan had known — not the soft, warm smile that had brightened his hours in the dusky garret and haunted his dreams ever since. Thinking upon it now, the knot in his stomach twisted and tightened until its tautness surpassed the tension he had recently shaken off, and he felt suffocated by its grip.

In that moment, Ethan knew that he could abide it no longer.

It was impossible. Something must give way.

He could not give his all to the Patriots' cause while simultaneously battling himself.

With fierce resolve, he turned away. He could not look upon the scene before him. Not upon the girl. Not upon the river. Not upon the merchant ship.

He could not stay in Merrilltown.

He would go to Colonel Naismith first thing in the morning.

ETHAN DID NOT DELAY IN setting out the next day. He arose before the sun's first rays had touched the river and put his horse to a gallop upon the high road, just as the shopkeepers and tradesmen of Merrilltown were unlatching their doors and exchanging sleepy "good mornings".

Even after he had left the town far behind, Ethan did not slow his horse. He wanted to achieve the Patriots' military encampment as soon as possible, before he changed his mind, before his pride got the best of him.

He dreaded the forthcoming confrontation with the colonel. And more compelling, he despised himself for what he was about to do. Ethan Shaye had never in his life been defeated, never surrendered, never backed away from danger. And now he must stand before his superior — a man whose faith in him had never wavered — and forfeit his mission. To any who knew Ethan, it would be unthinkable. He would be betraying his very nature, committing treason against his own character. Yet there he was — racing north at lightning gait, the pounding of the horse's hooves echoing the self-inflicted blows thrashing his conscience.

His mind was racing as well. What could he say to the colonel? Ethan's sense of honor and integrity would not permit him to lie. But neither could he be absolutely forthright in his explanation. He was about to relinquish his assignment and request a transfer to another regiment — one as far away from Merrilltown as he could get. How could he truthfully account for his unprecedented decision? He had skillfully defended against every kind of enemy and taken in stride the respect of his comrades. Yet, like indomitable Achilles, he had discovered within his own courageous soul one point of weakness.

ETHAN STOPPED OFF AT DOWLING'S outpost on his way to the Patriots' encampment. Henry would likely see him pass by on the high road in any case, and Ethan could attempt to calm his own agitations with some fraternal camaraderie before facing the colonel.

Despite the passage of many weeks since the assignment's inception, Henry had evidently remained duly vigilant in his delegated task, for he immediately came out to greet Ethan, before the latter had even dismounted.

"Ethan Shaye! This is an unexpected — but very welcome — surprise! You must have known I was in want of some diversion today."

In spite of his own distracted state, Ethan mustered a smile at this enthusiastic reception, for Henry's ready grin bespoke of his unabashed delight in seeing his comrade.

Ethan shook his friend's hand.

"'Tis a fine enough morning for a ride, Harry, and I thought you wouldn't object to an early visitor."

If the breezy cheerfulness of Ethan's greeting sounded a bit forced, it went quite unnoticed. Henry did perceive, however, that Ethan's horse had been put to a brisk pace, and he lost no time in querying the rider. "What news do you bring?" Henry demanded eagerly. "Did Colonel Naismith already send word to you about the wagon? Have you captured the perpetrator?"

Ethan was entirely perplexed by Henry's words. He shook his head. "I have heard nothing from the colonel. And I have no news to speak of. What is it you say about a wagon?"

Henry was more than willing to share what he knew. "Colonel Naismith sent a message late last night. Another of Porter's supply wagons was detained at the blockade yesterday. The guards practically tore it apart in their search and discovered some arms and powder, though it had been well-concealed. The Redcoats seized everything, including the wagon and horses."

Ethan was keenly attentive to this short narrative — forgetting for the moment his own tribulations — for his thoughts immediately turned to the undated, signed pass and the vessel moored at Porter's landing. "What about the driver?" he asked briskly.

Henry shrugged. "He was unharmed — though I would guess he had no choice but to turn back without the wagon or its contents. They would never have allowed him to cross the border. Probably made his way back to Porter's."

Ethan nodded thoughtfully. "Aye. And 'tis Porter's word we must take regarding this episode, I daresay."

Now it was Henry's turn to look perplexed. "Do you doubt the accuracy of these events?" he asked. "Do you think Porter himself to be an accomplice to treason?"

Ethan did not immediately reply, but rather pondered a moment before uttering a cautious, "No." Then, with a shake of his head — "I cannot say, in truth." He reflected for another moment, then looked at Dowling with a gleam of conviction in his eye, as if a new thought had just occurred to him. "But I can tell you what I *have* learned. It may . . . serve you well to know." Ethan did not elaborate, but in his own mind he had reason enough to turn over to Sergeant Dowling the knowledge he had gained while in Merrilltown.

Henry — after so many solitary days at his post and still anxious to prove himself a competent collaborator — was eager to be a party to this insight. "Come inside," he bid, leading the way toward the door of the little farmhouse that was his temporary home.

Ethan followed his friend into the simple structure, which consisted of a single room with a ladder at one end leading up to a loft. The loft apparently went unused, though, as a rather crude bedstead could be observed opposite the dirt-floor hearth. Other than that, the room was sparsely furnished with a few rustic remnants left from the previous occupants.

The two men took seats at the only chairs to be had, set at a tilting wooden table near the center of the room.

Ethan did not waste time nor wait for prompting, but directly set about apprising Henry of the evidence he had discovered confirming Joshua Porter's participation in the Patriots' campaign, the merchant's methods for recording the date and contents of the supply shipments, and the placement of the logbook in the study. He told him about the proceedings at the dock as the cargo was unloaded and of the pass he had seen but two days prior.

A silence fell over the room after Ethan had concluded his account.

Then, Henry voiced what must be apparent. "The pass you saw had surely been in the possession of the wagon-driver yesterday."

Ethan nodded. "Aye. But how did the Redcoats know it was counterfeit? It looked as authentic as any I have ever seen, and it was accompanied by an original signature which had been flawlessly reproduced by the forger's hand." Ethan rose from his chair and began to pace restlessly. "I wish we could determine whether it is the pass itself that betrays the shipment's purpose, or whether the guards have some other means of identifying the driver or wagon." He looked sharply toward his friend. "What did you observe here yesterday? Did you have aught to report to the colonel?"

Henry shrugged. "I did see the wagon pass by, though I had no way of knowing at the time that it was our provisions. I see any number of wagons pass here every day, but given the time of the interception, I am fairly certain I know which one was ours."

"And did you see anybody or anything of interest upon the road nearing the time the wagon went by?"

Henry shook his head bleakly. "Nothing out of the ordinary that I can recall. I cannot say that I was paying any special heed, though, as I was not anticipating that Porter should have sent out a wagon that day." Henry's eyes lit up with an idea. "Perhaps if you see another blockade pass in Porter's study, you could send word to me, so I could be particularly watchful that day."

But Ethan knew this simplistic suggestion was not practical. "It was fully two days ago I saw the pass," he pointed out. "How many wagons have you seen in that time? A dozen? More? How can we know at precisely what time, or even day, the shipment is to be sent out? . . . How does *anyone* know?" he added under his breath.

Both men once again fell into silent reflection.

"It would seem that Porter is the only one who can know for certain," Henry ventured.

Ethan said nothing. He was still reluctant to accuse Joshua Porter, though he had nothing beyond his own instinctive impression to substantiate his belief.

"Have you learned of any others who might have access to Porter's information?" Henry prompted.

Ethan responded with caution. "There are any number of people in and about the Porter house at all hours. Business associates, neighbors, friends — to say nothing of family members and servants. I must confess, though, that unless Joshua Porter himself is personally relaying information to another party, I cannot see how the perpetrator should get his information except by seeking it in the documents in the study. And to do so on a regular basis . . ." Ethan could only shake his head at the unlikelihood of it.

But Henry refused to be daunted by practicalities. "Can you think of no one who might have such consistent access?" he further queried.

Again, Ethan took his time in answering, though he himself had pondered the same question a thousand times.

"There is a Frenchman lodging with them," he began cautiously. "He is in Virginia on an extended visit relating to his business dealings with Mr. Porter — or so Mr. Porter tells me, for I have never discussed any matters in detail with the Frenchman himself. Porter indicated that Monsieur Brisonneau owns some of the ships which bring the merchant goods from overseas."

Henry's eyes were bright with interest. "A foreigner staying beneath Porter's roof!" he exclaimed. "That is rather extraordinary, given the circumstances. Do you think it likely he is in league with the British? Would he betray his country and ours?"

But Ethan could give no satisfactory answer to those questions and responded with measured restraint. "I know nothing about the man's character or loyalties. He has been often enough in Porter's study, although I cannot say I have ever seen him enter or emerge from that room unaccompanied." Ethan did not mention his own antipathy toward the man, for it was as unsubstantiated as his personal conviction regarding Joshua Porter's innocence. "Then there is Porter's elder son," he continued. "I have only recently made his acquaintance, but I would judge him to be quite capable for a youth of only eighteen. He has joined the colony's militia, though he seems to spend a fair amount of time in his father's house."

Henry's forehead wrinkled in perplexity. "His affiliation with the militia must surely bespeak of his loyalty to the Patriots' cause."

But the period of diversion had ended for Ethan, and, in recalling his present tribulations and the purpose of his journey, his patience gave out. "*Somebody's* loyalties are evidently deceiving," he retorted irritably. "It is as likely to be Porter's son as anyone."

Ethan's abrupt gruffness caught Henry off guard, and he looked at his friend in some concern. Henry could only guess as to the cause of this sudden change in demeanor and, based upon self-drawn conclusions, he attempted to offer encouragement. "Naismith does not expect that you should have sorted it all out in only a few weeks. It has been only a little more than a month since we departed the encampment. You have learned a great deal already. Given more time, you will root out the traitor."

Ethan said nothing, only shifted rather uncomfortably in his chair.

Henry seemed not to notice his friend's uneasiness. "Shall I ride out to the encampment and impart to the colonel what you have related?" he asked, his eye eager once more.

Ethan shook his head. "No, 'tis not necessary," he responded, perhaps a bit too quickly. "I am riding there myself to speak with him."

"But he said—"

"I know what he said," Ethan interrupted, impatient once more. Then, checking his agitation, he added in a milder tone — "There are . . . other matters . . . which I must discuss with him."

He said no more, but felt a twinge of guilt as Henry looked at him questioningly. Henry — who had no family or home to speak of, and who had always looked upon Ethan as a brother — had surely never kept any confidence from Ethan's ear. Yet Ethan could not tell him what now weighed upon his mind nor the true purpose of his errand. He liked not to think how its outcome may have ramifications for his well-meaning comrade. He had already determined to rectify that to the best of his ability.

In seeking to alleviate the constrained silence with some new object of focus, Ethan's eye fell upon Henry's knife in its bejeweled scabbard. It was sitting on the table beside a half-carved ball trap . . . an indication of Henry's occupation before Ethan's arrival. And even in his state of uneasiness, Ethan could not help but be momentarily amused by his friend's superficial endeavor. Indeed, it provided the necessary opportunity to redirect the course of conversation with an attempt at lightheartedness:

"I see that you have been hard at work," Ethan said, with a nod toward the objects on the table. "Have you mustered a contingent of rural lads for trap-ball?"

Henry, subsequently diverted, grinned. "Nay," he responded, "but next time you come, I shall have the trap finished, and then we can have a match of sorts. I stowed in my knapsack the bat and ball from our camp. The other men will not have missed them, do you think?"

Ethan chuckled. "Oh, I've no doubt. You've only deprived them of their chief amusement."

Henry's merry smile widened. "Well, I've left them their trap, at any rate. 'Tis no difficult endeavor for Whitcomb to carve out a new bat—," Henry suddenly snapped his fingers as if recalling something of importance. He jumped up from his seat. "But here, I am a pathetic host!" he exclaimed. "I've offered you no food nor drink— and there's a pot on the hearth, just waiting for the fire to be stoked."

Ethan started to protest that he required no sustenance, but Henry cut him off:

"You cannot say no to chicken fricassee with parsnips. Especially when it is seasoned with a bit of sage. I'll wager 'tis the best you've ever tasted."

Ethan scrutinized his friend with an expression of quizzical incredulity. "Do not tell me you have set out to alleviate the monotony of country life by taking up cookery? You will never hear the end of it when you return to the regiment."

Whatever reaction Ethan may have expected at this mild jesting, it was not that Henry's face should turn two shades of red, as it subsequently did.

"'Twas not myself 'as fricasseed the chicken," Henry maintained, still red-faced. "'Twas Miss Dennis, who brought it over yesterday ev'n."

Upon hearing this confession, Ethan's eye sparkled with merriment. "Ah, I see. 'Tis no wonder the floor's swept so tidily for such a bachelor's abode. You have charmed some farmer's pretty daughter, who's now intent on gaining your favor with her domestic talents. You shall break her heart, I've no doubt." Ethan could not resist this bit of drollery at his friend's expense, for Henry had never had much luck in winning the attentions of the fairer sex and was undoubtedly elated to have found an admirer amongst the rural populace.

Indeed, Henry did not deny Ethan's good-humored conjecture, but seemed rather to corroborate it with a self-conscious grin. "You would likely not consider her so very pretty," Henry replied, "for she is ginger-haired and plump as pudding . . . but as even-tempered as a saint, and so agreeable that you would readily overlook the coarseness of her features. She is already a widow and not yet thirty, living with her brother's family on the farm just behind this one. 'Tis a pity I must refute every invitation to sup at her brother's table — I shall run out of excuses by and by. But she's taken to bringing over a bit of whatever she's been cooking — and always insisting that I'm sorely in want of decent sustenance, with no wife to tend to me." His smile broadened, thinking of these neighborly attentions.

But Ethan did not grin back, and indeed remained quite silent. Somehow he did not wish to pursue this topic further, and his momentary good humor diminished as suddenly as it had come on, giving way to dour moodiness once more.

Henry turned his attention to the cooking pot and was there occupied for the next half-hour or so, but he evidently had not completely put the previous topic from his mind as was evidenced once the fricassee was heated through and he had resumed his seat at the table.

Ethan had hardly taken one bite of the savory meat before Henry recommenced his discourse:

"I tell you, Ethan . . . all these days to myself with nothing to do but watch and wait — it's given me time to think, to . . . well, ponder — is that the proper word, ponder? You always were more learned than I about words and what they mean — but as I say, I've been thinking . . . when this war's over and our soldiering days behind us . . . well, for myself at any rate, it may not be such a bad prospect to take a wife and settle down. Maybe even have a bit of land to farm. Oh, I know you would scoff and avow to be a soldier all your days, and I've always thought as much for myself, but now . . . well, I cannot say for certain that I would fare so well as you in the military profession. Of course, I am loyal to our cause through and through. But once we've put the Redcoats down for good and all . . . well, 'tis natural enough that a soldier should seek the comforts of home, is it not?" Henry paused in his oration, sensing perhaps that his words had not been particularly well-received. Noting Ethan's brooding silence, Henry lightened his tone, cheerfully waggling his spoon in Ethan's direction. "I predict that even you, Lieutenant Shaye, might someday tire of dallying with tavern maids and set your sights upon someone with truer character. You would see that women are not all silly chits. Take my advice, if only in this matter," Henry continued with mock sagacity, "get yourself a plump one . . . 'tis a sure sign of her cooking prowess."

Ethan made no response to this jocular suggestion, for his own mind could only conjure the image of a graceful little figure whose slender waist his arm had once encircled, however briefly. And he slipped into a state of melancholy, so to remain for the duration of the meal. Thereupon did he take leave of the rustic farmhouse and set out upon the road once more. He had hoped that his friend's good-natured demeanor would distract his troubled mind, but in the end, the visit had merely served to delay the impending interview and cast a somber shadow across his resolve.

EVEN WITHOUT MEETING THE COLONEL'S eye, Ethan sensed the superior officer's stern, uncompromising scrutiny fixed upon him.

Though the prolonged silence was ominous, Ethan kept his own eyes trained straight ahead, focused upon the soot-smudged wall of the tent. He did not need to look upon Colonel Naismith's countenance to be conscious of the frown there; indeed, when the colonel at last spoke, his tone was as severe as his frown:

"Would you please specify as to the reason for this request of reassignment?"

Ethan made no immediate response.

Colonel Naismith's eyes narrowed and he began to pace the dirt floor as he continued speaking, his voice losing none of its sternness. "I confess, I am utterly astounded by such a request, Lieutenant Shaye. You are the last man on earth from whom I should expect to hear it, and I trust there is some extraordinary circumstance which has prompted you to put it thus before me? Out with it now, Lieutenant!" he commanded.

Ethan turned to face the colonel and spoke firmly, but respectfully. "Sir, I am well aware of the singular nature of my request, but the fact is . . . 'twould be better for me to serve with a regiment in the North — in New York or Massachusetts — where I can put to use my skill upon the battlefield. As it is . . . I am ill-suited to this assignment."

Colonel Naismith stopped his pacing and looked squarely at Ethan. "Ill-suited? What do you mean? Do you mean to say that executing the task entrusted to you by General Washington is beyond your abilities?"

As the colonel uttered these words, he observed with some satisfaction the spark of defiant pride ignited in the young lieutenant's eye.

"No sir," Ethan countered, a bit hotly, then added with a measure of reason: "You yourself voiced at the outset some misgivings as to my suitability for this commission. You know my temperament well enough, and you surmised then — as I can confirm now — that the assignment's requirements were ill-matched to my abilities." He frowned reflectively. "I did not join the Patriots' cause to attend dinner parties and exchange pleasantries with the provincial gentry. I could have done as much by staying in North Carolina! I have not the patience for such trivialities . . . not when there are victories yet to be won on the battlefield and behind enemy lines."

Colonel Naismith remained unmoved, his grey countenance reproachful. "Is your impatience, then, to take precedence over the welfare of General Washington's men?"

Though Ethan did not waver in his bearing, he felt the sting of this reprimand. "No sir, not at all," Ethan asserted steadfastly. "You mistake my intent. I did not mean to suggest that the mission should be abandoned, but rather that it should be completed by someone whose skills are more accordant to the task's requirements. There are any number who would readily take it up."

"Indeed?"

Ethan ignored the superior officer's unappeased frown and continued: "Aye. Why, Dowling would be a natural choice. He is already a participant and is well-apprised of the situation's details."

But the colonel dismissed this suggestion with a derisive shake of his head. "Sergeant Dowling is a dedicated, well-meaning soldier, but there is absolutely nothing which would recommend him for such a weighty commission. He possesses not your tactical expertise nor your physical resourcefulness nor your boldness; neither has he the breeding nor the education necessary to consort with gentlemen such as Mr. Porter and his associates." The colonel then added rather severely, "Do not for one moment think I am in any way attempting to flatter you, Lieutenant. I could just as easily enumerate your faults . . . 'tis certain that pride and stubbornness would top the list."

Ethan was undaunted by this mild reproof, even as the colonel turned back toward his desk, indicating that the matter was concluded. But Ethan would risk insubordination, for he would not be deterred, and he moved a step nearer to the colonel. "Yet, suppose that my alibi should unravel?" he persisted. "What if my identity as a spy should be revealed to Porter and his associates?"

Colonel Naismith turned back toward Ethan. "Why should that be a concern?" the colonel asked sharply. "Have you been careless in some way?"

Ethan's mind was yet in turmoil. He had begun to sense that his chance of escaping Merrilltown was slipping away, yet he could not bring himself to reveal that which would assuredly release him from his present assignment. In only a momentary pause, he settled upon a more conventional rationale:

"I fear that unforeseen circumstances have rendered our scheme susceptible to discovery. I arrived unannounced in Merrilltown under the pretext of carrying out a surveyor's duties, and it was under that pretext that I gained admittance into Porter's circle. But I cannot hope to sustain such an alibi, for my continued access to Mr. Porter's establishment is contingent upon my completing a survey of Porter's own property. 'Twas his idea, and at the time it seemed to me a feasible way of gaining regular access into his household, for he would allow me to utilize his study as often as I pleased, and so I agreed to his suggestion. But I now perceive that it was a foolish move on my part, for my knowledge of surveying is not nearly adequate to hold up against any scrutiny, and he will soon enough expect me to produce some evidence of my progress."

Colonel Naismith remained silent after this speech, his grey brow wrinkled shrewdly as he considered Ethan's words.

And for his part, Ethan felt some apprehension as he waited, for he had presented his best case — without having to reveal the full truth of his situation. But when the colonel at last responded, his words brought Ethan no reassurance.

"It is quite remarkable," asserted the colonel, with a gleam in his eye. "I know not whether to ascribe it to competence or luck — for you seem to possess both in abundance — but you have truly established yourself most advantageously. So Joshua Porter has commissioned you to make some measurements of his land . . . Play along with it. Take your time. You have adequate tools and a rudimentary knowledge of the procedures involved. Porter is not an expert in the field of surveying, and he is not likely to scrutinize the caliber of the plans before they are completed. By then, your mission should be accomplished and your true purpose revealed to him — whether to his detriment or favor remains to be seen." Colonel Naismith paused long enough to observe Ethan's dour countenance. The superior officer shook his head. "No one else could hope to make such progress as you have made, nor to gain such un-precedented access to Porter's enterprise. You know as well as I that it would be no simple matter to send another in your place. It would mean starting from the beginning again, conjuring up a new story, a new set of circumstances — losing the weeks of progress you've already made. General Washington's men could be soundly defeated by then, if they have not already perished from hunger or disease. Shall they be forced to longer await relief merely because of your disinclination to complete your assignment?"

A resurgence of patriotic zeal gripped Ethan in equal measure to the unmitigated shame he felt as he was reminded of his brother soldiers and of the sacred cause to which he had long ago allied himself.

Colonel Naismith continued: "I know you crave adventure. I was much the same way when I was your age — wanting every moment to count, wanting to fight for victories that are physical . . . tangible . . . decisive. But winning wars is not only about defeating the enemy; it is also about the ability of your own men to survive. History presents many examples of wars in which outcomes were determined not so much by one side's victories, but rather by the other side's inability to endure harsh or perilous conditions. Be assured that General Washington's men are at the precipice of such tribulation. It is not only their bodies that will suffer from lack of food and supplies . . . their morale will suffer grievously. And in reducing our men to a state of despair — that is when the British will carve out an easy victory."

Colonel Naismith paused, allowing his grim words to permeate the tent's austerity.

Ethan was not unaffected by them.

The colonel sat down again. Leaning back in his chair, he studied Ethan for a moment, casting a critical eye upon the silent lieutenant. After a time, the colonel resumed speaking: "I don't believe that any of your professed justifications are legitimate . . . nor do they warrant a moment of my consideration, or yours. You are far too intelligent to believe that I would release you from your duties based upon such unsubstantial rationale as you have presented. Therefore, I can only surmise that you had counted upon the longstanding friendship between our families to persuade me. But you know very well, Lieutenant, that I would be betraying not only our cause and my military responsibilities, but also my respect for your father — who was one of my most esteemed compatriots, as well as my friend — if I allowed you to relinquish this assignment. So, unless you wish to disclose the complete truth as to why you felt compelled to request this release from duty . . .?" The colonel did not immediately finish his sentence, but looked to Ethan expectantly.

Ethan knew it was his last chance. If he did not divulge the full truth now, he would never win the reprieve he sought. But he remained silent.

The colonel nodded somberly. "Then I presume you understand where it is your duty lies."

So it was that Ethan returned to Merrilltown, reinvigorated with a sense of genuine conviction concerning the vital significance of his task.

But for the other matters which weighed upon his mind . . . he had no plan nor strategy.

Fortunately, he had never depended solely upon long-deliberated strategy to survive or succeed, relying instead upon the spontaneity of his wit and instinct; so lacking a plan in one area did not hinder his progress in other measures, and he plunged into his work with renewed energy.

The day after returning to Merrilltown, he took his surveying tools and rowed across the Rappahannock's calm grey waters to the far bank, where he began to take measurements of Porter's property there. And in the following days he did the same, allotting ample time not only for taking measurements, but also for observing all that went on at Porter's landing. From the opposite shore, he familiarized himself with the daily procedures, the faces on the pier, the coming and going of the vessels upon the water. The vessels were not abundant in number, but he noted what a substantial share of them had French names engraved upon their sterns.

While measuring and observing occupied many of his daylight hours, Ethan devoted a fair number of evenings to working in Joshua Porter's study. This allotment of time was not due to mere convenience, but rather was a conscious choice on Ethan's part, for he knew that he was unlikely to encounter any members of the household during those hours when they were customarily seated around the dining table or sequestered in the drawing room engaged in conversation or other af-ter-dinner amusements.

But though he did accomplish a substantial amount of work during those evenings — while simultaneously keeping a vigilant eye upon the entries in Mr. Porter's logbook — he could not entirely overcome the distractions created by the presence of the residents and guests of the house. Sometimes the murmur of their conversation would carry into the study — not distinct enough to be able to discern any individual voices, yet audible enough that he was ever reminded of the activity transpir-ing beyond the study's seclusion. And on more than one occasion, his concentration had been diverted by the musical strains of the spinet, its silvery dulcet tone drifting across the hall from the drawing room, stirring up memories. While it was surely the youngest of Matthew Jameson's daughters at the keys, Ethan thought not of her but of another daughter — one who had been at his side when the spinet's distant melody had floated up into the hushed space beneath the garret's rafters.

Ethan's own presence in the Porters' house did not go entirely undetected, at least not by the master of the house. Joshua Porter — whether on a word from his servants or his own perception — would sometimes step into the study while Ethan was at work there and converse for a few minutes. These brief exchanges were always cordial and amicable in nature and served to reinforce in Ethan's mind the sincerity of Porter's hospitality. Mr. Porter never left without extending an invitation to join his kin in some refreshment and fellowship, but Ethan always respectfully declined, under the pretext of time constraints. For the most part, though, he was left to his own devices and made some progress in his work, though he observed nothing further of notable interest in Mr. Porter's logbook.

One late afternoon, Ethan approached the Porters' house a bit earlier than his usual hour, and he slowed his pace as he perceived a figure standing just outside the white gate at the front of the property. He recognized at once the dark-skinned, stately-attired slave Thaddeus, the manservant of Mr. Zachary Merrill. As Ethan reached the fence, Thaddeus saw him and gave a slight but very proper bow as Ethan passed through the gate.

Knowing that Thaddeus's master was bound to be in the vicinity, Ethan was not surprised to see that gentleman standing just ahead at the Porters' door, which was just opening to admit him. But Ethan again slowed his step, realizing that the state of inconspicuousness he wished to preserve upon his own arrival would be compromised should he enter the house at the same time as Mr. Merrill.

It was too late, however; the cheerful housegirl had already sighted Ethan and was waving him in, which of course caused Mr. Merrill to turn to see who was following upon his heels. That gentleman seemed pleasantly surprised as he recognized Ethan.

"Good afternoon, Mr. Shaye!" Mr. Merrill called out in greeting as Ethan mounted the porch steps and entered the house. "This is a fortunate coincidence! I've heard Mr. Porter tell that you were still in the region, but I'd begun to doubt whether he was right. I'm glad to see you are taking some respite from your work."

Ethan had no time to respond, for at that moment Mrs. Porter came gliding into the hallway from the parlor, her smile warm and welcoming.

"Mr. Merrill!" she started to greet her guest, then interrupted herself when she saw Ethan. "Why, you've brought Mr. Shaye with you! How lovely!"

Mr. Merrill chuckled. "Aye, it seems that I have at that."

"I am so glad to see you, Mr. Shaye!" Mrs. Porter went on blithely. "How ever did you convince him, Mr. Merrill? He has turned a deaf ear to our entreaties and insists on shutting himself up in the study every evening . . . as if work must take precedence over good company!" She laughed merrily. "But never mind — I shall forgive you, Mr. Shaye, as you've redeemed yourself by your appearance here today. What a delightful assemblage we shall have at dinner! Betsy—," she addressed the young housegirl, "set an extra plate at the table for Mr. Shaye, near Mr. Porter."

Ethan was about to protest, but before the servant girl had yet departed, Mrs. Porter was already set upon another topic, now directed toward the other guest:

"Why, Mr. Merrill, what is it you have there?" she inquired, looking with interest toward some papers Zachary Merrill held rolled in his hand.

"Ah yes." Mr. Merrill held the papers aloft. "'Tis the music we had up at the Hall last week. Miss Polly seemed quite taken with it, so I thought she might like to have it here to practice and play at her leisure. Perhaps we might even convince Miss Constance to give it voice, though she would not sing at the Hall."

"But you sang it yourself so enchantingly!" Mrs. Porter enthused, slipping her arm through Mr. Merrill's as she confided to him: "We must both of us put our efforts into convincing her tonight, for she is far too self-conscious about such things and will surely be at ease in these familiar surroundings if you offer to sing it with her. But come now, Mr. Merrill, the others are waiting to greet you. You too, Mr. Shaye!"

Ethan decided not to protest after all and, nodding in acknowledgement of Mrs. Porter's beckoning, followed her and Mr. Merrill into the parlor.

The other members of the household were there assembled, having not yet sat down to table, and it was at once evident to Ethan that by merely entering the room he had irreparably marred what remained of Miss Constance's day. Constance's face immediately paled, so manifest was her discomfiture at his appearance. This palpable transformation unsettled Ethan profoundly, and he summarily regretted that he had thus discomposed her by his presence. But he could not now withdraw himself without offending his host, whose continued trust and friendship were crucial to his mission's success. And so, as before, he did not address Miss Constance personally but gave only a nod of greeting in the general direction of where she stood with Polly and Tristan before turning his attention to safer company — in this case, Mr. Porter and Monsieur Brisonneau at the opposite end of the room. Before those gentlemen had opportunity to discern Ethan's distracted state, however, they were all summoned to the table, and the dinner was served.

Mrs. Porter's directive had been obeyed, and Ethan found his seat at Joshua Porter's right, across from Monsieur Brisonneau. Constance was seated on the opposite side of the table, between Monsieur Brisonneau and Zachary Merrill.

Although Ethan did not converse with Constance, he was never oblivious to her presence.

And yet, she did not know that. How could she? How could she know that he had very nearly forsaken his mission because of her? How could she know that his every latent sensation came alive when she was near? Or did she feel it, too?

Ethan quickly reined in his thoughts as they strayed into precarious territory.

Indeed, what could Constance feel except confusion, doubt, and betrayal?

Ethan scowled, thinking about it. Once again, he attempted to mitigate the guilt with rationalization. After all, he reasoned, how could he have conducted himself differently without endangering the integrity of his mission?

Yet, neither his mind nor his heart seemed to concur with such rationalization.

While he did not direct any conversation toward Constance, Ethan did cast an eye in her direction more than once during the course of the dinner. She remained subdued throughout, engaging only in quiet discourse with Zachary Merrill beside her, for that gentleman politely endeavored to draw her out, though he was met with only moderate success.

Neither did Ethan entirely forget his own purpose in joining the dinner party, for even with the distraction of Miss Constance, he was attentive to the interactions between the other individuals present.

Those in nearest proximity provided scant opportunity for any insight, as Tristan Porter was seated to his right and Monsieur Brisonneau opposite, both of whom said very little, although their reticence did not signify apathy.

Ethan noted that Brisonneau's wandering eye encompassed now not only the mistress of the house but also that lady's two younger sisters.

Once again, Ethan's dislike of the Frenchman was reinforced.

And Tristan Porter's sullen taciturnity doubtlessly offset a very alert mind, for he was intently heedful of the discussion transpiring at the opposite end of the table. There, Miss Polly Jameson was at the center of a lively dialogue, though whether Tristan was listening with approval or objection Ethan could not tell, for the subject matter would hardly have elicited approbation from most present. Indeed, though Anne Porter presided at that end of the table and attempted to maintain the expected decorum by steering the conversation toward only superficial topics of general interest, Polly would not acquiesce and persisted in returning to the decidedly controversial subject of the war — controversial because her viewpoints on the matter were in clear opposition to anyone professing allegiance to the Patriots' cause.

Ethan himself considered the discourse to be of no consequence, despite his own ardent loyalty to the Continentals, for he knew that Polly's assertions were only the ramblings of a very young and naïve girl who was, after all, the offspring of Loyalists and was undoubtedly only repeating sentiments upon which she'd often overheard her father expound. The others, too, indulged her, no doubt out of politeness and deference to her youth, though Ethan suspected there may be at least one present — other than perhaps Constance — who was in silent agreement with Miss Polly's views. But if that was the case, none gave himself away by countenance or word.

By the end of the meal, Mrs. Porter had managed to introduce several new topics — in between Polly's criticisms of the war — and the hostess had even succeeded in eliciting from Constance agreement to sing the duet with Mr. Merrill, though it was with tremendous reluctance — and only after Mr. Merrill put forth his own good-natured entreaty — that Constance agreed.

The Porters and their guests might have tarried longer over conversation at the dinner table but for the entrance of another visitor, whose arrival was discreetly imparted to Mrs. Porter by the toothy housegirl. The mistress gave a nod of assent, and the new guest was promptly admitted into the presence of the assembled company. Introduced to Ethan as the Reverend Wynn (and the necessity of an introduction brought Ethan some discomfiture, for he alone amongst all the company was not acquainted with the clergyman, having never set foot inside the parish church), the unexpected visitor refused to partake of any sustenance, proclaiming that he had already supped. Consequently, instead of directing another chair to be set at the table, Mrs. Porter proposed that all should adjourn forthwith to the drawing room. None objected, and it was at a leisurely pace that the guests proceeded across the hall, still conversing amongst themselves.

Ethan was one of the last to exit the parlor, and as he entered the hall, he slowed his gait further upon perceiving that Zachary Merrill and Constance were just ahead of him.

As the pair reached the drawing room door, Constance withdrew her hand from Mr. Merrill's arm, and in so doing, her lace shawl slipped from her shoulders and fell to the floor.

"Oh!" she breathed in soft dismay, glancing over her shoulder just as Ethan came to a halt before the shawl.

Zachary Merrill, turning also, took note of the lost article and would undoubtedly have moved to recover it but that Ethan was already standing over it.

Unhurried, absorbed in thought, Ethan bent to retrieve the length of white lace. And as he rose, he became aware of a light floral fragrance permeating his senses. As ethereal as the lace between his fingers, it was the delicate scent of lavender — a scent so instantly recognizable, so familiarly evocative, so unexpectedly transporting that it gave him pause, if only for a fraction of a moment. Without a word, he stepped forward to where Constance stood and handed the shawl to her. She took it with a nod of acknowledgement, and in so doing, raised her eyes to meet his. It was but a brief glance, yet it was the first time since their meeting at the staircase that Ethan had truly looked into her eyes, and the silent affliction that he saw there dealt him a harsher blow than would have been wrought by any words of castigation.

Constance turned away and continued into the drawing room, followed by Zachary Merrill, who gave an affable nod of thanks to Ethan before passing through the doorway.

But Ethan stood where he was for some minutes, lost in reverie. When at last he moved into the drawing room, he maintained a distance between himself and the others, remaining just inside the door, where he might observe in solitude.

The singing did not commence at once, as the arrival of the late visitor necessitated some requisite inquiries as to his well-being and toward the general news of the church, but Polly did sit down at the spinet and played quietly to herself, with Tristan behind her turning pages until Polly impatiently sent him away, vexed by his inept timing.

Reverend Wynn proved to be something of an anomaly, at least to Ethan's mind, for the clergyman fit not at all Ethan's notion of the profession. The Reverend was quite young and convivial of manner — even jovial, as evidenced by his hearty, frequent laugh — and 'twas he who suggested at length that they commence with some music, proposing to begin with some lively and popular tunes.

Here Zachary Merrill, too, proved himself to be not above such conventional indulgences and lent his fine, rich baritone to some rousing country airs, much to the delight of the listeners.

Most listeners, that is. Tristan, after being banished by Polly from the spinet, had sullenly retreated to a chair near the fire. And Ethan tarried near the doorway, an air of discontent about him, seemingly indifferent to the music's cheerful mirth. The others took no notice, though, and, excepting Miss Constance, all were quite caught up in a dozen rounds of rollicking song — even Monsieur Brisonneau, for the melodies were readily recognizable even if the English words eluded him.

Eventually, though, the revelry gave way to a quieter ambience, for Polly wished to demonstrate the full range of her skill upon the instrument and set to playing more sophisticated, wordless pieces, while the rest of the company took refreshment and fell back to hushed conversation amongst themselves.

But Anne Porter was not neglectful of her little design, and after a time she spoke up: "I do believe the interval should have been adequate for Mr. Merrill to rest his voice, and he must now give us the promised duet with Constance."

Zachary Merrill laughed good-naturedly. "I assure you, Madam, the cessation of song was none of my doing and had naught to do with the state of my voice, for I could have carried on without pause or fatigue, even as I am now prepared to do so again. But come, Miss Constance...," he turned to that young lady with a kind smile, "your sister is determined that we shall sing this piece, so let us accommodate her at once, that she might then direct her bidding elsewhere."

Constance looked as if she had hoped the matter might have remained forgotten, but she obediently gave a little nod of acquiescence and rose from her chair, as Polly reached for the printed music supplied by Mr. Merrill.

Constance took her place, not at the front of the spinet as may be expected, but rather behind Polly's chair, where she might ostensibly see the music from a good vantage, though Ethan surmised it was more a matter of self-conscious modesty than of necessity. Merrill, too, seemed to understand as much, for he followed her without objection and, positioning himself beside her, gave a nod to Polly that she might proceed with the accompaniment.

The piece was an old Scottish ballad — melodic and wistful and charming — to which Constance's sweetly pleasant voice was well-suited and paired quite nicely with Mr. Merrill's. The listeners evidently concurred, as was made plain by their thorough attentiveness, and none appeared more satisfied than Anne Porter, whose complacent smile bore testimony to the merit of her persistence.

But Ethan was hardly enchanted. A frown creased his brow, though it was not the singing that displeased him, for he paid it scant heed; instead, his preoccupied glower was fixed upon the man who had provided the music and was now giving it voice alongside Constance Jameson. Indeed, as Ethan observed the two of them, it occurred to him that Zachary Merrill had been spending a great deal of time at the Porter house of late. Despite the fact that Ethan himself had, from the first, been a welcome guest within the household, he had never encountered the judge's grandson on the premises until the arrival of Mrs. Porter's sisters; since their arrival, however, Mr. Merrill had established himself as a regular guest. The two events were assuredly not linked by mere coincidence, and the realization of such irritated Ethan, thus provoking his discontent.

Being in no mood to debate the logic of this sentiment, nor to be concerned with the constraints of decorum, Ethan's restlessness won out over the music's charm, and, without waiting for the song to conclude, he silently took his leave.

⸙

ETHAN'S ABRUPT DEPARTURE DID NOT go unnoticed. Indeed, Constance was very much aware of it, even as she kept her eyes fastidiously trained upon the music notes.

Unhappy girl! Her misery knew no bounds.

As unsettled as she had been by Ethan's presence that afternoon, she was even more disconcerted by his unceremonious exit.

Somehow she could no longer concentrate on the music; the duration of the song passed in a blur, for her thoughts were obscured — held captive in a haze of distant memories and haunting questions.

Though her voice continued to articulate the song's words, it was only perfunctorily so, and the others must surely have noticed the alteration in her tone and countenance. Both Mr. Merrill and Polly glanced at her with some concern as she stumbled over the words during the familiar refrain — an occurrence which quickly restored her sensibilities, but which only compounded her disquietude.

The song's conclusion was met with exceedingly polite applause, which Constance acknowledged with an acutely self-conscious inclination of the head, and then, before anyone might propose an encore — though even Mrs. Porter made no immediate suggestion of such — Constance murmured a faltering "Pray, excuse me" to Mr. Merrill and hastened from the room.

"Whatever can be the matter with that girl?" queried Anne Porter with an incredulous frown.

Polly shook her head. "Poor Constance has been much affected by our family's misfortune, I fear."

"And 'tis no wonder," added Mr. Merrill sympathetically, still looking toward the side door through which Constance had departed. "Her whole world has been turned upside down."

Polly started to rise from her chair. "Perhaps I ought to go after her . . ."

"No." Anne Porter spoke with quiet firmness as she motioned her youngest sister to sit. "Let her be. She will return when she is ready." Her tone was unexpectedly benign and thoughtful — a departure from her previous incredulity — and it occurred to more than one present that, in spite of differing allegiances, the eldest daughter of Matthew Jameson was not untouched by her family's tribulations.

KEEPING ONE HAND UPON THE wall to steady herself, Constance wound her way up the narrow, unfamiliar back stairs, her disconcerted mind fixed upon but one purpose: attaining the sanctuary of solitude.

She emerged at the far end of the upper corridor, only a few steps from the door of her bedchamber; yet, as ill-fortune would have it, even that short distance would not be achieved without obstacle.

As she passed an open doorway, a dark, imposing figure suddenly and unexpectedly stepped out into the corridor, blocking Constance's path and forcing her to an abrupt halt.

"Oh!" Constance exclaimed, startled. "J—Jenny!"

Jenny was momentarily caught off-guard as well — nearly losing her grip on the laundry-laden work basket she carried — but she recovered almost at once, unlike Constance whose sustained pallor and breathlessness attested to some deeper tribulation.

The slave woman did not give way, and Constance somehow could not move nor speak further. It was with almost fearful apprehension that she looked into Jenny's round blinking eyes. She knew that Jenny — more than any other person in the household — might suspect the true cause of her discomposure. Indeed, what could Constance hope to conceal from the faithful servant who had raised her, who had shared her every confidence since the time of her childhood? Jenny would perceive in an instant any trouble that weighed upon the heart of her young mistress.

Even now, Jenny's gruff, dark visage reflected both pity and concern as she stood before Constance in the silent corridor.

But Constance could not confide in Jenny — not now, not this. How could she disclose to another what she dared not articulate even to herself? She desperately wanted to be alone, and her mind — already in turmoil — could fix upon nothing else but achieving that solitary state. Unable to think with reason or logic, she spoke words that would assuredly raise further suspicions, for they were uttered in a tone so unnaturally brusque that anyone familiar with Constance's gentle nature would know at once that the words were forced under the strain of affliction. Her voice truly quivered as she spoke.

"Do not just stand there like a statue, Jenny — you'd best get those linens out to the laundry at once! Now stand aside, that I might pass."

Despite issuing this injunction, the young mistress did not wait for her servant to acquiesce, but instead initiated her own hasty removal, stepping around the slave woman and hurrying away down the corridor to her bedchamber.

Once inside, Constance closed the door noiselessly behind her, and, taking a deep, shaky breath, she crossed to the window, as if keeping her back to the door might somehow shield her from the inquisitiveness of the other members of the household beyond.

She needed the tranquility of knowing — if only for a few moments — that she did not have to worry about putting on a brave face or concealing her emotions, as she had done now for so many weeks, ever since her life had been thrown into upheaval — a chaos which had touched her father and sisters as well, but which was surely most acutely felt by Constance, for her grief was compounded by other circumstances of which they knew naught.

But even now, enclosed within her solitary haven, Constance was not afforded the luxury of peace. She could not calm her mind.

She had snapped so at Jenny. However much it was within her right, it was not true to her nature, and she was ashamed of it. That feeling of guilt only intensified her already-unsettled emotions. And it seemed that the haven she had sought could offer her no real respite. Jenny herself could open the door at any moment, under the pretext of collecting the bed-linens or the curtains but in actuality looking to resolve whatever ailed her mistress. If not Jenny, it would assuredly be Polly, for it would be natural enough that Polly would come to look in upon her sister who had departed the drawing room so hastily. Or it may be Anne. Or Caleb, looking for his toy soldiers which were constantly strewn about the place. Indeed, there was the potential for any number of intruders.

And so, as she stood there at the window, gazing across the deserted garden toward the grey river below, Constance remained on edge — her heart pulsing and her ears very much attuned to the slightest noise within the house, half expecting to hear a footfall on the other side of the door or a whisper in the corridor.

This would not do.

Turning from the window with a sigh, Constance surveyed the room distractedly, then tensed suddenly as the soft patter of footsteps neared her door.

Whomever it was continued past without pause, though, and as the footsteps receded down the corridor, Constance moved with new resolve.

Crossing to the bed, she knelt beside it, and, with one hand upon the wooden floorboards, she reached with the other hand and pulled out from beneath the bed a small basket, its contents covered with a handkerchief. Still kneeling upon the floor, she began to remove the handkerchief, but, with a nervous glance toward the door, changed her mind almost at once and replaced it. Rising to her feet, she slipped the basket's handle over one arm and crossed back to the door. As quietly as she could, she opened the door and peered cautiously into the corridor. Ascertaining that it was quite deserted, she stepped across the threshold and made her way back toward the rear stairwell, intent upon reaching the ground-floor landing where a side door gave easy access to the garden.

ALTHOUGH A BENCH RAN THE length of the vine-covered pergola, Constance perched on the very end, just inside the long structure's leafy shade, where she might make use of the bits of waning sunlight which penetrated the edge of the covered walk.

Setting her basket beside her on the bench, Constance took from it a folded piece of paper. It was familiar in her grasp, and indeed the worn edges and slight wrinkles suggested that it had been folded and unfolded many times throughout numerous perusals. And yet, by the way she unfolded it now, it might have been again the first time — slowly and consciously, almost with reverence or trepidation.

But assuredly did she know well the words written upon the page, for her eye immediately fixed upon one line near the bottom:

I know you will understand why I must leave before you wake.

She did not really need to look at the page; she knew the text as well as she knew her own being, but somehow she liked to see it — the scrawled, faded letters — and to feel the already-brittling paper upon which the words had been scripted so many months ago.

That sentence never failed to awaken a stirring within her. But now, as she gazed upon the words, a different sort of sensation gripped her heart. A desolate pang conflicted with the familiar wistful tremulousness . . . a pang that was not entirely new, for it had taken root well over the course of recent weeks. But never had it manifested itself so dauntingly as upon this occasion.

She became lost in thought . . . thoughts most poignant, yet tinged with sadness. How her gentle heart ached!

So absorbed was she in her reverie that she heard no approaching footsteps, but when she looked up, Ethan Shaye was standing there, leaning up against the pergola's entrance, looking at her.

Startled and abashed, Constance blushed to her fingertips and hastily thrust the letter back into her basket, silently grieving over the additional creases she unwittingly inflicted upon it in her flustered haste.

Ethan did not move, but regarded the basket within which the letter had been so unceremoniously stowed. After a long moment, he shifted his gaze back to Constance. "I had wished at the time that I could have penned it in ink," he murmured low. "Now I truly wish I had."

Constance was mortified at being thus apprehended in her weakness and would not look him in the eye. "I — I did not know you were still here," she stammered, adopting a tone she hoped came across as loftily cold. "You spend a great deal of time at this house."

Ethan frowned, clearly displeased at this chilly reception. His own tone took on a slightly hardened edge. "I am sorry if my presence here vexes you. I yet have work to complete in this town. It would appear to be your misfortune that my endeavors require me to frequent these premises. I must expose a corruption whose perpetrator is conclusively linked with this household."

Constance stared at Ethan in astonishment, her furrowed brow plainly showing her consternation at this suggestion. Ethan did not waver in his bearing, however, and maintained his resolute stance.

Constance could not remain thus confronting him. She rose, reaching for her basket. "I must go—"

But Ethan stepped quickly forward, still frowning. "Will you not speak with me, then?"

Constance, though, could endure no more. There, in all of her broken-hearted wretchedness, did she turn upon Ethan Shaye. "I am amazed that you would even suggest such a thing!" she exclaimed, struggling to maintain the evenness of her tone. "It would seem by your recent actions that you would have nothing to do with me!"

Ethan scowled more deeply, his eyes darkening stormily.

But Constance gave him no opportunity to interject. The rising tide of her emotions carried her onward and gave her courage to voice what would ordinarily be restrained: "I understand that you cannot openly acknowledge any prior acquaintance with me, but surely that would not preclude offering me at least the same courtesies as are extended to other members of respectable society." Though she saw the mounting vexation in Ethan's scowling face, Constance did not pause, her voice inadvertently rising as she further succumbed to the intensity of her sentiment: "I cannot think what I have done to deserve such hard-heartedness, such complete lack of civility as you have shown me! You have seen fit to shun me and to look upon me with a coldness that can only be contempt. And now . . . now you would further insult me by accusing my family of gravest wrongdoing!" And unable to face him more, Constance turned, that she might make her way to the opposite end of the pergola and thus escape his presence.

But Ethan's own temper was aroused, and he would not permit this. He grasped her arm quickly and fiercely, forcing her to face him.

Constance gasped, but Ethan did not relinquish his hold and gave vent to his seething frustration: "I made no mention of your family," he asserted heatedly. "Do not twist my words. I merely alluded to someone with connections to this household. That situation has no bearing on my acquaintance with you."

Constance had not wanted Ethan to see the tears brimming in her eyes, but as she could not turn away she was helpless to conceal them, and so she looked up into his face, her faltering voice echoing her misery as she responded: "How do you deign to speak of an acquaintance? In your eyes, I am nothing but a — a threat to your alibi, a hindrance to your efforts!" In the dusky twilight she could see the anger flashing in Ethan's eyes and hear the feverish rapidity of his breathing. Yet the surging pulsation she felt within her own breast was a familiar sensation and only intensified as Ethan tightened his grip upon her, pulling her close.

"Do not presume to know my feelings for you," he growled under his breath, even as Constance was aware of his hand, warm upon her cheek . . . even as she felt the heat of his fervor.

And in his anger and in his passion, Ethan kissed her there under the pergola — hungrily at first, as the pent-up emotions ignited in the shadows of the garret were turned loose, and then very tenderly, for she submitted very willingly, her soft lips warmly and earnestly pressing against his.

Indeed, Constance could not think, could only feel; could only know that the yearning pang had fled, to be replaced by a wondrous exhilaration that now coursed throughout her body; could only be aware that everything was suddenly made right in the embrace of Ethan Shaye.

And for his part, Ethan would not surrender her after one kiss, but continued to hold her close, as if solidifying his claim upon her.

Constance found immeasurable comfort in his strong, sturdy arms . . . she did not want to be anywhere else. She could feel the cadence of his heart beating against her own throbbing breast, and she remembered that night in the garret — feeling the rise and fall of his chest beneath her fingers in the dim light of a single candle.

Memories of the garret stirred in Ethan's mind as well, though it was upon a different episode that his thoughts dwelt.

"The last time I saw you in the garret," he whispered low into her ear, "you were afraid of me. You did not want me to touch you."

Constance could feel the movement of his lips against her hair as he spoke. She closed her eyes, remembering well that last encounter. "No, you are wrong," she murmured, shaking her head slightly. "I was afraid — but not of you. I was afraid of . . . myself. Because I . . . I did want you to touch me." And, blushing and ashamed, she buried her face against his chest, not daring to look into his eyes.

But even as Constance hid her face, she felt Ethan's reassuring arms tighten about her, his cheek pressing lightly against her head.

There were no more words. They did not need to speak. One was content to hold, the other to be held. Neither dared to think beyond the present moment, though, for the kiss had been stolen, and the serenity of seclusion was bound to be fleeting.

Indeed, after an interval that was all-too-brief, their haven was penetrated by the sound of distant laughter.

With one accord they separated, each taking a step back as they turned their heads in the direction of the mirthful voices — now emanating from the vicinity of the house, but sure to trespass upon their presence soon enough.

Ethan was instinctively alert, as if evading the enemy in hostile territory — at once on his guard, his sharp eyes narrowed and vigilant, every sense attuned to the danger of discovery.

Constance's eyes were wide with apprehension as the lighthearted — and nearing — voices floated obliviously over the neatly-trimmed hedges. She seemed rooted to the spot . . . knowing well that they must part, yet unable to take such initiative.

But Ethan knew they must not tarry. "Go on now," he urged her, with a nod toward the house.

Still Constance did not move but stood looking up at him, her dark eyes filled with uncertainty.

Ethan hesitated a moment — thus betraying his own reluctance — but swiftly regained his purpose and reached for the basket upon the bench. "Here, do not forget this." He extended the basket to her, but not before seamlessly withdrawing from it the folded paper.

Constance did not take the basket, but watched in dismay as Ethan slipped the letter into an inner-pocket of his coat.

Noting her disquietude, Ethan shook his head. "You will not need it more," he assured her. "And I shall keep it as a promissory note . . . to remind me of the debt I must pay."

Constance's eye yet lingered somewhat anxiously upon Ethan's coat, where he had concealed the letter.

Ethan took Constance's hand and gently closed her fingers around the basket's handle. "'Twill be all right." His voice was low and reassuring, as his own hand enfolded hers.

Constance lifted her eyes to once more meet his, but before anything more could be spoken, a sudden peal of laughter alarmingly near the arbor's entrance abruptly recalled them to the precariousness of further delay.

Ethan glanced past Constance toward the pergola's leafy opening before addressing her with renewed conviction. "You must go," he charged her, gently propelling her toward the house.

Constance needed no further urging, reawakened to her senses by the sudden proximity of the voices. Clutching her basket, she hurried the short distance to the passage's entrance, but as she emerged from beneath the vine-covered arch into the garden's fading light, she paused and turned her head, casting a glance down the length of the pergola's walkway. Ethan had already made his way to the far end of the darkened path and in a moment was out of sight, undoubtedly headed toward the river gate.

Turning to the garden once more, Constance drew a deep breath, which did little to allay her rapidly beating heart. Even so, there was assuredly a lightness to her step as she hastened along the garden's edge toward the house, praying she would encounter no one along the way.

THE EFFECT RENDERED BY A single kiss should not be underestimated, even if the kiss had been stolen in the twilight and must remain a secret. For Ethan and Constance, it freed them from their torment, released them from the bondage of uncertainty and denial. And they were no strangers to secrecy; the garret gave testament to that.

Neither did it matter that they did not see one another again in the days immediately following. Ethan was able to concentrate on his work with a clarity of focus he had not had since Constance's arrival in Merrilltown. And Constance was again cheerful — her sweet smile once more gracing her pretty countenance.

Their paths did not cross again until the occasion of the Merrill's barbecue.

The barbecue was, Ethan learned from the local tavern talk, an annual event — a gift from Judge Merrill to the town and was, in fact, a Merrill tradition that harkened back several generations. Every year, at summer's end, the gates of the Merrill estate were opened to the townsfolk, who were invited to a day of festivities, food, contests, and merriment. It was an event that was eagerly anticipated by the citizens of Merrilltown, and as the occasion neared, one could not walk into a shop or tavern without overhearing lively discourse, animated conjectures, or mirthful reminiscing upon the subject.

Having spent his fair share of evenings in the town's public rooms, Ethan was not oblivious to this anticipatory chatter, and it was with a certain degree of interest and expectation that he rode through the Merrills' gate on the appointed morning.

He dismounted at the top of the hill, before the grand Hall, and was there greeted by Zachary Merrill, who came forth to shake his hand.

"Mr. Shaye! It is good to see you! You are most welcome here. Now at last you can meet my grandfather. He's been anxious to make your acquaintance, you know, ever since he'd heard you were here surveying property for Mr. Clymer. He likes to keep abreast of all the land acquisitions in the region . . . all of the land that doesn't belong to him, that is," he added with a wry smile.

Ethan nodded good-naturedly. "I look forward to meeting him."

"He's down at the river landing now, greeting those who are arriving by boat," Merrill explained. "You must head down there yourself, for that is where most of the festivities shall commence. But first," he went on, motioning toward the house, "I am sure you wish to greet your friends. They have only just arrived before you."

Indeed, the party from the Porter household was assembled a short distance away, near the steps leading up to the grand Hall — the ladies attired in fresh, floral-printed gowns, and young Caleb Porter sporting his cockaded hat.

With a nod to Zachary Merrill, who was already turning to greet the next arriving guests, Ethan left his host and made his way along the cobblestoned drive to the front of the house.

He first encountered Monsieur Brissoneau, who was nearest the drive. The Frenchman greeted him with a bow and a brief salutation, which Ethan returned in kind before turning his attention to the next member of the party, who happened to be Miss Constance Jameson.

Outwardly, neither showed any sign of a deeper acquaintance than would be expected between Mr. Shaye and one of Joshua Porter's kin, but an astute observer would assuredly have noted that Constance's cheek betrayed a soft pink glow that had not been there a moment before; or that Ethan, reaching for her hand, pressed it to his lips with a warmth that was hardly mere formality. As he released her hand, he whispered into her ear—

"You, my girl, look far too pretty for your own good."

Constance beamed, even as a blush rose upon her neck, as Ethan moved on to greet the other members of the party. To each of Constance's sisters he gave a hasty, perfunctory peck on the hand — for he must acknowledge them in a similar manner, so as not to raise suspicions with overt attention to Constance — and Joshua Porter he met with a hearty handshake, for that good man hailed Ethan's approach with the most convivial of greetings, and the two men conversed for quite some time while the ladies retired to the shade of the porch. Tristan Porter was there, too, at his father's side, but short of giving Ethan a nod of acknowledgement, Tristan contributed nothing to the conversation, remaining silent throughout. There was nothing remarkable in this, though, as Ethan had come to expect such reticence from Porter's elder son.

The friendly discourse would undoubtedly have continued for some length of time, had it not been interrupted by young Caleb Porter, who, caught up in the excitement of the day, ran up and tugged impatiently upon his father's hand, begging him to come and look at a puppy he'd discovered under the porch. Mr. Porter frowned and would have reprimanded the boy for interrupting, but Ethan bid him to acquiesce with the child's request, assuring him that he himself was anxious to get down to the river and partake of the festivities there.

So, while Porter and his sons went off in the direction of the Hall, Ethan made his way around the side of the house and proceeded along the path which wound down the hill toward the river. As chance would have it, he found himself following behind the remainder of the Porter contingent.

Constance, taking note of this with a glance over her shoulder, discreetly slowed her own gait so as to unobtrusively distance herself from her party.

Ethan soon caught up with her, and the two of them continued down the path together, both in fine spirits.

"I hope you've placed your wager upon me to win the race," Ethan put forth with cheerful immodesty and twinkling eye.

Constance's eye sparkled as well. "Indeed I have not," she countered. "Anne said I must wager upon Mr. Merrill to win. He breeds horses for speed."

Ethan shook his head and tsk-tsked her in mock reproach. "'Tis very unwise to wager upon the advice of another. You will come to regret it, I fear. Did *she* put her own wager upon him?"

"Of course not," Constance replied disdainfully. "Naturally, she must place hers upon her husband."

"Ah, 'tis even more imprudent — placing a wager upon the advice of one who has placed hers elsewhere."

Constance sniffed primly. "And who is to say that I would not have placed the exact same wager of my own accord? After all, the Merrills have the finest horses in the county. Yours is . . . probably stolen."

Ethan merely laughed at this — which would seem to neither confirm nor deny the conjecture — and continued: "What your sister may not know is that there has been a change in the course, as of only yesterday. It is my understanding that one of Mr. Merrill's dinner guests suggested an alternative to the usual straight run and proposed a circular course, which will pass partially through the wood, as well as over and across several natural obstructions. I have heard that Mr. Merrill agreed to the scheme. So, you see, 'twill not be only the speed and stamina of the horse that will be tested, but also the cleverness of the rider." He shook his head again, though his tone remained undeniably jocular. "'Tis a pity the wagers have already been laid."

There was a pause before Constance replied. "Well . . . indeed, it promises to be an exciting race," was all she said, but as she glanced sideways at him, there was a distinct brightness to her eye, for she truly had no doubt that Ethan's spirit of daring adventure would serve him well in such a race.

The path split into two at the foot of the hill, and there they parted — Constance turning off in the direction of the pavilion where the other ladies were laying out food upon wooden tables, and Ethan continuing to the river, where a contingent of his town-fellows had gathered with cane-poles, ostensibly to see what contributions they might make to the occasion's fare, but in truth, the mirthful carousing among them was so boisterous that it was doubtful a single fish remained anywhere near the vicinity of the pier.

The day's festivities commenced with a series of contests and games — foot races, sack races, cricket, quoits, and stool-ball — of which the men and youths from every class partook with equal enthusiasm while the women and children looked on, cheering and laughing in turn, and a climate of lively merriment encompassed all.

But it was the much-anticipated horse race which was the afternoon's culminating event, and it seemed that nearly the entire population of Merrilltown converged beside the river at the appointed hour, eager to take in the sporting competition.

Judge Merrill himself underscored the event's importance by giving an introductory speech before its commencement. The Judge was a somewhat imposing figure, with his flowing powdered wig and dignified manner, but he was nonetheless impeccable in his display of hospitality, and his words were gracious — addressing the assemblage as "fellow citizens of Merrilltown" — even if his delivery lacked the warmth and conviction of one who truly believed that all present qualified as peers. His wisdom showed through, though, in the brevity of his speech-making, for while his audience listened with polite attentiveness, they were truly impatient for the race to begin, and when the eminent Judge was handed his ornately embellished ancestral firearm, a ripple of excitement visibly swept across the assemblage. Hoisting it in the air, the Judge fired a single shot, and the crowd erupted in boisterous huzzahs as the mounted riders took off.

Constance stood with her sisters near the front of the company of onlookers. Polly was the only truly vocal member of the trio — cheering on Tristan Porter, upon whom she'd placed her wager. But the other two sisters were plainly enjoying themselves as well — Anne laughing and exchanging comments with Monsieur Brissoneau, and Constance's eyes dancing with excitement as she followed the progress of the riders. Those soft brown eyes were assuredly fickle, though, for they did not remain entirely fixed upon the rider with whom her wager lay, but instead strayed time and again to the man who had hinted at his own ability to cross the finish line first.

With their backs to the river, the throng of spectators had a fine view of the race, although there was no vantage point which would allow unobstructed observation of the entire course, for portions of it took the riders into the wood and to the far side of the ridge beyond the broad creek bed.

There was disparity among the contestants nearly from the outset, for the creek was one of the first barriers to be overcome, and its width and depth prevented any means of traversing other than by a wooden bridge which was well within sight of the onlookers. The bridge was so narrow, however, that two could not ride abreast at once, and this circumstance led to a chaotic disarray as fully a dozen riders converged upon the bridge's near side at approximately the same moment, each desiring to cross before any other. A rather comical melee ensued, and more than one man was unseated as horses reared and collided amid the din of cries, shouts, laughter, and cursing, which emanated as much from the spectators as from the tangle of riders and steeds.

This disruption caused such a marked delay in the progress of most contestants that only a half-dozen could be said to truly remain in contention once across the bridge, among them Zachary Merrill, Tristan Porter, and Ethan Shaye, all of whom — by skill or speed — had managed to circumvent the commotion at the water crossing.

As the riders disappeared into the wood, a quietude fell over the onlookers, for there was naught to see or applaud during the next few minutes — the men and youths marking the forest trail being the only individuals privy to witness the proceedings during that portion of the race.

But once the first rider emerged from the thicket, the crowd picked up again with their rallying cheers, and none more so than those who had wagered upon Zachary Merrill, for he was the first to appear. His lead was short-lived, however, for Tristan, Ethan, and two others were fast upon his heels, and indeed, first one than another of the contestants took the lead by turns, so closely aligned was their progress.

It was just as the riders were about to disappear from sight again around the far side of the ridge when another mishap forced the subsequent elimination of another contestant. Toby Harrow, the cabinetmaker, was leading at that moment, with Zachary Merrill a near second. Whether by chance or design, Ethan Shaye and Tristan Porter both spurred their horses on with a burst of speed at the same instant in order to advance past Mr. Merrill, so that they were at first flanking him, one on either side, and then overtaking him altogether. But once past Merrill, both horses were pulled quickly even, effectively creating a moving barricade right before the nose of Merrill's steed and with so sudden a movement that the unsuspecting animal took fright and reared up without warning, tumbling Merrill to the ground.

A clamor arose from the spectators, for Mr. Merrill had been a great favorite to win, and many a wager was lost in the moment he fell to the ground.

"Oh dear," Polly intoned to Constance. "There's an end to your wager."

"I do hope he isn't badly injured," Constance murmured, even as the slave Thaddeus could be seen rushing across the field toward his master, an assortment of other concerned personages in tow.

"Well, he isn't killed, that's for certain," Polly observed as Merrill sat himself up even before the arrival of his attendants. "You can go to him if you like, though it appears he is not in want of assistance at the moment."

Constance had no chance to reply, for all at once the crowd started in again with shouts and hollers — Polly as audible as any — for the riders had reappeared, rounding the near side of the ridge, with Tristan Porter at the front.

Although Tristan's focus remained intently upon the creek bridge, for he must cross it again before reaching the race's end, an uncharacteristically broad smile illuminated his visage — a rare manifestation of exuberance from Joshua Porter's elder son.

Ethan Shaye was close upon him, though, and as they raced toward the bridge, Constance became distracted by a nearby voice calling out Ethan's name:

"Go to it, Mr. Shaye! Faster . . . that's it! Aye, Mr. Shaye, spur him on! Give it some pace now!"

The voice belonged to Maria Lethbridge, a vivacious young lady who waited upon patrons in the tap room of her father's tavern and who was not only well-acquainted with the lodgers at that establishment but undoubtedly with many of the townsmen as well, for Lethbridge's public room was a popular gathering-spot on the high street.

Maria Lethbridge's familiarity with her chosen wager became more evident, for her inhibitions diminished as her excitement mounted. All semblance of formality was cast off as she observed the two lead contenders pull neck and neck: "You've got it now, Ethan! Keep it up! Faster, Ethan, don't let him ahead of you there! Keep to it! Keep to it!"

Miss Lethbridge's enthusiasm was well apparent.

Having been momentarily distracted by Miss Lethbridge's rallying cries, Constance turned her focus back toward the rider at whom Miss Lethbridge's hearty encouragement was directed. But Ethan's concentration was entirely occupied with overtaking his opponent and commanding his steed, so as to render him oblivious to any of the din from the crowd.

Of a sudden, there was an escalation in the volume of the crowd's clamors, and Polly clutched at Constance's arm.

"Look!" Polly exclaimed, pointing toward the oncoming riders. "What is Mr. Shaye doing?"

Indeed, it appeared that Ethan had either abandoned participation in the race or had devised some unprecedented new strategy, for his horse had abruptly veered to the left, and instead of heading toward the bridge, was now setting a course directly toward the creek itself.

"What is he doing?" Polly repeated, forgetting her own wager for the moment. "He cannot cross the creek — 'tis too wide, even at its narrowest. He will never make it."

But Constance's gaze was fixed upon Ethan's countenance, and she knew the rider's intent. "He is going to try," she murmured, her heartbeat accelerating as realization gave way to trepidation.

Polly's brow knit in disbelief. "He is mad to attempt it! His horse will stall and throw him, else both could be the worse, for it will not result in a mere soaking. And yet—," she was at once subdued as a new thought occurred to her, "—should he chance to succeed, he would land nearly at the finish line and well ahead of the others." Polly frowned as she glanced once more toward Tristan, who had not yet reached the bridge.

By this time, the other spectators had perceived Ethan's intent, and their shouts took on a whole new tone, as some cheered and urged him on, while others hollered in reproach at such an audacious risk. More than one new wager was laid on the spot.

Still unheedful of the noise from the observers, Ethan's focus remained entirely on the steed beneath him and the waterway before him. He had deliberately set a course toward the creek's narrowest point, though in appearance it was still too wide for horse and rider to traverse. Leaning in, so that his body was nearly parallel with the horse's neck, Ethan urged his horse on, eliciting a burst of speed just before they reached the creek bank.

Like those around her, Constance's eyes were fixed upon the brash rider fast approaching the creek. Truly, her breath was suspended as the horse's hooves pushed away from the solid ground and stretched across the width of the channel. But as horse and rider cleared the creek, the animal's hooves touching down upon the opposite bank, Constance drew in a deep and audible breath — not merely in relief, but in exhilaration as well.

"He made it!" Polly exclaimed. "He has won!"

And as the crowd's hollers and huzzahs rose to a deafening clamor, Constance's smile was as radiant as if she herself had won the wager.

Even before crossing the finish line, Ethan was well aware of his victory, as evidenced by his own confidently satisfied visage, and those few who had wagered upon him were easily discernible by their elated shouts, chief among them Maria Lethbridge, who whooped in a decidedly unladylike manner before taking off at a run toward her champion. Others followed, many streaming across the field toward the winner, while some set off toward their own chosen contestants to offer consolation and, in some cases, a hand up.

Tristan Porter was the first to reach Ethan, though. He rode up only seconds after Ethan had dismounted. Shaking his head and smiling broadly, Tristan dismounted and extended to the victor a hand, which Ethan clasped congenially.

Polly followed the others across the field, for everyone was caught up in the excitement of the race's enthralling finish, and she could not harbor any real grievance, for Tristan had proven himself a worthy contender.

Constance stood where she was for a moment, uncertain . . . wanting to follow her sister, yet knowing full well that she herself had no claim upon anyone near the finish line.

It was her elder sister who reminded her of her immediate obligation.

"Constance! You must go to Mr. Merrill at once, else he'll think you care for nothing except your lost wager," Anne admonished before hurrying off to find her husband, who had been among those delayed at the bridge's first crossing.

Constance nodded and forthwith turned in the direction of Mr. Merrill's disqualification, but as she walked along the edge of the field, she glanced back toward the finish line, just as Maria Lethbridge reached Ethan. As Constance watched, Miss Lethbridge ecstatically flung her arms about Ethan's neck and planted a jubilant kiss upon his cheek.

Constance hastily cast her eyes frontward again, doing her best to suppress the pang which had risen within her, and continued toward her destination. But just before she reached Mr. Merrill — who was sitting quite easily upon the grass, laughing and conversing with those about him — Constance turned her gaze again toward the finish line and paused in her step, for Judge Merrill was just bestowing upon Ethan the victor's rewards — two "laurel" wreaths (which actually consisted of late-summer blooms), one to circle the neck of the victor's noble steed, and the other to adorn his three-cornered hat.

Well-pleased with his win, Ethan shook the magistrate's hand amid further huzzahs from those surrounding, and then placed one circlet about his horse's neck — giving the animal's muzzle an appreciative rub — but the other he gallantly surrendered to Miss Maria Lethbridge, who accepted with a gleeful bob and immediately set the wreath atop her own disheveled curls.

It was but slowly that Constance turned back toward Mr. Merrill. She did not notice that Ethan was quite indifferent to Miss Lethbridge once the wreath had been bestowed — indeed, he seemed to have taken it all in as a matter of course, well-satisfied with his victory but soon enough leading his horse back across the field toward the river, where some of the other riders had gathered to give their steeds a cooling respite.

Though Constance put forth a perfunctory smile to those about her, her thoughts remained yet distant. Still reflecting upon the scene she had just turned away from, the realization came upon her that there were aspects of Ethan Shaye's life she knew nothing about; that the sum of his experiences could not be neatly subdivided between his military career, the garret, and the twilight garden. She lapsed into a reverie thinking about it . . . wondering and reflecting and trying not to become too much aware of a slight twinge of heartache that had arisen shortly after Ethan's victory, casting a bit of a shadow across her afternoon.

ETHAN HAD NOT FORGOTTEN ABOUT Constance.

Later that day, after everyone had eaten and conversed and laughed and lounged to their hearts' content, some of the men — Ethan among them — devised an impromptu hunting party and set out upon horseback toward the nearby foothills.

As they rode off, Ethan broke away from his cohorts, guiding his horse upon a slightly divergent path that took him alongside the grove where Constance and Polly were watching the company's departure. He did not stop, but only slowed a bit as he passed, calling out jocundly:

"I hope you've learned a lesson today, Miss Jameson, on the cost of wagering against your inclinations!"

And without tarrying further, he spurred his horse on, that he might catch up to his party once more, but Constance's shining eyes as she looked after him attested to her comprehension of his words.

Polly, however, wrinkled her forehead, clearly puzzled, as she, too, watched Ethan ride away. "Whatever did he mean?" she queried. "Was Mr. Shaye addressing *you*?"

Constance was yet again spared the necessity of a response, as a sudden high-pitched wailing filled the air.

Both sisters turned in the direction of the sound, which did not abate and truly seemed to be coming nearer.

Indeed, it proved to be their elder sister's flaxen-haired child, approaching at a run, tears streaming down his reddened cheeks.

"Owwwww!" he howled plaintively. "He bit me! He bit me! That bad dog bit me!"

Polly frowned. "It serves you right if he did, you little fiend," she reprimanded crossly. "I saw you chasing him — trying to pull his tail."

"Here, let me look." Constance knelt beside Caleb and examined the arm he proffered. After a moment she shook her head. "I cannot see any marks at all."

"Well, he *tried* to bite me," the boy sniffled sulkily. "He's a bad dog — and he took my hat." He glared in the direction of the puppy, who was lying beneath some distant foliage, placidly chewing upon Caleb's cockaded hat.

Polly chortled. "Good for him!" she proclaimed. "He got the better of you in the end."

Caleb turned his glower upon her.

Constance sighed reproachfully as she rose. "'Tis truly a shame," she noted. "And I heard Mr. Merrill say he'd make a present of the puppy to you if you minded your manners today."

This merely set the boy to howling again.

"Oh, run to your mama, you naughty boy," Polly impatiently shooed him away. "You'll find no sympathy here."

Caleb stuck his tongue out at her before running off, still wailing, in the direction of his doting mother, as Polly added under her breath, "She'll no doubt persuade Mr. Merrill to give you the unfortunate puppy anyway, in spite of your horrid behavior."

ETHAN AND CONSTANCE DID NOT meet again for the remainder of the day.

After the sun had set, though, and most of the townspeople had returned to their homes, those few who remained into the evening gathered near the river, where chairs and benches were placed for their comfort, and cressets were lit, creating a festive and congenial ambience for hushed conversation and low-toned laughter.

Constance and Ethan were seated a fair distance apart from one another — she amidst her kin and he with some acquaintances from town — but across the light of the fire's dancing flame, Ethan caught Constance's eye and winked at her with a grin. Constance's heart was at once filled with an overflowing warmth, for that roguish grin was well familiar to her.

And though the moment was but fleeting, within it lay a deeper significance; an acknowledgement of the secret that they shared . . . and a wordless understanding that had never faded.

So it was that Ethan had indulged in one day's respite — and the following afternoon a wagonload of food and medical provisions was confiscated at the blockade. He learned of the incident even before Colonel Naismith or Henry Dowling sent word of it, for he chanced to be working in Mr. Porter's study that evening, when he saw the entry already marked in the logbook's register, dated the same day, its final column inscribed with the single ominous word: "*Intercepted*".

Bringing his fist down upon the logbook's page, Ethan silently blamed his own lack of vigilance, although in truth it was unlikely he would have gained aught had he foregone the festivities of the previous day and remained instead on the premises, for he knew next to nothing of the perpetrator or his methods. And yet . . .

He sat for a long while, staring at the logbook entry, pondering.

How was it that the wagon was intercepted so soon after the town's holiday? Ethan knew for certain that the only new vessel docked upon the river had put in but two nights ago. And surely there had been no activity at Porter's landing the day after the cargo's arrival — with both master and overseers away at the Merrill estate — nor could there have been opportunity to conduct any business upon that day. Surely information could not have been passed to an accomplice before the present day? Had the whole episode been plotted, carried out, and recorded in only a few hours' time? It seemed unlikely. Given the circumstances, Ethan knew that no one except Joshua Porter, or a member of his household, could have had such advantageous access to the necessary information.

And yet, Porter himself evidently trusted implicitly those nearest him, as he took no extraordinary measures to safeguard his study or conceal the logbook. This fact always made Ethan's mind uneasy, for it more than anything pointed to the possibility of Porter's own guilt. But, in spite of such substantiation, Ethan still could not convince himself that the benign merchant was the perpetrator of such heinous treason, although he had no evidence — other than his own instinctive sensibilities — to refute such a possibility.

Ethan determined that his vigilance would not lapse again. An alteration of strategy was in order, however, and he concluded that he must concentrate his efforts less upon the logbook and more upon the happenings at the wharf, for it had proved futile to try and link the traitor with the logbook's scribe or to identify who might truly have the most opportune access to the register. Indeed, for such a diminutive, lightless room, purposed solely for business, the study seemed inordinately frequented by nearly every person under Porter's roof — from the youngest member of the household, whose tin soldiers were always underfoot; to Tristan Porter, who used the room for his own correspondence when he was at home; to the mistress of the house, who was apt to flutter in on occasion with the housegirl in tow, measuring ribbon in hand, and with a sprightly "Don't mind us at all, Mr. Shaye, we shall be just a moment and won't disturb you a bit" proceed to push the furniture aside and generally cause a great deal of disturbance, despite her best efforts, as she endeavored to take measurements and lay out plans for her future china closet.

And it would be impossible to account for the servants who passed through the room daily, though Ethan had no cause to believe any would be capable of deciphering the logbook's entries or abetting the treasonous scheme's progression.

The only person whose presence in the study Ethan could not ascertain was the one he would most readily suspect: Monsieur Brisonneau. He had no doubt that the Frenchman was regularly in the study during the day, discussing business matters with Joshua Porter, but he had neither seen nor heard anything which could lead him to conclude that Monsieur Brisonneau had ever entered the room unaccompanied, even for a purportedly innocuous objective. Ethan knew well enough that this lack of evidence was fairly meaningless, for Monsieur Brisonneau — being a guest in the house — would have ample opportunity to access the room, perhaps during the night, when everyone was sleeping; such a circumstance, however, would be nearly impossible to discover, even should

Ethan conceal himself outside in the dark, hoping to catch a glimpse of a lighted candle or some movement inside, for the study itself was entirely enclosed and windowless.

Ethan came to the conclusion that he could not depend solely upon the logbook to provide him with the information he needed; he must look elsewhere if he was to learn anything of substance pertaining to the perpetrator's actions, and he must make swift progess, for summer had already given way to autumn, and winter would be fast approaching — too fast for General Washington and his men in New York, where winters could be brutal and unforgiving even under the best of circumstances. Without adequate food and supplies, they would assuredly perish along with the colonies' hopes for independence.

Ethan closed the logbook and pushed back his chair with resolve, gathering his loose papers as he rose. He must focus his observations once more upon Porter's landing and the proceedings there, beginning on the morrow. The merchant's newly-acquired property on the opposite bank would afford an excellent view, and it was fortuitous indeed that Ethan had a ready and conspicuous justification for traversing thence.

ETHAN AWAKENED WITH A START, instantly alert to the sound of the drumbeats calling him to grab his musket and march. He was on his feet at once, for his body was trained to respond to the drum's orders, but a momentary disorientation followed as his senses caught up with his instinct, and he remembered that he was not in his regiment's camp but inside his room at Lethbridge's, where the day's sunlight had barely begun to cast its hazy beams upon his windowpane.

The drums were not a remnant of his slumber, though. They were real enough and reverberated still through the morning air.

Quickly, Ethan pulled on his clothes and hastened down the stairs and outside. There he encountered Maria Lethbridge standing on the front steps of the tavern, broom in hand.

"Good morning, Mr. Shaye!" she greeted him brightly, happy to see the establishment's handsomest lodger.

"Good morning, Maria," Ethan responded absently, his attention diverted by the activity upon the street before him where a group of children were running past, shouting and calling to one another excitedly. Several men and women were also hurrying by, all headed in the same direction.

Maria flashed her vivacious smile at Ethan. "You were drummed right out of bed, I daresay!"

"Aye." Ethan was at once impatient and perplexed. "Where are the drums? Are there soldiers in the town?"

Maria nodded, her eyes gleaming knowingly. "'Tis the militia. They are mustering here in Merrilltown today." She laughed. "You can see the great excitement it's brought about! You ought to go watch them march. They are assembled upon the Green."

"Yes, I will." Ethan needed no urging; he had already begun descending the steps.

Making his way along the street, he cut across the wheelwright's yard and arrived at the central Green in a matter of minutes. As he approached, the drumbeats commenced once more, and he saw a company of men at the far end of the Green begin to march toward the center, their rows nearing straight and their marching fairly accurate for such a contingent of local civilians. It was not a large company — perhaps thirty or forty men in all — most of them shouldering muskets, a few bearing only fowling pieces, each man plainly armed with whatever he was able to supply for himself.

Despite their contrast to the well-trained, well-armed regulars who were Ethan's military colleagues, he could not think less of the men before him, for he knew that a militia's composition must reflect the resources — however limited — of the populace at hand, and it was impossible for him to look upon any brother-at-arms without feeling a surge of pride, for any characteristic differences in rank or affiliation were overcome by their common alliance in the fight for justice.

A good number of the town's citizens stood along the edge of the Green, observing the proceedings, and a cluster of exhilarated boys convened to one side, eagerly following alongside the militiamen, attempting to replicate their movements. Among them was little Caleb Porter, easily discernible with his flaxen head shining in the morning sunlight.

Scanning the perimeter, Ethan spotted Caleb's escorts — Mrs. Porter and Monsieur Brisonneau, who were standing at the near side of the Green. Turning in their direction, Ethan strode toward them, bidding a placid "Good morning" to Mrs. Porter as he approached.

Anne Porter, always pleased to see an acquaintance and never at a loss for words, responded with her usual vigor. "How very good to see you, Mr. Shaye! Look who is here, Monsieur Brisonneau — it is our *bon ami* Mr. Shaye! Or should I say our *perdre ami* — did I say that properly? I meant to say he is our long-lost friend, for we do not see him about as we used to, ever since his victory the day of the horse race." And here she inclined her head toward Ethan. "I daresay you have made many acquaintances in town after your heroic win on that day . . . yet I hope that you will not neglect your most devoted friends, Mr. Shaye! You really must come around — oh, I don't mean to do your work, though you are always welcome to use our amenities for such — but for dinner or cards or something likewise amusing. Have you quite recovered from your exertions upon the race course?"

Ethan humored this vacuous chatter with a wry smile. "It would be perhaps more fitting to inquire after the horse, Madam, as the exertion was all his doing."

Mrs. Porter laughed delightedly. "You are very clever, Mr. Shaye. And far too modest, I am sure, for I know the course must have put all the riders to the test— oh!" She started quite suddenly as a volley of gunshots, fired in relative unison, pierced the air. "Goodness!" she exclaimed with a nervous twitter. "That did give me a start!"

Monsieur Brisonneau spoke up for the first time. "It is a fine day for a muster, is it not?"

The question was directed toward Ethan, who nodded in response. "I cannot deny it," he replied, attempting to keep his tone pleasant and agreeable. Despite his dislike of Monsieur Brisonneau, he had reached a point where he had no choice but to put on an amicable front, for it was crucial now that he learn all he could about the Frenchman and his business with Joshua Porter.

However, to Ethan's disappointment, the ever-restrained foreigner made no further comment nor gave further indication that he was inclined to converse, though he seemed well-enough disposed and appeared to be enjoying the proceedings of the muster.

Mrs. Porter, however, was always easily engaged, and Ethan hoped that by maintaining discourse with her, Monsieur Brisonneau might be drawn into the conversation.

"I trust your husband and sisters are faring well?" Ethan inquired of Mrs. Porter. "They do not accompany you here today?"

"No." Anne Porter shook her head, her forehead wrinkling slightly. "Polly would not be persuaded to turn out, even to give a show of support to our Tristan."

Following Mrs. Porter's line of sight, Ethan's eye fell upon Tristan Porter, who was indeed among those marching upon the Green, intent upon his duties and seemingly oblivious to his stepmother's presence.

Monsieur Brisonneau commented upon Mrs. Porter's statement. "Miss Polly is not shy about expressing her views or her loyalties."

The frown quickly disappeared from Anne Porter's visage as she glanced at Monsieur Brisonneau. "You must not judge Polly too harshly," she put forth with a trace of an apologetic smile. "She is assuredly the product of her upbringing." She turned toward Ethan. "You undoubtedly have heard that our father is a staunch supporter of the Crown."

Ethan dismissed the gravity of the statement with a shrug. "It is understandable that your sister should share her father's viewpoint. I would imagine that you yourself must have once been influenced by the same perspective."

Now it was Anne Porter's turn to be dismissive. She gave a slight shake of her head. "It has been a long while since I lived beneath my father's roof. When I did, there was no talk of such loyalties or divisions, and I am sure I would have had no opinions on the matter. But Constance and Polly have been brought up with it, and they have not had an opportunity to hear the sound reasoning behind our Patriots' cause."

Mrs. Porter's patronizing tone implied that she had been privileged where her sisters had not, but Ethan doubted that Anne Porter would be capable of holding her own in any debate upon the subject of the Revolution.

It was again Monsieur Brisonneau who commented upon her assertion. "I cannot recall ever hearing Miss Constance express her views upon the subject."

Mrs. Porter concurred with a light and rather condescending titter. "I am sure you will find that Constance's absence today has less to do with her political convictions than with her loyalty to Polly and her aversion to anything having to do with the war or battles. She's really not very sporting when it comes to such things."

The idiocy of this statement did not merit a response from either Ethan or Monsieur Brisonneau.

After a few moments of silence, however — during which all three directed their focus toward the activity on the Green — Monsieur Brisonneau attempted to re-establish conversation:

"Your sisters appear to have adapted well to their situation, despite their circumstance."

"Do you think so?" Mrs. Porter sounded surprised, as if she had never really thought about it before. "I suppose they have at that. Although Polly certainly has her moments, hasn't she? There are times she is as sullen as Tristan."

Monsieur Brisonneau nodded, but there was an unmistakably fervent glint in his eye as he mused, "Oui. But at other times she has a certain — I do not know how you say it — *esprit de feu*, which is most . . . intriguing."

If Monsieur Brisonneau did not already occupy the lowest possible stratum in the hierarchy of Ethan's regard, this inordinately expressive remark upon a seventeen-year-old girl would assuredly have solidified the Frenchman's status there. As it was, Ethan's loathing of the Frenchman was merely reinforced yet again, and though he himself had no vested interest in Monsieur Brisonneau's regard for Polly Jameson, he could not help but wonder if the yellow-haired youth marching in the front line before them would have remained entirely passive had he been a party to the conversation.

Not surprisingly, Anne Porter seemed neither disturbed by nor even cognizant of the underlying implication of the Frenchman's words. "Esprit de feu?" Mrs. Porter repeated rather blankly. "If what you mean is 'willful', then aye, you've named it aright."

"And yet," Ethan pointed out, "in light of Miss Polly's overt animosity toward the Patriots' cause, I wonder that she shows no resentment in being exiled among them."

"Resentment? Toward her own kin?" Mrs. Porter was plainly incredulous. "I assure you, Mr. Shaye, in spite of her youth, Polly is old enough to differentiate between her family loyalties and political strife, however they may conflict. She is sensible enough to be appreciative of her present situation."

Monsieur Brisonneau inclined his head toward Mrs. Porter. "Your sisters are fortunate indeed to have such a safe and agreeable refuge. I think, though, that they must have some fears in their hearts, for what young lady would not, were she displaced from her home, and her father fled?"

Coming from anyone else, Ethan would have taken this statement as a common expression of compassion, but coming from Monsieur Brisonneau . . . it was merely baffling.

Yet however much Ethan questioned the Frenchman's sincerity, Mrs. Porter evidently took him at his word.

"Oh, Monsieur Brisonneau," the lady intoned, "you are very sentimental, I am sure. What fears have they? Our father is quite safe and amongst friends of his own convictions. My sisters know that. He writes to us regularly. And as for being displaced from their home . . . I am certain they cannot fully comprehend the depth of such a loss, nor appreciate its significance."

It was an odd thing to say, and both men glanced at Mrs. Porter, whose tone had been markedly altered upon utterance of the last phrase. Her countenance, too, was changed — no longer vibrant and animated, but now unexpectedly somber and distant. She lowered her eyes as she added, "'Twas more than just a house or a piece of property. They . . . would not understand."

Monsieur Brisonneau was undoubtedly puzzled by her words and altered disposition, but Ethan was not. How well he remembered Constance's wistful eyes as she gazed out the garret window toward her mother's grave and the tender, sorrowful manner in which she had spoken of the mother she barely remembered.

Anne Jameson Porter had been old enough at the time of her mother's death to have felt acutely the loss, and this rare manifestation of solemnity — which did not strike Ethan as insincere — undoubtedly reflected some emotional attachment to her mother's final resting place.

Nevertheless, Ethan found it difficult to conjure much sympathy for Anne Porter, even though she was Constance's sister. Indeed, he felt some indignation on Constance's behalf. Constance had so longed for a connection to her mother — a connection her elder sister could have provided, had that elder sister deemed it worth her while. But Anne Porter — who might have shared in Constance's grief and offered comfort — instead dismissed her sister's suffering with disdain.

Ethan scowled. "I think you do your sisters a disservice by minimizing their trials and therefore their fortitude."

Anne Porter did not deign to respond to this assertion, and Monsieur Brisonneau, perhaps attuned to the underlying bitterness in Ethan's tone, quickly diverted Mrs. Porter's attention by pointing out the militia's new formation on the Green.

Ethan remained taciturn. He was irritated by Mrs. Porter and frustrated with the conversation's direction. He had not succeeded in drawing out Monsieur Brisonneau to any purpose. Instead of elucidating a political stance or shedding light upon loyalties, the Frenchman had proven himself only more nebulous in those matters (and more reprehensible in others). Yet, to Ethan's mind, there was no person more likely than Brisonneau to be the transgressor or, at the very least, an accomplice.

Except . . .

He glanced toward the yellow-haired youth standing tall in the middle of the militia's front line. Ethan had wondered a great deal about the extent of Tristan Porter's knowledge regarding his father's covert endeavors. Ever since that first uneasy encounter in the study, Ethan had suspected that Tristan was at least cognizant of the situation, if not a party to it. But Joshua Porter's elder son was a difficult one to gauge. Mrs. Porter had earlier alluded to her stepson's sullenness — a trait that Ethan had observed in Tristan from the first. Yet, Tristan had showed a different side of himself at the horse race —eager, competitive, invigorated. He had let his guard down for the duration of the contest. In reflecting upon this, Ethan surmised that Tristan's customarily sullen demeanor was not, perhaps, reflective of any inherent temperament, but was rather an innate response to his present circumstance.

As it were, Ethan's reverie upon the subject was but brief, for his thoughts were soon absorbed by the activity of the militiamen upon the Green.

Marching, halting, loading, aiming, firing. Marching again. Dispersing and assembling.

How readily could Ethan have fallen into step beside them or asserted his rank and taken command.

But he knew that the militia's very existence might well depend upon his continued discretion. He must yet conceal his affiliation with the military and the task with which he had been entrusted. He must yet watch and listen and discern . . . and wait.

CONSTANCE FELT THE EYES OF the entire congregation upon her and her party as they filed into their pew, conspicuously late.

The hymn-books had already been closed and the litany was well under way by the time Joshua Porter and his family took their seats. As the family's pew was located halfway up the church's center aisle, it was quite impossible to proceed there unnoticed, and to make matters worse, Reverend Wynn paused in his invocation until the members of the Porter group were situated, thus calling further attention to their arrival.

Mortified, the three ladies of the party kept their eyes fastidiously downcast as they hasted to their seats, and even little Caleb, keeping close to his mother's skirts, seemed conscious of being the focus of so many watchful eyes. Joshua Porter appeared slightly vexed by the whole thing, for his family's tardiness was none of his doing.

Indeed, Constance herself was partially to blame (and how acutely did she feel the shame of it now!), for she had taken the time to mend the seam of her favored gown rather than choose a different one, thereby delaying the family's departure by more than a few minutes.

And the family had set out but a quarter of the way toward the church when Caleb, running ahead, had abruptly fallen and torn a sizable hole in his breeches. Against the background of the child's howls — for he had scraped his knee in the fall — Mrs. Porter insisted to her husband that they turn back, that Caleb could be outfitted in a new pair of breeches. But Mr. Porter was already impatient to achieve their destination, knowing that the service would soon commence without them — not to mention the fact that this was the second garment-related delay incurred that morning — so he bade his wife to take the child home, while he and her sisters would progress to the church ahead of them. Mrs. Porter had seemed doubtful at this injunction, but Constance offered to accompany her, and so the little party split into two.

Upon arriving at the church, however, Joshua Porter and Polly did not hasten inside, though they arrived just as the doors were being closed, but instead waited outside, for in truth, Mr. Porter — in spite of his previous impatience — was not hardhearted and would not allow his wife and kin to be unaccompanied during what was sure to be an awkward entrance in the midst of the service.

So it was under the watchful scrutiny of most of the town's citizens that Joshua Porter and his family made their very belated entrance that Sunday morning.

Once seated, and much relieved when the litany resumed, Constance kept her eyes fixed steadfastly upon the pulpit, hoping the parishioners would quickly forget the distraction of the latecomers.

She was not to be granted such simple reprieve, however. The prayer had not re-commenced for more than a minute before Constance felt an elbow's nudge beneath her ribs. She glanced at Polly beside her, who in turn motioned as discreetly as she could toward Constance's opposite side. Turning her head in the direction indicated, Constance observed with a sinking heart that the door to the pew had been left open, and she was seated nearest to it. She apprehensively looked back toward Polly but found herself met with not only her younger sister's continued prompting, but her elder sister's as well, for Anne sat on Polly's other side and was also nodding Constance toward the open door.

Constance glanced over her opposite shoulder toward the rear of the church where Mr. Lowry, the verger, sat upon his bench, placidly dozing off — his mouth open, his nose wheezing, his wig slightly askew, entirely oblivious to the issue of the pew door needing to be closed.

Constance sighed. It was plain that Mr. Lowry was not going to be of any help to her. She must undertake the task herself.

Trying to call as little attention to herself as possible — though knowing full well that she was undoubtedly creating a distraction — she rose from her seat as quietly as she could, and, taking two small steps, stretched her hand toward the pew's wooden door. Being unaccustomed to the task, however, she was prepared for neither the door's lightness of weight nor for the ease with which it closed; consequently, as she pulled it toward her, it swung shut with a clatter that resounded throughout the sanctuary.

Petrified, Constance froze. Every eye in the church was assuredly fixed upon her. She could only imagine the look of reproach which was undoubtedly manifest upon her elder sister's face at that moment. Reverend Wynn, though, mercifully gave no pause this time, nor even any indication that he had seen or heard the disruption — though he must have been cognizant of it — but continued along in his prayer without so much as a stammer or a glance in the direction of the noise, for which Constance was truly grateful.

As Constance turned back toward her seat, however, she chanced to glance up at the gallery above and there unexpectedly sighted an individual who was gazing down upon her, though not in any reproach; indeed, his mouth was drawn up in an amused half-smile, and his eyes shone with approval.

Constance's heartbeat — which felt to have ceased entirely the moment the pew door slammed shut — suddenly resumed with rapidity, and she hastily took her seat, fixing her eyes intently upon the pulpit once more. It had not occurred to her that Ethan Shaye would be at church. She had never seen him there before, not in all the weeks she'd been in Merrilltown. And try as she may to remain duly attentive to the service, as the litany gave way to the sermon she found herself thinking on him still.

After a time, she ventured to lift her eyes toward the gallery once more. Ethan was no longer looking at her. He was leaning forward in his seat, elbow propped up on one knee, chin resting in his hand. But though the object of his focus would seem to be the vicar, Constance could tell that Ethan's mind was not upon the sermon. Indeed, he was not hearing a word the Reverend spoke nor even seeing the man behind the pulpit. Constance had no doubt that Ethan's thoughts were far away, absorbed in other matters.

And upon what did his thoughts dwell? Constance could only guess. The war, perhaps. His military unit. The comrades whom he longed to join. The mission that had brought him to Merrilltown, of which Constance had no knowledge other than that it was as of yet unfinished. But she knew Ethan well, and she knew that he would succeed in his endeavor. And once his mission was accomplished . . . he would depart from Merrilltown and return to the life he loved . . .

Her face suddenly flushed, Constance averted her gaze and turned her head back toward the clergyman's pulpit. She ought not to be thinking about Ethan Shaye during the sermon . . . any more than she ought to be wondering if she was as far from his thoughts as she purported to put him from hers.

ANNE PORTER RATHER QUICKLY GOT over her embarrassment at their late arrival, for when the service had ended she had no desire to hasten home, but instead wished to stay and exchange pleasantries and gossip with her neighbors, as was the custom of a Sunday. Neither did Joshua Porter intend to forgo his weekly discourse with the other men of the town regarding the prices of cotton and tobacco or the latest news of the war.

So Constance found herself standing at the edge of her sister's circle of acquaintances, only half listening to the ladies' chatter, and finding ample opportunity to take note of the surrounding environs.

She sighted Ethan a short distance away, standing near the church building, conversing with a young lady. Constance recognized the girl to be the same one who had so impetuously run to Ethan after his horse race victory and upon whom he had subsequently bestowed the wreath of blossoms. The girl was not beautiful nor smartly-dressed, but she had a disarming smile and radiated a mirthful confidence as she conversed with Ethan in an easy, familiar way. After several minutes, a plain-ly-attired man of middling years emerged from the church and joined them — standing beside the girl in a fashion that led Constance to believe they were likely father and daughter. The man greeted Ethan with hearty goodwill. After some more discourse between the three of them, the man took his leave of Ethan with a handshake and walked away toward the high street. The girl did not immediately follow, but instead spoke again to Ethan, nodding toward the departing man, evidently requesting Ethan to accompany them. Though Constance could not hear Ethan's reply, she could see that he was declining with a good-natured shake of his head. The girl persisted, though, smiling and coaxingly placing her hand upon his arm. But Ethan did not concede — only shook his head again, and, with a slight bow, turned and took his own leave, as the girl gave a final wave and hurried away to overtake her elder relation.

Constance, by this point, was so far removed from the discussion amongst her own circle that she had no trouble slipping away unnoticed.

Ethan had disappeared round the corner of the church, and Constance found him there in the quiet churchyard untying his horse's bridle, which he had unceremoniously tethered to a mossy gravestone.

He looked up as she approached, and she could tell at once by the glimmer in his eye that her appearance was welcome — and indeed, not unexpected.

He greeted her with good-humored warmth. "Good day, Miss Jameson. 'Tis a fine day to turn out for a church service, is it not?"

Constance blushed a bit self-consciously. "You would tease me about our late arrival, but truly I have no defense, for it was my own fault. I so wanted to wear this gown today," and she looked down at her dress, nimbly fingering the soft-hued skirt, "but I forgot to mend the seam this week, and I'm afraid that I — that is to say, I ought to have — well, with one thing or another . . . it did set everyone to a late start."

For one who knew Constance well, it was a charmingly charac-teristic explanation, and Ethan's countenance betrayed the hint of a smile — which somehow both pleased and flustered Constance, prompting her to hastily turn the subject away from herself, stammering slightly as she did so:

"At any rate, I — I cannot recall having ever seen you at church before."

Ethan's grin was hardly penitential. "Aye, I have been rather negligent in my ways, it is true. But a few days ago I received an invitation which I thought would be unseemly to ignore."

And in response to Constance's puzzled look, he produced from his pocket a letter, which he handed to her, and which she perused as quickly as she could, in spite of its length:

Mr. Shaye,

Please accept my humblest apologies, as I have been delinquent these several months in properly welcoming you to Merrilltown. While I realize that you are not a permanent resident of our community, I hope that the warm reception and laudatory congratulations of our town's citizens upon your recent acclaimed victory at Judge Merrill's race, as well as the lengthened tenure of your stay here, have persuaded you that you are truly and graciously regarded as an honorary resident, and as such, I hope that you will not hesitate to rightfully avail yourself of the town's resources.

As a long-time citizen of the community and as vicar of the general parish, I feel it is my duty to reach out to all newcomers and to offer my services and assistance in any way I can. As each colony has made its own laws, there is bound to be some understandable confusion when moving across borders as to the intricacies of each region's regulations. That is where we must entrust true friends and upstanding citizens to look after our welfare and hope that they will point out with courtesy and tact those very intricacies of law which would hitherto be unknown to one newly-arrived. And it is in that self-same spirit of fraternity that I wish to render you assistance in bringing to your attention the fact that the laws of Virginia require every free-born citizen in good health to attend church services each Sunday. As the penalty for repeated absences is left

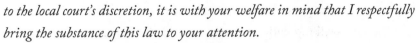

to the local court's discretion, it is with your welfare in mind that I respectfully bring the substance of this law to your attention.

However, I am confident that it will not be due to the avoidance of repercussion, but rather in deference to the natural and sincere inclination of a devout heart, that you will accept this invitation to present yourself at the parish church this Sunday and henceforth.

It is with forthright anticipation that I look forward to your attendance. I remain

Your servant in the Lord,
Reverend A. Wynn

Constance could not conceal her own smile as she came to the missive's end. "Reverend Wynn is most tactful and discreet." She handed the letter back to Ethan. "I suppose you would not have such a law in your new nation? Though I do not know why you should object to something that serves the best interest of men's souls."

Ethan raised an eyebrow. "You are a bit presumptuous. I have no objection to it. It is a common enough law across the colonies — commonly broken and seldom enforced, from what I've seen."

Constance shook her head. "If Reverend Wynn truly knew you, he would not have chosen such a tactic — though it is undoubtedly effective upon others — for threat of retribution shall never deter nor motivate you."

Ethan laughed. "That is true. However, it is a rather cynical view that would assume most men are in attendance at church merely to avoid censure."

"I did not mean to suggest that," Constance hastily countered. "I have no doubt that there are many upstanding and virtuous men who attend services every Sunday out of genuine piety and righteousness. Yet, there are assuredly others who come for reasons that are . . . less commendable."

As she spoke the last words, she inadvertently glanced toward the road.

Following her gaze, Ethan's eye alighted upon Maria Lethbridge in the distance, walking with her father toward the town.

And Ethan understood.

He shook his head, attempting to make light of it. "Nay, pity the man who seeks to meet with a tavern maid at church. She's better kept to her tap-room."

But Constance continued to gaze absently after the retreating pair. "'Tis undoubtedly a lively scene," she murmured, "even of a Sunday."

Ethan looked at Constance for a long moment, sensing her solemnness, and when at last he spoke, his tone was both grave and gentle. "I would not know, for I shall not be there."

Constance's eye strayed back to meet his. She was ever quiet and thoughtful. "Where will you go today? Shall you be about your work of a Sunday afternoon?"

Ethan nodded. "Aye, there are no days of rest during a war; not in my profession. But first," he added, "I shall take my horse for a run in the country, I think. He is surely in need of some exercise, and 'twill do us both some good to be away from the town for a bit."

He might have spoken further — yet, somehow he could not. Somehow, with Constance's soft brown eyes trained upon him like that, his thoughts were flown. Neither could he sever his own gaze.

It was not the first time they had found themselves transfixed in silence — under a spell that neither wished to break. Once, the silence had been filled with unanswered questions; now, it was filled with answers they dared not profess.

For just one moment, though, the quiet churchyard corner was all their own.

Yet in the next moment, Ethan averted his eye, distracted by some movement in the distance behind Constance.

Looking back to her with a rueful smile and a knowing gleam in his eye, he nodded in the direction toward which his attention had been diverted. "I think it is not only men who have ulterior motives in attending church. It is assuredly a fine place for young ladies to meet with their beaux."

Constance glanced over her shoulder and saw Mr. Zachary Merrill crossing the churchyard toward them.

"Oh!" With flushed countenance, she turned back to Ethan but had no opportunity to speak more, for Mr. Merrill was already within earshot, and Ethan must acknowledge his approach.

Never one to flatter, Ethan greeted the judge's grandson with an easy nod and a nonchalant "Good day, Merrill."

Constance turned to face the newcomer, but she lacked Ethan's composure — indeed, she still dwelt upon his last remark to her — and so she said nothing, allowing Zachary Merrill to speak first.

Mr. Merrill was as cordial and agreeable as ever. "Good afternoon, Miss Jameson, Mr. Shaye. It is a pleasure to see you both."

By this time, he had reached the spot where they stood, and he bent over Constance's hand with gracious gallantry, while she lowered her eyes and murmured a nearly inaudible greeting.

Mr. Merrill appeared not to notice her tepidity — truly, he might well have taken it for demure bashfulness — and he moved on, stepping forth to shake Ethan's hand. "How are you, Shaye? Still hard at work on the surveying? One of these days you must come up to the Hall and dine with us. I've been meaning to ask you ever since the horse race. My grandfather and I had quite a dialogue going, you know, leading right up to the day of the race." He smiled ruefully. "I was plum confident I would win again this year, and he was just as certain that I would not — *'pride goeth before destruction, and an haughty spirit before a fall'* — I must have heard him utter it at least ten times in the days before the race." He laughed and shook his head. "I shall not soon live it down if he has his way. Aye, you must come up one of these days — he'd be pleased as punch to have you, as would I."

"Thank you, I'm much obliged." Ethan's response was proper enough, but entirely noncommittal and even slightly aloof. He had no interest in befriending the local gentry, nor in endearing himself to their esteem, beyond what was necessary for his work.

Zachary Merrill seemed satisfied with the response, though, and continued speaking: "And now, I hope you will not object if I steal away your charming companion. I have promised her a ride along the river road in my Landau."

"No, of course not," was Ethan's offhand reply.

Both men looked toward Constance, who had yet remained silent.

A rather long pause followed, until Zachary Merrill smiled at her and said, "That is — if the lady is still interested."

Constance glanced from one face to the other. There was surely only one correct response, but in that moment she could not seem to recall what it was. Her mind had stalled — caught up in the struggle between honesty and propriety. And to her dismay, when at last she did hear herself uttering the appropriate response — "Yes, yes I am" — it sounded so unconvincing that there must be some doubt as to whether propriety really had triumphed over truth.

But Ethan was ever vigilant where Constance was concerned. He was aware of her unsettled state, as well as the cause thereof, and he rescued her from what would assuredly have been another awkward silence.

"I'm sure that Miss Jameson has been looking forward to it. I believe all young ladies take pleasure in an open carriage ride."

Constance glanced at Ethan, then back to Mr. Merrill. "To be sure," she softly corroborated with a nod.

"Very well then," asserted Zachary Merrill amiably. "We'd best be on our way, for it is a route of some distance that I have in mind, and your sister prevailed upon me to have you back before supper."

Constance obligingly took the arm he proffered, as the two men bid each other good day. For Constance and Ethan, a parting glance must suffice for good-bye.

But a few minutes later, as she sat in the elegant open carriage, waiting for Zachary Merrill to finish giving instructions to Thaddeus, Constance turned her head and looked back across the churchyard, where Ethan

was just mounting his horse. And as she beheld him there, she was overcome with a sudden, profound yearning. It very nearly overwhelmed her.
And as she watched Ethan ride away — tall and strong and sure of himself — the yearning only intensified. There was no logic or sensibility to
it. Indeed, she knew not even where he was going. Yet, just then, more
than anything on earth, she longed to be with him.

She continued to gaze after him even after he had disappeared from
sight, and it was not until the carriage started forth with a slight jolt that
she came to her senses, though she remained distracted for quite some
minutes and paid only scant heed to her companion's discourse.

Poor Mr. Merrill! He could not have known how ill-timed was his
approach in the churchyard nor how significant was the silence he had
breached.

ANNE PORTER HAD DEVELOPED A passing fancy for games of forfeit,
so that — for a time — every gathering at the Porter house was bound to
include some sort of frivolous wagering, particularly upon the occasion
of that lady's birthday, when her whims were most likely to be indulged.
Indeed, it was in the very midst of the dinner given in honor of the occasion that she conceived of such an opportunity.

Ethan Shaye was among the company gathered around the Porters'
dinner table that evening when Joshua Porter quite innocuously broached
the conversation that would ultimately become the occasion's most significant diversion.

"We have more than one cause for celebration today," Mr. Porter put
forth as the main course was cleared from the table. "One of Monsieur
Brisonneau's ships arrived this afternoon, on schedule and intact."

Mrs. Porter was unimpressed. "You would compare my birthday to
the ordinary arrival of a ship?" she lightheartedly admonished her husband. "Nay, I see your ploy — it is your way of introducing talk of business at the dinner-table. I shall not have it on my birthday."

"Ah, but Madame," interjected Monsieur Brisonneau, "this ship should be of interest to you, for it does indeed bear a connection to your birthday, and its arrival today was most timely. You see, Madame, amidst its cargo is something particular that I had requested with this occasion in mind, and which shall be presented to you shortly."

Mrs. Porter was at once intrigued. Her eyes widened with interest. "What is it?"

Monsieur Brisonneau smiled at her. "You must wait and see. I shall bring it in after the last course has been cleared."

"Oh, you are very cruel to tease, Monsieur Brisonneau!" Mrs. Porter bemoaned. But no sooner had she uttered the words than her face lit up once more. She leaned forward eagerly. "What if we should guess it? Would you tell us then?"

Polly groaned. "Oh no, do not encourage her in this, else she shall have you making a wager of it!"

"Well, why not?" Mrs. Porter's enthusiasm was growing. "We might each have a guess at it, then Monsieur Brisonneau has only to reveal which of us has guessed correctly. 'Tis a simple enough game."

Zachary Merrill laughed. "And what prize would go to the victor? Would you give up your gift to him?"

"Certainly not!"

"Or would you expect Monsieur Brisonneau to make another present from his ship's inventory?" Polly put forth drily.

"Not at all." Anne Porter dismissed her younger sister's suggestion with a wag of her head. "The winner shall be rewarded without costing anyone a shilling nor even a penny." Her eyes danced mischievously.

"Why, you've already thought this through!" Polly exclaimed, her tone unapologetically accusatory.

Anne laughed. "I had such an idea the other night when we were playing at cards in the parlor. Only, there weren't enough of us then to make it worth the while."

Polly nodded knowingly. "And you've been waiting to put your scheme into practice ever since."

Mrs. Porter ignored her sister. She leaned forward once more, quite caught up in the delight of her own plan. "Here is my proposal, and I guarantee — none of you shall say nay when you hear of it, so give heed: If any gentleman should correctly guess what the gift might be, he may bestow a kiss upon the lady of his choice!"

A young lady seated next to Polly — Miss Lindley by name — covered her mouth to stifle a delighted giggle. "Goodness!"

"And what if it should be a lady who guesses aright?" demanded Polly.

Mrs. Porter's smile widened. "Then," she went on, "the lady may name any gentleman here, who must then do her bidding for the duration of the evening!"

This proposal was met with resounding approbation in the form of applause, laughter, and even a jovial "Hear, hear!", so that those sitting at the opposite end of the table — Mr. Porter, Ethan, and several other gentlemen — who had heretofore been occupied with their own conversation, turned their heads at the sound of the merriment before returning to their discourse.

Even Polly was diverted at the prospect of such a delectable reward. "Is the prize meant to reward the winner or punish one of the others?" she laughed.

"It is indeed a clever game," acknowledged Monsieur Brisonneau. "Nevertheless," he added, "I shall not tell you what the gift may be. You must wait until the last course is cleared away and see it for yourself."

"Oh, very well!" Anne Porter yielded easily now that she had a new divertissement. "This shall at least keep us occupied until that time. Now, who shall start?"

"You ought to go first, as it is your birthday," suggested Miss Lindley's mother, who sat across from her daughter.

"Aye," seconded Zachary Merrill convivially, "'tis only fitting."

"Very well." Mrs. Porter was readily persuaded. "I confess, though, I have nothing particular in mind."

She fell silent as she pondered what her guess might be, and the others obligingly refrained from distracting her, the only sound being the conversation transpiring between Mr. Porter and his associates at the other end of the table.

It took but a few moments for Mrs. Porter to summon a guess. "I know!" she exclaimed suddenly, her face brightening with an idea. "A cameo!" She uttered the words with the confidence of assured victory, unwittingly looking to Monsieur Brisonneau as she did so.

The Frenchman merely smiled. "It is a good guess," was all he would say.

Zachary Merrill laughed. "'Tis no use glaring at him like that, Mrs. Porter. 'Tis plain, he shall not give in. Who shall be next? Miss Constance?" He turned to that young lady, who was in her usual place at his right hand.

Although Miss Constance had no aspirations to win such a prize, she did enjoy games, and as she had no idea of what Monsieur Brisonneau's gift might be and was in no real danger of predicting correctly, she was more than happy to submit a guess.

"A length of silk, perhaps?" she ventured. "Or lace?"

"A length of silk or lace?" Polly echoed questioningly. "Is that two guesses?"

"She cannot have two guesses!" Miss Lindley objected petulantly. "'Twould give her an advantage!"

"Oh, very well," Mrs. Porter interjected impatiently. "Which shall it be, Constance? Silk or lace?"

"Why not simply guess 'textiles'?" suggested Zachary Merrill to Constance. "That would encompass both and is somewhat broader, so as to increase your odds of winning."

"Oh . . . no," Constance murmured, shaking her head slightly. "No, I shall go with . . . lace. Yes, lace."

Mr. Merrill nodded agreeably. "Lace it is then. The finest from Bayeux, I've no doubt. And now, Miss Lindley — have you a guess of your own?"

Miss Lindley was slightly flustered, being thus singled out by the illustrious Mr. Merrill. "Yes, yes, I — that is, I was going to suggest a — a lace fan, but since Miss Jameson has guessed lace . . . perhaps I ought to make a different guess."

"Nonsense," countered her mother briskly. "There is plainly a difference between a length of lace and a lace fan. If the item is one or the other, it shall be evident to all of us which of you should win."

"Better just to guess 'a fan' in general," put forth Polly with a mischievous gleam in her eye and a grin in Mr. Merrill's direction. "Such a broad category will assuredly give you an advantage."

Zachary Merrill tipped his glass to Polly, his own eyes sparkling in appreciation of her mild jest.

Miss Lindley, however, took the suggestion to heart. "Aye! A fan shall be my guess," she pronounced with conviction.

"Oh! I've just thought of something!" exclaimed Anne Porter. "Supposing nobody guesses aright? What shall we do then? It won't do to have nobody win."

There followed an interval of silence at that end of the table as everyone pondered the dilemma. But after only a few seconds' cogitation, Zachary Merrill put forth a solution:

"If no one's guess is exact, why not have Monsieur Brisonneau decide whose guess he deems to be most nearly correct?" he proposed.

Mrs. Porter beamed, relieved to have such a ready solution. "Aye, that is good thinking, Mr. Merrill! Is that agreeable to you, Monsieur Brisonneau?"

The Frenchman inclined his head graciously. "*Mais oui, Madame. C'est bon.*"

"Oh!" Anne Porter giggled and leaned in to Mrs. Lindley. "He means to say, 'yes, it is good'."

"Now, who has yet to put forth a guess?" proceeded Mr. Merrill, as a servant brought in some sweets upon a tray. "Miss Polly Jameson?"

"I believe that Monsieur Brisonneau will give my sister a looking-glass!" Polly declared confidently — and even decisively — so that everyone looked at her in some surprise. "I overheard them talking about it only recently," she added, by way of explanation. "Monsieur Brisonneau was telling my sister about some palace or other in France, where gilded mirrors hang on the walls of every room. Anne sighed over the fact that she has not even one gilded mirror in her own house. And I remember thinking at that moment that her husband is bound to procure one for her, as he likes to give her whatever pleases her, but it would work out very well that Monsieur Brisonneau should be the bearer of the gift, as his ship arrived only today, and my brother-in-law has assuredly already procured a different gift for the immediate occasion." Her eye gleamed triumphantly.

Monsieur Brisonneau chuckled and inclined his head toward the youngest Jameson sister. "You are a very perceptive young lady, Miss Polly," he asserted, eyeing her appreciatively. "Nevertheless, you must wait to see if your perception is validated."

"Oh — this is delicious!" Mrs. Lindley suddenly interjected amidst the discussion. "The pudding," she added, as heads turned in her direction. She motioned toward the plate which had been set before her. "It is flavored with molasses, is it not?" she inquired of her hostess. "It really is divine."

Anne Porter smiled. "Aye," she affirmed. "It is indeed."

"But how did you come by it?" queried Dr. Harwood, one of the gentlemen seated near Mr. Porter. "It is nigh impossible to obtain molasses in Merrilltown these days."

By that time, the men seated at that end of the table had been served their own portion of the pudding and were attentive to the related conversation.

Mrs. Porter's smile broadened. "Monsieur Brisonneau is not the only one who bears surprise gifts today," she related, evidently well-pleased at her singular knowledge of such.

Polly glanced at the faces round the table. "Well, if it was not Monsieur Brisonneau, then it was surely Mr. Merrill, for who else here would have the means to procure something so scarce?"

Anne Porter laughed. "Well, what have you to say, Mr. Merrill? Will you own up to the deed?"

Zachary Merrill's eyes twinkled. "I will own that I've been in Norfolk this week, and that I sent my man down to the lower wharves to see what he might find amidst the storehouses there. It would seem that practically anything may be had for a price, if one knows where to look."

"No doubt such a commodity came to these shores aboard a French ship," intoned Monsieur Brisonneau shrewdly.

Mr. Merrill smiled placidly. "No doubt," he agreed. "Thaddeus knows better than to pour any of my money into the Crown's coffers, though I hope I may be objective enough to state that the molasses from the British West Indies is far superior to that of . . . other origins."

Monsieur Brisonneau did not concede this point. "With all due respect, Monsieur Merrill, I beg to disagree. Your objectivity is commendable, but there is no circumstance on earth which would impel me to give credit to the British for anything, unless it be treachery and deceit — vices at which they excel."

This unnaturally blunt statement from Brisonneau was met with an unsettled silence. The remark's pronouncedly bitter tone strayed from the customary neutral cordiality of conversation at a dinner-table where ladies were present.

But Mr. Merrill's gentlemanly sense of decorum served him well in bringing the matter to a close. "I shall not argue with you, sir. I bear no more love for the British monarchy than do you, and your partiality toward your own country is natural enough, even in such matters of triviality."

Ethan Shaye listened to this exchange with interest. Like the other men seated near Joshua Porter, he had paid no mind to any of the conversation at the other end of the table until the pudding had been brought in. But this last dialogue he heeded well. Was there some animosity between Zachary Merrill and Monsieur Brisonneau? He had never noted such before — but then, it was rare for Monsieur Brisonneau to engage so emphatically in a conversation to which so many attended. Ethan had always been under the impression that the Frenchman liked not to draw attention to himself. Yet here, Brisonneau had not only audibly contradicted Zachary Merrill's opinion but had also — and perhaps more tellingly — denounced with vehemence the British contingent.

Ethan could not help but wonder if either of those facts was significant to his own objective. Was Brisonneau's bitter statement sincere? While it was not uncommon amongst groups of ardent Patriots to disparage or jeer their red-coated adversaries, and certainly it was well-known that the French and the English bore a long and deep-seated hostility toward one another, the circumstance and the tenor of Brisonneau's remark seemed quite out of place.

But if the Frenchman intended to speak further upon the subject, Ethan would never know, for Mrs. Porter artfully interjected at that point.

"Why, Mr. Merrill!" she exclaimed. "You have orchestrated everyone else's turn, but you have yet to put forth any guess yourself. You must do so now. And you, too, Mr. Lindley," she added, addressing Mrs. Lindley's husband, who had as of yet not contributed two words to the discussion.

Mr. Merrill gave a laugh, then addressed his hostess with mock contrition. "Alas, Madam, you have caught on to my scheme. By keeping everyone's attention occupied with their own conjectures, I have succeeded in putting off my own. For indeed, I haven't any idea at all of what Monsieur Brisonneau's gift might be. Nonetheless, I'll not pass up my chance at winning such a reward." He laid down his spoon for a moment as he pondered. "Hmm . . . a music box?"

Ethan ceased attending to the conversation at that point. His senses had been unexpectedly diverted by something nearer at hand — a fragrant aroma, sweet and distractingly familiar. Glancing down, he regarded the plate which had been set before him.

The molasses pudding was covered with what appeared to be a sour cherry sauce and adorned with bits of candied orange. Ethan appraised it for a moment, keenly aware of the aroma — pleasant enough with its mingling of fruit and spice . . . and yet, beguiling, for in alerting his senses it had somehow awakened something in his memory.

But what?

Picking up his spoon, he carefully broke off a corner of the pudding, along with some of the sauce, and raised it to his mouth. While the flavor was exactly what had been anticipated — a mixture of sour cherry, molasses, cinnamon, and ginger — it brought no further enlightenment as to the source of the awakened memory.

With the edge of his spoon, he scraped off a bit more of the cherry sauce — so deep a crimson, it was almost purple — and tasted it in isolation.

But no, it was assuredly not the flavor but the aroma itself which had called up some distant association. What it was, though, he could not identify. Nor could he establish why it beguiled him so.

Regardless, he had little time to ponder it, for before he had yet finished his portion of the pudding, Mrs. Porter (who had just finished her own) commandeered everyone's attention:

"Well, I do believe everyone has finished the last course! Betsy! Come and clear the plates."

The housegirl standing at the sideboard obediently took a step toward her mistress's place.

"What?" Mr. Porter interjected. "I'm afraid you are quite ahead of yourself, my dear. Miss Lindley has not yet finished her pudding, and neither has anyone at this end of the table."

"Oh! No — no, I am quite finished, thank you," Miss Lindley twittered, hastily pushing her half-eaten portion away and looking to her hostess, smiling eagerly.

Monsieur Brisonneau chuckled and addressed the host. "Your wife is most anxious to receive her gift, I think, Monsieur Porter, and those about her are equally anxious, for they have wagers riding upon it."

"Aye, you'd best pay heed, Porter," declared Zachary Merrill blithely. "You could be on the losing end of this one. Should your wife win, she may choose any man here to be her servant for the remainder of the evening."

Mr. Porter smiled in amusement and gave a good-natured wink.

"Well then, she'd best not choose me, or 'twould be no novelty in it. 'Twould be no more than an ordinary evening about here."

Mrs. Porter, however, was not so amused and was impatient to move on. "Have no fear, dearest; you are ineligible to lose — or to win — as you did not participate in the wager. You kept everyone about you occupied with discussing highly secretive issues in low tones — undoubtedly regarding the war," she added to Mrs. Lindley with some distaste, "and so have thus deprived these lovely young ladies of the chance of being kissed by any of the gentlemen at that end of the table."

"On the contrary, Madam," countered Dr. Harwood jovially, "it would seem that your husband has instead saved us from an evening of servitude to those young ladies!"

"Oh, I do hope it is a lady who wins the wager!" Polly exclaimed with a rare show of enthusiasm.

Monsieur Brisonneau regarded her with a glint in his eye. "Indeed, Miss Polly? It would undoubtedly amuse you to have a gentleman to do your bidding."

Polly frowned at him and tossed her head. "I did not say it had to be me. 'Twould be equally amusing to be an observer of the consequences."

Monsieur Brisonneau was not put off by her disdain. He merely smiled and rose from his chair. "Well, I think it is time to present our charming hostess with a gift in honor of her birthday." He gave a slight bow toward that lady. "If you will excuse me, Madame, I shall return momentarily."

There was a perceptible flutter of excitement amongst the ladies as Monsieur Brisonneau exited the room.

"It was a brilliant idea of yours, my dear," Mrs. Lindley confided to the hostess. "The wager. I confess, I am as excited as if I were to be the recipient of the gift!"

"I hope he does not need to go far to fetch it," fretted Mrs. Lindley's daughter plaintively. "The anticipation shall be too much for me, I am sure!"

Ethan's patience was sorely tried by this tiresome chatter, and, though he remained silent, he, too, hoped that Monsieur Brisonneau would re-appear quickly, so that the ladies might withdraw from the room and leave the men to resume their discourse, which centered around topics of far greater interest to Ethan, and from which he was more likely to glean pertinent information than the present dialogue.

Fortunately, no one was required to wait long. Monsieur Brisonneau's imminent approach was heralded not by footsteps, but by another sound: a soft, silvery trill — unmistakably high-pitched, but not unpleasant.

Heads were already turned expectantly toward the door when Monsieur Brisonneau stepped into the room, holding aloft his gift.

Mrs. Porter immediately gasped in delight. "Oh, how lovely!" she breathed, her eyes dancing as Monsieur Brisonneau set the gift before her.

It was an elegant little cage — quite exquisite in and of itself — and inside were perched two dainty songbirds: one pale green, the other blue.

"How very lovely," Anne Porter repeated, thoroughly charmed.

The other ladies were no less enchanted, echoing their own murmurs of approbation. Constance's eyes shone softly as she beheld the delicate little creatures.

"They have come to you from the markets in Paris," Monsieur Brisonneau informed his hostess, then added with a smile, "but I think they will like better the peacefulness of Virginia."

"Hmm . . . if they are partial to peacefulness," noted Joshua Porter, "then you'd best keep them out of Caleb's reach."

"Aye!" concurred Polly. "Put them well out of his grasp, or you shall find them flown."

Mrs. Porter was still captivated by her beguiling gift, even as the Frenchman moved the cage to the sideboard. "Thank you very much, Monsieur Brisonneau. What a marvelous gift."

"I am sure there is not another such charming pair of songbirds in Merrilltown," Mrs. Lindley asserted.

This thought pleased Mrs. Porter greatly, and she beamed at her friend.

"But what of the wager?" Miss Lindley asked somewhat anxiously. "None of us thought to guess a living creature."

"Monsieur Brisonneau shall have to decide," Polly pronounced matter-of-factly. "Although," she added, with a rather resolved shake of her head, "I do not suppose he shall choose my guess as the closest. I cannot think how to relate a looking-glass to songbirds."

There was a brief silence.

"Well . . . they are both contained in a sort of . . . metal . . . encasing," offered Miss Lindley, in a faltering attempt at encouragement.

Monsieur Brisonneau laughed aloud. "*Mes cheres* Mademoiselles, I wish I could bestow the reward upon each of you," he declared, his smile falling unambiguously upon Polly. "But alas, I cannot make the case for any lady here when there was a gentleman's guess so plainly aligned with the correct answer. It was, of course, Monsieur Merrill's."

"Hear, hear!" Mr. Lindley raised his glass in concession to the victor.

Polly was not so willing to concede. A slightly pouting frown creased her lips. "I hardly see where there lies an obvious connection between a birdcage and a music box," she muttered.

Anne Porter dismissed this comment with a wave of her hand. "Oh come now, Polly, it is evident that Mr. Merrill is the winner. Of course a pair of songbirds must be comparable to a music box. He is plainly the victor."

During this repartee, Ethan glanced at Constance, who had gone quite pale — undoubtedly sensing that she was about to be made a party to the victor's claim.

And indeed, their hostess encouraged the winner to take his prize at once. "Well, Mr. Merrill," Mrs. Porter smiled at that gentleman, "you must not subject us to further waiting, but claim your reward without delay!"

"He shall choose Constance, of course," Polly murmured to Miss Lindley, who managed a giggle even as she looked slightly crestfallen.

"Choose judiciously, Merrill," Dr. Harwood advised cheerfully. "This could be your only chance to kiss a married woman without requiring her husband's permission."

Zachary Merrill chuckled and shook his head. "I'm sure we would all be interested to know which one in particular *you* have in mind, Dr. Harwood. However," his demeanor became more solemn as he turned to the young lady beside him, "I should very much like to bestow the kiss upon Miss Constance — if she does not object." And he smiled very kindly at her.

With so many eyes fixed expectantly upon her, Constance was not at liberty to voice any objections, as she had willingly participated in the wager. She had no choice but to give Mr. Merrill a slight nod of her head, though any who was studying her closely — and there was one — would assuredly detect her reluctance.

As Zachary Merrill pushed back his chair and rose from his place, Constance kept her eyes cast downward and turned her head, plainly expecting him to kiss her upon the cheek. In a rather surprising display of assertiveness, however, Mr. Merrill craned his neck and planted the kiss squarely upon Constance's mouth.

It was nothing more than a peck, but Constance — quite taken by surprise — recoiled at once, raising the back of her hand to her lips and uttering a dismayed, "Oh!".

While everyone observed this episode with eager attentiveness, Ethan alone remained withdrawn. Leaning back in his chair, he watched with a seemingly cool detachment. Nevertheless, the slight furrow of his brow betrayed an inward discontent, for though a wagered kiss was but meaningless, he could not like seeing Constance so discomposed.

Anne Porter, however, saw a different meaning in Constance's reaction. "See now, how sweetly she blushes!" Mrs. Porter exclaimed, nearly simpering. "You have assuredly touched her with your romantic gesture, Mr. Merrill."

Polly scoffed at this sentiment. "I hardly think being the recipient of a wagered kiss can be deemed 'romantic', as I'm sure even Mr. Merrill will agree."

That gentleman's blue eyes sparkled, and he seemed set to concur, but before he could get a word out, Miss Lindley voiced her dissension.

"That is not so!" she cried. "Out of every lady here, he chose Miss Jameson especially. It must speak of some regard he has for her."

"Even so," contended Polly, "unless Constance returns that regard, there can be no plausible suggestion of 'romance'."

"'Tis true enough," asserted Zachary Merrill good-naturedly. "Miss Constance undoubtedly has many suitors and may already have one whom she esteems."

Constance had remained fastidiously silent during this exchange and looked as if she dearly wished the conversation would turn to other topics.

Those who were thoroughly invested in the discussion, though, gave not a glance in her direction as they continued upon the subject:

"What a ridiculous notion!" laughed Anne Porter. "She has shown no preference toward any other, I assure you. I would have observed it if she had, for I am very astute in these matters."

"You do not know everything," retorted Polly. "You have only observed her here in Virginia. Did it occur to you that she may have demonstrated some regard for an individual in Pennsylvania, where her home is?"

Constance glanced up at her younger sister, her eyes wide and incredulous. "Why Polly, that isn't so! I never have done such a thing."

But Polly persisted. "What about Daniel Bennett?"

Constance's brow creased in dismay. "Daniel Bennett? I've never shown him undue regard, and hardly even know him for an acquaintance."

Anne Porter took this opportunity to interject. "Well there, you can see plainly enough that you are mistaken, Polly." Then, reassuringly to Mr. Merrill— "You cannot doubt the veracity of Constance's words, for she is seldom so forthcoming amidst company."

Polly was still scrutinizing Constance, though. "I do not mean to put you ill at ease, Constance, but you cannot deny that whenever

Daniel Bennett came calling with his mother and brother, you were always quite attentive." Then, to the others— "Even when she spent half her time shut upstairs in the garret, endlessly working on our father's gift, she made a point to be in attendance downstairs whenever the Bennetts called."

Constance stared at Polly, taken aback by this insinuation on the part of her beloved sister.

"I cannot think what you mean to imply," Constance said in some distress and a great deal of embarrassment. "I did enjoy listening to his violin, as I enjoy hearing any musical instrument, but other than that, I hope I never gave him — or you — the impression of anything more."

She was quite disconcerted by now, and it was her elder sister who put an end to the subject:

"Now Polly, I hope you will be satisfied and leave the topic alone. You have put our poor sister through grief enough." But Mrs. Porter could not resist pointedly adding to Mr. Merrill — "It is true, though, that Constance loves music. I am sure she would only ever show preference to one who is musically inclined."

Whether or not Mr. Merrill discerned any personal implication in this statement remained unknown, for Miss Lindley at that moment took it upon herself to introduce a new course of conversation.

She turned to Constance.

"What was it you were making for your father?" Miss Lindley asked curiously. "In the garret, did she say?"

The heightened blush upon Constance's cheek, which had scarcely begun to abate, rose once more. "It was only a — a gift for his birthday," she stammered. "'Twas nothing to speak of."

"Do not believe her," Polly asserted. "She spent months working on it, but never will tell what it was."

Miss Lindley's mother laughed. "But that is absurd! Surely there is no harm in telling us here, where the recipient is not present."

"And our father's birthday is long past," added Polly. "Wouldn't we have discovered what it was, had you given it to him at that time?"

But Constance only shook her head, her eyes averted. "Nay, I — I cannot say. You will see it when I give it to him . . . someday."

Miss Lindley frowned, disappointed. "But we shall not *all* see it then. I shall never learn what it is, if you will not say."

"Where is it now?" Anne Porter wondered. "Did you bring it with you to Virginia?"

Constance shook her head despondently.

There was quite an awkward silence after that, as all were much too polite to voice what each was surely thinking about the fate of Constance's gift, left in the house which had been confiscated by her father's adversaries.

Mr. Merrill did eventually, and even gallantly, resume upon an entirely different topic, which took the focus off of the unhappy young lady beside him.

But Constance remained subdued. What had once been a pleasant, festive occasion had, for her, been rendered a discomfiting ordeal. It was not the first time such an occasion had been marred for her.

And Ethan knew that the only way he could protect Constance was by remaining silent. Indeed, anything he might have interjected during the discourse would have cast inordinate suspicion upon them both, so he had no choice but to hold his tongue and remain silent.

Even so, he wished she would glance his way, just for an instant, that he might reassure her with a look.

She did not, though, and in fact, she avoided his eye for the remainder of the evening, nor did she utter more than a few brief, murmured replies to anyone who addressed her.

The guests eventually all removed to the drawing room, and as the evening wore on, Constance was among the first to unobtrusively take her leave, bidding a general "good-night" to those remaining, then curtseying demurely before making her way toward the hall door. Just as she reached the threshold, though, she paused for only the slightest moment and, turning her head, cast a look in Ethan's direction.

It was only a glance — swift as a heart's beat — but so poignantly expressive that Ethan had to summon every ounce of his self-control in order to refrain from going to her at once.

He must speak with her.

But what could he say? Here, before this company, what words of any significance could he impart?

There were none. There was nothing to do but watch as Constance set foot across the threshold and disappeared into the hall.

Ethan did not move for some minutes thereafter. Ruminating, he stared absently at the doorway through which Constance had departed, quite oblivious to the conversations transpiring about him.

And when the remaining guests began to take their leave throughout the course of the next hour, Ethan deliberately delayed his own departure, taking care that he should be the last to bid his hosts good-night.

A short while later, as Ethan stood in the Porters' stable yard — his hand extended to grasp the lantern proffered for his ride back to the tavern — he abruptly changed the course of his movement, retracting his hand and turning his head in the direction of the house from which he had just exited.

"I meant to get some papers out of the study before I left," he muttered, as if the thought had just occurred to him. He took the lantern from the servant. "Just leave my horse at the post. I'll see myself back out."

And with the lantern in hand, Ethan hurried away across the stable yard back toward the house, easily admitting himself through the door which opened into the rear of the main hall, now deserted and darkened save for the lantern's flickering light.

Making his way across the hall toward the study, he paused beside the staircase. Keeping his lantern at his side, he gazed up into the dark abyss of the stairwell.

She was up there somewhere.

For one ephemeral moment, an illusory thought flitted across Ethan's brain — a senseless notion that he might ascend the steps and find her and speak with her.

The thought was, of course, thoroughly irrational and entirely implausible.

But there it was, all the same.

He lingered a moment beside the staircase, then, lifting his lantern slightly, proceeded across the hall and slipped noiselessly into the study, closing the door behind him.

Once enclosed inside the windowless room, Ethan moved swiftly, as one who is easily familiar with his surroundings. Setting the lantern atop the desk, he opened a drawer and tore an edge off of a sheet of paper inside. Pulling a pencil from the same drawer, he moved the torn edge of paper closer to the light and hurriedly scrawled a single sentence:

Meet me at sunrise in McCreary's orchard, near the pasture gate.

– E

Replacing the pencil in the drawer, he started to push the drawer shut, then paused, his fingertips still upon the drawer's edge. He glanced across the desktop, then quickly scanned the room. In truth, he had left nothing in the study which he might now ostensibly collect. He started to pull the drawer open again, when he became suddenly aware of a footfall without.

At once alert, he glanced toward the door, but saw no evidence of light emanating beneath it. Nevertheless, he had heard the creak of trodden floorboards . . . and again the footsteps resumed.

Whomever was treading in the hall was taking no particular care at discretion, and as Ethan listened, his senses registered something else — an awareness of recognition; recognition of the rhythm, of the uneven weight of the footfall. He had heard it so many times before, up and down the steps and across the floorboards of the garret. The lapse of time had not diluted his memory.

And now, it was a stroke of luck, for it was the very person he would have momentarily sought out.

Clutching the torn bit of paper in his fist, he strode back to the door and pulled it open.

"Jenny!" he hissed into the darkness.

The lantern on the desk behind him gave off the only light to be had, but it was enough to discern the large, swarthy silhouette before him in the hall — a silhouette which had immediately frozen upon the study door's sudden opening.

Ethan pushed the door open wider, that the slave woman might see him more clearly.

"Jenny," he repeated, his voice inadvertently gruff, even as he attempted to moderate it.

Jenny's feet remained planted to the spot, her head turned toward Ethan. A frown creased her dark forehead as Ethan stepped into the hall.

He moved toward her slowly, only a few steps, deliberately restraining his pace.

Looking her directly in the eye, he extended the paper toward her, addressing her in a low tone. "Would you give this to Constance?" He paused, then added, "Tonight." It ended as a statement rather than a question. Ethan was not accustomed to asking favors of slaves, and his natural sense of command momentarily usurped any deferential endeavor.

Jenny remained unmoved. She eyed the bit of paper suspiciously, her frown deepening.

Ethan's own brow furrowed impatiently at this familiar reception. Frustrated, he looked away, that he might collect his thoughts. When he met Jenny's eye once more, he spoke plainly:

"Jenny, I know you will not do this for me, but — will you do it for her?"

If he had expected a softening of Jenny's austere visage, he was bound to be yet frustrated, for he saw no change in those round, glowering eyes. He knew Jenny doubted that anything he might impart would benefit her beloved mistress. Yet he maintained his stance, arm extended, proffering the bit of paper.

It was a cavernous silence in which they confronted one another — Ethan defying Jenny's resentment with his own unyielding resolve.

It was the slave woman who at last ended the stalemate, though without any hint of concession or any indication that she intended to fulfill Ethan's request. She merely took the paper from him and without further acknowledgement shuffled away into the darkness toward the drawing room.

Ethan remained where he was. When Jenny had reached for the bit of paper, she had stepped into the pale circle of light emanating from the study, and Ethan had glimpsed her dark face more clearly. His recognition of the familiar had been tempered by the realization that Jenny's countenance was not entirely the same impervious face he had so often seen begrudgingly bending over him in the garret. The slave woman's face was now creased about the eyes and showed lines etched about the mouth, giving her a tired and somewhat careworn appearance. Her face had aged considerably in the months since Ethan had left the garret. He could not help but wonder if these changes in Jenny's appearance were due to the trauma of her master's eviction or perhaps to her new situation at the Porters' residence.

Ethan's sympathy was tinged with some irritation, though, for Jenny had not departed in the direction of either staircase, where she might ascend to convey the note to her young mistress, but rather had departed in quite the opposite direction, leaving Ethan to further doubt that his message would be received.

As he gazed absently in the direction of the main staircase, his thoughts were interrupted by the unexpected appearance of a faint glimmer of light penetrating the darkness above.

Glancing upward, Ethan saw the unmistakable flicker of a candle's flame upon the upstairs landing, accompanied by the dim outline of a white-clad figure. But both figure and light disappeared as quickly as they had emanated, for the figure had spotted the shadowy entity in the hall below and had retreated with haste.

Ethan frowned to himself as he stared up into the black void where the figure had appeared. Who was it, and why had they fled?

Though he had glimpsed nothing more than a momentary perception of white, something about the figure — whether shape or size or movement — left Ethan with the impression that it had been a woman.

Assuredly it was not Constance, for she was so familiar to him that he would have immediately recognized her form, her movement, even the sound of her footfall; neither was she likely to have fled upon sighting him.

Nor could Ethan think that any of the servants should have so hurriedly retreated, unless one of them was straying from duty.

But that left only two possibilities: either the eldest or youngest of Matthew Jameson's daughters.

Certainly Anne Porter was the likelier of the two, for who but the mistress of the house would have any errand which might summon her from her bedchamber after dark? But why did she not carry out her errand then? Even was she about some business of questionable nature, a hasty retreat was surely more subject to suspicion than a fabricated excuse.

Yet, he could not think that the figure was Polly Jameson, for what possible reason could such a young girl have for prowling about the house at night?

It was, perhaps, Ethan's own situation which caused him to dwell at length upon the incident, for standing as he was, in the doorway of the room which guarded the information so crucial to his purpose, his mind invariably sought to link the white-clad figure on the landing with his own pursuit, as improbable as such a connection seemed.

The longer he reflected, though, the more he began to doubt his senses. He could not be certain that the figure had been a woman. Any member of the household was likely to be clad in white at such a late hour, and it was only the size and carriage of the figure which had led to his initial impression. But there was another member of the household whose interest in the study after dark would fit in very neatly with Ethan's instinctive suspicions. Truly, it might have been Monsieur Brisonneau . . .

As Ethan fetched his lantern and proceeded back through the hall toward the rear door, he could not help but regret that he had lingered so long where he stood after Jenny's departure. Had he stepped back into the study instead, the white-clad figure would perhaps have descended the stairs, and Ethan might have discovered the nature of the errand his presence had unwittingly deterred.

THE AUTUMN AIR WAS BRISK and the mossy ground soft with dew, as the first rays of sunlight penetrated the early morning greyness with a yellow haze.

As Ethan made his way through the orchard's uneven rows, he thought back upon his encounter with Jenny the previous evening and wondered anew whether she had carried out his bidding. He had cause enough to doubt, and unconsciously frowned as he remembered Jenny's mistrustful glower.

It was one question, at least, to which he would not have long to wait upon an answer.

While the pasture gate was as yet beyond his view through the tree's branches, the slightest sound carried clearly and easily across the thin, brisk air, and though Ethan gave no pause to his step, he became cognizant of a light, musical sound which reached his ear. Faint as it was, he knew at once that it was Constance, and as he turned to cut across a row of trees, he sighted her in the distance, standing at the wooden fence beside the gate.

She did not see him, for she faced away toward the pasture . . . and she was singing, very softly, doubtlessly unaware that any other than the sleepy, slow-moving cows across the fence could hear her.

There were no distinguishable words to her song; it was more of a "lully-lee" humming, but the tune was melodious and undeniably cheerful, as would be attributed to a gladsome state of mind.

Ethan's spirits rose upon hearing her thus, and he took some satisfaction in the thought that he may have played a part in mitigating some of the unhappiness she had suffered the previous evening.

He greeted her as he approached, and her soft smile as she turned from the fence affirmed her pleasure at seeing him.

And Ethan reciprocated — the corner of his mouth turning upward as he beheld her face.

He spread his coat upon the ground for her at the edge of the orchard — for there was no proper seating in the vicinity — then settled himself opposite her, at the mossy base of one of the trees, leaning his back up against its weathered trunk.

And there, amidst the peacefulness and isolation of that pastoral setting, Ethan imparted to Constance everything.

He told her how he had been summoned by Colonel Naismith and assigned a covert mission from General Washington. He told her of the dire situation faced by the general's men and of the waylaid supply shipments. He told her of Joshua Porter's involvement with the Patriots' cause and of the logbook discovered in his study. He told her of Henry Dowling's watch upon the high road and of the ongoing sabotage in spite of their efforts. He told her of his frustration at his lack of success as the weeks progressed to months.

Only one thing did he refrain from imparting: he made no mention of the fact that the sabotage had resulted in the death of one of the Patriot emissaries. Somehow, he felt it best to omit that grim detail.

And Constance, for her part, listened just as she always had . . . with a silent, thoughtful demeanor — her eyes sometimes trained upon Ethan, sometimes looking solemnly off into the distance across the meadow — but ever attentive. When he had finished his tale, she yet remained silent for some moments, pondering his words, and when she at last looked at him once more, there was a puzzled furrow to her pretty brow.

"There is no one here who professes allegiance to the Loyalist cause," she asserted.

Ethan gave her a wry smile. "Excepting only your younger sister and yourself."

The color heightened a bit on Constance's cheek as Ethan shook his head.

"No," he went on, "in the months I've been in Merrilltown, I have neither heard a single soul admit loyalty to the Crown. And yet — assuredly there is someone here who bears no love for the Patriots' cause. Someone who goes to great lengths to conceal his allegiance and his actions."

Constance's soft brown eyes remained troubled. "You speak of treason — a hanging offense under British law."

"Aye." Ethan restlessly threw a grounded apple toward the pasture fence. "And rightfully so."

Constance made no further remark upon the subject, but cast her eyes downward, reflecting once more. When she spoke again, she did not lift her eyes, and her words were put forth with marked hesitation. "I think that you must suspect my sister's husband. Or one of his associates."

"It would be natural enough, given Porter's involvement with the supply shipments." Ethan did not elaborate nor give any indication of his own reservations regarding Joshua Porter's connection to the ongoing sabotage.

Constance looked at him for a long moment, then spoke quietly but evenly. "I have lived under my sister's roof these several months now. I have grown familiar with the household's activity and come to know those you most suspect. Yet you have never asked me anything in this regard, not even indirectly."

Ethan would not meet her eye. "No." He scowled and hurled another rotting apple under the pasture fence. "Nor shall I."

Had he looked at Constance, he would have seen the glimmer of tender warmth which shone in her eyes at that moment; but he remained obstinately focused on the spot where the apple had landed on the other side of the fence, toward which some curious cows were now ambling.

Constance lapsed into silence once more, and her next words indicated that her thoughts had turned to a new and unexpected subject:

"You spoke of a colleague who is helping you in your endeavors here."

Ethan glanced up at her, the scowl dissipating from his visage. "Aye, Sergeant Dowling. He keeps watch upon the high road, out on Clymer's farm."

"Sergeant Dowling," Constance repeated thoughtfully. "He is a subordinate officer then."

Ethan nodded. "'Tis true — Dowling was not born into circumstances which would accord him a commissioned officer's rank. But no man is more deserving of the advancement in status he has achieved, for he has earned his rank through his own merit and tenacity."

"You esteem him greatly," Constance observed.

Ethan gave a shake of his head. "A truer friend and a truer soldier I have never known. Dowling's life has not been an easy one — he has no family to speak of and few resources. The regiment is as a brotherhood to him."

Constance listened with interest, for she had seldom heard Ethan speak of his comrades, and his next words affirmed that his own thoughts were not entirely disparate:

"'Tis strange to think of it," he mused. "Dowling . . . the regiment . . . the skirmishes, battles, drills . . . It is a world apart from—". He did not finish his sentence, rather letting the thought trail off into obscurity.

"It is a world you love," Constance put forth with an understanding, but unmistakably wistful, smile.

"Aye." Ethan nodded absently. After a few moments, though, he turned to Constance and spoke with sudden conviction. "Should you like to see him?"

"See him?" Constance repeated blankly. "Do you mean your friend — the sergeant?"

"Aye."

Constance was still perplexed, but her brown eyes were bright with interest. "Is he coming to Merrilltown?"

"No." Ethan shook his head. "No, I would need to take you out to Clymer's farm to see him." He looked at Constance thoughtfully. In truth, the idea had come upon him so suddenly, and he could not rightfully account for his own impulsiveness in verbalizing it so hastily, but as he discerned the rosy tinge of anticipation flush softly upon her cheek, the merit of the plan was solidified in his resolve. "It would undoubtedly provide a much-needed diversion for him," Ethan speculated. "Indeed, I think Dowling would be well-pleased to make your acquaintance."

Constance was momentarily distracted by the prospect of such an excursion, but when she looked toward Ethan once more, she met his eye, for his was already trained upon her face, though he might not have seen her at all, so deep was his contemplation.

"What is it?" Constance murmured with a smile. "What are you thinking?"

A flicker of awareness lighted Ethan's eye, for Constance had summoned him from his reverie, though he did not avert his gaze. Neither did he make immediate reply, and when he did, he chose his words with care:

"I was thinking . . . how fortunate I was that it was you and not one of your sisters who came across me in the snow that day."

Constance was yet again caught off-guard, and this time by a subject which must expose her vulnerabilities more than perhaps any other. And how apparent it must have been, for she could not sever her gaze from his; indeed, the solemnity which overtook her countenance made such emotions manifest.

She was rendered speechless for a long moment — her thoughts flown to a distant, snowy field beside a creek bed; and though the image was but fleeting, it took concerted effort to extract herself from the memory and to make adequate response.

"Whatever your impression of my sisters, I hope you do not believe that either one would have left you there to . . . perish." Her voice quavered upon the last word as a shadow passed across her visage — so afflicting was the thought to her.

Ethan regarded her yet intently. "They would have turned me over to your father."

"Aye." Constance's tone took on new conviction. "It was my own in-clination as well. Our father is a learned physician; it is natural enough to think that they — or anyone — should have given you over to his charge without thought to further ramifications."

"Yet . . . you did not," Ethan maintained steadily.

Constance finally averted her eyes. "No," she murmured and did not elaborate.

Ethan sensed her reluctance to pursue the subject more, and he did not press her further. His eye lingered a moment on her face, though, before he spoke again, putting forth a subject he presumed to be less precarious:

"I have not seen Jenny about much."

While this topic was indeed a safer one, it succeeded not in lighten-ing the mood, but instead appeared to produce quite the opposite effect.

Constance shook her head dejectedly. "No . . . Anne has put her to the laundress's duties."

Ethan understood the implication. "It is a lower status than she was accustomed to at your father's house."

Constance sighed. "Polly and I have spoken with Anne, but she will not be swayed. You see, she entertains guests much more regularly than we ever did in the country, and . . . it is important to her that her home and servants are . . . just so," she finished rather feebly.

Ethan fully comprehended. "Just so," he repeated, rising to his feet and extending his hand to Constance as he went on: "I daresay Jenny is as anxious as you are to return to your father."

Constance had begun to reach her hand up toward his, yet now she paused and looked up at him, slightly retracting her hand.

But Ethan merely gave her a knowing smile and took hold of her hand, gently pulling her to her feet, and not indulging her hesitation.

"Listen," he bade her, as he bent to pick up his coat from the ground.

Indeed, now Constance could hear what Ethan must have perceived earlier — the sound of a bell, tolling the hour from the distant church-yard at the far end of the town.

And whatever had given Constance pause a moment earlier was suddenly flown from her mind, as her eyes grew wide with apprehension. "Oh, it is late!" she exclaimed in dismay. "The breakfast will have already been laid out. I must be back before they sit down to table! Whatever shall I say if I— oh, I must go!"

The urgency of her predicament took precedence over any formalities of leave-taking, and she hastened away down the lane between the pasture and the orchard. But she had not gone far when she suddenly stopped and looked back.

"Ethan!"

Ethan, who yet remained at the spot from which they had just arisen, raised his eyebrows inquiringly, as Constance continued speaking:

"You — you won't forget? You will take me to meet your colleague?"

Ethan nodded. "Aye. I must think on it for a bit. But I will find a way." He gave a nod in her direction. "Go along now, or you shall have to make excuses to your family."

Constance cast him a parting smile over her shoulder and hurried on her way.

Ethan did not depart so hastily, however, but donned his coat slowly, lost in thought. He gave one more glance down the grassy lane where Constance had departed, then turned and walked in the opposite direction, making his way back toward the town.

ETHAN HAD ATTEMPTED ON SEVERAL occasions to covertly follow the wagons which left Porter's dock and headed north along the high road. His efforts were to no avail, though. Each wagon he had followed turned off the high road well before reaching the Maryland border. Given the number of loads assembled at Porter's landing each day and the infrequency with which shipments were sent to General Washington, it would take an extraordinary stroke of luck for one man to chance upon the right wagon at the right time.

Consequently, Ethan had devised another strategy: For three days, he positioned himself at the border blockade, concealing himself high upon a ridge in the adjacent wood, that he might observe the exchanges between the posted blockade guards and any emissary who approached them.

It was an exercise that proved both invigorating and frustrating.

To Ethan, those three days in the wilderness — watchful, solitary, and self-reliant — recalled his previous endeavors of tracking and spying; the adventurous, independent commissions upon which he had always thrived and which he hoped to win again through the success of his current assignment. And yet, despite this reconnection with the life to which he was partial, there was also an unfamiliar sense of discontent, and though he dwelt not upon it, as he rode back toward Merrilltown at the end of the three days — his vigilance having proved futile, for he observed nothing suspicious at the blockade — he was aware of this trace of unrest where he had expected to find fulfillment and liberation.

It was but a fleeting discontent, though, and was soon forgotten as he entered the town and there resumed work upon his mission's objective.

It was shortly after Ethan's return to his lodgings in town that he determined to revisit the peaceful river tributary beyond the eastern wooded hills. He could not say what drew him there; it was not merely the fact that the quiet tributary or a solitary swim had once soothed his unsettled mind — for indeed, it was now far too cold for a swim, nor did he longer feel such a need to divert his thoughts. No, it was something else . . . something he could not quite put his finger on, but which had been prodding at the back of his mind for some weeks. Perhaps a return to the spot would clarify the purpose.

He had no access to a boat other than that at the Porters' landing, which he utilized whenever he needed to row across to the opposite shore under the pretext of surveying Joshua Porter's recent land acquisition; but though the workers and tradesmen about the landing were accustomed to seeing him row to the far shore, they may raise questions should he set a course deliberately downriver.

So it was that Ethan decided to forego the swifter method of transport, and he once again set out on foot. He would take the same route he had the first time — through the dense forest which covered the hills behind the Merrill estate — though it would take the better part of the day to traverse there and back.

He had not yet achieved even the lowest foothill, however, when his plans were met with an abrupt alteration. As he tread upon the silent dirt road across a wide field, a sudden gust of wind penetrated the tranquil autumn air.

Scanning the horizon before him, he beheld nothing but a bright blue, cloudless sky; yet a quick glance over his shoulder presented him with a darkly contrasting perspective. There, low clouds had gathered in an ominous grey mass, heavy with moisture and swiftly following the advancing movement of the harbinger wind, which did not abate after that first unexpected gust.

Though rain showers were not uncommon in the autumn, this one had arisen without warning, and Ethan found himself in an unanticipated predicament — on foot, with only his hat and coat for cover, and surrounded by miles of fields and woods and hills.

He quickly surveyed his environs, seeking any discernible shelter. The only structure in sight was the small schoolhouse, set back from the road within its neatly-fenced enclosure, but as the pupils were undoubtedly in attendance, that option could not be deemed practical.

Looking further up the road, he could see in the distance the entrance to the Merrill estate at the base of the tall hill upon which stood Merrill Hall. But even if he achieved the gate in a matter of minutes, the Hall itself was at least another mile's trek from the gate's head, though he might find shelter in any dependencies located between the gate and the house.

Even as he contemplated this possibility, thick droplets of rain began to spatter his coat.

Just as the foreboding clouds had gathered so quickly at his back, so did the precipitation gather momentum in its intensity, so that after only a few moments, what had begun as scattered droplets became a steady shower, as the blue sky before him quickly turned to somber grey.

Ethan proceeded with rapid step in the direction of the Merrill estate, the rain beating ever more steadily upon his shoulders.

He had hurried forth but a scarce measure when, in the distance ahead, a sudden movement agitated the hazy mist, as a splashing bulk of darkness surged through the Merrills' gate.

It was a figure on horseback, riding headlong into the ever-accelerating torrent of rain, and Ethan slowed his step as the rider approached.

The mounted figure did not sight Ethan until he had practically come upon him, and he reined in his horse so suddenly that the startled creature reared up under the duress, though the rider maintained his bearing with a sure hand upon the rein.

It was Zachary Merrill, and he recognized Ethan at once.

"Mr. Shaye!" he shouted against the cascading din. "This will soon be a downpour! I am heading to the schoolhouse. Follow me — you can take shelter there!"

And Mr. Merrill pulled his horse to the left and urged the creature off of the main road toward the picket fence which enclosed the schoolyard.

Ethan wasted no time — for the rain shower was intensifying — and hurried toward the fence's opening, continuing swiftly on in the direction of the small wooden structure at the far end of the yard.

By the time Ethan reached the schoolhouse, Zachary Merrill had dismounted and tied his horse to the post at the side of the building. As there was no covering over the structure's entrance, Mr. Merrill did not tarry outside, but hastily pushed open the door, motioned Ethan inside, then quickly followed, closing the door behind them.

Their entrance was hardly subtle and was certainly unexpected, as evidenced by the way the schoolmaster jumped up from his stool and the concurrence with which a dozen youthful heads turned toward the door at the back of the room.

"Mr. Merrill! I — I did not know you were coming today," the schoolmaster stammered. "Up, gentlemen!"

And a dozen fidgeting boys promptly rose from their benches.

Zachary Merrill remained collected. "It makes no difference," Mr. Merrill remarked to the schoolmaster with an even smile. "Is your instruction not of the same excellent caliber every day, whether or not I am expected?"

"Of course, sir." The schoolmaster — hardly older than some of the pupils he taught — wrung his hands a bit nervously.

"I am glad to hear it," Zachary Merrill asserted genially, "as I have brought a visitor today and hope to impress him with your pupils' academic achievements."

The schoolmaster nodded in acknowledgement, though he appeared quite ill-at-ease.

"I know him," a small but familiarly piping voice proclaimed in a loud whisper.

All eyes turned upon Caleb Porter, who had made the none-too-discreet announcement to a slightly taller boy standing next to him.

"I know that man," Caleb reiterated, with some unconcealed smugness. "'Tis Mr. Shaye."

But Zachary Merrill played no favorites in the schoolroom, nor made exceptions, even for the child of his personal acquaintances. He turned a stern eye upon young Caleb. "Master Porter," he intoned with some severity, "you are speaking quite out of turn."

Caleb looked immediately contrite.

"You must excuse Master Porter's misconduct, sir," the schoolmaster put forth hastily. "He has been absent from school these several days and has only just retuned, having recovered from an illness."

Zachary Merrill shook his head. "Spoiled by his mamma, no doubt, during his time abed, and now has quite forgotten his manners. I must speak to his mamma about it next time I see her."

Merrill's tone was firm, but not unkind. It was effective enough, though, as Caleb's wide eyes attested.

Merrill did not pursue the subject further, but rather turned his focus back to the schoolmaster. "And now — this sudden rain has left Mr. Shaye and me quite drenched, and we would much appreciate a seat before your fire."

The schoolmaster nodded, undoubtedly relieved to have moved on to a new topic. "Yes, yes, of course." And he motioned accommodatingly toward the bench before the fire at the front of the room.

Merrill indicated to Ethan that he might take a seat, and Ethan did not delay in so doing, for the autumn day was chilly as well as damp, and the warmth of the fire upon his back was most welcome.

From his seat before the fire, Ethan observed with some interest the activity taking place before him in the tiny microcosm that was the little schoolroom — with its simple wooden benches and, at the front, the schoolmaster's podium, which seemed oversized and ostentatious in the modest, sparsely-furnished room.

Mr. Merrill did not join him at the fireside but instead removed his dampened cloak — hanging it alongside the other, smaller ones upon the hooks lining the back wall — and circulated amongst the pupils, inspecting their work, hearing recitations, and asking them questions. Just as his grandfather was the magistrate for the county, so Zachary Merrill apparently considered himself a sort of "magistrate of the schoolroom". There was nothing of strict or harsh taskmaster about him, though. Indeed, he seemed to take a genuine interest in the progress of each young scholar, and his pale eyes were benevolent, yet intent, as they studied each face and each copybook. When he had concluded his rounds, Mr. Merrill stood at the back of the room beside the cloaks and hats (Ethan noted among them a familiar small black-cockaded hat) and observed with a keen eye the still-flustered schoolmaster's instruction. Ethan was certain that, had the schoolmaster been at all slacking in

his duties, such negligence would be remedied at once upon this unannounced visit from the school's patron, who suffered no fools.

It seemed the occupants of the little schoolroom were not yet to be
reprieved of disruptions that day, for nearly a half-hour after Mr. Merrill's
and Ethan's arrival, the door at the rear of the room suddenly burst open
again, and once more a dozen startled heads turned to see who was
entering.

This time the schoolmaster was given no cause for alarm, and indeed,
Ethan immediately recognized the dusky figure who had entered with
such an unceremonious clatter and who was even now indecorously wiping his wet and muddied shoes upon the floorboards. There was slung
over his shoulder a small cloth sack, its unseen contents bulging within.

Zachary Merrill nodded toward the newly-arrived visitor. "Ah,
Thaddeus," he greeted his manservant. "Your timing is impeccable, as
always." He strode over to the slave and took from him the cloth sack.
As he did so, one corner slipped from his grasp, and a round, bright object fell from the sack onto the floor, where it promptly rolled under the
nearest bench.

An audible murmur of excitement rippled across the room, and more
than one whispered exclamation of "Oranges!" could be discerned.

Thaddeus expeditiously retrieved the orange and placed it back into
the sack.

Merrill's eyes sparkled as he extended the sack toward the schoolmaster. "I shall entrust these to you to distribute as you see fit before
these gentlemen are dismissed for the day."

The schoolmaster, still flustered and fawning, hastened forward to
take the proffered sack from his benefactor.

"Thank you, sir. It shall be my pleasure. I am glad that the pupils'
progress has met with your satisfaction."

Zachary Merrill nodded with a smile, giving one last glance over the
little schoolroom before turning to take his leave.

But the schoolmaster had a sudden thought come upon him. "Mr.
Merrill, sir!"

Zachary Merrill turned.

"What of Master Porter?"

All movement in the room ceased as Mr. Merrill's eye fell upon young Caleb Porter, whose own blue eyes were wide with trepidation.

"Ah, Master Porter . . ." Mr. Merrill seemed to be considering the situation, and though the child was duly grim under such scrutiny, an astute observer would detect a twinkle in Zachary Merrill's eye as he regarded the impudent child.

Merrill took a step toward the schoolmaster, holding one hand aloft.

"I shall take custody of Master Porter's orange," Mr. Merrill said, as the schoolmaster reached into the sack to procure one. "I had intended to pay a visit to the Porters' house this evening, and this shall serve as a reminder to address there the topic of young Master Porter's comportment." He pocketed the orange. "We shall let his mamma decide whether or not to bestow it upon him."

It was an effective tactic, for the child remained quite subdued, though Ethan knew as well as Mr. Merrill that Caleb's adoring mamma would unquestioningly deem her precious son worthy of the reward.

Merrill then turned to Ethan, who yet remained silently observing before the fire.

"Mr. Shaye, I must take my leave, for the rain seems to have abated somewhat, and I have other matters to which I must attend. However, you are welcome to stay here as long as you like. And now—," he once again addressed the schoolmaster and the room at large, "I bid you all a good day."

The schoolmaster gave a bow as Mr. Merrill departed, followed by the ever dutiful — but ever dignified — Thaddeus.

And despite Mr. Merrill's hospitable bidding, Ethan subsequently quit the premises as well, for the downpour had given way to a cold, dismal drizzle which gave no indication of subsiding but afforded him an opportunity to make his way back to town, his objective necessarily postponed for the time being.

ETHAN LEANED HIS HEAD AGAINST the windowpane. The rain had fallen relentlessly over the course of days and even into weeks, and the foggy glass of the window was damp and cold, as the unceasing rain pelted mercilessly against it.

Assuredly the afternoon was waning, though in the absence of any sunlight the hours of the day could scarcely be differentiated, each one as desolate and grey as the one before. And although the chamber was amply illuminated by both firelight and candlelight, the bleakness of the day yet penetrated the room.

From his seat at the small table beside the window, Ethan was indifferent to the draft from without and to the dampness of the windowpane. Indeed, the dreariness of the day seemed to have robbed him of any initiative, and he idly tapped his pencil against the pewter base of the chamberstick, looking with some distaste at the crudely-sketched, half-finished map on the table before him.

His work had been all but halted during the consecutive days of precipitation, and so he had set himself upon the task of putting the measurements of Clymer's property into a proper map, intending to first lay out the basic grid before taking it to Joshua Porter's house, where he might make use of the study to work on it over subsequent days, for he yet believed that the key to discovering the identity of the traitor lay within Porter's household.

But mapmaking was a slow and tedious process even under the best of circumstances, and in this situation — where the task had no genuine purpose — Ethan found the exercise especially onerous, giving rise to a restlessness that could not be alleviated so long as he must remain confined indoors.

Although the usual noise from the tavern's public room could be discerned, it was but faint and distant, so that Ethan's room was, for all intents, quite silent, save for the patter of the rain against the window and the soft idle tapping of his pencil upon the candle's base.

The gentlest of rappings upon his chamber door was therefore very audible, and Ethan raised his head, roused from his state of listlessness by the unexpected knock. As he rose from his chair, another knock reverberated upon the door, slightly louder, but still hardly forceful.

He crossed the room and opened the door to reveal the proprietor's daughter standing in the dim corridor.

Although the corridor was dim, the gleam in Maria Lethbridge's eye was not. She smiled coquettishly.

"Good afternoon, Mr. Shaye."

Whatever her errand, she was in no hurry to reveal it and waited for Ethan to return the greeting, which he did with a brief nod and a nonchalant acknowledgement of "Maria".

"There is someone asking to see you," Maria related, still without haste, evidently content to linger in the presence of her favorite lodger.

Ethan was somewhat puzzled by the vagueness of her message, for in peering past her into the darkened corridor, he saw no one.

"Very well," he prompted her. "You may show him up."

"Oh, I cannot show him up," Maria declared airily. "For it is not a *him* at all, but rather a *her*. It is a lady. And you know the rules of the establishment — no ladies in the rooms of single gentlemen." And she smiled at him saucily, for indeed, by that time she herself had crossed the threshold and was standing well inside the room.

Ethan frowned impatiently, ignoring her flirtatious implication. "What lady is it?"

Maria shrugged carelessly. "I cannot say. She did not give her name, and I do not know her. Shall I tell her you are occupied?"

Ethan gave no heed to the question, but took a step in the direction of the corridor, motioning for her to follow. "Come, Maria, you must take me to the lady, for I do not know who she may be."

Resigned that detaining him was futile, Maria followed him into the corridor and scurried past him into the stairwell, leading the way down the stairs to the landing below. The door to the tap-room was open, as always, and Maria paused there but a moment, for Ethan was directly behind her.

The tavern's public room was crowded, as it had often been of late, as the incessant rain prodded people to seek indoor amusement.

Ethan did not wait to be led to his visitor, though, for in following Maria's line of sight, he spotted a young lady sitting apart from anyone else, on a low chair beside the fire, her face partially obscured by the rain-spattered hood of her dark green cloak. And Ethan knew at once that it was she who had asked to see him. Indeed, it was the lady his own eye had unconsciously sought.

He strode past the proprietor's daughter and hastened forth to meet the unexpected visitor, disregarding the acquaintances who called out to him in greeting as he crossed the room.

And Constance, for her part, had been keeping her eye trained anxiously upon the doorway. She immediately rose from her chair when Ethan entered the room.

As Ethan neared her, he saw that her face was pale and drawn, her brown eyes afflicted.

When he reached her, she addressed him at once, without pause for greeting, nor formalities of any kind:

"Ethan, I must speak with you," she implored breathlessly. "I — I do not know what to do."

Ethan's brow knit, troubled by her state of distress. He instinctively took command of the situation, placing his hand upon her shoulder.

"Aye, of course," he reassured her. "But not here," he added, glancing round the crowded room.

Constance also looked about, realizing for the first time the density of the company around her.

Ethan's hand slid effortlessly from her shoulder down the length of her arm and grasped her hand.

"Come with me," he charged her, as he turned back toward the door.

Still clasping Constance's hand, Ethan led her across the room, past Maria Lethbridge — who had been detained at the room's entrance by an overly-friendly patron — and out into the deserted hall.

Moving swiftly, he led Constance up the staircase and into the dim corridor above, where he stopped before the door to his chamber. Pushing it open, he stepped aside and motioned her inside. With one hasty glance back down the corridor, Ethan followed her into the room and closed the door behind him.

He crossed directly to the fireplace and set before it a chair, then turned back to Constance.

"Here," he said, motioning toward the chair. "Please, be seated."

Constance only shook her head and remained where she was at the center of the room, wringing her hands nervously. "I cannot tarry. No one knows that I . . . that I am here. I am truly in a wretched predicament!"

Still frowning in concern, Ethan crossed to her.

Constance removed her hood and lifted her troubled eyes to meet his.

"What has happened?" Ethan demanded. "Tell me."

Constance took a shaky breath in an attempt to collect herself, then proceeded: "My sisters and I went into town today to look in some of the shops, though our sojourn was cut short due to the rain's persistence. When we returned to the house, we learned that Thaddeus — Mr. Merrill's Thaddeus — had been there in our absence, delivering a — a gift on Mr. Merrill's behalf. It was . . . it was for me."

She hesitated a moment, then, unfastening her cloak, she produced from within its folds a small velvet pouch, bound with a silken cord. Untying the cord, she reached into the pouch and withdrew the object within, holding it aloft for Ethan to see.

Having discerned that Constance was not in any immediate peril, the troubled crease in Ethan's brow dissolved, and he regarded the trinket she held aloft.

It was a necklace — a delicate silver knot entwining a stone of rare crimson.

Its brightly glittering brilliance presented a marked contrast to Constance's desolate visage, for her misery was apparent.

"'Tis a true-love knot," Constance whispered, her eyes downcast.

"Aye," Ethan nodded, taking the necklace from her and inspecting it more closely. "Plainly a token of affection." He looked at Constance, a warm gleam in his eye. "The giver must be well-familiar with his recipient, for I know Miss Constance to be fond of pretty things."

And with one finger, he lightly tapped the end of her pretty nose, so that she raised her eyes to meet his once more.

But his gentle teasing had done nothing to assuage her. She shook her head. "I care nothing for it!" she exclaimed with fervor, looking upon the necklace as if it were an object to be reviled. Then, ashamed of her outburst, the color rose upon her cheek. "That is, I — I know it was meant as a gesture of kindness on Mr. Merrill's part — and I do not wish to be ungrateful — but it is no mere trinket given between friends. A true-love knot implies something more . . . a higher regard between two people, which I do not feel toward Mr. Merrill . . . and even a — a promise of sorts. A promise I cannot give." She was very somber, her eyes once more cast down.

Ethan looked at her for a long moment, suddenly subdued. "No," he murmured. "No, you certainly cannot."

Constance met his gaze, momentarily diverted.

But once she had regained her senses — or perhaps been alerted by them to the precariousness of her position, with Ethan's head bent so near to her own, and her heart's pulsation suddenly accelerated — she turned away, forcing herself to resume her course of thought.

"Yet, neither can I refuse it," she continued disconsolately. "Anne is furious with me for even hesitating upon the matter — and rightfully so, for to refuse any gift is to offend the one who gave it, and to refuse such a gift as this would be a blatant rejection of Mr. Merrill's regard. It would bring disgrace upon my family, for such an affront cannot but put distance between the households implied. Mr. Merrill is no common suitor; he is a man of prominence and influence whose friendship has elevated my sister's family into the top circles of society and whose affiliation and generosity has allowed Mr. Porter's business to succeed and flourish, even under the shadow of the Merrill estate's trade. Even Caleb's education is owed to his benevolence."

Constance paused in her discourse, but though she yet remained with her back to Ethan, Ethan sensed that she had not finished and so did not interject.

Indeed, after a moment Constance continued, her tone diminished and remorseful: "For Polly and myself . . . our sister's husband has taken us in when he was not bound to do so. He has extended to us every hospitality, as would be accorded to his own blood relations. We are much indebted to him, though he would never allow us to utter such a sentiment. I cannot show myself so ungrateful as to bring disgrace upon his household." And here she ended, her head bowed under the ponderous weight of her cares.

A long and doleful silence followed. Neither did she turn to face Ethan, and so she gave a start when she suddenly felt something cold alight upon her breast, for Ethan had noiselessly stepped up behind her and placed the silver pendant about her throat. She turned her head slightly, but nothing more, for her breath was suspended in that moment as she sensed his nearness and felt his fingers brush lightly against the back of her neck as he fastened the clasp there.

It was undoubtedly a mutual heightening of awareness, for his touch lingered softly upon her neck even after the clasp was fastened.

Constance closed her eyes, succumbing to her senses, allowing them to transport her for one fleeting, yearning, tremulous moment. And even when she lifted her eyelids, she managed but a quivering breath as she felt Ethan's hands move across her shoulders as he gently turned her about to face him.

He spoke in a low, even tone. "I think that you must accept the gift . . . and pray that your father sends for you soon."

Tears welled in Constance's soft brown eyes. She nodded resignedly, as one who had known all along what the answer must be but had hoped against hope for an unperceived alternative.

Ethan reached forth and lightly fingered the pendant which hung at Constance's breast. "You would be the envy of all you see," he murmured. "Every girl in the county would wish to have such a token and the attentions of Mr. Zachary Merrill."

Constance's grief was not allayed. "I would be deceiving them all!" she cried out with unexpected vigor. Her momentary ardor dissipated at once, though, as she shook her head and repeated in a hushed, forlorn tone, "I would be deceiving them all." She thereupon looked up at Ethan, her eyes wide and beseeching. "But you . . . you know the truth. You know I harbor not this affection for Mr. Merrill."

Ethan gazed upon her. He sensed that herein lay the true heart of her affliction. Gently letting the pendant fall back upon her breast, he laid his hand upon her cheek, a reassuring warmth kindled in his eye. "Aye," he whispered. "I know."

Whatever might have happened next can only be conjectured, for at that moment — for the second time that day — a jarring knock upon the door abruptly breached the silence.

Neither Constance nor Ethan made any hasty movement, though. Their desire to remain near to one another temporarily eclipsed any other impetus. But it was a futile attempt to hold onto a moment that had already vanished with the reverberating intrusion of the world outside.

Turning his hand over, Ethan gently stroked Constance's cheek, then murmured, "Stay here," before he crossed to the door and pulled it open.

The tavern's proprietor stood in the corridor, looking wholly ill-at-ease. "Beggin' your pardon, Mr. Shaye," he began, evidently flustered, "but I . . . that is . . . well, the fact of the matter is . . . it's been brought to my attention that you have a . . . a lady in your room." The tavern-keeper inadvertently glanced at Constance before quickly reverting his focus back toward Ethan.

Ethan frowned. He knew well enough where Mr. Lethbridge had learned this information, and, glancing past Lethbridge's shoulder, he saw in the shadows of the dim corridor a familiar figure peering inquisitively at the young lady within the room.

Mr. Lethbridge went on: "We ask that our lodgers adhere to the rules of the house, one of which states that single gentlemen may not bring ladies to their rooms. I am sorry, Mr. Shaye, if that rule was not made known to you before today — although it is a common enough standard among reputable establishments."

Ethan looked upon his landlord severely. "Take care, sir, lest your words be construed as insulting to this lady and to my judgement."

Mr. Lethbridge's face reddened. "I meant no disrespect, Mr. Shaye. Indeed, you are one of our best lodgers, and anyone can see that your lady is as genteel as can be."

Constance blushed, as Mr. Lethbridge continued addressing Ethan:

"It is only that I must consider the other guests. It doesn't reflect well upon me if some are given an exception to the rules while others must abide by them." Even as he concluded his speech, Mr. Lethbridge yet appeared discomfited at having to thus confront one of his best patrons.

Ethan was truly irritated — primarily at the proprietor's daughter — but, for Constance's sake, he did not wish to prolong the scene. He made response to the tavern-keeper, though his words offered the landlord no reprieve: "At such a 'reputable establishment', I'd expect you to provide a room where a young lady may sit and wait in comfort instead of showing her into the tap-room."

The proprietor's countenance reddened further at this reproach.

"As it is," Ethan continued, "we have just concluded our discourse, and I shall be escorting the lady home."

Here, Constance stepped forward for the first time. "Oh no— you mustn't do that," she interjected, then immediately blushed again, realizing how peculiar her words must have seemed to those in the corridor. "I – I mean, Jenny accompanied me," she murmured, her face still flushed. "She is waiting in the stable yard."

Maria Lethbridge at last spoke up, peering round her father's shoulder. Her eyes were bright as she very deliberately addressed Ethan:

"You will not wish to miss your supper tonight, Mr. Shaye, for I've laid out a young rabbit for you. 'Tis your favorite, I well know." She cast a smugly triumphant look towards Constance.

Ethan merely glared at Maria and would not indulge her with a response.

Mr. Lethbridge, who truly did wish to mitigate the situation, bowed slightly to Constance. "I would be most pleased to escort the young lady downstairs. Maria— run down and fetch her servant and bring her round to the front."

Maria was not pleased at this command, as evidenced by her pouting visage, but she obeyed, sulkily retreating toward the stairwell.

Mr. Lethbridge smiled kindly at Constance and courteously extended his arm to her. "You'd best let me lead the way, Madam, for the stairwell is dark and narrow."

Constance smiled back at the old man, for she could see how well-meaning were his intentions. She graciously inclined her head and — casting a parting glance in Ethan's direction — took the proprietor's arm and allowed him to guide her toward the stairwell.

STILL THE RAINS PERSISTED, UNTIL the Rappahannock's banks were flooded, and every tributary footbridge and low-water crossing was washed out. The Porters' house and garden were set high enough to be spared, but all commerce upon the river was halted for a time, leading to much inconvenience for the townsfolk, as supplies in the shops could not be replenished.

But then, as suddenly as it had started, the rain stopped. After seemingly endless days of dreary, damp grey, the citizens of Merrilltown awoke to the unexpected warmth of sunlight cascading through their windowpanes, the nearly-forgotten brightness of sunbeams streaming across their faces and illuminating every corner of their chambers.

Throughout the town, shutters and doors were thrown open, and the citizenry emerged as if in accord, eager to break free from their weeks of confinement, descending upon the saturated streets as if it were a holiday, paying no heed to the lingering autumn chill, nor to the mud, nor to the massive puddles that stretched in every direction.

Constance did not venture into town that day, but instead settled herself with a book upon the sunny front steps of the house (for the lawn and garden were still water-logged), taking great pleasure in the quiet brightness of the sunlight falling across the words upon the page.

The stillness of the morning was interrupted by the sound of splashing hooves, and, glancing up from her book, Constance beheld a rider approaching from the Merrilltown road.

It was Ethan Shaye, reining in his horse at the Porters' gate.

Upon seeing him, Constance beamed, her countenance rivaling that of the radiant sunlight, for the glorious day had just grown even brighter for her.

Setting aside her book, she rose to her feet as Ethan dismounted, but before she had even started down the front walk, she paused in her step, for Ethan — having secured his mount to the post and retrieved some rolled documents from his saddle — had not turned in at the gate, but instead tarried there, his attention distracted by something further down the road.

Turning her own head to see what had distracted him, Constance saw approaching from the opposite direction another familiar figure — this one on foot with a musket slung over his back and hair as yellow as the sunlight which dappled the road before him.

As the two men exchanged good-natured greetings, Constance's smile widened, and she hastened down the path toward them, darting about the puddles with a light step.

"Tristan!" she exclaimed when she reached the gate. "We were not expecting you! How happy everyone shall be to see you! Good day to you, Mr. Shaye," she added as nonchalantly as possible, though her softly shining eyes betrayed a warmer sentiment.

Ethan made no reply (for indeed, Tristan had already commenced to speak) but momentarily shifted his gaze to meet Constance's — the hint of a knowing smile about his visage — before reverting his focus back to Joshua Porter's elder son, who was explaining his unexpected arrival.

"We've been given three days' leave before we muster on Thursday," Tristan said. "I must confess," he added, with a slight shake of his head, "after all these weeks in the rain-drenched camp, I am much looking forward to a warm, dry bed and a hot meal."

"Do come inside and put your things down," Constance beckoned graciously. "Everyone else has gone out, except Polly and me, but I am sure your stepmother would wish the cook to fry up some bacon for you, and we can open Polly's jar of black-currant jam. How pleased she shall be to have an appreciative patron!"

Tristan beamed, as Constance turned to Ethan, noting the documents in his hand. "I hope you will also take some refreshment, Mr.

Shaye," she bade, a bit shyly. "I know you must be about your work in the study, but perhaps you could delay it for just a short while — it is such a lovely occasion, with the sun out and Tristan returned."

She was so eager and appealing, Ethan could not help but give affirmation. Constance was clearly relishing her temporary role as mistress of the house. Ethan knew it was a role she had cherished at her father's home in Pennsylvania. Indeed, she made a charming hostess.

It was with a lighthearted gait that Constance led the way back up the path toward the house. The two men followed at a more leisurely pace, for Ethan wished to hear the news Tristan brought from the militia's camp.

Upon entering the house, however, the trio's buoyant mood quickly subsided, as it became immediately apparent that Constance had been mistaken about those present within.

As she crossed the central hall toward the parlor, Constance suddenly stopped where she was. Tristan, too, came to a standstill.

Although the parlor door was closed, there were muffled sounds emanating from within that room.

Constance's eyes widened in bewilderment.

It all happened so quickly — before anyone could have reacted. There emanated from the parlor a sort of scuffling sound, accompanied by a shrill exclamation, and then an indignantly feminine *"Oh! How dare you!"*. Then one more *"Oh!"*, as if in great exertion, and the parlor door was flung open, revealing Polly, her face flaming, her hair and gown disheveled. She came to an abrupt halt when she saw the three figures standing in the entrance hall. Gasping, her eyes filled with tears. Without a word, she darted across the room and scrambled up the stairs, stifling a choking sob.

Ethan, who had joined the others belatedly — having stopped to place his documents and Tristan's musket just inside the front door — arrived at Constance's side just in time to see Polly emerge from the parlor. But he quickly grasped the situation, as Monsieur Brisonneau appeared in the parlor doorway.

Brisonneau's voice trailed the fleeing girl: "Miss Polly you must not think—." The Frenchman broke off as he beheld the trio in the hall. His entire expression changed. "Ah, good afternoon," he greeted them with a saccharine smile, smoothing back his hair. "Or is it still morning? I have quite lost track of the time today. Master Tristan — I did not know you were at home. It is good to see you, as always. And now, you must excuse me. I have some business I must attend to down at the wharf. We must assess whether or not we can have any ships come through yet, though I suspect the water levels may yet be too high." And with a nod, he crossed the hall and departed through the back door.

Tristan emitted a sort of husky grunt and, with fists clenched, made as if to follow the dissolute Frenchman.

But Ethan swiftly reached out and gripped Tristan's arm, detaining him.

"Constance," Ethan murmured to that young lady, who still stood at his side, motionless. "Go up and attend to your sister."

Constance needed no further urging. Indeed, her eyes — full of dismay — had remained fixed upon the staircase, where her younger sibling had fled moments before. She hurried up after her now and disappeared down the corridor at the top of the steps.

Ethan did not yet loosen his grip upon Tristan's arm. "It is not your place to confront him," Ethan cautioned firmly. "You must leave that to your father."

Tristan's eyes — still upon the door through with the Frenchman had exited — blazed with anger. "How I should like to pummel him! He is a worthless bastard."

"Aye, that he is," Ethan agreed, as he released Tristan's arm. "Your father will undoubtedly turn him out."

But Tristan shook his head and responded in an unexpectedly bitter tone: "My father will not turn him out."

Ethan glanced sharply at him. But before he could elicit any further elaboration, the front door suddenly burst open, and, with a yelp, a small dog bounded into the hall and up the stairs, followed by Caleb Porter, who, with a *"Whoop!"* scampered up the steps after his pet.

The voice of Caleb's mother came drifting through the open door: "What is this? My book lying upon the damp steps?" The nearing voice was plainly vexed. "I lent it to Constance only this morning . . . and the pages left wide open to be bleached by the sunlight! Really, this is too careless of her." Still talking — to no one in particular, apparently, for she was alone — Anne Porter entered into the hall, holding the book gingerly before her. "I shall have to scold her and advise her that if she is entrusted with—." She broke off as she beheld the two men. "Goodness! Mr. Shaye— and Tristan! I had no idea you were— But how lovely that they let you come home when the sun is shining! Caleb will be so excited! You will have to be in with him again, of course, as Monsieur Brisonneau is still occupying your usual chamber. Has no one attended to you yet? Do run up and put on a clean shirt and breeches. I'll send Jenny in to fetch the ones you have on. I'll have her put them to the laundry at once."

But Tristan, who was still agitated by the earlier incident, merely glared at his father's wife and stalked sullenly out of the hall through the rear door.

Mrs. Porter stared after him, gaping. "Good heavens! What has gotten into everyone today? Constance being inordinately careless and quite absent in her duties as hostess . . . and Tristan entirely forgetting his manners! I must apologize, Mr. Shaye, for this aberrance in our usual hospitality. I shall leave Tristan for his father to deal with, and I shall have words with Constance at once." She gave a quick — but rather severe — glance at the book in her hand as she proceeded to the staircase. "I know you will want to get straight to your work in the study, Mr. Shaye. I shall send Betsy in with some coffee for you."

If Mrs. Porter was expecting Ethan to alleviate the strained atmosphere with a word of acknowledgement, she was bound to be disappointed, for her remarks were met with only austere silence. Hence, she tarried not, but continued on her way up the stairs.

❦

I⊤ SEEMED THAT TRISTAN DID indeed speak to his father about Monsieur Brisonneau, although the result was not entirely what Ethan had anticipated, for Brisonneau and Mr. Porter appeared to continue their business association. Several days after the incident, however, the Frenchman moved out of the Porters' residence and took up lodgings in town. Neither was Brisonneau present at any of the Porters' meals or social gatherings; indeed, Ethan never saw him set foot inside the Porters' house again, although he did occasionally glimpse the Frenchman in town or at the Porters' wharf, where he appeared to be still very much a part of the shipping operations.

It was a singularly odd situation. The fact that Brisonneau continued his association with the Merrilltown merchant assuredly spoke to the significance of their business dealings, although what those dealings entailed beyond customary trade, Ethan had not discovered.

❦

AFTER THE WEEKS OF RAIN and chill, it seemed that Nature was doing her best to appease the citizens of Virginia, for shortly after the rains ceased, a warm spell enveloped the region, bestowing unseasonably mild, pleasant days upon the Rappahannock valley.

Although the river itself remained swollen, the saturated earth quickly recovered, and on one such mild day, Ethan set forth across the eastern hills toward the river's tributary, determined to complete the endeavor begun more than a fortnight before, when the rains had commenced. He still knew not what drew him back there — only the sense that something must be reconciled in his mind, something that might be discerned once he was there.

He traversed the wooded hills more quickly this time — giving only a cursory glance in the direction of the ravine, where the sound of running water proved eminently more prominent than it had in the summer — and stayed upon his course, compelled by a specific purpose and destination.

Despite his swifter steps and higher degree of familiarity with the terrain, the forest was yet dense, even at the threshold of winter, undoubtedly spurred into new growth by the weeks of precipitation followed almost immediately by sunlight and warmth, and it took Ethan the better part of the morning to reach the tributary's bank.

Once there, he found that the landscape itself was altered, as the mossy bank upon which he had once stood was presently underwater; neither was the dilapidated pier visible, although its decaying wooden planks would undoubtedly reappear once the water receded.

The cacophony of the rushing water and exuberant birds lent a different air to the once silently-still haven, but it retained its familiarly, recalling to Ethan the emancipating hours he had spent beside and immersed in the tributary's waters.

He lingered at the spot but a moment, though, before turning his course northward, retracing the path that he had once followed toward the now-immersed pier. As he walked along the forest's edge, he recalled that there had been a series of piers at regular intervals, now all covered with water, but as he scanned the landscape before him, his eye fell upon a low wooden building, sagging in its dilapidated state. It was the abandoned warehouse, which had once sat at a comfortable distance from the tributary but was now perilously within the water's reach.

As he neared the structure, Ethan became aware of an awakening of his senses, and he paused in his step, turning his head first toward the water, then back toward the warehouse. He inhaled deeply, noting the heady, sweet aroma which pervaded the air and which he had noted once before, during his swim. Or was it twice that he had perceived the sweet fragrance? During his swim, he had attributed it to something growing near the bank — some sort of blossoming vegetation. But now, a different association arose in his mind . . . only a vague stirring of familiarity, but it was somehow linked with a memory. And somehow it did not reconcile with his previous notion regarding the plant growth along the bank. No, he must clear from his mind all preconceived inferences, for they were inhibiting his ability to identify the aroma's source. Frowning in concentration, he resumed his course in the direction of the abandoned warehouse, though his pace was slower as he attempted to reconcile the present infiltration of his senses with an ambiguous memory. The fragrance grew more and more conspicuous as he neared the dilapidated building.

And then, all at once, Ethan remembered.

And he paused again in his step.

He remembered . . . remembered where he had been the second time he had perceived that sweet aroma. It was at the Porters' dinner-table the night of Anne Porter's birthday. Ethan recalled how the fragrance had made an impression upon his senses then. The sweet pudding with the sour cherry sauce. But now he knew . . . it was not the aroma of the sauce that had formed a connection in his memory; no, it was the pudding itself, with its heady fragrance of molasses — the same fragrance of which he had been vaguely aware, but had failed to identify, during his invigorating summer's-day swim in the tributary's refreshing waters.

Now, with his eye fixed upon the wooden structure before him, Ethan strode with purposeful step up to the warehouse's door.

Here was assuredly the aroma's source, for the fragrance quite engulfed him — its sweetness almost repulsively pungent.

Facing the river, the structure's wide door, though nearly falling off its hinges, was bolted and secured with a padlock. Two narrow windows, set quite high in the wall, were boarded up.

Ethan circled the building and observed two more windows, similarly boarded, set into the structure's rear wall. Here, though, the plank covering one of the windows was poorly attached and rotting. This plank was easily dislodged, and through the narrowest of openings which was subsequently exposed, Ethan was able to peer into the warehouse's interior.

It took a moment for his eyes to adjust to the darkness, for the bit of sunlight which traversed the window's meager opening gave scant illumination. But slowly he was able to discern tangible elements of the structure's interior. It consisted of a single room; indeed, he could see along the opposite wall slender threads of light seeping through the cracks around the warehouse's wide door. But, contrary to his initial assumption — and substantiating his present one — the ancient warehouse was most definitely not abandoned. Barrels — row upon row of them, uniform in dimension — filled the dusky space. They were stacked nearly to the ceiling, and the heady fragrance enveloping everything left no doubt as to their contents.

Shifting his focus slightly downward, Ethan scrutinized the stack of barrels nearest the window.

Despite the warehouse's age and the dankness of the atmosphere, the barrels were quite intact and showed no signs of deterioration or neglect. In the dim light streaming through the window's narrow opening, Ethan could even make out a merchant's insignia etched onto one of the barrels. The insignia consisted of a triangle trisected by two lines at forty-five-degree angles, creating a diamond within the triangle. It was a mark with which Ethan was unfamiliar.

Ethan surveyed the warehouse's contents with perplexity.

With the trade restrictions imposed by the British at the start of the war, molasses was all but impossible to obtain in the colonies. If a blockade runner had succeeded in smuggling a shipment into Virginia, the merchants there would unquestionably pay a pretty sum for the rare commodity.

So why was a formidable quantity of the prized substance sitting locked up in a remote, seemingly-abandoned warehouse?

Every aspect of it suggested a desire for covertness. But why?

Ethan could not conceive of any explanation.

Stepping away from the window, Ethan made his way back around the building's exterior to the front. Standing at the river's edge, he surveyed his surroundings.

Upon his previous expedition to the spot, he had assumed this tract of land belonged to the Merrill estate. Was the eminent Judge Merrill the owner of — or at least cognizant of — the stock of molasses? While that possibility would appear to tidily correspond to the fact that the judge's grandson had acquired a supply of the substance, it was yet a very unsatisfactory explanation.

Ethan racked his brain, trying to recall the conversation at the table upon the occasion of Anne Porter's birthday, wishing he had paid closer heed to the discourse. Zachary Merrill had admitted to providing the molasses for the pudding, but where had he acquired it? An explanation had been given, but Ethan could not recall the details other than a vague recollection that the molasses had been purchased somewhere. Ethan was certain that Zachary Merrill had made no mention of his grandfather in connection with the substance. It was, of course, entirely possible that the judge's grandson knew nothing of the barrels stowed in the warehouse or of his grandfather's possession of such. It was equally possible, however, that Zachary Merrill *was* aware of it and had fabricated an explanation in order to conceal his grandfather's affiliation with the acquisition.

Ethan's brow furrowed as he gazed unseeing into the rushing water before him.

None of this seemed plausible, as he could not conceive of any reason for Judge Merrill to have hidden a large quantity of molasses to begin with. Even had it been embezzled, which was likely, that was hardly a crime in this region and would, in fact, be a welcome commodity for the merchants of Merrilltown and beyond.

Although Ethan had no personal stake in the matter and no real reason to take any interest in it, the situation nonetheless aroused his curiosity, and he pondered it further.

While he had assumed this tract of land to be part of the Merrill estate, he had no real foundation for such an assumption, other than the fact that he had crossed the Merrill property en route to this spot. But he did not truly know where the property lines were drawn, as there were no fences or other demarcations visible in the wilderness. Neither was he familiar with the other landowners in the vicinity surrounding

Merrilltown, and he must concede that it was entirely possible the warehouse and decaying piers belonged to someone whose property was adjacent to the Merrill estate.

Or —

A third possibility presented itself.

The area was so remote, so seemingly untraversed . . . it was conceivable that some cunning smuggler might be utilizing the decrepit warehouse without the knowledge or permission of the property's owner, whomever that might be. The cache was unlikely to be discovered, at least for some period of time.

In the end, Ethan could only shake his head and turn his course back toward civilization. He had spent far too long puzzling over something which likely had an innocuous explanation. While the circumstance had temporarily awakened his curiosity, he must own that he was not likely ever to learn the explanation behind the barrels of molasses or the reason for their presence in the decaying warehouse beside the tributary's rushing waters.

As he walked back through the woods, Ethan determined he'd pay a visit to Henry Dowling. After so many days confined indoors during the rain, Ethan had completed nearly all he could on the maps without taking more measurements, and he decided to concentrate on the survey of Clymer's property. Indeed, he'd nearly finished Joshua Porter's survey and was getting concerned that he'd have little excuse to remain in the area if he didn't slow the pace of the map-making. Moreover, he would welcome a chance to visit with his friend, whom he had not seen in many weeks, and to hear the latest news from their regiment.

So, when he emerged from the forest and descended the hill, he took not the road before him, which led back to town, but turned his course westward toward the river path, for he must stop at the Porter house to retrieve some drafting tools he'd left in the study there.

Although the main path along the river was yet damp, it was intact, for the waters of the wide Rappahannock had already begun to recede upon the rain's cessation, and Ethan could quite easily and quickly traverse the narrow footpath.

However, as he rounded a thicket which grew at a bend in the river, he came to an abrupt halt as he spotted a familiar party standing on the riverbank a short distance ahead. The ensemble consisted of Anne Porter and her sisters, Tristan Porter, and Zachary Merrill. Merrill's slave Thaddeus stood nearby. Two wooden boats — a small, white-painted wherry and a somewhat larger bateau — were moored alongside the bank. Constance and Polly Jameson were each holding a covered basket, and an earthenware jug was set upon the ground at Tristan's feet. Several members of the party appeared to be engaged in animated discourse.

Although it was yet some distance from them that Ethan had paused in his step, Anne Porter spotted him nearly at once. She smiled and waved at him, bidding him to approach.

"Mr. Shaye!" she called out eagerly, as the others turned their heads in his direction.

Ethan proceeded along the path unhurriedly — to the chagrin of Mrs. Porter, who was plainly impatient that he should reach them. It was she who stepped forth to meet him as he neared.

"Mr. Shaye! You cannot know how well-timed was your appearance!" Mrs. Porter exclaimed.

Ethan regarded her with cautious silence as he came to a stop where the group was assembled.

Brief nods and murmurs of greeting were put forth by the others as Mrs. Porter continued:

"We had the loveliest plan for an outing — a picnic at Mott's Point."

"Or, more rightly, Mott's *Island*," Polly Jameson interposed, her eyes bright with uncharacteristic animation. "That is the true purpose of our outing. The peninsula has been flooded over, except for the tip, which sits on higher ground, making an island in the midst of the channel! It shall disappear when the water recedes, but for now it shall make the most cunning spot for a picnic!"

Mrs. Porter, who had temporarily deferred to her youngest sister's enthusiasm, now took up the discourse again: "We were to take the bateau, but then Mr. Merrill showed us the little wherry, which has just received a fresh coat of paint, and Polly was quite enamored of it and insists that she and Tristan ride in the wherry — though I set the condition that Constance and Mr. Merrill must have it on the way home. But therein lies our dilemma, Mr. Shaye; the wherry is fit for two, but one hand cannot row the bateau. However, if *you* would graciously consent to join our party . . . you and Mr. Merrill could each take an oar and handily take two ladies in the bateau!"

Though Mrs. Porter was evidently delighted with the scheme, Ethan frowned.

"The water is yet too turbulent," he asserted. "It is too soon to venture out upon it, especially in such small craft."

This unexpected dissent was met with momentary silence from the others.

Polly frowned.

Mrs. Porter tittered incredulously. "Why, Mr. Shaye! I am surprised at your opposition! One needs only look at these boats moored here to see that the river is nearly as calm as it has ever been. And we cannot wait another day, or our island may disappear, and there would be an end to our plan!"

Ethan shook his head, his scowl deepening. "The river is wide here, but the channels are still flooded well over their banks. I have just seen the tributary north of here — its waters are far too rough to navigate, and 'twould be foolish to attempt on an even narrower channel." Though he ostensibly spoke to the whole group, he looked directly at Constance as he added: "It is too dangerous an endeavor."

Wide-eyed, Constance held his gaze for but a moment, then turned away, casting her eyes uncertainly toward the river.

Polly was not pleased with the course of the conversation. "You needn't come at all if you don't wish, Mr. Shaye," she pronounced contrarily. "Mr. Merrill has already stated that Thaddeus might take an oar."

"Oh no!" Mrs. Porter objected fretfully. "We don't want any servants along! That would spoil everything!"

Thaddeus remained properly aloof at this reference, as Mrs. Porter continued entreatingly:

"Mr. Shaye, with all due respect, you are still relatively new to this region, and I think we must defer to the judgement of Mr. Merrill and Tristan, who are well familiar with these waters. I am sure they would not have consented to such an expedition if it posed any possibility of danger or discomfort to us."

Neither Zachary Merrill nor Tristan seemed eager to corroborate this, though, as both were eyeing the river with new wariness.

Polly positively glowered and tossed her head impatiently. "Oh! I am tired of this tarrying. Let us be off! Come, Tristan!" And still grasping her basket, she flounced off toward the boats.

Tristan hesitated a moment, then followed.

But Constance had been watching Ethan throughout this discourse. She had seen his eyes flash darkly beneath his furrowed brow, his temper manifestly provoked at the obstinacy of the eldest and youngest sisters. And when he glanced then at Constance, she knew that he was further frustrated by his inability to speak to her directly. He would forbid her to go; and she would obey. But he did not know . . . he did not know how she trusted him, how she knew him to be the most capable of the party in assessing the natural environment, for she could not speak out so before the others. She could only remain helplessly silent, and he must remain thus vexed.

Neither did his dark scowl abate as he stepped forward and took Constance's basket from her.

Then — as his eye chanced to fall upon her neckline — he added rather acerbically, "Charming bauble you're sporting today."

Constance blushed as her hand instinctively rose to her throat, fingering the silver and crimson true-love knot that encircled it. She knew

Ethan had only remarked upon it because he was cross, but nevertheless, she averted her eyes as he proceeded down the footpath toward the boats.

Mrs. Porter followed, smiling blithely at the prospect of their undelayed outing.

Constance and Mr. Merrill were left in a rather awkward situation, as Mr. Merrill had not thought to assist Constance with her basket, and Ethan had taken it up with seemingly casual ease. Nevertheless, after only the slightest uncomfortable pause, Mr. Merrill gallantly proffered his arm to Constance — which she took as graciously as she could — and, following a directive to Thaddeus to fetch the earthenware jug, Merrill escorted Constance down to the boats.

Ethan and Tristan had already loaded both baskets onto the larger bateau, and Tristan and Polly were starting to push off in the small wherry.

Ethan stood in the stern of the larger boat, and Anne Porter had situated herself at the front, for she insisted that Mr. Merrill and Constance take the wider bench at the boat's center. (It was surely mere coincidence that the narrow bench at the front would afford Mrs. Porter the best view.).

Ethan said nothing — still glowering, still not reconciled to the judiciousness of the endeavor.

Mr. Merrill handed Constance into the boat, settled himself beside her upon the middle bench, and took up his oar.

Ethan took the jug from Thaddeus and placed it beside him in the stern. Then, as Thaddeus bowed and retreated at Mr. Merrill's command, Ethan loosed the ropes that held fast the boat and pushed off, guiding the vessel slightly away from the riverbank in the wake of the little wherry.

At first, no one spoke, as the men were engaged at their oars, and the ladies were taking in the scenery and acclimating themselves to the boat's motion. But after a time, Anne Porter and Polly began to call out to one another, pointing out interesting sights along the riverbank or exclaiming over the delight of their adventure.

Constance said very little, only occasionally responding to a comment directed at her from one of her sisters, but she remained quietly watchful of both the landscape and the river . . . and every now and then stole a glance at the man in the stern, who yet remained broodingly reticent as he guided the vessel along.

In truth, all three of the men kept silent, for the river's current, though traversable, was stronger than usual, and their energies were necessarily focused upon keeping their boats on course.

But the day was truly lovely and the ride pleasant for the ladies, and it appeared that Ethan's cautions may have been overstated.

However, when the boats were guided off of the river into a narrower channel, the situation changed nearly at once. The current intensified, speeding the vessels onward with little regard to the rowers' maneuvering, and Tristan and Polly's lighter craft was swiftly carried ahead of the other, despite Anne Porter's admonishing cries of "Tristan! Slow down! You are getting too far ahead!"

The bateau, with its pair of oarsmen and weightier load, was somewhat more manageable, but the narrow channel's churning waters rocked the vessel perilously, as Ethan and Zachary Merrill struggled to overcome the current's will in bringing the boat nearer to the bank.

Even Anne Porter fell silent in deference to the rowers' exertions and the rushing water's momentum.

Constance, wide-eyed and pale, clutched onto the side of the boat.

To the further dismay of the party in the larger boat, Tristan's small wherry suddenly surged out of sight.

"Oh, what has happened to them?" Anne Porter uttered anxiously, her voice barely audible against the current's din.

Zachary Merrill momentarily stilled his oar and scanned the horizon. "They have just rounded the bend," he assured Mrs. Porter. "We shall see them again in a moment."

Indeed, the bateau was fast approaching the channel bend, and though they did regain sight of Tristan's boat on the other side, it brought them but little comfort, for the lighter craft was yet far in the distance and moving still rapidly. The waters on the far side of the bend, in fact, proved to be more treacherous than those previously encountered, for though the channel widened, its course became more winding, its swift current giving way to swollen rapids.

A stone bridge appeared in the distance.

"Mott's Point is just on the other side of the bridge!" Merrill called back to Ethan.

But Ethan did not respond. He suddenly straightened, his vigilant eye fixed upon the scene before him, his brow knit ominously. "Tristan!" he shouted. "Look sharp! The bridge! Turn your boat!"

Constance, turning in her seat, saw what had precipitated Ethan's warning, and her heart was gripped with fear. The stone bridge's broad arch, under which a pleasure boat could easily pass, seemed to have disappeared. Instead of the wide arch, there was visible only a narrow slit, the channel's water having risen so high as to leave only a few feet of space beneath the bridge; certainly it was not enough clearance to allow passage of even an empty vessel, yet Tristan's small wherry was careering toward it, in spite of Tristan's frantic efforts to turn the boat toward the bank.

The imminent danger to the smaller craft had scarcely registered with the occupants of the bateau when their thoughts were suddenly diverted by the precariousness of their own situation.

Striking some unseen protrusion beneath the water's surface, the larger boat lurched violently, pitching the vessel's objects and occupants into upheaval. One of the baskets was propelled overboard, and the earthenware jug shattered as it smashed into the side of the boat.

Mrs. Porter shrieked, clutching desperately at the bow-plank in front of her.

Constance was likewise distressed. "Ethan!" she cried out in fright, instinctively reaching for him and nearly losing her balance as she did so.

Ethan, turning his head at the sound of her voice, managed to keep one hand upon his oar and grab hold of her with the other. "Steady now," he murmured, his voice reassuring, as he lowered her onto the bench nearest him.

Breathless and relieved to be thus situated at his side, Constance grasped onto the low stern-wall, as Ethan quickly resumed command of his oar.

Zachary Merrill did not recover as quickly, for in the tumult he had momentarily lost hold of his oar, and it was only with a stroke of luck that he was able to retrieve it without himself plunging overboard, though he was thoroughly soaked in the process.

And when the boat, caught suddenly in a strong undercurrent, began to turn sharply and swiftly, it took the full strength of both men upon their oars to prevent the vessel from capsizing.

"Merrill!" Ethan shouted amidst the din. "Put your shoulder into it! I'm going to bring her around toward the shore!"

It was then plain to all that there would be no chance of reaching Tristan and Polly, nor was the prospect of altering the course toward the bank comforting, for nothing resembling a soft landing-place could be observed.

"We're taking in water!" Zachary Merrill bellowed of a sudden.

Ethan glanced quickly downward and saw that there was indeed a narrow gash in the flat bottom of the vessel, where the bateau had struck the underwater protrusion. He did not pause in his efforts, though, but redoubled his exertions upon the oar, gritting his teeth and directing every ounce of his strength into turning the boat eastward, until the bateau was facing the shore.

Propelled against the current, the vessel moved slowly, heaving and pitching in protest against a noisy backdrop of rushing water, creaking oars, and Anne Porter's wailing about the water pooling at her feet, for the breach had occurred in the bow.

"Hold her steady!" Ethan suddenly called to Merrill, as he himself let off his oar.

Moving swiftly, Ethan seized the coil of mooring-rope at his feet and tied one end of it onto the stern-latch, looping the other end into a wide knot.

Constance watched Ethan's face as he intently scanned the shoreline.

He frowned as he scanned it again, finally fixating upon a leaf-bare tree several yards from the bank.

But as Constance followed his line of sight to the tree and back again, she saw that his look of discontent yet remained. Nevertheless, with his eye still fixed upon the distant tree, he swung the knotted rope up over his head, then cast the length of it toward the bank. The rope's loop narrowly missed a low-hanging branch of the tree.

Still frowning, Ethan gave a shake of his head and quickly retracted the rope, shifting his balance to counter the boat's incessant rocking. Wasting no time — for in truth, Merrill was having great difficulty maintaining the boat's position with his single oar — Ethan cast the rope once again toward the shore. It caught upon the tree's branch, but immediately slipped off again, falling to the ground below.

Ethan cursed under his breath.

Reeling in the line of rope once more, he made no further attempts at casting it, but instead transitioned swiftly to another course of action. Sitting down momentarily on the bench beside Constance, he hastily pulled off his boots, then, grasping the rope's end, coiled it beneath his arm, never slowing his urgent pace of motion.

Constance watched apprehensively as Ethan stepped up onto the bench, the rope still wound about one shoulder — his movements so swift as to permit no unsteadiness against the boat's heaving.

At once, Constance was filled with alarm. "What are you doing?" she cried out imploringly.

But Ethan did not pause. "Stay there," he charged her, then dove over the side of the boat into the churning waters below.

Anne Porter screamed. "Mr. Shaye! What is he doing? Oh, he shall be killed!" she shrieked hysterically.

Constance remained silent, her face ashen, her knuckles as white as her face, as, in her anxiety, she gripped the side of the boat with tense rigidity. Her eyes remained fixed upon the head bobbing in the rushing water below.

A man could easily get swept away in that current.

Ethan was a strong swimmer, but the force of the water's turbulence and the friction of swimming sidelong against the current hindered any notion of speed. He kept on with unrelenting purpose, though, for what seemed an eternity to the boat's breathless occupants, until, at last, he reached the steep bank.

Despite his exertions, Ethan scrambled up the bank with alacrity, compelled by the urgency of the situation, and moved swiftly to anchor the rope around the solid trunk of a sturdy oak tree. Running back to the bank's edge, he pulled the rope taut and called out to Zachary Merrill, who once more pulled upon his oar, and the two men working in tandem — Merrill rowing and Ethan reeling in the rope —managed to maneuver the vessel toward the shore.

"All right, ease up now!" Ethan shouted to Merrill, securing the rope about a burgeoning root that protruded at the water's edge. Merrill stayed his oar, and Ethan — still soaked from his swim — positioned himself on the ledge nearest the boat's stern.

Constance, yet petrified, remained seated fast upon the stern-bench and looked uncertainly up at the steep bank, which was still several feet above her.

Ethan crouched down and extended his hand toward her. "Here, take my hand!" he commanded.

Constance rose, wobbling a bit due to the boat's movement beneath her feet, then reached her hand up toward Ethan's. He grasped it firmly and pulled her up just far enough until he could put his arms about her to lift her onto the bank.

Depositing her thus safely upon solid ground, he then turned back toward the boat, where the two remaining occupants were having some difficulty.

Mrs. Porter, in her haste to exit the waterlogged vessel, had stood before she was bidden and immediately lost her footing as she tried to climb over the benches toward the stern, thus redistributing the weight within the boat and causing it to tilt precariously, half submerging the bow, where the water had already penetrated the floorboards from the rift. With a high-pitched yelp she flung herself toward Mr. Merrill, clutching wildly at his waistcoat. Merrill, unprepared for this sudden weight thrown upon him, fell backward, scraping his back and shoulder upon the oar shaft. After some moments of confusion, the two of them somehow managed to extricate themselves from the awkward heap into which they had fallen, though Merrill's shirt was torn and blood already seeping through its back. Keeping a tight grip upon the lady, lest she once again unsettle the boat, Merrill maneuvered her over the benches to the stern, where she was within reach of Ethan, who quickly pulled her up to the bank.

Merrill hastily gathered what items he could from the boat — Ethan's boots among them — and tossed them up onto the bank before himself scrambling to safety; and none too soon, for scarcely had Mr. Merrill set foot upon the ground when the poor, beleaguered bateau sank completely beneath the channel's undulating waves, with only a corner of the stern, still held fast by the taut rope, yet visible above the water's surface.

There could be no respite for the two men of the party, though, and as soon as Zachary Merrill reached the bank, Ethan set off running in the direction of the stone bridge, where the cries of the pair in the smaller boat could be heard above the current's roar.

Merrill followed upon Ethan's heels but had taken only a few strides when he perceptibly slowed his gait.

Ethan, glancing over his shoulder, observed that Merrill had fallen behind. Pausing in his own step, Ethan saw the judge's grandson stagger, grimacing. As Merrill turned slightly, Ethan could see that the back of his shirt near the right shoulder was saturated with blood.

"Look after yourself, man!" Ethan charged him, then turned back toward the distant bridge, redoubling his efforts to achieve it.

As Ethan approached the bridge, he quickly grasped the situation.

Tristan had managed to steer the small boat to one side — thus avoiding the bridge's low arch — but had very nearly crashed the vessel into the bridge's stone wall, averting collision only by thrusting his oar out before him, thus breaking the force of impact upon the boat, but snapping his oar in two.

When Ethan arrived at the bridge, Tristan was applying every ounce of strength to keeping the boat from smashing into the stone wall, pressing the remnant of his oar into a space beneath one of the bridge's stones — the splintered oar and the length of his own arm all that separated the small craft from disaster.

Ethan ran up onto the bridge and leaned over its low stone wall just above the spot where the wherry bobbed in perilous proximity to the structure.

Polly looked up at him, her eyes wide with fear. "Oh, Mr. Shaye!" she cried, manifestly terrified. "Please help us!"

Ethan swiftly surveyed the scene below. The boat was a good distance from the top of the bridge, and Tristan — struggling to keep the wherry from slamming into the stone structure — could do naught besides maintain his stance. Getting them off the boat would prove a formidable task. Ethan quickly scanned the bridge's surroundings, then once again looked down into the boat, gauging the resources immediately available to him. He must act quickly, before Tristan's strength was spent or the oar slipped free.

Ethan called down to Polly: "Listen — do exactly as I say!"

Polly gave a tense nod.

Ethan went on: "Untie the mooring rope from its shaft," he directed, "then toss it up to me."

The rope's shaft was only inches from where Polly sat, and she quickly set about untying it. In her anxiety, though, her usually-nimble fingers moved clumsily, and the rope was tightly knotted, so it took some minutes before it came loose in her hand. As the remaining length of rope already lay coiled in the bottom of the boat, Polly was able to quickly gather it up and wind the loose end into the coil, standing shakily once she had finished.

She glanced up at Ethan, who extended one hand.

"Toss it up to me!" he reiterated somewhat gruffly, for Polly had hesitated with the rope in hand.

Palms upward, Polly flung the rope coil out of the boat, the momentum compelling her back into her seat.

The rope, however, propelled by neither a great amount of strength nor intensity, fell far short of its mark, forcing Ethan to extend the full length of his torso over the bridge's low wall in order to grasp onto the rope with his outstretched hand. This he did adroitly, though, and without delay straightened himself and took hold of one end of the rope.

To Polly's astonishment, Ethan then tossed the remaining coil back into the boat below, where it landed only inches from her feet.

"Tie it about Tristan's waist!" Ethan shouted to her over the wall. "Tight as you're able!"

Polly just sat there, gaping at him.

"Do as he says!" Tristan growled through clenched teeth. "Hurry!"

And for once, Polly made no retort, but rose gingerly to her feet, the end of the rope in her hand. Moving as quickly as she could, she positioned herself behind Tristan and circled the rope about his abdomen, pulling it snugly.

Tristan nodded. "That's all right," he affirmed between gasping breaths. "Knot it well," he added, shifting his weight slightly against the bracing oar.

Polly tied the rope into a rather overly-large but secure knot then glanced up at Ethan, who had in the meantime loosely fastened the opposite end of the rope to a low branch just beside the bridge.

Ethan then established himself upon the near end of the stone structure, where it curved downward to meet the river bank. When he saw that Polly had finished securing the rope about Tristan, he motioned to her.

"Come this way!" Ethan called out to Polly. "You must move to this end of the boat!"

Polly shifted her gaze uncertainly to the boat's stern. "But how—," she began, for Tristan, with his bracing stance, stood between her and the far end of the boat.

"Go under," Tristan urged with heaving breath, nodding toward his extended arm.

Polly stood fixed for but a moment, then stepped carefully around Tristan, bending to take hold of the wherry's side as she ducked beneath his arm. Despite the urgency of the situation, she moved slowly, taking care that she should not touch him or his arm, lest she upset his stance. Moving her hand carefully along the rim of the boat, she edged her way past Tristan and did not right herself until she reached the stern-wall, where the bridge's contour was much lower as it sloped downward to the bank.

Even so, it was still a fair distance to the top of the bridge wall.

Ethan, however, seemed unconcerned about this distance. Straddling the bridge's stone wall, with one foot upon the bridge's surface and the other dangling over the water, he bent down toward the boat's stern.

Polly slowly started to reach upward, then abruptly shrank back, shaking her head. "The weight will be too much," she intoned plaintively. "'Twill bring us both down."

Ethan frowned impatiently. "There is no time for fretting. You must trust me! Now, give me your hand."

Polly yet hesitated, then once more reached her hand upward, stretching as far as she could upon her toes until she felt a firm hand grasp her by the wrist. Before she could so much as utter a fearful "Oh!", she felt herself being pulled quickly and forcefully upward. She was conscious for the briefest second of her legs dangling high above the river, then was dimly cognizant of her own weight bearing down upon her feet as she was released upon the blessedly solid surface of the bridge.

It had all happened in a blur, but she managed to stay aright, steadying herself upon the low wall and gulping in air.

Ethan, though his exertions had left him winded, had not the luxury of tarrying on the bridge, and after only a moment's pause to catch his breath, he made his way quickly back to the riverbank and to the rope which he had fastened about the low branch there.

Swiftly loosing the rope — the other end of which was still cinched about Tristan's waist — Ethan braced it against the smooth trunk of a nearby smaller tree, then ran back to the water's edge, clutching the rope's end.

"Tristan!" he called out to Joshua Porter's son. "You're going to have to swim. I've got the rope and will pull you to shore, but you must look out for the boat. Hold fast to the oar until I give the signal, then jump from the port side as quickly as you can and head for the riverbank."

Tristan gave a curt nod, though his face was grimly taut. And Ethan, despite the forthright manner with which he had issued the instructions, knew that Tristan comprehended the danger of the plan. There was no alternative, though, under the circumstances, without anyone else to give aid and every passing minute increasing Tristan's fatigue.

Ethan's eye remained fast upon the boat, watching it rise and fall with the current. "Don't move," he murmured, though Tristan could not hear. "Not yet . . . not yet . . ." Then— "Now!" Ethan shouted. "Jump!"

And Tristan moved without hesitation, dropping the oar and plunging over the port side as the boat pulled away from the bridge.

There was a brief moment of disorientation as Tristan surfaced amid the rollicking waves, but Ethan lost no time on his part and pulled with all his strength upon the rope. Tristan sputtered amid the whirling current as the boat came crashing down not three feet away, but he felt the rope's pull and hastily started swimming toward the bank.

In spite of Ethan pulling on the rope, progress was slow against the force of the river, but just as Tristan neared the shore, Ethan suddenly felt a lurch upon the rope, the unexpectedness of which nearly caused him to lose his grip upon it.

Turning his head, Ethan found himself face to face with Zachary Merrill. Merrill was bereft of shirtsleeves and fitted with a rudimentary bandage about one shoulder (undoubtedly Constance's handiwork), but he was nonetheless positioned directly behind Ethan and lending additional force to the rescue effort.

With no time to express either surprise or gratitude, Ethan merely nodded in acknowledgement of Merrill's assistance, then resumed his own endeavors upon the rope. With the combined strength of both men, the rescue proceeded at a faster pace, and within minutes, Ethan was grasping Tristan by the hand, pulling him up onto the steep bank.

Tristan — exhausted and soaked — promptly collapsed upon the coarse grass.

Polly, who had by that time made her way off of the bridge, rushed to Tristan's side, and her sisters, too, hurried forth, much relieved to see their kin safely on dry land.

The pretty little wherry, with no weight inside and no brace separating it from the bridge, had crashed into the structure's stone wall, splintering its boards, the remnants of which continued to heave against the merciless stone until the vessel was battered beyond recognition and sank beneath the waves.

As Ethan climbed back up to level ground, he glanced in the direction of Zachary Merrill, who was unloosing the rope from the tree.

And Ethan halted mid-step.

For an instant, he forgot about his fatigue, his drenched body, and the group upon the riverbank.

Indeed, he was quite astonished by what he saw.

For Zachary Merrill, with his arms divested of shirtsleeves, had imprinted upon his broad upper arm a conspicuous mark which Ethan immediately recognized. It was the mark Ethan had first observed only hours earlier — the triangular insignia which was etched upon the barrels in the decrepit warehouse.

But whereas the figure on the barrels was but carved in wood, the same design marked upon Zachary Merrill's arm was rendered in vivid color, clarifying the insignia's details. And with that illumination, Ethan realized that he had been mistaken in his initial impression of the symbol's attributes. The angled lines trisecting the triangle's interior were not intended to form a diamond, but rather constituted the central angles of a more familiar symbol, now plainly discernible with its red hue inlaid against the black shaded triangle's congruent sides.

It was the letter M . . .

Ethan did not tarry, for the rest of the party was making its way up the bank, where they settled upon softer ground to rest.

Ethan and Tristan, both soaked to the skin, shed their shirts, and Polly fretted over Tristan, who — with a grimace upon his face — cradled one wrist precariously. Zachary Merrill, too, seemed to be in some discomfort, as he adjusted the improvised bandage about his shoulder.

Constance, who had emerged from the ordeal quite the driest member of the party, silently seated herself at the edge of the group, and Ethan, his chest heaving after his exertions, stretched out upon the ground beside her.

Though his body at last could rest, there was no respite for Ethan's mind, which remained very much alert, attempting to sort out and process what he had observed.

The barrels in the warehouse . . . imprinted with the same insignia marked upon Zachary Merrill's arm . . . the symbol's attributes now so clearly delineated:

M for Merrill.

And the black triangle — branded onto the wooden barrels of molasses — no doubt signified more than just a geometric adornment.

Yet, rather than elucidate circumstances, the correlating symbols did little more than raise new questions. While Ethan could assuredly ascertain now that the warehouse and its contents were the property of the Merrill estate, he could not help but wonder, considering the warehouse's location and condition, if both grandfather and grandson were aware of its existence. And if Judge Merrill was somehow involved in the clandestine purchase of embargoed goods, what could he hope to profit beyond the commerce of the Virginia merchants, who would undoubtedly be willing to pay a great deal for such a precious commodity? Was the Judge merely keeping it in reserve, waiting for a time when profit margins would be even higher? That seemed hardly plausible, when the stock was already utterly depleted, even in the port cities. Truly, it would cast the respected and benevolent Judge in a very contradictory light.

Then, too, while Ethan had spent very little time on the Merrill estate or in the presence of the illustrious magistrate, he could not recall ever seeing the symbol before. If it adorned the Merrill carriages or livery, he had taken no notice of it.

But what did it all mean, if anything? Like as not, he was looking for controversy where there was none.

His thoughts were disrupted when, out of the corner of his eye, he glimpsed some movement.

Turning his head, he saw that Constance was staring at him — not at his face, but rather at his chest, now barren of cover, and it was her hand, slowly stealing toward it, that he had perceived. Constance seemed to be entirely lost in thought, however . . . her gaze unseeing, oblivious to her own movements. But Ethan knew well enough what it was she saw upon his chest that so arrested her, and, raising his own hand, he gently obstructed hers.

Startled out of her reverie, Constance glanced at Ethan's face as he shook his head in warning.

Blushing furiously, Constance hastily retracted her hand and quickly looked away.

But when she shifted her gaze past Ethan toward the other members of the party — for it was her instinctive reaction to ascertain that no one else had witnessed her momentary lack of discretion — she was dismayed to meet the eye of her elder sister, who was looking at Constance so fixedly, so contemplatively, that Constance could have no doubt that Anne had indeed observed the preceding incident, brief and subtle though it had been.

IT WAS AN EXHAUSTED, BEDRAGGLED party that trudged through the Porters' front door two hours later, having been compelled in their state of disarray to avoid the main roads and keep to the river bank.

Mrs. Porter, too weary to pay heed to the housegirl's gaping at her unkempt appearance, immediately sent one servant to fetch the doctor and another to summon her husband, who, upon arrival, was duly astonished at the sight of his wife, son, and guests — indecorously disheveled as they were.

As the rest of the company filed into the parlor to await the doctor and take some refreshment, Constance laid a soft hand upon Ethan's arm, detaining him until the others had exited the hall.

Then— "Come with me," she whispered, beckoning him toward the staircase.

If Ethan was surprised or puzzled by her bidding, he did not voice such, but instead acquiesced, silently following her up the stairs. They ascended with some haste, despite their fatigue, for Constance was perceptively anxious and scurried up the steps quickly, glancing more than once over the banister, lest anyone should suddenly appear in the hall below and observe them.

But once they had achieved the upper corridor and were safely inside her bedchamber — the door shut tight behind them — Constance breathed a sigh of relief and looked up at Ethan with earnest eyes.

"Ethan — you were right about the river, and we ought to have heeded your words. It was foolish of us to endeavor — and I was most foolish, because I more than any know that you . . . And then it all went so — so terribly—," she broke off, shaking her head remorsefully. "I am sorry you were put to so much trouble today."

Ethan sought to reassure her. "Do not dwell upon it more. 'Tis a shame about the boats, though."

Constance smiled shyly at him, the warmth in her eyes more eloquent than any words of gratitude. "You must be weary; truly, you exerted yourself far more than anyone else today. You can rest here until the doctor arrives." She crossed to the bed and propped up the pillows. "'Twill be far more comfortable than sitting in the parlor with the others."

Ethan gave a shake of his head. "I am not in need of a doctor. But," he added with a rueful grin, "I cannot deny, that pillow looks immensely appealing right now. I could do with a bit of rest before heading back to town."

As he took a step toward the bed, Constance looked at him with a newly-critical eye. "Goodness, you cannot possibly to go back to town looking like that. Give me your things—" She blushed, then hastily added, "Your shirt, I mean. I'll set it to dry before the fire."

Ethan duly handed over his shirt then leaned upon the bed to remove his boots as Constance crossed to the fireplace, shirt in hand.

"I wish there was time enough to launder it," she mused, spreading the shirt out upon the back of a chair before the fire. "Jenny could— oh!" she interrupted herself. "Oh dear," she murmured, examining the dampened garment more closely. "I'm afraid you've torn the sleeve. And here, too, at the seam." She proceeded to inspect the rest of it. "I can mend it once it's dry, but—," she sighed resignedly, "I'm afraid you will look rather a sight going into town."

She glanced down at her own frock, which was also less than pristine after the day's adventure, and, as she busied herself before the fire, silently contemplated whether she dared slip out into an adjacent chamber to don a fresh gown. Before she could come to a resolution on the matter, though, her train of thought was unexpectedly diverted by the sound of Ethan's voice:

"Is this your mother?"

Glancing back toward the bed, Constance saw that Ethan had settled himself against the pillows and was holding a framed miniature which he had picked up from the bedside table.

Smiling reproachfully, Constance rose from the hearth and crossed to the bed. "You are supposed to be resting," she reprimanded, though any attempt at reproachfulness faded as she neared, her eye upon the diminutive portrait. She gave a nod of her head as Ethan handed the miniature to her. "Aye," she murmured. "My father gave it to my safe-keeping before — before we parted."

The slight quiver in her voice was not lost upon Ethan.

Constance reverently ran a light finger over the portrait's delicate surface. "He bade me give it to Anne. He knew that it would be safer here than — than where he was going." She shook her head sadly. "Even so . . . I know how difficult it was for him to part with it. 'Tis the only likeness he has of her."

Constance slipped into a reverie, and Ethan — well-aware of the depth of her emotions — broke not the silence with movement nor word.

After a moment, Constance recovered her senses with a sigh and placed the portrait back upon the table. "Anne lets me keep it in here sometimes. She knows it brings me some comfort. But truly—," Constance turned her attention back to Ethan, "you'd better rest a bit while you can. For you mustn't stay here long, else Polly will surely be up, or Anne will come looking for me. And besides . . . I must tend to your shirt."

In spite of this pronouncement, Constance lingered at the bedside, for Ethan was regarding her in such a manner that Constance was reluctant to sever her own gaze.

They did not need to speak to each know the other's thoughts . . . indeed, with Ethan stretched out upon the bed and Constance at his side, they could not help but recall the garret and all that had transpired there so many months ago.

It was the second time that day that Constance had been drawn into the past, and as she had done earlier upon the riverbank, she allowed her eye to fall upon Ethan's chest . . . and the scar yet visible below his shoulder. This time, though, as her hand slowly and inadvertently stretched toward it, Ethan did not impede her.

Thus transfixed, her expression both tender and troubled, Constance softly touched the scar's surface, her fingers as tremulous as her heart's beat. Her voice was not more than a whisper: "This should have healed long ago, had you been given a physician's proper care."

Ethan's own gaze remained intent upon Constance's face, even as his hand encircled her fingers, gently lifting them from the scar. He spoke low, but with conviction. "No doctor could have cared for me so tenderly, nor looked after me half so well."

Ethan was rarely so forthright in his sentiment, and the color rose prettily upon Constance's cheek. And even as she withdrew her hand from his, she moved closer, perching on the edge of the bed, facing him. "Truly, I cannot take credit," she asserted. "'Twas Jenny who did most of the labor in healing you."

Ethan ruminated over her words, his visage gradually transformed as his brow furrowed. "She did it only to please you," he said. "She bears no regard for me. I thought I knew why, in the garret, but her mistrust is yet evident here, where you are safe."

Constance did not immediately respond but cast her eyes downward, reflecting. When at last she spoke, it was very softly. "Jenny is somewhat protective of me, I think. She—" Constance paused, hesitating. She lifted her eyes to meet Ethan's once more. "She knows there are some wounds that cannot be healed with a splint or a bandage."

Ethan gazed at her a long moment, frowning broodingly. Then, slowly leaning forward, his fingers took hold of the pendant about her neck — Constance's throat blushing furiously beneath the touch of his hand.

"To whom would Jenny entrust you, I wonder?" Ethan murmured sullenly, even as Constance's breast throbbed with increasing intensity.

All at once, Ethan gave a sudden and forceful flick of his wrist, breaking the clasp of the delicate chain and releasing the love-knot into his grasp.

Constance gasped, but before she could so much as comprehend what had happened, she felt his lips press against hers and heard the soft "clink" of the bauble falling to the floor as his arms enfolded her. After that, she was aware of nothing except the rapturous surging of blood within her veins as Ethan Shaye kissed her for the second time.

Just as in the twilight garden, there was no uncertainty in his embrace — it was charged with the intensity and purpose of one who was taking full possession of what was rightfully his own.

And when at last he released her lips, he yet bent his head close to hers, and Constance became aware of the rapid rise and fall of his chest — a testament to the depth of his passion.

They lingered there, suspended in the moment, until Ethan somehow mastered his senses and whispered:

"Now . . . you'd best go tend to your things at the fire."

And Constance, yet unable to speak, could do no more than nod breathlessly and obey, for she well understood his meaning and the precariousness of their situation. Scrambling to her feet, she hastened to the fireside, thus putting the necessary distance between them, though her breast still pulsated fervently, and her cheek remained flushed crimson.

Seated upon her wooden chair before the hearth, with Ethan's shirt upon her lap and her sewing basket at her feet, Constance kept her focus fastidiously before her. She dared not even a glance over her shoulder in the direction of the bed, for if she should find Ethan looking at her in the way that he had — with that fire kindled in his eye — she knew she would be utterly lost to her resolve and would fly to his arms once more.

As it was, it remained yet a long while before she could steady her heart's beating and truly concentrate on her mending.

A stillness enveloped the room, and for the next half-hour the only sound to be heard was the occasional crackling of embers upon the fire.

Constance heard no stirring behind her, and she presumed that Ethan had at last fallen asleep. Once the mending was completed to her satisfaction, however, and she finally arose from her seat and turned toward the bed with the repaired garment in hand, she saw that Ethan was not sleeping at all, but was instead lounging against the pillows, very much awake, although he appeared to be deep in thought.

It was with the softest of treads that Constance approached, and not until she had reached the bedside did Ethan emerge from his reverie and take note of her. Even then, he regarded her for a long moment before he finally spoke:

"I think that I shall ride out to Harry Dowling's place tomorrow. I would take you with me, if you will go."

He could not help but smile at Constance's reaction to his words, for her eyes immediately lit up, and — heedlessly discarding the shirt upon the bed — she clasped her hands together with an eagerness that both pleased and amused Ethan.

"Let us hope that Dowling will be as delighted to see us," he said with a laugh. "We may need to shake him out of bed, as early as we'll be presenting ourselves. We must set out from McCreary's orchard at sunrise, before any travelers are out upon the high road."

Constance's expression turned to one of puzzlement, and she tilted her head inquisitively to one side. "But how shall I — shall we—"

She had no chance to complete her sentence, but broke off suddenly with a sharp intake of breath, for at that moment the sound of the door latch was heard. Turning her head quickly toward the door, Constance had not time to take more than two steps back from the bed before her elder sister's voice preceded that lady into the room.

"Constance? Oh, you are up here! Doctor Harwood is just leaving, so you'd—" Mrs. Porter's voice broke off abruptly as she sighted Ethan. "Why, Mr. Shaye!" she exclaimed in surprise. "I had no idea that you were still here."

The lady's astonishment was evident — not only at Ethan's presence in the room, but at his state of undress, for the shirt still lay upon the bedcovering beside him where Constance had deposited it only moments before.

Ethan, however, remained coolly composed. Whereas Constance had scrambled to distance herself from the bed, Ethan — who was far more practiced at diverting suspicions — maintained an air of nonchalance.

"Aye, Miss Constance was good enough to mend my shirt, so I'd be fit to return to town without drawing attention. I would not have presumed to ask such a deed of her if I'd known it would consume so much of her time. I confess to knowing nothing of such domestic tasks and thought it would take but a moment. As it is—," he rose from the bed and took up the shirt, "she had just finished it and was insisting that I go down to see the doctor before I head back."

And he proceeded to don the shirt as Anne Porter glanced at Constance, who remained yet silent.

After a pause, Mrs. Porter again addressed Ethan, who was by that time fully clothed and in the process of pulling on his boots. "Yes, well . . . I am glad that Constance was able to assist you. If you hurry, you may yet detain the doctor before he leaves." Mrs. Porter looked once more to Constance, whose eyes were self-consciously averted. "I would have some words with Constance before she goes about her business."

Constance glanced up at her sister. Something in Anne's tone filled Constance with trepidation and made her dearly wish to avoid the imminent dialogue. As always, though, her virtue would best her, for try as she might, she never could come up with an excuse where she had none, and so she could do no more than remain silent as Ethan took his leave with a curt bow to the mistress of the house, who reciprocated with a staid nod.

Once the door had closed behind him, however, Anne turned — a visibly cool, accusing gleam in her eye. She addressed Constance slowly and with purpose, punctuating each word with steely precision:

"You are in love with Ethan Shaye."

It was not a statement; it was an accusation.

Constance was so stunned by her sister's words and tone that she could not immediately think or react, but could only stare speechlessly, at last emitting a faintly murmured, "No . . . no—"

But Anne cut her off sharply. "You are in love with Mr. Shaye," she reiterated vehemently, "when you know full well it is Mr. Merrill who is the only man worthy of your regard."

Constance felt her face flaming, and she shook her head. "It — it isn't true—," she faltered.

"Do not deny it!" Anne interposed. "I have watched you on more than one occasion, though you have never displayed your preference more conspicuously than this afternoon. I pray that no others were observing you so closely. Foolish girl! You would cast your affections on a merely handsome figure rather than on a truly worthy gentleman — a worthy gentleman who elevates your status by his very association and who has visibly demonstrated his esteem for you above all others — an esteem which you have appeared to reciprocate, I might add!"

Shrinking wretchedly under her sister's contemptuous eye and harsh tone, Constance struggled to give voice to her own defense. "No, I — I—," she stammered miserably, "I am not in love with anyone. Besides," she added, averting her eyes, "I cannot see that it is any concern of yours whom I should love."

"Well, there's a pretty contradiction if I ever heard one!"

The scorn in Anne's voice cut into Constance like a dagger, and whatever slight measure of composure Constance had remaining evaporated as tears sprang into her eyes.

Sensing this further weakening, Anne took a step nearer her sister, merciless in her purpose. With narrowed eyes, she spoke to Constance in a low, even tone which had lost none of its hardness: "You have always been a silly, foolish little thing, but you are no longer a child. You must come to your senses and think about your future — and that of your family. Or have you forgotten about all but yourself and your petty fancies? Have you forgotten that your father has lost nearly all that he — that *you* — possessed? Have you no thought for him or for Polly? Or did you intend that I should continue to provide for you indefinitely? Would you take advantage of my husband's benevolence in order to indulge your girlish fancies?"

Constance turned away, anguished by her sister's acerbic castigation.

Still, Anne did not relent. "Mr. Merrill could provide for all of you — and more! Not to mention the fact that you have certainly led Mr. Merrill — and indeed all of us — to believe that your favorable reception of his attentions was based upon your manifest regard for him. Was it all a ruse on your part? You have many faults, I am sure, but I never would have thought deceit to be among them!"

Poor Constance, whose heart had never known an ounce of deceit, was overcome with distress at the nature of such an accusation, and though her back remained turned, her affliction was apparent to her elder sibling.

Anne at last took some scant pity on her sister. She moved a step closer to Constance, her voice taking on a tone of reason: "I am sorry if this topic discomforts you, Constance. In the absence of our mother, it is my duty to guide you in these matters and to remind you of your obligations; just as it is your place to acknowledge and defer to my wisdom and experience, for I have already tread the path upon which you now venture. Certainly no one can blame you for having your head turned by a man like Mr. Shaye — he has, on more than one occasion, demonstrated a . . . physical prowess . . . that would naturally appeal to any young girl. But you are past the age of childish notions. You are a woman, however young, and must embrace the responsibilities of your sex. I need hardly remind you that a woman's primary obligation in life is to marry — and more than that, to marry as well as she can. And you—," Anne's voice heightened with conviction, "you have been presented with an opportunity far beyond what most in your position could expect. An opportunity to secure a future of comfort and prosperity for yourself and your offspring; to aid your family; to ally yourself with a man distinguished not only by the prominence of his lineage, but by the very worthiness of his character, which is assuredly of paramount importance to one of your sensitivities. Such an opportunity will not present itself again, and I urge you to accord it the weight it entails."

If Anne expected the strength of her words to elicit a response from Constance, she was bound to be disappointed, for Constance remained yet silent nor did she even turn to face her elder sister.

Indeed, Constance stood as motionless as a statue, her eyes fixed dully upon the window before her — yet seeing only a dark abyss. A pang which had taken root in her abdomen upon mention of an alliance with Zachary Merrill had spread slowly throughout her body, rendering her whole being inert with bleak numbness.

Anne, dissatisfied with this lack of response, frowned silently at her sister's back for a long moment. Then, emitting a weary sigh, she stepped up beside Constance, slipping her arm though her sister's. "There now," Anne intoned soothingly. "You must not let this trouble you. I am not upset with you. I know what it is to be young and in need of guidance. You simply needed someone to set you back upon your course. I am glad that we nipped this in the bud while there is still time to set everything aright."

Constance remained yet mute.

Anne was not deterred, though. With her arm yet entwined through Constance's, she gently eased her around and guided her toward the door.

"Now," Anne continued, her tone yet pacifying, "let us go back downstairs and see if Mr. Merrill isn't—"

She broke off, halting suddenly in her step.

Constance at last glanced at her sister and, with a terrible sinking feeling, realized at once what it was Anne's eye had fallen upon.

Relinquishing Constance's arm, Anne stepped closer to the bed, and Constance watched in dismay as her sister bent to retrieve from the floor the shining silver and crimson object that had caught her eye. As Anne picked up the delicate chain, the pendant fell from it, for the clasp was truly severed.

Constance stood as if frozen, as her sister stared contemplatively at the love-knot for what seemed an eternity before bending once more to retrieve it.

Cradling both pendant and chain in one hand, Anne rose slowly, and her eyes, when she raised them to meet Constance's, flashed with icy fury.

When Anne at last spoke, the frigid tone of her words cut through the air with a sharp, deliberate chill:

"You ungrateful, deceitful girl. Have you no shame?"

And Constance, who must remain silent as to the cause of the necklace's state, succumbed to her misery and — unable to bear the cold severity of her sister's condemnation — buried her face in her hands.

Constance's anguish only served to pique Anne's ire. "Aye, it is right you should cover your face, wretched girl! I think you'd better stay in here after all. You have a great deal to ponder — and I am grateful that I bear not your burden of atonement, for you have an onerous task before you in determining how you shall make amends to Mr. Merrill. At present, you are unworthy to even look upon his face."

And, knowing well the effect such a scathing rebuke would have upon her tender-hearted sister, Anne swept out of the room, leaving behind the broken necklace and the bitter sting of her displeasure.

Constance was not the only one to witness an unforeseen alteration in demeanor of a member of the Porter family that day.

After leaving the upstairs bedchamber, Ethan did not directly depart from the premises, nor did he seek out the doctor as proposed, but instead, upon descending the stairs and finding the lower hall deserted, he stole noiselessly into Joshua Porter's study, that he might examine the logbook once more, for he yet hoped its chronology would reveal to him the evidence he sought.

Leaving the hall door slightly ajar in order to provide some illumination to the windowless room, Ethan crossed to the shelf behind Porter's desk. But as he reached for the familiar logbook, he paused, for he became aware of the sound of voices in the vicinity. Turning his head, Ethan saw that the door to the parlor was not closed tight upon its hinge, thus allowing the muffled sounds emanating from that room to filter into the study.

Ethan hesitated, debating whether he should attempt to secure the door before proceeding, for it was open but a fraction and could conceivably be closed without drawing attention.

Moving silently, Ethan laid his hand upon the door-latch . . . but there paused again. Although he could not see into the parlor beyond, the voices therein became audible and diverted his attention.

"—keep it bound tight, and you will have use of it again in a few weeks," came the hearty voice of Doctor Harwood. "The pain may yet worsen before it subsides, but you will find it to decrease significantly after four or five days. I am sure you will take it in stride, Master Tristan — and by the sound of it, we should be thankful it was not worse that befell ye, eh?"

The doctor's tone was jovial, but Tristan's response — which Ethan could not fully discern — sounded characteristically abrupt.

The doctor then continued: "I shall be off then. I must look in on Mistress Nolan before returning home; she's been ailing again, and I fear the worst for her. Good-day to you, Porter . . . Master Tristan."

Ethan heard Joshua Porter's voice congenially reciprocate. Then, the sound of receding footsteps indicated the doctor's departure.

What Ethan heard next, though, caught him off-guard, for Joshua Porter — now apparently alone with his son — addressed Tristan in a tone Ethan had never heard the merchant adopt.

"Damn it, Tristan!" Porter growled angrily. "A broken wrist! What were you thinking?" Tristan started to respond, but his father cut him off— "Nay! Do not speak. 'Tis plain you were *not* thinking. And you talk of going to sea one day! A fine sailor you will make . . . you cannot even command a rowboat upon a stream! 'Twas a foolish endeavor all round. And now — you have jeopardized all that we have worked to achieve."

Ethan listened intently. Joshua Porter's uncharacteristically harsh words had been underscored not with a tone of cruelty, but rather that of consummate frustration.

Tristan would yet attempt to defend himself. "What would you have had me do?" he rejoined heatedly. "You cannot fathom what the—"

"What would I have had you do?" Porter interjected, his voice low but unmistakable in its authority. His next words were not uttered hastily, but with precision. "I would have you act as a man. But I must remember that you are yet a boy."

The ensuing silence was long and acute in its depth.

When Joshua Porter spoke again, it was with resignation, his tone markedly weary. "Now go. I must have time to think — to contemplate how we shall extract ourselves from this entanglement."

Tristan made no further attempt to defend or explain his actions, and after another long pause, the sound of quiet footsteps indicated that he had retreated from his father's presence.

Ethan remained where he was for a moment, straining to hear any nearing footfall which would indicate that Joshua Porter was crossing toward the study door, but stillness enveloped the room beyond, and Ethan guessed that Porter had situated himself in one of the parlor chairs.

Leaving the door as it was, Ethan crossed silently back to the desk and swiftly pulled the logbook from its shelf. Placing it upon the desk's surface, he hastily flipped through its pages until he came to the registry's last entries. Straining to see in the dim light, he scanned the page's contents, running a finger down the list of dates and names until he came to the column's end. And there, as his eye rested upon the most recently-dated records, his heartbeat quickened. For beside the last two entries was scrawled the single, stark word: *Intercepted*.

IT WAS NEARLY DARK WHEN Ethan departed the Porters' house; yet he did not hasten in his steps, but tread slowly the road back to Merrilltown. To be sure, his body was weary after the long and physically-demanding day; but his mind was ever active and had much to ponder upon the trek back into town.

All that had come to light that day — the barrels in the warehouse, the triangular inscription, the mark upon Zachary Merrill's arm, the heated confrontation between Joshua Porter and his son, the ominous entries in the logbook — Ethan turned it all over in his mind again and again, attempting to synthesize the seemingly disparate circumstances. He felt certain there must be connections among at least some of them . . . but which ones? And which — if any — were relevant to his mission?

He could make no sense of it, yet at the same time he felt he was on the brink of discovering something — *something* — which would shed illumination upon the treasonous scheme he was attempting to uncover. And though he had not yet laid plain the facts or uncovered the perpetrator, his consciousness was infused with a new and indomitable conviction; for fomenting beneath the myriad of unanswered questions was a familiar vitality — the instinctive, invigorating command of a hunter closing in on his prey.

WHEN POLLY TENTATIVELY PUSHED OPEN the door to Constance's bedchamber later that evening, she found a despondent Constance sitting upon the bed, still wearing the rumpled frock she'd had on during the boating incident.

"Why Con, whatever is the matter?" Polly cried in concern, hurrying to her sister's side. "Are you still shaken by our mishap upon the water today?"

Constance stared at Polly blankly for a moment, as if she did not comprehend the question. But then, lowering her eyes, she gave a slight shake of her head.

Polly had ready insight, though, and leaned nearer in confidence. "'Twas something Anne said to you, wasn't it? She came down the stairs earlier today looking black as daggers, and I knew she'd had words with someone . . . she was positively seething all through dinner. But dearest Con — you did not make an appearance at the dinner table, and I am certain she must have said something to distress you."

Polly waited patiently for her sister's response, and when Constance finally spoke, it was yet listlessly, with eyes remaining downcast.

"Anne says that I . . . that I am not in love with Mr. Merrill as I ought to be."

Polly's brow knit into a practical frown, and she made no immediate response but instead pondered a moment before giving a shrug of her shoulders. "Well, what of it?" she said. "Mr. Merrill's qualities are rather insipid, and I cannot imagine that he would be any girl's ideal suitor, except that he has money. Anne is thinking only of herself and of the increase in her own prestige should her sister form an alliance with the local gentry. You have merely upset her scheme to put herself at the head of Merrilltown society, that is all. Think no more on it. Besides, she knows that our father would never give his blessing to such an alliance, however wealthy the suitor, for Mr. Merrill is at the front of the Patriots' cause. Undoubtedly, Anne thinks that her own relations with Father would be eased under such circumstances. You must not fall prey to her tactics, though, nor allow her to intimidate you with her accusations. Father will likely send for us soon enough, and then we can put all of this behind us." Polly concluded her speech by giving her sister's hand a squeeze.

Constance, however, made no reply, for though she knew her younger sister meant well, in truth she could glean little comfort from Polly's assurances, nor could she confide in Polly the entirety of their elder sibling's displeasure.

CONSTANCE SPENT A SLEEPLESS NIGHT, as a torrent of divergent thoughts assaulted her slumber. She tossed and turned upon her pillow, as the previous day's events played out over and over in her mind — from the anguish of her dialogue with Anne, to the breathless exhilaration of being held in Ethan's arms; from the strenuous fright of the misadventure upon the river, to the eager anticipation of the next morning's excursion — her thoughts and emotions vied with one another throughout the duration of the long, restless night.

But with the nearing of dawn, one train of thought came to supersede all others, and it was thus with a sense of anticipation that she slipped noiselessly out of bed before the first rays of sunlight were prominent enough to be discerned by any but the most watchful eye.

PART III: THE TOWN

Though it was still dark at the hour Constance left the house, when she reached McCreary's orchard she found Ethan already there waiting for her. She could not discern him at first in the darkness as she approached, but she spotted the flickering light of his lantern through the silhouetted trees. It was a welcome sight and sped her steps, so that in only a moment's time she had achieved the end of the orchard's rows.

Ethan, who had perceived her approach, came forward to meet her with his lantern in hand, and as he led her back toward the pasture fence, Constance slowed her step, for in the burgeoning grey light of dawn she discerned before her the equipage intended to convey her to Clymer's farm. It was, by its appearance, a lightweight two-wheeled chaise, and as they neared, Constance hurried forth to inspect it.

Hitched to the chaise was an unfamiliar and unremarkable horse, toward which Constance gave only a cursory glance; but the vehicle itself was quite handsome in its sturdy simplicity.

"Why, it is very pretty!" Constance exclaimed admiringly. She started to reach her hand up to touch the side of the chaise, when she paused, as a thought occurred to her. She looked back over her shoulder at Ethan. "Where did you come by it?" she asked, a bit dubiously.

Ethan's eye twinkled in amusement. "You are a suspicious little thing! I pray you may never be called upon to give witness to my character in a court of law — I shall be convicted for certain."

Constance bit her lip to conceal her own smile at his gentle teasing.

"If you must know," Ethan went on, as he set about attaching the lantern to the side of the chaise, "I procured it quite legitimately from an acquaintance at Lethbridge's, who very cheerily lent it to me after I paid out his wager for him at the card table. I assured him I'd have the equipage returned intact by half past one. And—," he added, turning back toward Constance, "I even promised to throw in a bushel of oats for the horse. How should that please you?"

326

His grin was as jaunty as his stance as he leaned against the wheel's rim, and Constance's eyes danced merrily as she hastened to him.

"It does indeed!" she laughed happily, for truly her pleasure at the excursion was evident, as was the warmth of her smile for Ethan Shaye.

And it was with equal pleasure that Ethan observed her thus, because, somehow, Constance's happiness mattered a great deal to him.

"Let us be off then!" he declared. "Dowling is sorely in want of company, and though he knows nothing of our visit, once we present ourselves he shall undoubtedly be eager for us to tarry as long as possible." And taking from Constance the basket she held in one hand — into which she had thoughtfully tucked a jar of figs and a wedge of cheese for their unsuspecting host — Ethan placed it inside the chaise, then handed Constance up. After untethering the horse, he moved swiftly round to the opposite side of the chaise and hopped agilely up into the box, taking up the reins and urging the horse toward the high road, just as the sun's rays broke through the trees with certainty.

So it was with light hearts and contented smiles that the party of two left Merrilltown behind them and set out for Clymer's farm.

It was the pleasantest of journeys; Ethan regaled Constance with tales of his adventures with Henry Dowling, which elicited from Constance by turns wide-eyed breathlessness and merry laughter, for the two men had undertaken as many lively exploits — both daring and jocular — as any two brothers might have.

The journey, in truth, took a good bit longer than it might otherwise have, for Ethan did not hurry the horse but kept it at a steady gait, for though both individuals in the chaise looked forward to the achievement of their excursion's destination, they were truly content to tarry upon the journey . . . to savor the rare opportunity to be thus together in solitude.

The venture was lengthened further when they were compelled to stop for a herd of cows crossing in the road before them, driven to pasture by a youth of thirteen or fourteen. Though the herd was not large, the youth made no effort to speed his charges, but rather let them amble at a leisurely pace; indeed, the boy seemed happy at the unexpected meeting with the occupants of the chaise, conversing with them in a friendly manner and eagerly inquiring as to the news from town and upon the war front. This exchange was prolonged beyond the herd's passage, but the cows were treading a well-worn path and appeared amenable to their master's tarrying a bit. The youth, once apprised of the news from town, imparted to his new acquaintances the latest hearsay from the country-side, which amounted to an account of Widow Hansen's runaway mule and his own father's acquisition of a secondhand ox cart.

Just before departing, the boy leaned in toward Ethan and confided in a loud whisper, "'Tis a very pretty lady you have, sir", which implication caused Constance to blush profusely. Ethan, however took it in as a matter of course, and, stealing a glance at his fair companion, nodded his concurrence with a grin and a warm, "Aye, she is," which further intensified both Constance's blush and her delight.

And so the boy, quite satisfied at having passed the time of day so pleasantly, ran off to catch up with his herd, happily munching the figs which Constance had presented to him from her basket; and Ethan and Constance resumed their journey.

They had not gone far, though, when Constance bade Ethan to stop once again, for she had spotted along the wayside a cluster of wildflowers blooming quite out of season, their delicate blossoms coaxed forth by the previous week's misleadingly mild temperatures.

Ethan obliged and waited good-naturedly as Constance gathered the blossoms. He noted with satisfaction as he observed her how prettily was her cheek tinged with a soft, rosy glow, and how brightly her eyes shone as she smiled up at him from amidst the flowers.

"I only hope they shall last until we reach Mr. Dowling's," Constance declared earnestly, as Ethan helped her back into the chaise, "for I am certain that such a bachelor's house must be in want of some color and adornment."

Ethan laughed and could not deny it.

He took up the reins once more and set the chaise again upon its course, this time to continue without further interruption until the horse was drawn to a halt in the stable yard of Clymer's property.

As Ethan attended to the horse, Constance waited beside the chaise, looking about her with interest. Everything about the little farm was modest, from the house itself — unpainted and so small as to be assuredly but one room and a loft — to the stable and handful of tiny dependencies surrounding the stable yard. At first glance, it was typically picturesque in its simplicity, though closer inspection would have revealed that the buildings and yard were in some state of disrepair, owing to the property having but a sole proprietor — and a temporary one at that — who had no real vested interest in maintaining it beyond the appearance of habitation and who had not even a servant to assist in the upkeep.

This train of thought led Constance to contemplate further the farm's tenant, to whom she would momentarily be introduced. Was Henry Dowling like Ethan — handsome and daring and sure of himself? Constance felt suddenly bashful and pulled her cloak tighter about her.

After securing the horse, Ethan also looked about him, not observing as Constance did, but assessing. The late hour of their arrival all but assured that Dowling was no longer abed, but as he had not come out to meet them, Ethan thought it likely that his friend was not in the house nor in the vicinity of the stable yard at all. He glanced toward the house's smokeless chimney, wondering if Henry had set off upon some errand or other. Ethan frowned. Perhaps he ought to have sent word of their visit.

Uncertain as to how long they may have to wait for Dowling's return, and conscious of the morning's briskness, Ethan determined to settle Constance inside the house — it would take but a moment to light a fire for her comfort — then he himself would take a look about the dependencies and fields.

He beckoned to Constance and started toward the house.

Constance did not hurry forth, though — her sudden bashfulness having taken hold of her — but tarried a moment before following him at a distance.

So it was that Ethan reached the house well before Constance, and

he gave a cursory rap upon the door, which, as expected, produced neither response nor movement from within. He pushed the door open,
calling, "Dowling? Dowling, are you there?"

Ethan did not immediately enter into the house's single room, but
paused upon the threshold, allowing his eyes to adjust to the grey dimness of the interior.

But then, once his eyes could discern, how quickly did his manner
change, as his senses were jarred violently into realization. It was, indeed,
a brutal assault upon his perception which caused him to start fiercely.

For the room was not unoccupied as he had suspected.

Henry Dowling was in the room.

And Henry Dowling was dead.

Even as Ethan's mind reeled savagely, his soldier's instincts took
possession of his faculties as he heard Constance's light footfall behind
him.

"Stay back!" Ethan commanded gruffly, barring the door so
Constance could not see into the house. "Get back — back!" he repeated,
then, without waiting for her reaction or reply, he entered swiftly into the
house, shutting the door behind him.

He could not allow Constance to see what lay beyond the door, to
see that which had so savagely hammered his senses moments before
and which now presented itself before him again with the grim horror
of reality. For death had not merely entered Henry Dowling's house, but
had overtaken it by the most appallingly sinister of means.

Like a spectral puppet upon a string, the grey, lifeless body of Henry
Dowling dangled ominously before Ethan's eyes, suspended from the
dwelling's rafters by a rope about the neck, pivoting slightly in the draft
of the hastily-closed door.

From the moment he had comprehended the situation, instinct rather than intellect had gripped Ethan's faculties, and it was that visceral
reaction which propelled him toward the silent corpse. It was that sus-
pension of logic and perception which overpowered the intensity of his
heartbeat — fiercely pounding against his ribcage — and which led him

to right the overturned chair at the room's center, to climb upon it and reach up to sever the rope that hung taught from the rafters; nor was he yet wakened to reason when the full weight of the lifeless body fell with a thud to the floor of the room.

But then, only seconds later, Ethan's faculties were jolted into wakefulness once more. For as he dismounted from the chair, knocking it over again in his haste, his eye fell upon Henry Dowling's back, and Ethan's brow knit darkly as he crouched beside the overturned body.

Henry's linen shirt was stained red with blood — blood that had been violently expelled from the jagged, gaping crevice between his shoulder blades, where a lead ball had torn through flesh and muscle.

Ethan contemplated the wound for but a moment; he had seen enough of battle and bloodshed to know that the lead ball had been fired at no great distance and that such a point of entry would prove instantly lethal.

As his mind assimilated this stark revision of circumstance, Ethan turned the body over upon its back and examined the corpse's neck, which, in spite of the rope, was only slightly bruised. Neither was the noose pulled tight about it.

Frowning in deliberation, Ethan stood up and surveyed the room, his sharp eye quick to discern anything therein that may provide insight into the circumstances of Henry's death.

His eye fixed nearly at once upon a small wooden table pushed up against the opposite wall. Henry had utilized the table as a makeshift writing desk, and the chair beside it — identical to the chair which had been left beside the body at the center of the room — was likewise overturned.

As Ethan crossed toward the table, he noted that the floorboards were spattered with blood, the mottled stains creating a crimson-black trail across the room.

In addition to the overturned chair beside the table, everything upon the table's surface was in disarray. Papers were strewn about; the inkstand was pushed precariously close to the table's edge; the chamberstick was tipped over upon its side. Near the table, several sheets of paper lay scattered upon the floor alongside a feathered quill. All of the articles upon the floor were bloodstained; none more so than the chair, from which the trail of blood originated, leading to the noose across the room.

As Ethan bent to inspect the chair, his eye chanced to pass over the papers scattered around it, and at once his attention was arrested by the words upon one of the pages.

It was his own name that caught his eye.

Leaving the chair as it was, Ethan hastily retrieved the paper from the floor, noting how the page was smeared with ink and blood, rendering some of the words nearly illegible. There were, indeed, not many words upon the page, but their significance was not lost upon Ethan, and his heart pounded as he read the message penned in Henry's familiar, crude hand:

Lt. Shaye,

You must come at once. I cannot give details here, but I have discovered the identity of the—

The final word was scarcely discernible, the ink having smeared through most of the letters, as if the author had been abruptly startled, his task interrupted, never to be completed.

Ethan stood there a long moment, staring at his friend's last missive. Though unfinished, the message's intent was clear: Henry Dowling had learned the identity of the informant to the British guard. And Ethan had no doubt it was that knowledge which had cost Henry his life.

And by what nefarious means had Henry's assailant undertaken to murder in cold blood.

Ethan frowned as his mind worked to piece together the circumstances of his colleague's death. It was plain that the hangman's rope had played no part in it. Henry had been killed as he sat writing at the table, shot in the back, perhaps even unaware of his adversary's presence behind him.

But then . . . why the noose? Why hang a man who was assuredly already dead?

Ethan shifted his gaze to the frayed rope yet dangling opposite him.

The hanging corpse had been intended as a warning. A gruesome, sinister warning, brazenly issued to . . . whom? To himself, perhaps; to whomever would find the body and would know of Sergeant Dowling's endeavors.

Ethan's blood surged in anger. It was a senseless killing, a cowardly assassination. A murder, justified in the assailant's mind by loyalty to a cause which was divested of all honor by this heinous deed.

Ethan clenched his fists, crumpling the paper in his hand.

Of only one thing was he certain — whomever was responsible for this vile crime would be held accountable; he would ensure it.

But who was the assailant? Was it a single perpetrator or a band of cohorts who had ambushed the unsuspecting sergeant? And where were they now? Were they yet in the vicinity or long departed?

In the midst of these deliberations, a new and terrible thought suddenly gripped Ethan's mind.

Without wasting another breath or tarrying another moment, he dropped the crumpled paper and bolted toward the door, shouting "Constance!" as he raced outside into the stable yard.

"Constance!" he bellowed again, his heart pounding, for Constance was not in his immediate sight, though she appeared in but the briefest moment's time, making her way round the far side of the chaise, where she had wandered during the lengthy interval.

Ethan waited not for her approach, but ran toward her, and upon reaching her, his chest yet heaving, placed his hands on either side of her face, as if to ascertain for himself that she was manifest and unharmed.

Constance looked up at him, wide-eyed. "What is it?" she asked, much bewildered. "Have you learned anything of your friend's whereabouts?"

Ethan did not answer — indeed, did not even seem to hear her. Instead, he took firm hold of her hand and started leading her toward the chaise.

"I must take you away from here," was all he said, his tone uncompromisingly austere.

Constance was yet startled and perplexed by both his manner and his actions, though she had no choice but to acquiesce as he pulled her toward the vehicle.

"But what has happened?" Constance asked in dismay. "Am I not to meet Sergeant Dowling?"

"No," Ethan replied, an edge of bitterness to his voice, as he set Constance up into the seat. Then he paused and looked up at her from where he stood beside the chaise. "No," he repeated, his tone slightly subdued, though his demeanor remained somber, "you shall not meet Sergeant Dowling."

That was all he said, but Constance, looking back at him, sensed a greater implication in his words, and her brow knit in concern. "Has . . . has something happened to Sergeant Dowling?" she ventured.

Ethan made no response, but his grim visage conveyed more than words, and Constance's own heart beat faster, as her mind formulated the gravest of conclusions.

She said no more, nor did Ethan tarry longer; he hurriedly untethered the horse then leapt up into the box, taking up the rein as he did so, and with a sharp command to the horse, swiftly guided the chaise out of the stable yard and onto the high road.

The journey back to Merrilltown was much the opposite of that which had taken Ethan and Constance to Clymer's farm. There was no lighthearted conversation, no diversions along the way, no keeping the horse at a leisurely pace in order to prolong the drive. Not a word was said between them during the return journey; Ethan kept his eyes fixed upon the road before him — though, indeed, he seemed so preoccupied that he might not have taken any notice of the road nor the horse nor the lady at his side. His countenance retained a grim austerity, with rigid jaw and darkly furrowed brow. To the horse he gave a very liberal rein, so that the light vehicle sped briskly past fields and trees, farms and pastures, never slowing.

They might have continued on in such a manner and achieved the edge of town in half the time, had Ethan not at one point chanced to glance over at Constance, whose face was pale and drawn with fright, her white-knuckled hand clutching the side of the speeding chaise.

Ethan immediately slowed the horse, silently rebuking himself, for he never wished to frighten Constance.

So it was at a more restrained pace, though yet in unmitigated silence, that the chaise was at last brought to a halt beside the pasture fence in McCreary's orchard.

There, Ethan renewed the swiftness of his own movement, quickly disembarking and hurrying round to the other side of the equipage.

As he lifted Constance from the chaise, though, and set her upon the ground, she detained him, grasping his hand in both of hers.

"Ethan—," she intoned, her voice softly tremulous.

He looked into her wide, troubled eyes, as she continued:

"Are — are you going back there?"

Ethan paused hardly at all before nodding in affirmation. "Aye," he replied. "First I must fetch my horse and ride out to the military encampment. I may be gone for several days."

Constance looked up at him entreatingly. "Please . . . please take care of yourself."

Ethan gave but a nod — hardly reassuring to Constance, who knew well both his fearlessness and his resolve.

Gently but firmly he disengaged himself, and in only a moment's time he had departed, urging the horse with all haste along the road to Merrilltown.

Constance lingered in the orchard. Though she knew not what had transpired at Clymer's farm, a sense of fear — of ominous danger — yet permeated her being, and as she watched the chaise disappear in the distance, she sent after Ethan a silent, earnest prayer on his behalf.

The day of Henry Dowling's funeral was befittingly dismal and bleak, with the winter-grey sky nearly indistinguishable from the chilly drizzle that fell from it.

The melancholy of the day was commensurate to the austerity of the burial itself, for only Colonel Naismith, Lieutenant Shaye, and a clergyman brought from the military encampment were in attendance, gathered stiffly about the mound of dirt which marked the grave that they themselves had dug out of the soft, wet earth on a low ridge behind Clymer's farm. The body had been interred upon a wooden plank, wrapped in a plain linen sheet, without ceremony or eulogy, and with only a simple wooden cross implanted into the ground above.

For Colonel Naismith, the occasion of the burial proved to be both insightful and perplexing. He stood to one side of the grave, with the clergyman at his right and Lieutenant Shaye opposite, and as the clergyman uttered prayers at the grave's head, the colonel studied Lieutenant Shaye's face, frowning at what he observed.

Though Ethan's eyes were fixed upon the mound of dirt, it was plain he paid no heed to the clergyman's invocations. Nor did his countenance convey grief or sadness, as would be natural in reflecting upon the loss of his comrade. Instead, a scowl creased Ethan's brow; his eye gleamed with defiance. Yet it was neither the scowl nor the defiance that troubled the colonel — but rather the hardness, the bitterness, behind them.

In thus observing, Colonel Naismith surmised that the dark seeds of revenge had taken root in Ethan's mind, and this thought caused the superior officer to ponder such implications, for he knew that vengeance could be a powerful catalyst; but so, too, could it consume.

Ethan's natural boldness, courage, and skill had well-served the Patriots' cause, for these traits had been tempered by his intelligence and breeding; but his loyalties ran deep, and his determination made him fearless — a trait that could easily turn to recklessness if stoked by the fires of vengeance.

For the briefest moment, a new but very real consideration entered the colonel's mind — should he recall Lieutenant Shaye from this assignment? Had it become too personal? But no sooner had the thought arisen than the colonel extinguished it. It would be no use. Ethan had demonstrated time and again a disregard for regulations, and if the defiance the colonel observed in the lieutenant's eye was any indication, there would be no stopping him from pursuing that which he sought. No, Colonel Naismith could not doubt now that Ethan Shaye would succeed — would see his mission through at all cost.

But at what cost?

The colonel had no opportunity to further contemplate, as his attention was unexpectedly diverted by the appearance of two figures approaching over the ridge.

It was two women, both unfamiliar to the colonel. One was a young lady — slender and pretty — enfolded in a green hooded cloak. The other woman was a servant by her appearance — swarthy and stout — her dark, ample girth wrapped in a woolen shawl. Although the women walked at an unhurried pace, it was evident that their object was the funeral gathering. The young lady held in one hand a cluster of tiny white flowers.

Colonel Naismith glanced at Ethan and saw that he, too, had perceived the approach of the two women. Yet whereas the colonel was entirely ignorant of their identities, he saw by the look of recognition in the lieutenant's eye that these women were not strangers to him. But what was even more significant to the colonel was the change in Ethan's manner. It was subtle, to be sure, but to an astute observer it was perceptible — the steely defiance in Ethan's eye diminished, the hardness of his countenance mitigated.

Frowning in puzzlement, the colonel shifted his attention back to the young lady, who by that time was approaching alone, the slave woman having stopped at the perimeter of trees that surrounded the burial site.

The colonel truly wondered at the identity of the young lady. He knew that Henry Dowling had no kin. Could she be an acquaintance made during his tenure at Clymer's farm? She had not the appearance of a common farm girl; both her attire and her manner suggested a more cultivated breeding. She made no intrusion upon the graveside service — for the clergyman was yet offering his supplications — but rather made her way silently toward Lieutenant Shaye and stood unobtrusively near, slightly behind him.

Ethan had, by that time, affixed his attention back upon the burial, but the colonel sensed that he was well aware of the girl's presence, and indeed, as the colonel watched out of the corner of his eye, Ethan reached his hand back and took hold of the girl's hand, drawing her closer to him.

It was an action that bespoke of a familiarity — of an intimacy even — that quite astonished and perplexed the colonel. Even as he reverted his focus back upon the funeral proceedings, he continued to ruminate over what he had seen. When next he glanced at Ethan, he saw that the lieutenant was yet scowling sullenly at the mound of dirt before him, but the bitterness in his gaze had dissipated.

The clergyman's prayers were concluded shortly thereafter, and after a moment of respectful silence, the young lady slipped away from Lieutenant Shaye's side and approached the grave. Her eyes yet modestly downcast, she bent and reverently laid the little cluster of wildflowers upon the burial mound. As she arose, though, and lifted her solemn dark eyes, her gaze was suddenly arrested by something in the distance, giving her pause.

The colonel instinctively turned to see what had captured the young lady's attention, and he was quite incredulous at what he saw, for approaching over the low ridge at the rear was another woman.

The approaching woman was perhaps caught as unaware as the colonel, for upon perceiving the company before her, she came to an abrupt halt. She was plain-featured in appearance — ginger-haired and ginger-complexioned, plump, and coarse in both her carriage and her attire, as was common amongst humble country folk. She carried in her arms what appeared to be a black iron soup kettle, and by the way she stood gaping at the scene before her, it was apparent she had not expected to encounter a funeral party upon the rise of the hill.

The colonel turned his glance back toward the grave and the pretty young lady who yet stood beside it, and he saw at once by her blank expression that she did not recognize the plump stranger.

Neither did Ethan's perceptive eye reflect any trace of recognition, yet he appraised the woman with a contemplative frown, as if ruminating over her identity.

As for the woman, she walked a few more hesitant paces, then paused again in her step, evidently bewildered and uncertain as to the proceedings before her.

There was an awkwardness which was felt by all, until Ethan took command of the situation; breaking away from the funeral party, he strode across the grass toward the unknown woman, hailing her as he approached. The woman nodded a bit tentatively, for it was apparent that the lieutenant was unfamiliar to her, and indeed she may have been in awe of the handsome young officer in his regimental blue coat. Ethan spoke to her but briefly, and though the colonel could not hear what was said, it was evident by the woman's reaction that she was being apprised to some extent of the situation, and furthermore, that she was affected quite profoundly. The colonel saw her eyes widen in disbelief, in utter dismay. She shook her head, her face contorted with affliction. The colonel observed Ethan gesture toward the burial site, and the woman — glancing in the direction toward which he motioned her — tarried for a moment where she was, timid and apprehensive, clutching her soup kettle, before she gave a slight nod and moved slowly past him toward the circle of trees which surrounded the newly-hallowed ground. Ethan followed, resuming his place opposite the grave.

The woman seemed unaware of the presence of the others until she neared the burial mound, beside which yet stood the pretty young lady. The woman eyed the young lady uncertainly, but the young lady stepped to one side, as if to reassure that she herself had no claim upon the coveted graveside position. And so the ginger-haired woman advanced and rather clumsily knelt beside the mound, setting her cooking pot upon the ground as she did so. As she reached forward to reverently touch a bit of the fresh-turned dirt, her pale eyes suddenly filled with tears, which subsequently streamed down her plump cheek. She emitted a snuffling sob, and, ashen and overcome, she buried her face in her freckled hands, shaking her head all the while.

The younger lady, meanwhile, had been silently standing nearby, her dark eyes filled with sympathy, and when the ginger-haired woman began to weep, the young lady knelt quietly beside her and placed a graceful arm lightly about the coarse woman's rounded shoulder. The woman lifted her head at this unexpected gesture and glanced with gratitude at the girl who was so gently offering comfort. And even the colonel was not unmoved by the tableau before him, for though it was plain that these two women knew nothing of one another — indeed, appeared to be from very different realms of society — they were in that moment joined by a tenderness elicited from loss and sympathy; and while men might scoff at the softness of the fairer sex's heart, assuredly such softness could be in such a moment revealed as not weakness but virtue, brought to light by the heartfelt grief of one and the unaffected kindness of the other.

"I—I am sorry, Miss," the ginger-haired woman sniffled. "I just cannot believe that . . . in truth I have no right to . . . 'tis just so—so hard to believe . . . only last week I spoke to him and . . . promised him a pot of stew, and n-now—," the woman broke down sobbing again, as the young lady murmured soothingly, "There, there."

Ultimately, Colonel Naismith attributed the plump woman's tears to shock and pity more than anything, for they soon subsided, and he heard her lament to the young lady, "Twas a lonesome life he led, bein' out here all on his own. But have no doubt, Miss — he were a good man."

The young lady patted the woman's arm reassuringly. "I know," the young lady murmured softly and cast a shy smile in Ethan's direction, blushing slightly as she met his eye, for indeed, his gaze was already fixed upon her, and though he did not return her smile, an intensely ardent warmth was kindled in his eye.

And in that moment, as the colonel observed this shared gaze, it became apparent to him that whatever existed between Lieutenant Shaye and this girl was far deeper than mere acquaintance.

It was an unexpected revelation and gave the colonel much to ponder, not just at the funeral, but in the days to follow.

The ginger-haired woman was the first to depart from the burial. She rose heftily to her feet — aided by the young lady — and with a bob and a nod toward the three men and an appreciative smile toward the young lady, she picked up her soup kettle and started on her way. She had not gone more than a few steps, however, when she paused and turned back toward the burial site. She stood there but a few seconds, then slowly returned to the side of the grave. Bending over, she carefully placed the kettle upon the mound of dirt alongside the cluster of white flowers.

It was an odd memento, to be sure, but the woman seemed quite satisfied with her contribution, and she departed with a more purposeful gait than that with which she had approached.

After the woman had gone, Lieutenant Shaye stepped forward and approached the young lady, who yet remained beside the grave. "Come, I will see you home," the colonel heard him say.

But though the girl gave him a soft smile, she shook her head. "No, it is better if you stay here," she murmured, glancing in the direction of the other two men, her cheeks turning pink as she did so, for both men were already looking at her. "Jenny has accompanied me," the girl continued, indicating the stout slave woman who stood in the distance beneath the trees.

Lieutenant Shaye glanced toward the trees, then back at the young lady. After a moment's consideration, he conceded with a nod, and, taking her hand, pressed his lips first against her fingertips, then her palm, in a manner whose swiftness in no way diluted the very personal nature of such a gesture.

There was no more spoken between them, and the young lady thus departed, pausing but briefly at the perimeter of trees to say a word to the slave woman, who duly joined her mistress, walking alongside her toward the distant ridge.

Lieutenant Shaye, in joining his superior officer and the clergyman once more, said little to them before they parted — Ethan back to his lodgings in Merrilltown and the others to the military encampment. Ethan had made no attempt to introduce the young lady to the colonel, nor to account for her presence at the burial. He made no mention of her, nor of the funeral proceedings, nor even of his comrade now buried beneath the earth. His demeanor was once again sullen and preoccupied, and he took his leave with little more than a brusque promise to keep the colonel informed as to his progress.

So was concluded the humble burial of Sergeant Henry Dowling.

COLONEL NAISMITH HAD BEEN ASTUTE in his observations of Ethan Shaye during the burial service and justified in his concern at the Lieutenant's defiant scowl.

Indeed, in the days since Ethan's discovery of Henry Dowling's lifeless body hanging from the farmhouse rafters, any sentiments of natural grief Ethan might have felt at his friend's death had been compounded — usurped even — by bitterness and anger; anger at himself for not having prevented the grisly deed; anger at the injustice of a life cut short; and most especially, anger toward the perpetrator of the heinous crime.

Ethan's mission — once focused upon the higher causes of justice and liberty — had become personal, fueled by the desire for vengeance.

So it was that in the days following the funeral, Ethan threw himself into his work with relentless determination, resolved to let nothing distract him from his purpose until he had discovered the identity of the saboteur, and thereby identified Dowling's killer, for he felt certain that they were one and the same. He would not rest until he had put an end to the traitor's enterprise, using whatever means he must . . . even should the adversary be Joshua Porter himself.

JOSHUA PORTER HAD BEEN ON Ethan's mind ever since the day of the boating mishap, when Ethan had overheard the merchant's uncharacteristically bitter exchange with his elder son. In the few encounters he'd had with Porter since that day, Ethan observed a subtle, but notable, change in the merchant's comportment. While Porter retained an outwardly cordial manner on these occasions, Ethan sensed an air of persistent agitation about him and had observed exchanges with servants and household members that were marked by a conspicuous irritability on the part of Mr. Porter. Something was surely weighing heavily upon the merchant to cause such an unnatural turn of disposition . . . but what? Had it begun with the boating incident, when Ethan had first witnessed Porter's alteration of temperament? Or had something already been pressing upon the merchant's mind, which that day's misadventure had merely exacerbated? Ethan could not help but wonder if there could be some connection between Mr. Porter's agitation and the circumstances surrounding the interception of General Washington's supplies. Indeed, there had been no new entries recorded in the logbook since Ethan had last inspected it. He could only conclude that any attempts to send supplies to the Patriot troops had ceased for the time being, although the Porters' wharf remained as busy as ever, with vessels arriving and unloading their cargo with some regularity.

Ethan had, in fact, begun to concentrate his efforts once more upon the activity at the wharf, spending long hours observing the movements of the workers and the ships' crews, walking amongst the barrels and crates which were deposited upon the landing or stacked in neat rows within the warehouse, getting a sense of the comings and goings of the wagons and light vessels upon which the cargo was loaded. Truly, Joshua Porter's business appeared to be thriving — in spite of the war and the naval blockade — which made the merchant's state of discomposure all the more confounding.

It was, therefore, with mindful perception that Ethan observed the merchant upon the landing one afternoon, less than a fortnight after Henry Dowling's burial. Ethan was just making his way toward the wharf when he spotted Joshua Porter ahead of him, standing in conversation with his overseer. While there was nothing unusual about Porter's manner or presence upon the landing, Ethan nevertheless paused in his step, for the two men before him were just concluding their discourse, and Joshua Porter — though he appeared intent upon following the overseer toward one of the docks — instead tarried where he was, his attention diverted by a figure approaching upon the river path. It was his elder son.

Tristan's musket and haversack were slung across his shoulder, and though he would likely not soon put the musket to any use — for his wrist was still wrapped and bound — it appeared that he was set upon returning to the militia camp that day.

His father was undoubtedly not expecting to see his son thus outfitted, for he did not go forth to meet Tristan, but rather tarried where he was, scrutinizing the lad's approach with a wary eye.

Ethan was not near enough to hear the exchange between father and son, but it was evident by the frowns upon both countenances — one disapproving and one sullen — that they were at odds in their discourse. Their conversation was but brief and conducted in low tones, but Ethan surmised that Joshua Porter had not anticipated his son's imminent departure, nor did he sanction its merit. Tristan evidently held fast to his purpose, however, his stubborn frown unyielding, until his father, in frustration, dismissed him with an impatient gesture and strode away toward the wharf.

Tristan remained where he was, staring resentfully after his father. Their disagreement had perhaps only increased his resolve, for after a moment he re-shouldered his musket and proceeded with deliberate step in the direction of the high road.

As for Ethan — he did not continue on toward the harbor, but rather tarried for a long while at the spot from which he had observed the contentious exchange, his brow furrowed in rumination, oblivious to the movements of the workers or the activity about him on the landing. When at last he emerged from his contemplation, he proceeded not toward the river but instead made his way back along the road to town, back to his lodgings at Lethbridge's, where he shut himself in his room, that he might be left undisturbed to further deliberate. For indeed, a thought had taken hold of him as he observed Joshua and Tristan Porter upon the landing . . . an idea of significant implication. It was a theory only, and yet — should it prove true, he would at last have gained definitive insight into the covert process behind the military supply line operations.

Verifying the accuracy of the theory was a dangerous proposition, however. It would require such a degree of risk as to potentially jeopardize his entire mission and put a swift end to his career as a Patriot spy.

But it was a risk he must take, and in characteristic fashion, once he had determined upon it, he thought no more of the potential hazards, but rather sprang forthwith into bold action, undaunted by the audacity of such an endeavor.

❧

A WAVE OF EXCITEMENT RIPPLED through the militia encampment as the blue-coated officer of the Continental Army rode into their midst, reining in his spirited horse with agility.

But there was one among the enlisted who looked upon the unexpected visitor not with admiration but with astonishment; indeed, Tristan Porter well-recognized the able-bodied officer, though he could not conceal his bewilderment at seeing Ethan Shaye thus attired and with a lieutenant's insignia.

For his part, Ethan spared not a glance toward any of the inquisitive onlookers, but quickly dismounted and went straight to his purpose, exchanging hasty salutes with the militia commander, who was as eager and curious as his men to learn what had brought the Continental officer into their camp.

But Ethan was impatient to proceed with the task at hand and could not be troubled with assuaging the civilian commander's curiosity.

"Forgive this intrusion," Ethan said brusquely. "I must have a word with one of your men — Tristan Porter."

The militia commander raised his eyebrows in some surprise, but nodded and summoned Tristan, who stood with some comrades about a fire at the far end of the small encampment.

"He's only just returned to us today," the commander noted as Tristan approached. "Injured," he added grimly, "though he can yet make himself useful keeping watch."

Ethan made no response, for indeed, his mind was set only upon his objective.

The militia commander thus addressed Tristan as he neared: "Master Porter, this officer has requested to have a word with you."

Ethan wasted no time in greetings or explanations, but forthwith drew Tristan aside to the edge of the wood which surrounded the camp and spoke to him firmly and directly, putting forth his purpose not as a question but as a statement: "You are the forger."

An immediate but fleeting gleam in Tristan's eye told Ethan that his assertion had not fallen upon incognizant ears. Nevertheless, Tristan remained silent, eyeing Ethan warily.

Despite his impatience for definitive verification, Ethan realized that he must substantiate his premise, and so, after a pause, he proceeded to give a brief but straightforward account of himself:

"I can well understand your astonishment at seeing me here and in this manner. Though I presented myself in Merrilltown as an acquaintance of Mr. Clymer, intent upon surveying his land, that was a pretext only, for in truth, I am commissioned a lieutenant in the Continental Army, operating under direct orders from General Washington himself, tasked with discovering the identity of the person or persons responsible for sabotaging the Patriot troops' supply shipments — and putting an end to their treachery, if I am able. A company from my regiment, under the command of Colonel Naismith, is situated north of here, near the Maryland border, awaiting my word and prepared to intervene, should it prove necessary."

Still Tristan made no response but remained yet fixed, his eyes distant and narrowed — evidence of his mind's struggle to comprehend and assimilate ideas which would necessarily compel a drastic alteration of perception. When at last he looked at Ethan, there was yet uncertainty in Tristan's eyes.

"Does my father know that you're a spy?"

Ethan gave a slight shake of his head. "No. Until we have identified the traitor — and any possible collaborators — it is imperative that my affiliation with the Patriot army remain a secret."

Tristan's brow knit. "Then why have you revealed all of this to me?"

Ethan looked him steadily in the eye. "It is a risk, to be sure," he maintained evenly, his tone deliberate and unwavering. "But I am at a point where I must have an ally, someone I can trust. I believe that you can be trusted — that, indeed, you have well-proved your loyalty to the Patriots' cause."

Tristan inadvertently glanced down at his bandaged wrist. The gesture did not escape Ethan's notice, and he leaned forward, speaking with level conviction:

"You can yet be of service to the cause . . . to General Washington . . . to our soldiers fighting in the North."

Tristan looked up, simultaneously uncertain and attentive.

Aware of the impact of his words, Ethan continued, unrelenting in his objective, putting forth again the question of his purpose: "You are the forger, are you not?"

There followed a long silence before Tristan, at last, gave an affirmative nod. He did not say anything, but looked to Ethan questioningly.

For his part, Ethan acknowledged Tristan's admission with a curt nod of his own, then, after only a brief pause, proceeded upon the course at hand: "What do you know of the supply operation? Of the men chosen to transport the provisions? Of the inventories or the schedule upon which a shipment is dispatched?"

Tristan shook his head. "I know nothing about any of that. My father makes all of those decisions, and — other than my own part in forging the signatures — he has never taken me into his confidence regarding details of the process. I know that he seldom utilizes the same driver twice in the conveyance of the provisions. The British officers' names upon the passes are likewise varied, that the guards at the blockade would not take note of any pattern. But I play no part in determining which name shall be forged upon each pass. In truth, I know of no man with whom my father consults upon such matters. Ever since the wagons began to be turned away at the blockade — and worse — he has kept all of his decisions close. I know that this sabotage has weighed heavily upon him these past months."

In spite of Tristan's willingness to share this insight, Ethan chose his next words carefully:

"And yet, your father himself is not beyond suspicion in this matter. Can you attest to his unmitigated loyalty to the Patriots' cause?"

Tristan stared at Ethan incredulously. "My father has dedicated nearly every waking hour — and many sleepless nights — to the oversight of this operation. His chief concern is the welfare of our Patriot troops! If you need further evidence of that, you need look only to his reaction at my injury," Tristan lifted his bandaged wrist, "which has, for the time, effectively brought the entire enterprise to a halt. Such vexation on his part can only be attributed to his concern for the general's men and frustration at his inability to render them aid. Although," Tristan added, with a sulking frown, "I will not admit to any wrongdoing on my part, for it was a misfortune that could not have been prevented, however grave its consequences. I am as frustrated over it as he, and likely twice so, for now I cannot help in any useful capacity, but must sit idly by while others do the work that I cannot."

Ethan was well-attentive to Tristan's words.

"Has your father found another forger then?"

Tristan shrugged. "He says he has. Someone from Gloucester County is set to arrive in the next day or so to take up the task."

Ethan nodded thoughtfully, then quite abruptly put another question to Tristan: "Do you have any thought yourself as to the traitor's identity?"

Tristan appeared momentarily caught off-guard by this abrupt change in subject, but after a pause he shook his head. "I cannot fathom who amongst my father's acquaintances would betray the Patriots' cause . . . nor even how that person would acquire the information necessary to effect such a betrayal."

"What of Monsieur Brisonneau?" Ethan persisted. "What role does he play? Why does your father continue to do business with a man who has outrightly insulted a member of his household?"

Tristan scowled darkly. "That baseborn maggot! Nothing would give me more satisfaction than to see him go down in one of his own ships! I wish he was the traitor — how I should love to see his neck stretched upon the gallows!"

"But you do not think he is the traitor?" Ethan asked sharply.

Tristan shook his head, his anger giving way to sullen resignation. "Nay, I cannot think that he is, though his character be the vilest, most contemptible I have ever known. But his sole purpose in coming here was to give aid to the colonists' cause against the British."

Ethan listened intently as Tristan went on:

"It is Brisonneau's ships that bring all of the supplies we send north to the Patriot soldiers. His vessels have consistently been able to maneuver past the British naval blockade, where others have not. I wish to God my father could find another competent blockade runner, that he might sever all ties with Brisonneau." And upon that bitter pronouncement, Tristan lapsed into silence.

Ethan frowned. "How do you know all of this?"

"My father told me," Tristan replied, his face reddening slightly, "when Brisonneau first arrived."

Ethan looked at Tristan levelly. "I must ask you again," he said, his tone stern and deliberate. "Can you ascertain — absolutely and unequivocally — that your father plays no role in the sabotage of the Patriot army's provision shipments?"

Tristan hesitated. "I — I cannot swear to such," he admitted uncertainly. "But—," his voice gained in conviction, "I truly do not think there has been any deception on his part. My father and I have our disagreements, but I believe him to be a man of integrity and honor."

Ethan silently contemplated this avowal for a moment before he nodded, apparently satisfied. "Thank you," he said. "I will not detain you further."

Tristan accompanied Ethan back into the camp, where Ethan's horse was tethered.

As Ethan prepared to mount, though, he turned back toward Tristan. "I may yet have need of your assistance in this matter," he said, "but for now — you must swear to absolute silence regarding my purpose here in Virginia. There are many lives that may depend on it."

Tristan nodded. "Aye," he affirmed solemnly. "I understand."

AFTER HIS DISCOURSE WITH TRISTAN, Ethan determined to keep an acutely watchful eye upon Joshua Porter's study and logbook over the course of the next few days, that he might take note of any slight change or addition to the logbook's entries, even throughout the course of a single day; for indeed, Tristan had provided information that Ethan had previously sought in vain — a prediction as to when he might anticipate the dispatch of the next shipment of provisions.

So Ethan devised pretexts for visiting Porter's study twice daily, both morning and afternoon, so that nothing should escape his notice.

Upon the first day — though he was able to gain access to the room in the morning, as Mr. Porter was away from the house at an unusually early hour — Ethan observed nothing of any significance.

The second day found Porter sequestered in his study with a business associate all morning, frustrating Ethan's attempt to view the logbook at regular intervals. However, his visit to the Porter house upon that occasion was not entirely without value, for he was informed by the smiling housegirl that a new guest had arrived the previous evening — a Mr. Danforth of Gloucester County — and was expected to stay on for several weeks. Ethan was, of course, most attentive to this news, as it would seem to corroborate Tristan's conjecture regarding the imminent introduction of a new forger into the operation. It was, then, with some disappointment that upon admittance into the study later that day Ethan yet discovered no changes made to the logbook's entries.

However, upon the third morning, Ethan's efforts were at last rewarded, though the day would ultimately raise more questions than yield answers.

He was greeted, as always, by the cheerful housegirl, but as he passed through the main hall toward the study, he noted the uncommon quiet that pervaded the house; no murmur of voices nor clink of cups and saucers emanated from the drawing room or parlor; no footfall was heard in the upper corridor or upon the stair. Indeed, it seemed that every member of the household was away that morning. It was, for Ethan, an advantageous circumstance, as he would therefore not be required to make explanation for his presence so early in the day.

He went straight to the study, and, after the housegirl had brought him a candle, he closed the door to the hall, taking no chances of interruption or discovery, despite the quiet of the house.

Scanning the shelf behind the desk, his eye was drawn at once to the logbook, for it protruded slightly, as if it had been hastily put in its place, though Ethan himself had looked at it but the previous evening and was certain that he had not been so careless in replacing it. This circumstance incited in him a sense of heightened expectation, and he quickly took hold of the logbook and began thumbing through its pages until he reached the last entry in the ledger. And there his burgeoning anticipation was proven justified, for he found not only that the last entry was newly-scribed, but that a small scrap of paper had been tucked into the page since the previous night. The entry was incomplete — a status he had observed upon one previous occasion. And as upon that previous occasion, it was the two center columns which had been completed, one inscribed with two names — *Benjamin Fuller/Colonel Patrick Whitmore* — and the other column containing a long list of inventory, written in a miniscule but very legible hand.

Glancing at the scrap of paper that had been lodged between the pages, he saw that upon it was written, as he expected, the signature of Colonel Patrick Whitmore.

Ethan slowly closed the book and sat down in the chair at the desk, his mind turning over the implications of the new entry. It was undated. Notable, too, was the absence of a blockade pass. Yet the presence of the scrap of paper with the signature would surely suggest that a pass had not yet been forged. Even so, the new names and inventory inscribed in the ledger indicated that a shipment was ready to be dispatched . . . but when? Ethan determined that it was not likely to be that day, as it was already the ten o'clock hour, with no sign of Mr. Porter or the provisional forger on the premises.

It could well be dispatched upon the morrow, though . . .

Ethan's thoughts were interrupted by an unexpected sound of voices within the house. The voices were distant and indistinct — beyond the closed door as they were — but they diverted his attention nevertheless.

One of the voices was Constance's.

While it was not uncommon for Ethan to hear her voice within the Porter house as he worked in the study — indeed, his mind always instinctively discerned hers amongst any others — there was something different about it upon this occasion which called him out of his deliberation. It was difficult to establish what exactly had alerted his senses, for he could not discern any words being spoken, but there was something in the sound of Constance's voice . . . perhaps an uncharacteristic intensity of tone or register . . . something that did not sit well with Ethan.

Rising, he hastily returned the logbook to its place upon the shelf and exited the study, pausing just outside the door to listen and locate the source of the voices. His eye immediately lighted upon the door opposite, from behind which the voices seemed to emanate. He knew it to be the door which led to the rear staircase landing as well as to a side entrance into the house from outside.

Crossing the hall, Ethan pushed open the door and was there met with a most curious sight.

Directly opposite him, the door to the outside was open, giving ample light to the small, enclosed rear stairwell; standing at the foot of the stairs were three people, all familiar: Jenny stood in the center, her large dark hand clasped tightly around Constance's arm. Constance, standing nearest the door to the hall, was struggling to free herself from Jenny's grasp, and it was undoubtedly her repeated appeals of "Jenny, let me go!" which Ethan had discerned across the hall. The third member of the tableau, positioned on the other side of Jenny, was Zachary Merrill's man-servant Thaddeus, who had both his hands upon Jenny's arm, attempting to pry her away from Constance. His exclamations very nearly echoed Constance's, though with a deeper and far sterner resonance: "Let her go!"

Ethan witnessed only a brief instant of these vociferations, for as soon as he opened the door into the stairwell, all three people therein, upon perceiving him, fell silent and still, though neither Jenny nor Thaddeus relinquished their respective holds. Poor Constance, defenseless in the solid grip of her robust servant, was visibly distressed at her predicament.

In the silence that encompassed the small space, Ethan surveyed the three faces before him — his brow furrowed in brooding discontent — before demanding explanation. "What is this about?"

Constance shook her head, unhappy and perplexed. "I do not know what has come over Jenny. The others have all gone to the Merrills' to inspect the new orangery, but I was delayed in getting ready, so Mr. Porter said he would send the riding chair back to fetch me. But instead, Mr. Merrill has dispatched Thaddeus with a carriage. Yet, when I attempted to leave the house . . . Jenny interposed herself and . . . and seems intent that I should not go." Constance was truly dismayed at her beloved servant's conduct. "I— I do not know what to think. I have never known Jenny to be insubordinate."

Jenny herself made no concession but only glowered obdurately and maintained her firm grip upon Constance's arm.

Neither did Ethan forthwith move to free Constance but instead looked at Jenny with a thoughtful frown, then turned his gaze upon Thaddeus. "Release your hold upon that woman," Ethan commanded him. "You have no authority over her."

Thaddeus was plainly caught off-guard by this unexpected command.

He appeared to falter briefly, but quickly regained his composure; nor did he loosen his hold upon Jenny. "I was charged by my master with fetching Miss Jameson. This woman is preventing me from carrying out my master's orders."

The insinuation was plain as to from whom Thaddeus took orders.

Ethan, however, cared nothing about Thaddeus nor his inferences. He eyed Thaddeus coolly and addressed him in a tone that was level but uncompromisingly firm:

"Unhand that woman at once. She is your equal . . . whether you care to admit it or not, and you have stepped far out of your place in laying your hands upon her."

But Thaddeus, despite his subservient status, was proud, and he wavered for a moment — a moment in which Ethan observed a glint of defiance in the slave's eye — before grudgingly releasing his hold upon Jenny. Yet even in releasing her, Thaddeus did not defer meekly, but yet voiced his assertion: "She must unhand her mistress," he contended resentfully, "and be held accountable for her insubordination!"

Ethan frowned impatiently at this persistent insolence. "Not another word out of you!" he commanded — his forceful tone subduing the supercilious manservant, who, for the first time, averted his eyes. "To be sure," Ethan continued levelly, turning his focus upon Jenny once more, "I trust that this woman's actions would only ever reflect the highest regard for the welfare of her mistress."

Although Jenny had not surrendered her hold upon Constance, Ethan observed that the slave woman's stubborn stance and dour frown both appeared to be somewhat diminished after Thaddeus's begrudging relinquishment and Ethan's subsequent words.

Still, Ethan did not make any hasty attempt to extricate Constance from Jenny's grasp, but instead proceeded cautiously. Slowly, he reached forward and took gentle hold of Constance's free arm, keeping his eye fixed upon Jenny all the while.

"I shall escort Miss Constance to Merrill Hall," he pronounced evenly.

There was a palpable tension in the silence that followed, during which Ethan scrutinized Jenny's visage intently. He saw her round eyes flicker uncertainly.

It was not the first time Jenny had stood her ground where the issue of her mistress was concerned, but this time, after only a very brief interval, the slave woman unexpectedly conceded, releasing Constance's arm without opposition.

Ethan was, in truth, a bit taken aback at the ease of Jenny's surrender, and he stood fixed for yet another moment, regarding her contemplatively, before he gently pulled Constance to his side. He glanced at Constance — for indeed, that lady's welfare was ever his chief concern — and seeing that, though she was much bewildered at all that had transpired, she was nonetheless unharmed, he moved then with purpose to conduct her away from the premises.

As he guided Constance through the door into the hall, though, Ethan cast a glance back over his shoulder and found Thaddeus looking after him — a gleam of unmistakable animosity lighting the slave's intelligent eyes.

As he rode alongside the Merrills' carriage, a myriad of questions streamed through Ethan's mind, casting him into a state of deep absorption, so that he was scarcely aware of his surroundings or the passage of time upon the journey.

As he replayed in his mind the scenario in the stairwell, he grew increasingly confounded.

It was upon Jenny that his thoughts continuously focused. There was something disconcerting about her actions, both in the way she had physically impeded her mistress's departure — even to the point of insubordination — and in her subsequent voluntary release of Constance to Ethan. It was all very uncharacteristic behavior on Jenny's part.

Ethan knew Jenny well. He knew how protective she was of her young mistress; indeed, he himself had long been subject to Jenny's vigilant defense of her mistress's heart. And yet . . . here Jenny had willingly surrendered Constance to his care.

He could not reasonably conceive that Jenny had had a sudden alteration of attitude toward him. No, Jenny's actions must assuredly bespeak of something she felt the need to protect even more than her mistress's heart . . . something which, in her mind, posed a more formidable threat to Constance's well-being.

One thing was certain — Jenny had not been attempting to prevent Constance from going to the Merrills', as Constance had supposed, for when Ethan had plainly stated that he would be taking her to the same destination, Jenny had released her without opposition.

What was it, then, that Jenny so feared? In what regard would she trust Ethan more than Zachary Merrill's manservant? Did Jenny fear for Constance's physical safety? It was the only conclusion Ethan's mind could reasonably settle upon, yet such a premise was no conclusion at all, but rather the impetus for a host of further questions.

Ethan could conceive of only two vague possibilities: that Jenny had witnessed or overhead something which would lead her to believe that Thaddeus was not to be trusted as an escort, or that she feared some sort of assault by a third party enroute to the Merrill estate.

Ethan glanced about him as this second possibility arose in his mind. It was true that much of the terrain between the Porters' house and the Merrill estate consisted of unpopulated landscapes — forested hills and open fields; yet any notion of an assault upon the open road — an occurrence that was exceedingly rare throughout the colonies and of which there had never been, to Ethan's knowledge, a single instance in the immediate vicinity — seemed as unlikely as it was improbable.

Likewise, the alternative theory — that it was Thaddeus whom Jenny feared or mistrusted on behalf of her mistress — seemed equally irrational. Although Thaddeus had revealed himself to be scornful and even insolent, he was, nevertheless, Zachary Merrill's trusted servant and had undoubtedly attended to Constance upon numerous occasions. It was implausible that he should in any way threaten or harm the lady to whom his master paid suit.

Yet, where Constance was concerned, Ethan was not inclined to leave anything to chance, and so he continued to ponder the strange incident and determined that he must find an opportunity to speak to Jenny, to attempt to elicit from her the reason behind her anomalous actions.

Ethan was recalled from his contemplation by the party's approach to Merrill Hall. As they passed through the gate at the top of the hill, Ethan saw that Judge Merrill himself was standing on the steps of the main house, engaged in lively conversation with some other men — among them Joshua Porter, who turned and smiled in recognition as the carriage bearing his wife's sister came to a halt before the house.

Ethan quickly dismounted and handed Constance down from the carriage, detaining her for a moment as he bent his head toward hers.

"See that you go home with Mr. Porter and your sisters," Ethan instructed her in a low voice before turning her over to her distinguished host and Mr. Porter, who were approaching to greet her.

Not wishing to tarry at Merrill Hall nor to make explanation for his presence there, Ethan hastily mounted his steed once more and, with a nod toward the men, turned back in the direction of the main gate. As he passed beneath the latticed portal, though, he saw approaching up the hill another carriage, and as the drive was quite narrow, Ethan steered his mount onto a path which angled off into a wooded area and which he knew followed a semi-circular course back to the main drive a short distance down the hill.

He slowed his horse a bit upon the path, which was bordered on one side by fragrant pines and on the other by a red brick wall which ran about the perimeter of the Merrill estate's terraced formal gardens.

Though he paid but scant heed to these surroundings — for he was intent upon achieving the main road once more — as the path curved nearer the garden's enclosure, Ethan's attention was diverted by the faint sound of laughter drifting over the brick wall. It was very quiet laughter, to be sure — perhaps that of only two people, for he could discern both a man's low chuckle and a woman's lighter tone, suggestive of a moment shared in some intimate delight — but Ethan, uninterested in the garden's occupants, continued on along the path, casting but a cursory glance through one of the decorative geometric openings cut high into the garden wall — a view afforded him only because of his mount.

It was perhaps well that he caught only a glimpse of the secluded garden, for what he beheld in that split second was a tableau clearly not meant for any observer's eye; a man and woman, seated upon a garden bench, were caught up in a conspicuously amorous embrace, both blissfully unaware of the passing rider on the other side of the wall.

Yet as Ethan passed the opening in the wall and continued swiftly along the path, his mind was struck with a jarringly discordant perception . . .

The man he had glimpsed in the garden was Zachary Merrill.

It was an infinitely unsettling realization — one that cast a moment of doubt upon Ethan's faith in his own senses; but that moment of uncertainty quickly elapsed, to be replaced with an even firmer conviction. Ethan knew his senses had not deceived him; it was, without a doubt, Zachary Merrill whom he had seen through the opening in the garden wall.

As he cantered along the path and back out onto the main road, the rumination over what he had seen provoked in Ethan anger and antipathy. While he would ordinarily be indifferent to the amorous indiscretions among those with whom he was little acquainted, this instance consummately vexed him. Ethan loathed hypocrisy above all else, and Zachary Merrill — who had fashioned himself a paragon of upstanding virtue and benevolence — now betrayed a level of duplicity which must render him contemptible.

There was, of course, a more personal impetus behind Ethan's ire toward Zachary Merrill. Merrill had overtly wooed Constance — had presented her with gifts and affected a bashful blush at planting a chaste kiss upon her cheek, yet was even now deceiving her with clandestine trysts behind garden walls. Ethan knew that Constance did not love Zachary Merrill beyond the most platonic of friendships, yet even that friendship gave credence to the level of respect she had for Merrill — for a man who was unworthy of either her trust or respect.

In the brief glimpse he'd had into the garden, Ethan had not the opportunity nor the vantage point to discern the identity of the woman who was so enthusiastically receiving Zachary Merrill's attentions (and, indeed, upon whose bosom Merrill's hand was so conspicuously placed). It was plainly not Constance, whom Ethan had just delivered up to the house moments before, and beyond that he cared nothing about Merrill's paramour. But for Zachary Merrill himself — Zachary Merrill, who would undoubtedly in only a short while greet Constance up at the Hall, plant a doting kiss upon her hand, and gallantly take her arm through his — for that duplicitous blackguard, Ethan had nothing but contempt.

ETHAN HAD NOT THE LUXURY of dwelling upon Zachary Merrill's indiscretions, nor even Jenny's incongruous behavior, but was compelled to redirect his focus back upon his mission, for he was certain that, after the delay of several weeks, another shipment of supplies was about to be dispatched northward, likely upon the morrow. He had but little time to ascertain the whereabouts of the transporter, Benjamin Fuller, whose name had been inscribed in the logbook, so upon returning to Merrilltown Ethan set straight about the task.

He was able to draw aside Maria Lethbridge, for she seemed as likely as any to be acquainted with Benjamin Fuller, familiar as she was with the patrons who frequented the public room of her father's establishment; but that young woman, however eager to oblige her favorite lodger, could only shake her head perplexedly in response to the name put to her.

Ethan fared better with Widow Reid, the convivial proprietress of the dry-goods store.

"Benjamin Fuller?" she repeated, as she wrapped the parcel of ink and paper which Ethan had requested upon entering the shop. "Aye, to be sure, I know Mr. Fuller. His farm is just west of town. He doesn't come into the shop as often as he used to. After his wife died, he'd stop in often — I'd sometimes give him a hand with mending his shirts or offer some advice on cookery and the like, bless his soul — but I've heard he is about to marry again — Miss Eliza Prather — which, I daresay explains his not needin' my further assistance with such domestic tasks. But how good it will be for his boys to have a mother again! I always think boys need a mother's particular guidance, don't you? It cannot be good for them, growin' up in a household of only men. And I warrant Miss Prather will guide with a firm hand, as she is a purposeful sort of woman, I've always thought. Are you acquainted with Miss Eliza Prather?"

Ethan, who had been listening to this chatter with estimable patience, stated that he was not acquainted with the lady in question; and then, before the loquacious widow could launch into a dissertation on Miss Prather's character, he asked if she might provide direction to Benjamin Fuller's farm.

Once apprised of the location, Ethan took up his parcel, thanked Widow Reid, bid her a cordial "good-day", and hastily exited the shop, lest the widow set in to inquire after his purpose in seeking out Mr. Fuller.

Ethan had no trouble finding Fuller's farm — it was, as Widow Reid had described, about three miles west of town, with the house visible from the road beyond a grove of beech trees.

Ethan approached the grove just as the late afternoon sun cast its lengthening rays across the meadows and treetops. He slowed his horse, for he saw up ahead a flock of sheep crossing the road before him, guided by two boys, whom Ethan supposed were the aforementioned sons of Benjamin Fuller. He was yet a fair distance away, and the boys took no notice of him, intent as they were upon their task at hand. But Ethan turned his horse off the road, bringing it to a halt just at the edge of the beech grove, where he might observe further without drawing attention. And indeed, he had not long to wait before he saw a man of middling age crossing the pasture on the far side of the farmhouse, a reap hook in hand. The man stopped before the house and called out to the two boys, who were just closing the pasture gate upon their flock and who, after securing the gate-pin, promptly raced toward the distant barn, in accordance with the farmer's summons.

Ethan was confident in his assumption that the man was Benjamin Fuller, and as the farmer and his sons continued toward the barn, Ethan spurred his horse back out onto the road, setting off in the direction of Merrilltown, certain that he was on the brink of capturing the treasonous conspirator who had been sabotaging the Patriot supply shipments and who had killed his friend. But where this prospect of success would have once filled Ethan with the invigorating zeal of imminent triumph, he felt no surge of victorious exhilaration upon this occasion. Rather, he felt only the relentless drive of a predator closing in on his prey — an inexorable determination to pursue and to vanquish.

Ethan's plan was simple: He would set out at dawn upon the high road and stake out a position halfway to the Maryland border. He would make note of those who passed before Benjamin Fuller and any who returned upon the same road prior to Fuller's return. There were not likely to be many who passed twice within that timeframe, and he could then repeat the process with the next transport of supplies. While Benjamin Fuller's shipment might be turned away, Ethan was confident it would be the last time a shipment would be denied passage across the border.

As Ethan rode into Lethbridge's service yard upon his return from scouting out the transporter's farm, he determined to take several days' provisions with him when he set out for the high road, in the event that Fuller's shipment was not dispatched directly upon the morrow.

These thoughts were disrupted, though, when he entered the tavern's central hall and was met by Maria Lethbridge, who informed him that in his absence a message had been delivered by the Porters' stable-hand.

Ethan took from her the sealed, unmarked letter and — to the disappointment of the inquisitive Maria — proceeded directly up the stairs to his room, where he might examine the contents of the message in private.

Although the sky outside was already darkened, one of the establishment's dutiful servants had, upon Ethan's arrival in the service yard, prepared the fire in his room, and — taking not even a moment to light a chamberstick — Ethan crossed to the fire forthwith, that he might read the message by the light of its bright flames. Breaking the seal as he crossed the room, he held the paper low over the hearth, where the fire's light illuminated the words upon the page.

Ethan recognized the script upon first glance, for it was Constance's. Her message to him was brief and without detail:

Please come to the orchard at sunrise, if you are able.

-C

Ethan frowned broodingly. It was not like Constance to summon him; indeed, there was inherent risk to her in sending such a message and by such means, which must assuredly speak to some anxiety on her part . . . something pressing enough that she could not wait until circumstances should bring them together again, yet not so urgent as to necessitate an immediate meeting.

So, too, did the message's succinctness trouble Ethan. He knew that Constance would never make such a request of him without purpose; yet why she did not state the nature of that purpose was perplexing.

Constance could not, of course, know how unfortunate was the timing of her request, for Ethan could not both set out upon the high road at dawn and meet Constance in the orchard at sunrise. In truth, though, the dilemma gave Ethan only a moment's pause; while he knew full well that his mission should come before all else, he could never be indifferent to Constance, and he would not disregard her now. He would take to the high road directly from McCreary's orchard; it would not set him back any great distance, and any delay could be overcome by the speed of his horse, to which he would give free rein upon the open road.

ETHAN AND CONSTANCE MIGHT HAVE been of a single mind, for both arrived at the orchard before the appointed hour, each with a lantern in hand amidst the darkness of the early winter morn.

Although Constance knew nothing of Ethan's plan to set out afterward upon the high road, she might have discerned a certain restlessness about him, had her mind not been preoccupied with such weighty cares as rendered her incognizant of any ancillary circumstances.

But Ethan was ever observant and noted with some concern Constance's unsettled state, scrutinizing her anxious countenance by the flickering light of his lantern.

"I— I daresay you will think me foolish for summoning you here," Constance began, her soft voice unsteady as she struggled to articulate her thoughts, "for such a purpose as you are certain to perceive as trivial at best. I am truly sorry for any trouble you have been put to in arising at such an early hour, but . . . but I have not seen you much at the house of late, and I . . . I have not had an opportunity to . . . that is . . ." She faltered, her discomposure evident. She took a rather tremulous breath before continuing: "In truth . . . I am rather dreading this discourse; indeed, it was only after many hours of indecision yesterday that I sent the note to you, for it may be that what you will tell me here will only substantiate my fears, rather than allay them. But I— I cannot live with this uncertainty."

Her voice broke under the strain of her palpable distress, and Ethan, who had thus far been listening in a state of perplexity and concern, interjected:

"Constance, compose yourself," he charged her, "and tell me what it is you would ask of me, that I may put to rest whatever fears your mind has conjured."

But Constance could not be pacified. She shook her head unhappily. "I cannot quiet my mind," she uttered. "Ever since that day . . . that day when . . . when you found Sergeant Dowling in such a state—." She faltered again, averting her eyes, struggling to steady her voice as she continued. "I fear that he was . . . killed . . . because of the mission you pursue." She looked up at Ethan, suddenly beseeching. "Ethan, I must know— have there been other deaths?"

Ethan frowned. He had never revealed to her the full extent of the mission's dangers and had no desire to do so now.

But Constance pressed him.

"Please—," she entreated, "it is haunting me to no end. Have there been other deaths?"

Ethan's brooding frown turned darkly sullen. "We are at war," he contended bitterly. "There are bound to be deaths."

There followed a long silence. Constance stared at him, her eyes wide with fearful dismay.

"You— you think yourself impervious to danger," she at last stammered, her voice rising with anxiety. "You think nothing of the ruthlessness of these — these murderers — who have shown that they will stop at nothing to achieve their purpose. What will it take for you to see? How many lives must be lost before you realize the senselessness—"

"How many lives must be lost?" Ethan cut her off sharply, his tone unnaturally severe. "How many lives will be lost if we do not put an end to this treachery? How many soldiers will perish for want of food, medicine, or provisions? How many lives will be lost upon the battlefield because our men are too ill or frail to fight? Who shall send word to mothers and wives that their sons and husbands died, not fighting valiantly in battle, but of starvation or cold or illness because we could not get supplies to them? Because someone failed in his endeavor to secure safe passage for their provisions? Would you have me abandon my mission and bear that burden?"

He did not go on, for Constance — quite overcome — emitted a piteous sob and covered her face with her hands.

Ethan, yet breathing heavily after his declamation, forcibly lowered his tone, though he remained firm in his conviction. "I will not give up this cause," he maintained. "Do not ask it of me."

Constance raised her head, wiping her tears with one hand. "Your cause for freedom is admirable and just," she said slowly. "But I wonder if that is the cause you still fight for. I fear that a thirst for revenge has usurped your desire for liberty." She looked up at him, searchingly, fervently. "Would you risk your own life — your very *life* — for vengeance?" Tears sprang into her eyes once more. "Would you ever think upon the unspeakable pain such a loss would bring to those who love you?"

They stood there confronting one another, tears streaming down Constance's cheeks.

Ethan was not unmoved. Indeed, Constance had come near to professing what he himself had never dared. He could not trust himself to gaze at her for more than a moment, so he turned away, tormented by a love that was stronger than his desire for revenge, more profound than any allegiance to which he had bound himself.

But his portentous silence and dark scowl led Constance to believe that he had steeled his heart, and with a despairing sob she turned and fled into the nascent dawn.

"Constance!" Ethan called after her, every muscle in his body pulsating with an instinctive desire to go after her. He could easily outrun her, draw her into his arms, and there give her the comfort she sought.

But even as he watched her disappear into the trees near the river path, he was aware of the daylight's brightness pressing against the orchard's shadows, and he knew that he could not tarry further. He could not jeopardize the mission upon whose outcome so many lives depended, and it was already well past the hour he was to set forth upon his journey.

Matters of the heart must wait, though it was in a black mood that he set out upon the high road, reproaching himself greatly for the anguish Constance would endure before he could speak with her again and set things aright.

❦

ETHAN'S STATE OF DISCONTENT DID not soon abate as he rode north-ward upon the high road. His thoughts yet dwelt upon what had passed in the orchard, and the more he dwelt upon it, the more he loathed him-self — for speaking to Constance as he had, for imparting not one word of tenderness to her before she ran away, for causing her even a moment's pain — and the more he reproached himself, the faster did he uncon-sciously compel his horse, so that he nearly made up in speed for the late hour of his departure.

After riding for several miles in such an ill-tempered abstraction, Ethan's thoughts began to be encompassed by other grievous subjects as he neared the vicinity of Clymer's farm, the sight of which necessarily called to mind Henry Dowling's brutal death and awakened anew con-victions of retributive justice.

Ethan slowed his horse, determined to give the industrious animal a well-deserved respite at the stable-yard trough, while he himself could take a cursory look about the place, for he had not set foot upon the property since the day of Henry Dowling's burial.

As he turned the horse in the direction of the stable-yard, though, Ethan gave a sudden pull upon the rein, bringing the creature to an abrupt halt, for what he saw before him caught him completely off-guard.

There, in the midst of the service yard dependencies, stood another horse, placidly drinking from the stable trough. Furthermore, leaning up against the well, with his back to the road, was propped a man, drink-ing thirstily from a canteen. The man did not see Ethan nor hear his approach, and Ethan dismounted at a distance, that he might retain the advantage of discretion, though he kept at his waist his pistol, concealed beneath his coat.

As Ethan silently neared the well, he observed that the hands which grasped the canteen were dark, and as the man's profile came into view,

Ethan was further astonished as he realized that the individual at the well was none other than Zachary Merrill's manservant Thaddeus.

Upon this realization, Ethan halted where he was and glanced quickly about him, searching for any sign of Thaddeus's master. There was but one horse at the trough, though, and what would already be perceived as a suspicious circumstance was, to Ethan, doubly so, for he instantly recalled the incident in the stairwell, where both Thaddeus's conduct and character had come into question.

Ethan remained silent and motionless, waiting for Thaddeus to turn around.

It took but a moment before the slave had concluded his respite, and when he straightened, secured his canteen, and turned away from the well, he did indeed give a start at the sight of Ethan Shaye standing but a few feet away.

Ethan forthwith addressed the startled slave. "What are you doing here?" he demanded.

Thaddeus, yet rooted to the spot, seemed unable to give immediate reply.

Ethan strode forth and confronted Thaddeus directly.

"Where is your master?" Ethan further demanded.

Thaddeus found his tongue. "He — he is not here," he faltered, though he was fast recovering his senses. "I have a pass," he added more steadfastly, and proceeded to proffer the referenced document, meeting Ethan's eye with newly-regained self-possession.

Ethan glanced at the pass, which was signed by Zachary Merrill and permitted Thaddeus the use of a horse upon the high road in carrying out his master's tasks; it further specified that the slave was not to cross any borders and was to return by sundown.

Ethan eyed Thaddeus once more.

The slave, having fully recovered his poise, drew himself up with an air of pride and even a bit of smugness.

Ethan remained ever cool and stern. "You have made liberal use of the amenities of this place," he remarked evenly. "Have the proprietors given their consent? I do not see them about."

Thaddeus seemed momentarily unsettled under Ethan's unwavering scrutiny. He glanced toward the house before making reply. "I— was not able to find anyone within the house or stable-yard," Thaddeus contended. "The people who live here are well-known to my master and have often permitted me to take refreshment at their well."

Ethan's eye glinted with contempt at what he knew was a lie, though Thaddeus maintained his staunchly impervious stance. A prolonged silence followed, and the enmity between the two men, which had been first elicited during the stairwell confrontation, was again palpable in that moment.

Ethan was determined to learn what errand Thaddeus was about, for he could not relegate to coincidence two suspicious encounters with the slave across such a short duration.

Thaddeus, however, seemed equally determined to divulge nothing more, and indeed, he moved as if to take his leave, averting his eyes and giving a properly subservient nod to Ethan, stating, "I must be about my master's business," and took a step in the direction of his horse.

As Thaddeus moved, though, Ethan's keen eye glimpsed something beneath the folds of the slave's plain brown coat. It was but the briefest glimmer — the sun's rays catching a glint of azure — yet one glimpse was enough.

Like a flash of lightning, Ethan's movement was instantaneous and reflexive. With one hand, he reached for the handle of the dagger which was concealed beneath Thaddeus's coat, pulling it with swift precision from its bejeweled scabbard. At the same time, he grasped with his other hand Thaddeus's arm, twisting it round and forcing Thaddeus to turn his back, allowing Ethan to bring his arm around the front of Thaddeus's chest, rendering the slave immobile.

Ethan put the blade of Henry Dowling's dagger to Thaddeus's throat. "Where did you get this?" he growled between clenched teeth.

Any attempt on Thaddeus's part to extricate himself was in vain, for he could not match Ethan's strength or physical command. The slave's chest heaved under the sudden and unexpected strain of captivity.

"Where did you come by this dagger?" Ethan repeated more severely, pressing the blade closer to Thaddeus's throat.

"It is rightfully mine!" Thaddeus protested. "My master gave it to me."

Ethan did not ease his grip. "Where did he acquire it?"

"I— I do not know," Thaddeus faltered.

Ethan's brow furrowed in contempt. "You are a liar," he charged, re-exerting the force of the blade. "Where did he get it?"

But Thaddeus would disclose nothing. "I do not know," he maintained staunchly, adopting an air of stolid impassivity. "Likely it is from the West Indies, where he was born. I know nothing except what my master bids of me."

Ethan scowled darkly. "Aye, you do your master's bidding, and he is indeed implicated by your presence here."

Ethan feigned to loosen his hold upon Thaddeus — then reinstated it with ferocity, causing the slave to gasp in alarm.

"Did your master bid you to steal this knife from Henry Dowling after you'd murdered him?" Ethan growled, his tone dangerous and low, steeled with bitter intensity. "'Twas your finger that pulled the trigger, was it not? Your arm that dragged the body across the floor and hoisted it up to the noose? Your master would not soil his dainty white hands to do such a deed, though it be at his behest. You are even now set upon your master's commission, I've no doubt. Set to inform the blockade guard of the latest shipment from Porter's wharf. Dowling found out. He discovered it was you. And you . . . you discovered that he knew."

Ethan was by now pressing the blade so tightly against Thaddeus's throat that the slave's dark skin gave way beneath it — only slightly, but enough for a warm trickle of red to appear beneath the blade's edge. Thaddeus remained as taut as a board, undoubtedly too fearful to move — nearly to breathe — lest the blade should permeate further.

"Why is Merrill doing this?" Ethan demanded, loosing the dagger just enough that Thaddeus might speak. "What is his interest in the Patriot army's provisions?"

"He— he is loyal to the king," Thaddeus stammered.

Ethan's scowl darkened. "It is an uncommon loyalty that impels him to ordain murder several times over. What is his interest in this enterprise? What has he to gain?"

Thaddeus made no immediate reply, and Ethan once again pressed the knife's blade tight against his throat.

"Answer me!" Ethan commanded, relentless in his pursuit of the truth.

"I— I do not know!" Thaddeus sputtered. "There is a letter—," he continued, the words emitted between rapid, gasping breaths, "from the king . . . I do not know its contents. He keeps it hidden . . . so the Judge will not know. . ."

"Where is the letter?" Ethan interjected sharply.

"In the writing desk . . . in his chamber . . ."

Though Ethan yet retained his hold upon the slave, he made no further demands but gave pause for a moment, pondering Thaddeus's words. The only sound in the stable-yard was the slave's heaving respiration.

Then, Ethan moved swiftly, set upon a course of action. Moving the blade to the side of Thaddeus's neck, he forced the slave to the ground and cast the dagger's sharp point into the dirt beside Thaddeus's ear. While Thaddeus yet quaked at this unexpected action, Ethan drew his pistol upon the slave. Moving rapidly, Ethan withdrew the knife from the ground, and, setting the pistol upon the well within Thaddeus's sight, proceeded to sever the well-bucket's rope, which he then used to bind Thaddeus's hands.

Seemingly resigned to his disadvantage, Thaddeus made no effort to resist as Ethan roughly forced him to his feet. Taking hold of one of the slave's arms, Ethan led him across the stable-yard and into the furthest dependency, which had once been used as a laundry but was now in a state of dusty neglect.

"I do not know how . . . but somehow she knew," Ethan muttered as he untied the slave's hands then re-bound them about a post at the rear of the dependency. "Somehow Jenny knew."

Thaddeus held his head loftily rigid. "You would be surprised at what we know," he asserted stonily. "A slave must always be observing. We learn a great many things . . . things our masters would not have us know . . . would not have anyone know."

There was something of menace in the deliberateness of Thaddeus's words, and as Ethan finished securing the slave to the post and came round to the front, Thaddeus met his eye with cold directness.

"I have even learned something about you," Thaddeus continued placidly, his tone even, yet tinged with a sinister note. "Something my master was keen to hear."

Ethan glowered at the captive. He had no patience for such evasive ploys. "I care nothing about what you have told your master," he countered brusquely. "It will all come out soon enough now."

Thaddeus said no more, and Ethan continued to work in silence, binding the slave's feet together so that while he was sitting with his back against the post he might not maneuver about it.

Thaddeus must surely have been contemplating his own fate, though, for when Ethan stood in preparation to leave, Thaddeus spoke up once more:

"What are you going to do with me? Leave me here to starve or freeze? Better you should kill me now."

Ethan eyed Thaddeus with contempt. "Nay," he said as he unfastened the scabbard from Thaddeus's waist. "Nay, I am going to turn you over to someone as vile as yourself."

And securing Henry Dowling's scabbard about his own waist, Ethan sheathed the dagger and departed, hastening to his mount then riding with all speed back to Merrilltown. He stopped not at his lodgings but directly sought out an individual whom he loathed but to whom necessity now demanded he take into his confidence — the reprehensible Monsieur Brissoneau.

ETHAN KNEW HE MUST BIDE his time before setting upon his next course of action, so he retreated to his room at Lethbridge's and remained there for the next few hours.

Shortly before sunset, he departed again, riding eastward out of Merrilltown, heading toward the Merrill estate. He secured his horse in the wood beside the hill leading up to Merrill Hall, then made his way up the hill on foot — not along the dirt road, but keeping to the side, concealed amongst the trees that lined the drive.

Upon reaching the hill's summit, Ethan did not continue toward the main house but instead kept himself behind the periphery of trees, crouching down amidst the density of vegetation, where he might observe the activity outside of the Hall without himself being observed.

There he waited a long while, as he had anticipated. As the sun set, the activity about the house and service yard was nothing out of the ordinary. Servants went to and fro between the house and dependencies, intent upon their evening chores. Inside the Hall, the soft glow of candlelight appeared in upstairs windows, while the lower level was illuminated with the brighter incandescence of hearth fires warming the common rooms where the residents would gather for their meal and evening diversions.

After a time, however, the dusky serenity of the estate was disrupted by a marked increase of activity in the service yard. At first, it was just some heightened voices and hurried steps. But then, the quantity of lanterns and candles multiplied, and the voices intensified. Something out of the ordinary was decidedly afoot and was causing some agitation amongst the extended household.

A cresset was ignited in front of the Hall. Several figures emerged through the front door, as a half-dozen saddled horses were brought round from the stable. There was a sense of urgency about the movements and voices of the men assembled at the foot of the front steps, and by the cresset's bright flame, Ethan recognized Zachary Merrill at the center of the cohort, issuing sharp orders, to which the other men responded with nods and verbal affirmations. With all due haste, Merrill and several of the others mounted the horses and took up lanterns handed up by servants. Ethan saw reflecting in the fire's light the dark, metallic gleam of pistols and sabers, and then the sudden orange brightness of torches, ignited from the cresset's flame, in the grips of those remaining standing, who were to carry out their task on foot.

The terse, throaty barking of dogs gave Ethan but a moment's unease, for he soon realized that the dogs, in spite of their frenzied excitement, stayed close to their masters, well-trained and intent only upon the quarry of their prey.

It took only a few moments to issue commands before the company departed down the hill — the men on horseback in a tumult of clattering hooves and clamorous shouts, and those on foot following behind with their torches in hand.

As the horses clattered past, Ethan lay low in the brush, knowing full well that the party's search would be in vain. The slave they sought had long since been taken into custody and would, by this time, be well-removed from the vicinity of the high road.

Although it was all but certain that no member of the search party would return for several hours, Ethan yet remained where he was for a full twenty minutes, until the house was once more encompassed in tranquility, and the servants had fallen back upon their regular duties.

Ethan then emerged from the cover of trees and crossed the forecourt, ascended the front steps of the Hall, and rapped upon the door. It was a moment before he heard the scurry of footsteps within, and then the door was opened by a rather out-of-breath housegirl, who was evidently not expecting any visitors to call so late.

Ethan, however, made no mention of the lateness of the hour nor did he give his name, but only inquired in the most nonchalant manner, "Is Mr. Merrill at home this evening?"

The housegirl shook her head. "No sir. The Judge and his Lady have gone to Williamsburg and are not expected back for a fortnight."

Ethan received this unexpectedly felicitous information without so much as the blink of an eye, but rather maintained a facade of purpose and pressed to clarify his meaning. "No, it is not the Judge, but Mr. Zachary Merrill I have come to see."

"Oh, I beg your pardon, sir," the housegirl apologized. "Mr. Merrill has gone out, and I cannot say when he will return."

"Ah, that is unfortunate," Ethan ostensibly conceded. "But I think I shall wait for him if I may," he continued briskly. "I have ample time, and it is a matter of some importance."

The girl hesitated, then gave a slight bob of acquiescence and opened the door wider. "Of course, sir," she said, stepping aside, that Ethan might enter. "You can wait in the parlor," and taking up the candle from the hall table, she led him across the wide entrance hall and into the first room on the right, where a fire blazed hospitably upon the hearth. The girl used her candle to light several others in the room, while Ethan stationed himself at the fireplace, leaning casually upon the mantel.

Having made the room comfortably bright, the girl turned to go, but paused in the doorway. "What name shall I give Mr. Merrill when he returns?" she inquired.

Ethan turned from the mantel. He looked the girl in the eye and said with some deliberateness, "Mr. Shaye."

There was no point in subterfuge now. Ethan intended on being long departed before Zachary Merrill returned, and all would be disclosed upon the morrow.

After the girl had exited the room, Ethan remained where he was for some moments, listening intently. He heard the girl's footsteps recede then heard the slam of a door toward the rear of the house. After that was silence, save for the crackling of the fire and the occasional creak of a beam, as is natural in a structure settling after the movements of its inhabitants have ceased.

Leaving his post at the fireplace, Ethan took up one of the lighted candles the housegirl had left upon a sideboard, and he moved to the doorway, peering cautiously into the hall. There, all was deserted and still, save for the softly dancing flames emanating from sconces at the far end of the room on either side of the front door.

Stepping across the parlor threshold, Ethan glanced about him. An impressive staircase, its bannister of carved mahogany, graced one end of the hall, and the walls were hung with elegant paintings — portraits, mostly, of generations of Merrills.

His eye alighting upon one particular painting at the foot of the stairs, Ethan crossed toward it and paused before its gilded frame, holding his candle aloft and making a pretext of studying the portrait attentively, feigning great interest in its subject.

Still, there were no footsteps nor voices to be heard within the house, though Ethan was cognizant of distant activity in the service yard beyond the rear door. He knew that one of the servants could enter the house at any moment. Should he be found in the hall, he could make plausible enough excuse. But what if he should be discovered upstairs? He must not tarry in executing his plan.

He was already standing at the foot of the staircase. Ascending the first two steps, he again paused to inspect the painting hanging there upon the wall. Fortunately, the staircase emulated the theme of the entrance hall, its walls lined with portraits as well as some smaller landscapes. Ethan moved up another two steps, always feigning to inspect the artwork upon the wall.

He turned his head to gauge the remainder of the darkened stairwell before him. He could hardly ascend further without raising suspicion should he be observed.

Pausing once more, he listened for any conceivable indication of approaching footsteps or nearing voices, but he heard nothing other than a stray voice or two outside in the service yard.

Leaving behind the pretense of inspection, Ethan set a cautious foot upon the next step, then the next. Even with the slight creaking of boards beneath his feet, there was no reactionary movement from within any part of the house. And when Ethan moved again, he did so swiftly but stealthily, hastening up the remaining stairs with brisk agility.

At the top of the staircase he paused but briefly, finding himself in a long corridor unilluminated by any purposeful flame, save his own candle. Yet the corridor was not entirely darkened, for a flickering light could be seen emanating through an open door halfway down the passageway, and it was toward that door that Ethan strode.

Shielding his candle's flame with one hand, he peered cautiously through the doorway, finding — as he'd anticipated — a stately bedchamber, devoid of occupants but with a bright fire kindled upon the hearth, set to provide comforting warmth upon the occupant's return.

The Judge and his Lady were away; this bedchamber was assuredly that of their grandson, with the hospitable fire prepared for his eventual return.

But while the fire provided Ethan with welcome light, it also presented a heightened danger, for it must be tended. A servant might ascend the stairs at any moment to look in upon the hearth or to give the fire a stir.

Wasting no time, Ethan crossed the room to the opposite corner, where a small, handsome writing desk sat, its hinged front open, an inkwell, pen, and stack of blank pages arranged neatly upon its surface, awaiting the hand of the scribe.

Ethan reflected back upon his confrontation with Thaddeus at Clymer's farm. The slave had stated that the letter from the king was in Merrill's writing desk, but he had not specified any particular compartment, and Ethan had not pressed him.

Now, standing before the desk, he quickly appraised the object's structure, which was typically simple it its design, with a row of small niches above the writing surface and a single drawer below. It took but a cursory survey of the compartments to see that there were no papers tucked within — indeed, most of the niches were empty; the few holding items contained only ordinary accessories such as blotters and pounce.

Working quickly, Ethan pulled open the slender drawer and examined its contents. There were a few stray sheets of paper, which Ethan immediately seized. Upon inspection, though, they proved to be nothing of substance; the words scrawled upon them were merely random musings — snippets of poetry, quotations, and incidental names or dates. Casting the papers aside, Ethan quickly scanned the drawer's remaining contents, which were sparse indeed, consisting only of some mismatched brass buttons, a ball of sealing wax, and some half-spent candles.

Closing the drawer, Ethan glanced about the room, frowning in consternation.

Had Thaddeus deceived him?

It would have been a foolish exertion on the part of the slave, for now that Thaddeus was in captivity, Ethan could easily seek him out and confront him again. But — when could he hope to gain access again to Zachary Merrill's quarters? When would he again happen upon such a fortuitous occasion as to find both grandfather and grandson absent from the premises?

He could not count on another such opportunity.

He appraised the desk again. It was not uncommon for desks of quality to have a hidden compartment embedded in the framework. His own father's desk, larger and more elaborate than this one, had a drawer with a false bottom — of which Ethan, in his youth, had been granted knowledge only under the solemnest of vows.

Now, he pulled open the drawer of Zachary Merrill's desk again, and, getting on his knees, examined the underside, keeping one hand upon the bottom of the shallow drawer's interior. He could find no obvious discrepancy in the drawer's depth, however.

Still upon his knees — and ever aware of the passage of precious time — Ethan raised his head, scrutinizing once more the drawer's interior. His eye lingered upon the rear panel of the drawer. Dropping down once more, Ethan crawled beneath the desk, his hand reaching along the drawer's exterior until it came to the end of the rear panel.

Then, scrambling out from beneath the desk, Ethan took hold of the open drawer and pulled it completely out of its slot, setting it upon the desk's surface, where he could easily appraise the drawer's structure in its entirety. Sure enough, the rear panel of the drawer was unnaturally wide — measuring, at a glance, approximately four inches.

With hasty movement, Ethan pressed his hand along the bottom of the drawer, then its interior sides, a sense of urgency mounting as he heard nearing voices from the yard below. Shifting his hand to the exterior, his fingers moved deftly along the right panel, the rear, then the front, searching in vain for any kind of hidden spring which would trigger a mechanism within the drawer. But then, as his fingers slid across the left panel, Ethan suddenly gave pause and moved his hand back an inch or so, to where he thought he had felt something slightly raised upon the wood's smooth surface. And indeed, his fingers there alighted upon a sort of knob — so small as to be easily overlooked upon examination, for it was made of the same wood of which the panel was crafted, yet evident enough upon a finger's touch.

Ethan pressed down upon the knob, and at once — with a quiet springing sound — a narrow compartment opened inside the rear of the drawer. Narrow as it was, it extended the length of the panel, and nestled inside was a document, rolled and bearing a broken seal.

Seizing it at once, Ethan's pulse quickened as he noted the royal insignia upon the broken seal. Unrolling the document, he found it to be but a single page, a letter of sorts, penned in an ornately formal script, addressed to Mr. Zachary Merrill, and bearing the familiar signature of the British monarch.

Quickly scanning the letter's contents, Ethan skimmed through the first paragraph, which was an elaborate commendation of Merrill's loyalty to king and country. But it was the second paragraph which commanded Ethan's attention and to which he paid assiduous heed:

In appreciation of your unremitting allegiance to the British Crown, and in recognition of those direct efforts put forth in the rendering of assistance to the cause of justice and victory, you are hereby granted, upon that certain

victory, exclusive privilege to the right of importation of the commodity of mo-
lasses into the American colonies, such that no competitor may legally engage in
commensurate trade. This intractable right is granted you by the Sovereign au-
thority of the King upon the condition that those efforts on the Crown's behalf
are maintained to the extent that they are warranted . . .

Ethan had no chance to read further, for at that moment he heard a
door slam below. With swift and immediate movement, he shoved the
letter in his pocket, slid the drawer back into place, and took up his candle, leaving the desk's surface in some disarray, for he dared not take the
time to put it back in order.

Bolting from the room, Ethan hastened down the stairs, though he
abruptly slowed his pace at the stair's mid-point, for he saw in the hall
below the housegirl just emerging from one of the adjacent rooms.

She, likewise, came to a halt upon sighting him.

Sauntering nonchalantly down the remaining steps — as if it was the
most natural thing in the world that he should have been upon the stairs,
perhaps examining the portraits hanging there — Ethan addressed the
startled servant:

"I must take my leave," he said smoothly, setting the candle upon
the hall table. "I cannot wait longer upon Mr. Merrill's return. No need
to convey any message to him — I will undoubtedly speak with him
tomorrow or the next day."

The housegirl yet seemed a bit confounded, but Ethan made no further explanation and proceeded toward the front door. Pausing with his
hand upon the latch, he turned back toward the servant girl.

"Might I have a lantern for my journey?"

The girl, of course, could not have known of the audacity of his request, for when Mr. Shaye departed the premises a few minutes later, he
carried with him more than the Merrills' lantern.

IN SPITE OF THE DARKNESS, the ride back to his lodgings seemed but a fleeting moment, for so occupied was Ethan's mind that he took no notice of the passage of time.

He had upon his person unequivocal evidence that Zachary Merrill's allegiance lay surreptitiously with the king.

And everything was made clear to Ethan.

Zachary Merrill hailed from the West Indies — Thaddeus had affirmed as much earlier that day. Though now residing with his grandfather in Virginia, the younger Merrill undoubtedly yet retained his family's holdings in the islands — sugar plantations which yielded rich quantities of molasses, some of which was, even now, sitting in a decrepit warehouse beside the Rappahannock's tributary and was likely being traded by illicit means, providing a tidy subsidiary profit. It would pale, though, in comparison to the dividends Merrill would reap once he was granted exclusive rights to the commodity's importation. Merrill would do whatever it took to ensure the Crown's victory in war, thus securing his monopoly and an incomparable fortune.

But Zachary Merrill's scheme was about to unravel . . . and he would soon enough discover that he had lost far more than his trusted slave.

UPON RETURNING TO LETHBRIDGE'S, ETHAN secured the lock upon his chamber door then set about penning a missive to Tristan's commanding officer, for the militia, with its proximity to Merrilltown, could provide necessary assistance in the interim until a contingent from Ethan's own regiment would arrive.

Once the message was drafted and sealed, though, Ethan could take no further action until morning, so, latching the shutters and placing his pistol beneath his pillow, he extinguished the single light and went to bed.

Sleep proved elusive, however, for he could not still his mind. It was, perhaps, understandable, given the consequential events of the day; yet, strangely, it was not reflection upon such events nor even the anticipation of imminent victory which commanded his wakeful attention. Instead, as he lay there in the darkness, his thoughts strayed back to an entirely different tableau . . . one that had unfolded at the break of day — that very day — yet which might have been many days past, so much had since transpired. He could not help but think upon the orchard and upon the girl who had fled from him in tears.

How he loathed himself for hurting her again!

How he loved her.

Yet how unworthy was he of her love.

He lay quite awake far into the night, brooding and restless, heedless of the passing hours, until slumber at last descended upon him like a dark curtain, enveloping him in a deep and dreamless chasm.

PART IV
The Forest

T HE HOUR WAS ALREADY LATE when Ethan awoke the next morning, and it was with haste that he arose and dressed.

After dispatching the message to the militia camp, he set out at once from Lethbridge's, for he still had work to do before he could send word to Colonel Naismith. There were yet unanswered questions. He needed first to ascertain whether or not the previous day's supply shipment had successfully crossed the border, so it was to Joshua Porter's house that he headed. There, he could study the logbook's latest entry . . . and there, too, might he chance to encounter Constance.

When he was admitted into the Porters' entrance hall, however, he found the house — or at least the rooms leading off of the main hall — to be devoid of any activity and characterized only by pervasive silence; there was no sign of Constance nor of any other members of the household, save for the perpetually cheerful servant girl who greeted him at the door and affirmed that the study was unoccupied at present.

But while the study may have been momentarily vacant, there yet remained vestiges of recent occupants, for no sooner had Ethan entered the room than he felt something underfoot. Taking a step back, he saw that he had, indeed, stepped upon a small, hard object which lay upon the floor — one of Caleb Porter's toy soldiers. Other than the awareness of setting foot upon it, though, Ethan thought nothing of the plaything's presence in the study, for he had often seen Caleb's soldiers strewn about the place. As he bent to pick it up, Ethan noted with some measure of satisfaction that the tiny lead figure was attired in blue and not in red. Ethan was yet convinced of Joshua Porter's innocence to any complicity with Zachary Merrill or his henchman. Nevertheless, it was within the merchant's logbook that Ethan must again look for information.

Setting the toy soldier upon the desk, Ethan proceeded to the shelf and pulled the leather-bound logbook from its familiar place. Seating himself at the desk, he turned over the book's pages until he came to the one last notated. And there — it was with a surge of triumphant relief that Ethan's eye fell upon the last column, which remained unmarked. If the army's provisions had not made it across the border the previous day, Ethan was certain the word *"Intercepted"* — or worse — would have by now been inscribed.

So . . . Thaddeus had been enroute to the blockade and not returning from it when Ethan had apprehended him; and thus, the provisions were assuredly safely on their way to General Washington.

Reflecting upon the unequivocal significance of that circumstance and of what was now set in place for the Patriot army, Ethan looked up from the page, and as he did so, his eye chanced to alight upon the toy soldier he had set upon the desk only a few minutes earlier. It was no passing glance that he gave it, though, but rather his attention was momentarily diverted by the lead figure. He stared at it for a few seconds; then, leaning forward, he picked it up. He turned the small figure over in his fingers, contemplating it, for a new train of thought had arisen in his mind.

An image of the militia muster surfaced in his recollection — of little Caleb Porter eagerly cheering on the militia men, marching alongside them, imitating the movements of his brother Tristan, who had been present that day within the militia's ranks.

Such a recollection of the militia muster was a natural enough association to be paired with the sight of Caleb's toy soldier. Ethan reflected on how the child's evident preference and enthusiasm for all things related to the Patriots was unquestionably a testament to his father's guidance — and would seem to provide further testament to Joshua Porter's abiding loyalty to the Patriots' cause. Even so, it was, without a doubt, Caleb's mother who wielded the most influence over her son in other areas, for her oversight of his upbringing was meticulous, though her indulgence had rendered the child disagreeable and spoiled.

Yet, Ethan recalled that it was upon that very occasion of the militia muster that he had glimpsed another side of Anne Porter — when a momentary shadow had passed over the lady's countenance as she thought upon her mother's resting place. It had occurred to Ethan then that Mrs. Porter was, perhaps, not entirely flighty and frivolous, though it was but a rare manifestation of such gravity on her part.

Mrs. Porter's depth of emotion revealed itself far more perceptibly in the love she bore toward her child, though her coddling would, in time, undoubtedly prove only to the child's detriment. It was well that Caleb's father in some part provided a sensible counterbalance to the mother's overbearing devotion. Indeed, the only instance Ethan had ever observed Anne Porter to deny her son anything was when she had withheld permission for him to wear the Patriot's cockade upon his hat, which, in turn, endeared the privilege to Caleb all the more.

This thought led Ethan's contemplation to the subject of Zachary Merrill, for any recollection of young Caleb Porter must invariably be associated with the school which Mr. Merrill so munificently endowed and oversaw. As Ethan thought upon the day he had accompanied Zachary Merrill to the schoolroom — as he recalled the way that Merrill had stood at the back of the room, magnanimously presiding over the provincial microcosm — Ethan's brow furrowed. Truly, it was with bitterness that he reflected upon the hypocrisy of the man who had garnered the admiration of an entire town with his facade of benevolence and congeniality all the while surreptitiously orchestrating duplicity and murder. Everyone had been deceived — Constance, the Porters, the townspeople. Ethan remembered how Zachary Merrill's mere appearance in the schoolroom had merited Caleb permission to sport the black cockade upon his hat. Indeed, Ethan had noted it the day he and Merrill had visited the school.

And yet . . .

Ethan frowned as another memory surfaced. Surely it could not merely be Mr. Merrill's anticipated presence that persuaded Caleb's mother to allow the cherished cockade, for it had not been permitted upon the occasion of Caleb's recitation before the illustrious patron. Ethan well-remembered the first time he saw Caleb Porter — the child's disagreeable nature had been immediately revealed, vocalizing displeasure at being denied the chance to wear the cockade the day that Mr. Merrill was to hear his piece. The child had been told he might wear it only upon "special occasions", yet, indeed, Ethan wondered if it depended more upon the whim of Caleb's mother than upon any standard.

Ethan dwelt further upon this point, as inconsequential as it seemed, for there was a new idea arising in his mind . . . one that was not yet fully formed but gradually taking shape, and in such a manner as to dispel every divergent train of thought.

In beholding again the lead soldier in his hand, the image in Ethan's mind's-eye leapt from that of Zachary Merrill in the schoolroom back to the militia muster upon the Green . . . back to Anne Porter's face, tinged with a sorrow that was fleeting but unfeigned.

Yet, this time, the memory was not merely a recollection but a revelation, for in that moment everything was made clear to Ethan. In that moment, everything came together, and he knew . . . he knew how Zachary Merrill received his information; he knew why Merrill had made a point of courting Constance; he knew the identity of Merrill's companion in the amorous tryst behind the garden wall.

Ethan slowly placed the toy soldier back upon the desk, and he sat there a long while in silence, lost in thought, his mind assimilating the implication of such a consequential disclosure.

But in the midst of his rumination, it happened that the door to the study opened, and — as if on cue — Anne Porter stepped into the room.

She stopped just inside the doorway, evidently startled at finding the room occupied.

"Oh, Mr. Shaye!" she exclaimed. "I did not know that you were in here. I am sorry to disturb you. I'll just—" And she might have turned to go, but she broke off quite suddenly, as her eye fell upon the logbook sitting open on the desk before Ethan. Mrs. Porter's entire demeanor changed. "What are you about?" she asked, her tone taking on a markedly frigid, and even accusatory, edge. "Does my husband know that you are looking through his . . . his books?"

Ethan remained entirely unmoved by her disapproving manner. Neither did he make immediate reply, but only regarded her with such acute contempt that Mrs. Porter shifted a bit uncomfortably beneath such severe scrutiny.

"I might ask the same of you," Ethan at last responded, his voice low and unwavering.

Mrs. Porter paled slightly. "I . . . I am sure I don't know what you mean," she said stiffly.

"Indeed," Ethan went on levelly, rising from his seat, "I believe there is only one book here that holds any interest for you — this one," and he tapped his finger upon the logbook's open page. "The same one I have often examined."

"What on earth would I be doing looking at a musty old ledger?" Mrs. Porter began, but Ethan ignored her protestation and continued, moving around to the front of the desk, his eye yet fixed fast upon her:

"It is assuredly more convenient for you to visit this room at this hour — when your husband is away — than to come creeping down the stairs in the middle of the night."

Anne Porter's eyes flashed, but Ethan went on, his voice hardening with contempt:

"Shall I leave the logbook out for you? It is already open to the last entry. Or shall I spare you the trouble of reading it and inform you that the shipment sent out yesterday has safely crossed the border into Maryland without interception?"

Mrs. Porter's bosom heaved in tandem with her perceptibly audible breathing, even as she held her head rigidly erect. "I am sure I do not know what you are talking about," she said indignantly. "Nor do I care for your tone."

Ethan's eye gleamed with dark fire as his patience gave way. "Do not speak to me of tone nor mannerisms!" he admonished angrily. "Let us speak instead of a woman who styles herself a doting wife and mother, yet conspires to betrayal and murder behind her husband's back!"

Ethan's rancor was plain, and the flicker of fear which lighted Anne Porter's eye did not escape his notice.

Nevertheless, Mrs. Porter quickly regained an air of lofty self-composure, and when she made reply, her tone was as cold as her icy glare. "Your insolence knows no bounds. I must ask you to leave this room and this house at once."

"I assure you, I have finished here," Ethan replied heatedly, though he made no immediate movement to depart and, in fact, moved a step closer to Anne Porter, causing her to retreat several steps back. Indeed, the ominous darkness of Ethan's scowl would have unsettled a stronger soul than the mistress of the house. Ethan went on, forcefully, merciless in his castigation of Zachary Merrill's accomplice: "I am leaving, and I am taking with me the knowledge that you are the informant who has worked to sabotage your husband's efforts . . . the knowledge that you have used your own child as a pawn in your game . . . that the black cockade was the signal to your accomplice . . . the knowledge that you have betrayed your husband in more than just this endeavor."

Anne Porter blanched at these words, but Ethan continued:

"Your callous indifference to the brutality of murder and to the innocent lives lost and forever changed by your betrayal speaks more than any admission of guilt. You may yet feel some remorse when you find that, by your deception, you have lost everything you cherish."

And as Ethan uttered these forceful words, Anne Porter's composure suddenly disintegrated.

"Everything I cherish!" she cried out, her tone marked by equal measures of resentment and hysteria. "Everything I cherish!" she repeated. "What do you know of that which I cherish? I have already lost what I cherish! I have only endeavored to regain what is rightfully mine! And do not speak lightly of my child — you know nothing of a mother's love or anguish on behalf of her offspring! Everything I have done, I did for him! Aye, for him. What has Caleb in this world except what I may leave to him? What shall he inherit from his father? Nothing! *Nothing!*" She repeated the word with bitter vehemence. "Everything — all of *this*," and she extended her arms to indicate the house in which they stood, "—the land, the ships, what fortune is my husband's — all of it will go to Tristan. And what shall pass to Caleb? Only what is mine to give, for I, too, am the eldest among my father's heirs, and he has no sons to his name. It was all to come to me — my father's land, his house, his property!" By now, tears of desperation and of fury clouded her eyes. "All of it is my birthright. And all of it is lost — fallen into the hands of those baseborn Patriot rebels. Caleb's inheritance . . . stolen from my father — from *me!* My mother's grave . . . my family's legacy . . . everything we had — gone!" Here Anne paused, her vigor spent, her breast heaving under the duress of her indignation. When she continued, it was in a tone that was markedly lowered, though firmly intent. "When the opportunity presented itself to regain what was lost, to regain what is rightfully my father's, to re-establish my darling Caleb's inheritance . . . what woman would refuse such an opportunity? Surely you would not begrudge a mother her chance to secure a prosperous future for her son? Everything I have done, I did for him!"

Her voice implored Ethan to defer to reason and understanding, but he was only further incensed by her pleas.

"Lives have been lost!" he rebuked her fiercely. "Innocent lives — cut down in cold-blooded murder, to which you played a part."

"I know nothing of murder!" Anne bristled. "Besides," she added with disdain, "I'm sure even you would agree that lives lost to a higher cause are sometimes a necessary sacrifice."

Ethan's eyes flashed with fury. "I have done with you, woman!" he growled with such venom that Anne shrank back, again subdued by Ethan's forceful command. Ethan shook his head in bitter disgust. "How an angel like Constance can have a devil of a sister like you, I cannot fathom."

Anne drew herself up haughtily. "How dare you insult me?"

But Ethan paid no heed to her reprimand. "I will deal with you later," he said gruffly and strode past her toward the door. "There are other matters I must attend to now." And with that he departed, without another word, without any allusion to the fate that awaited Joshua Porter's wife.

As for Anne Porter — she remained where she stood, rigid in the cold paralysis of foreboding trepidation.

ETHAN QUICKLY MADE HIS WAY back to Lethbridge's, where he shut himself up in his room and once more put pen to paper. He remained thus engaged for well over an hour, for his missive was lengthy and detailed. It was addressed to Colonel Naismith, but it was not dispatched, for this message Ethan must himself deliver directly into the Colonel's hands. But he could not yet set out, nor could he even seal the report, for it was not yet complete. No, he must await the arrival of the contingent from the militia before he could write the ending to his missive, before he could make the long ride out to his regiment's encampment.

Having completed what he could, Ethan folded the document and, reaching for his coat, placed the folded paper into the pocket alongside the document he had retrieved from Zachary Merrill's writing desk.

He hung the coat back on its hook just as Maria Lethbridge knocked upon the door, inquiring if Ethan would take any sustenance. He bid her to bring a plate up to his room, for he felt the necessity of keeping close to his quarters as long as the two documents were in his possession, until such time as he must set forth to meet the militia contingent and see his mission through to the end.

He was restless in the interim, though, and after supping in solitude, he paced about the room a bit before settling in the chair before the fire, where — in an effort to occupy himself productively — he set about cleaning his pistol.

He had only just finished the task and had begun to load the weapon when he heard a sudden clatter upon the staircase in the hall accompanied by heavy footsteps and the sound of men's voices shouting angrily.

Ethan was instantly alert and on his feet. He hastily finished loading his pistol, and, securing it at his waist, he quickly crossed to the door, for the din outside was by then reverberating down the corridor outside his room. He paused but a moment with his hand upon the latch, formulating his course of action, then pulled back the pin and slipped swiftly into the corridor, intending to place himself between the staircase and his chamber.

He did not, however, step far beyond the threshold, for, regardless of what he might have anticipated, what he beheld in the corridor — by the light emanating from the chamber behind him — was so unexpected that he came to an abrupt halt just outside the doorway.

There before him, at the head of the stairwell, were three figures. Two of them were men from the tavern, whose shouts upon the stairs had been heard in Ethan's chamber. They were attempting to restrain the third individual, who was thrashing about, wildly desperate to be free from their restraint.

It was upon that third individual that Ethan's eye was fixed, his attention immediately arrested.

It was Jenny.

When she saw Ethan, she redoubled her efforts to free herself from the two men flanking her, straining to pull herself from their grip.

For the first time, Ethan heard sound emanate from Jenny's throat — not words nor speech, but a low, guttural sound, as that of an animal caught in a trap, desperate to extricate itself.

"Let her go!" Ethan ordered the two men, his brow furrowed, even as his eye remained fixed upon Jenny.

"Nay, she is mad," one of the men began, "—came barging through the front door like a—"

"Let her go!" Ethan reiterated with authoritative severity. "I will take responsibility for this woman."

"She is like to kill someone!" the other man protested.

But Ethan seemed not to hear. He stared at Jenny as if transfixed, then slowly approached her, a dark frown creasing his brow, for something had taken root inside of him; his heart began pounding and a sudden fear gripped his being as he beheld Jenny's frantic, wild-eyed countenance.

"Where is your mistress?" Ethan asked sharply, his chest tightening as Jenny's guttural vociferations intensified. Ethan's tone took on a terrible ferocity: *"Where is Constance?"*

And something like a sob emitted from Jenny's throat as two big tears rolled down her cheeks. The two men released their grip upon her, for indeed she had suddenly abandoned her struggling, and she clasped her hands before Ethan as if begging him to help her, her mouth working frenetically, uttering wordless sounds of desperation.

Ethan grasped her shoulders forcefully. "Take me to her!" he commanded gruffly, but Jenny did not move, and Ethan's sense of urgency increased. "Can you take me to her?"

Jenny shook her head, tears now streaming down her face.

"Then tell me where to go!" Ethan thundered, his grip upon Jenny's shoulders tightening roughly. His mind raced. "Porter's house? Shall I go to Porter's house?"

And Jenny nodded her head — rapidly, as if to urge him on.

Ethan needed no such prompting. He released his grasp upon Jenny's shoulders.

"Saddle my horse!" he ordered the men, then bolted back into his chamber. Moving swiftly, he pulled on his boots and donned his coat, taking care to secure the pistol beneath it. Then, slowing his step but for half a second, he reached for a second weapon — his rifle. Taking it up from its place beside the hearth, Ethan hastened from the room and raced down the stairs.

THE HORSE REARED IN AGITATION as Ethan pulled the speeding creature to an abrupt halt before the Porters' house. Indifferent to the animal's vexation, Ethan sprang from the saddle and hastened up the front steps without pausing to tether his mount. Neither did he knock upon the door, but thrust it swiftly open and proceeded straightaway into the main hall, where he very nearly collided with the docile young housegirl, who had been making her way toward the door and who gasped as it burst suddenly open before her.

Ethan paid the girl no heed, but glanced hastily about the hall, fixing his eye upon the parlor door, which was closed but from behind which the low murmur of voices emanated.

Indeed, three people were assembled therein: the master of the house, his wife, and his wife's youngest sister. They all turned in surprise as, without warning, the door suddenly burst open and Ethan Shaye strode into their midst.

"Where is Constance?" he demanded brusquely, glancing impatiently from face to face.

His question was met with grim silence.

Polly's eyes were red and swollen, as if she had been crying.

Even Anne Porter's countenance was unnaturally pale.

It was Polly who at last spoke up. "She is gone," she uttered hoarsely, and, knowing well that further explanation was in order, she crossed to the central table and picked up from its surface a piece of paper. "Here—," she extended the page toward Ethan. "You must read for yourself, for I—," she faltered, "I cannot myself comprehend it."

Ethan took from her the paper. It was a letter, written in a stately hand, addressed to Mr. and Mrs. Porter, and bearing Zachary Merrill's signature:

You must forgive what I am about to impart, for I know that upon first impression it may well astound and perhaps even alarm you, but I pray you to be assured of the noble character and intent of those implicated, such that you will determine, upon reflection, the merit and rationale behind their actions.

As you are aware, there has been a longstanding, deeply-rooted affection established between Miss Constance Jameson and myself, which has intensified profoundly over the course of these recent months. Though we have long since pledged our hearts to one another, the joy of our love must always be tempered with underlying sorrow, arising from the certain knowledge that her father would never bestow his blessing upon our union, due to the inexorable differences between his political loyalties and mine.

When I recently imparted to Miss Constance that I must return to my plantations in the West Indies for a time, the dear lady was overcome with grief at the prospect of our parting. I could not bear to see her thus distressed, and so we devised of a daring — yet necessary — scheme as the only way to secure our happiness.

She sends to you and to the rest of her family her abiding love and begs you to forgive whatever pain she may cause at such a drastic undertaking, imploring you to reflect upon the sorrowful circumstances put upon a young girl's heart which thus compelled her.

I, too, am compelled to add for your assurance that you must never doubt the sincerity of my intentions nor of my devotion to her. Attending to her every comfort shall be my greatest joy. You need never fear for her well-being.

Again, please think not harshly upon us, but remember us with love and tenderness, the same of which we extend to you all our days.

Zachary Merrill

Ethan cast the letter roughly upon the table. "This is rubbish!" he denounced angrily. He scowled darkly at Anne Porter. "You know this is rubbish!"

But though Anne Porter remained silent, it was apparent by her peaked countenance that she had not anticipated Zachary Merrill's actions.

Ethan's mind raced furiously. If Zachary Merrill intended to flee — why would he take Constance? And why would he pen an elaborate letter notifying Constance's family of her whereabouts and of his intended destination? Ethan could think of only one reason, and, even as his hand moved instinctively to his pocket, he wasted not a moment in setting about a course of action.

"When did you last see her?" he demanded.

"She — she was at breakfast," Polly faltered. "And afterward she set out toward the river path — she often walks there in the morning—"

"You cannot think of going after them," Joshua Porter interjected, frowning at Ethan. "Merrill has made their intentions known, and Constance is of age, though I like not to think what her father will say—"

"She would never go with Merrill!" Ethan countered vehemently. "Not of her own accord."

Polly emitted a cry. "See?" She turned suddenly upon her sister and brother-in-law. "I told you she would not do such a thing!" Tears welled in her eyes. "She does not love Mr. Merrill — she told me as much. And now, I truly fear for her well-being!"

Ethan paid no heed to this plaintive outburst, for indeed, every moment was precious, and his mind was working frantically.

"There were two ships at the Merrills' wharf yesterday," he contended, glancing at Joshua Porter, who gave a curt nod.

"Aye, they were yet there as of an hour ago."

That was all Ethan needed to hear. He turned swiftly and exited the room with all due haste, his pace yet increasing to a sprint as he tore through the hall and out the front door. Without slowing his step, he leapt up into his saddle, digging his spurs into the horse's side with such force that the animal shrieked in agitation, though it obeyed its master's command and bolted forward, so that only seconds later both horse and rider had disappeared from sight.

ETHAN BENT LOW OVER THE horse's neck as the animal raced along the riverbank, its hooves kicking up a storm of dust in their wake. The clatter of hooves, though, even at such a frenetic gait, could not outpace the pulsation of Ethan's heart, pounding against his ribcage, reverberating in his ears. But though the horse sped like the devil, straining at the bit, it could never be fast enough for Ethan, and he cursed the animal and the distance yet before him.

The horse pushed on valorously, though, even as the flat terrain gave way to a steeper incline, as Ethan guided his mount up a high ridge, where the path narrowed amidst the pines.

Still they pressed on, until horse and rider at last emerged from the trees at the top of the ridge, where the view of the river below stretched wide before them.

It was not, however, to the river or to its bustling wharves that Ethan looked, but rather he turned his head eastward, where from his vantage point he could see the Rappahannock's tributary — the quiet waterway toward which he had ventured in solitude upon multiple occasions and where the Merrills' ancestors had once moored their vessels. In observing the tributary now, though, Ethan's heart gave a lurch, for there — as he had both anticipated and dreaded — was a small ship parting the calm waters.

The momentary apprehension quickly dissipated as Ethan realized that the ship was moving slowly toward the shore; it had not yet reached its destination.

The realization of this circumstance offered but a fleeting reprieve, however, and meant only that a plan must be formulated all the more quickly.

Turning in the saddle, Ethan surveyed the surrounding landscape. The Merrill estate was directly to the north, shrouded by trees, with only the chimneys of the Hall emerging above the foliage. His eye lingered there for but the briefest second, for it was not upon Merrill Hall that he must focus; no — he must cast his gaze further, to the rugged, forested hills which lay between the Merrill estate and the tributary. He knew those hills well; he had ascended their wooded gradient in solitude; he was familiar with their dense, craggy inclines; and now — as he scanned the still, forested slopes, he knew that he must set his course again toward those distant hills.

He did not ponder further nor offer his horse more than that moment's respite before urging the creature onward again, back down the ridge with the same urgent alacrity with which they had ascended.

There was no course to take except that which they had already traversed, and Ethan again silently denounced the vastness of the terrain which cost him precious time.

Which cost Constance precious time.

Indeed, it was upon her alone that Ethan's every thought was focused; it was her image which was ever in his mind; it was the thought of her in harm's way which compelled him to urge his horse ever faster, rendering him indifferent to the creature's exertion or to any passing landscape as they reached the road at the foot of the ridge.

Neither did he allow the horse to slow as the wooded foothills came into view. Indeed, the sight of his objective only increased Ethan's sense of urgency, for he felt certain that Constance was there — somewhere in that interval between the hills and the tributary.

A figure appeared in the distance, crossing the road before him, but Ethan paid it no heed and steered his mount off the road and across an open field toward the hills. No sooner had he thus changed course, though, than he turned in the saddle, glancing back over his shoulder, for it registered with him that the figure was a familiar one, even at such a distance.

It was Jenny.

And Ethan's thoughts were momentarily diverted, for he had not only recognized Jenny's conspicuous figure, but it occurred to him that she was taking a very circuitous route back to the Porters' house, undoubtedly hoping to make her way along the river, that she might slip back to her quarters unobserved. It was likely she had already been missed.

But as he glanced back at Jenny, Ethan saw that she had come to a halt beside the road and had, in fact, sighted him.

He could not stop, though. He could not slow nor even call out a word to her. He could not lose a moment, and, indeed, after that cursory distraction, Ethan's thoughts immediately returned to his objective. He must achieve the foothills; he must find Constance; he must find her before it was too late.

As the open field gave way to wooded incline, Ethan had no choice but to slow his horse's pace. At first, the trees were amply spaced, so as to allow a horse and rider to pass among them, but as soon as the forest's density increased, Ethan abandoned his mount. He hastily tethered his horse, took up his rifle, and proceeded on foot, rapidly making his way up the ever-steeper incline.

He made swift progress, for the way was familiar to him, and the dormancy of early winter had greatly thinned the brush underfoot. So, too, did the sparseness of foliage lend itself to greater visibility amongst the trees, allowing Ethan to observe with clarity his surroundings, for even as he forged ahead, he was ever watchful. And indeed, as he passed near a thick cluster of pines, his eye alighted on something lying on the ground beneath the trees' fragrant branches — something small and starkly white, quite out of place atop the carpet of brown needles. As he bent to examine it, Ethan's heart skipped a beat. He reached forward and picked up the lightweight object, feeling its pliable softness between his fingers, even as his pulse accelerated.

It was a dainty linen cap, trimmed with lace, such as he had seen Constance wear on many occasions.

Frowning intently as he fingered the cap, Ethan rose slowly, his mind racing.

Constance had assuredly passed this way. But under what duress? Under what circumstances but those of forcible constraint would she lose her cap and fail to retrieve it?

Ethan quickly surveyed the forest about him but could see no other indication of Constance's or Zachary Merrill's presence in the vicinity. Yet Ethan was certain they were in these woods, and so, too, was he certain that Constance was in peril.

That thought compelled him swiftly onward toward the hill's summit, the stillness of the forest negated by the deafening pounding of his heart as he rapidly and adroitly made his way up the uneven ascent. He slowed his step as he entered a small clearing, pausing to quickly gauge the steep incline before him, which rose precipitously to the forested hill's highest point.

And then he heard it . . . a frantic, piercing scream, enunciating his own name, shattering the stillness of the forest:

"Ethan!"

Ethan's blood ran cold at the sound, for it was Constance's voice, filled with terror. And it was not only the sharp distress of her cry that chilled his blood; it was the enunciated word itself, for it was truly not the word "Ethan" that had been uttered but rather "Etha—". The scream had been cut off abruptly, as if something had suddenly severed its source.

With chest heaving, Ethan looked upward toward the summit, for the cry had come from a point above him.

"Constance!" he bellowed, but was met with only silence.

With redoubled intensity, he plunged forward, oblivious to any obstacles in his path, scaling the incline before him as rapidly as if it were level. Moving swiftly onward through the dense trees, Ethan sacrificed stealth for speed, though the dried branches and leaves upon the forest floor scarcely betrayed him, so sure-footed was his step.

Ethan's instinct for survival had always served him well, and he had never shied away from danger nor feared for his life, for his life was his own to risk as he saw fit. But it was an unfamiliar sensation that now gripped and propelled him: fear. For now it was another's life that was placed in peril — a life far dearer to him than his own; a life utterly innocent of any complicity in the matter which had precipitated the imperilment.

And when Ethan had last seen Constance . . . she had fled from him in tears.

A knot formed in Ethan's abdomen; his chest tightened. For indeed, it was assuredly by calculation and not by chance that Zachary Merrill had struck where Ethan was most vulnerable; it was Ethan's love for Constance that now placed Constance's life in jeopardy.

But he must not dwell upon that thought nor upon what might have caused her scream to so suddenly be silenced. No, he must think of nothing except reaching her; he must surrender to his senses and his physical resourcefulness. And indeed, while Merrill had the advantage of being further up the summit, where he could undoubtedly observe Ethan's progress, Ethan was well-aware of his own vital advantages — strength and speed; truly, one unencumbered, able-bodied man could move far more swiftly than a less physically-competent man bearing a captive.

Ethan pressed on and on with swift determination, reaching the craggy summit, barely cognizant of the sound of rushing water in the ravine far below. As he had done before, he set his course in the direction of the bluffs, for it was the easiest to traverse and the likeliest course for his quarry to follow. With one hand yet clutching his rifle, he made his way amongst the thinning trees, moving with agile step, steadfast in his pursuit, until at last, as he rounded a thorny bend, he sighted a figure just ahead.

It was Zachary Merrill.

And Ethan came to an abrupt halt, for Merrill, having levied his own advantage, had spied Ethan well in advance and now stood facing him at the opposite end of a rock-strewn clearing, in his hand a pistol levelled squarely at Ethan.

But it was not the pistol that commanded Ethan's attention, for his eye was drawn at once to a figure at Merrill's side; and Ethan's heart surged, for it was Constance.

She was entirely beholden to her captor; even as Merrill brandished the pistol in one hand, his other hand encircled Constance's slender throat.

Nevertheless, she was alive, and for a fleeting, suspended moment, Ethan was cognizant of nothing except her, as he looked into her frightened eyes. Instinctively, he started to move toward her, but Merrill reacted quickly.

"Stay where you are!" Merrill commanded, as he roughly forced Constance to the edge of the ravine, his hand yet about her throat, his pistol still trained upon Ethan.

Ethan immediately halted.

"Drop your gun!" Merrill ordered brusquely.

But this command Ethan did not forthwith obey. He had grasped the situation at once, and his mind raced, even as his fist tightened about his rifle.

He was an expert marksman and could easily finish off Merrill with a single shot from where he stood. Neither did he fear Merrill's pistol. Ethan was yet at a distance, and he doubted that Merrill possessed the skill necessary to fire a personal weapon effectively at such a range. But so, too, was Ethan aware of the sound of the rushing water in the ravine far below, at the precipice of which Constance was now being precariously held.

Merrill was impatient at Ethan's hesitation. "Drop your gun!" Merrill repeated with ill-tempered gruffness, pushing Constance even closer to the cliff's edge, so that she cried out in fear.

Ethan cast his rifle upon the ground.

"Now step away from it!" Merrill commanded further.

Ethan took a step forward, but Merrill quickly redirected him.

"Not forward!" Merrill bellowed. "Do not come one step nearer!"

Ethan paused. He was not about to put more distance between himself and Constance. Instead, he looked levelly at Merrill and kicked the rifle away.

"And your personal weapon," Merrill added expectantly.

Ethan was caught off-guard by this assertion, but he realized that Merrill must have glimpsed the pistol at his waist when he had moved to cast his rifle aside.

"Throw your pistol here," Merrill demanded, "and do not think of training it upon me. I assure you, my grip upon this girl is easily loosed, should it be with my dying breath."

Though Ethan's eyes gleamed defiantly, he slowly retrieved the pistol from beneath his coat. Holding it aloft by the barrel, he deliberately cast it several yards shy of where Merrill stood.

Merrill, however, did not move from his position at the cliff's edge.

Ethan shifted his gaze back to Constance, who yet remained silent and rigid with fear. Ethan had been so relieved to see her alive that he had initially taken notice of little else; but now, as he glanced at her again, he perceived her physical state, and his brow furrowed.

Her hands were bound behind her. Her hair was disheveled, and her face and gown smudged with dirt. The sleeve of her gown was torn, and—

Ethan's eye glinted with dark fire as he discerned a mark of bright red upon Constance's white skin, just below her neck.

It was unmistakably blood.

Though it was but a narrow streak, it was yet precariously near her throat, and its incision was undoubtedly what had silenced her scream earlier.

Ethan's blood surged wrathfully within him as he eyed Merrill once more.

"Free her," Ethan demanded heatedly. "She knows nothing of your scheme. It has naught to do with her."

"'Tis true," Merrill conceded calmly. "It has naught to do with her. Indeed, my quarrel is only with you now. But she has the misfortune to be loved by you. At least . . . that is what I am counting on. Such was conveyed to me by an astute observer, and this girl has blatantly confirmed her preference this day." He glanced scornfully at Constance before once more training his eye upon Ethan and adding with cool precision, "I am trusting that her ardor is not unrequited." After a pause, Merrill continued, his tone taking on an air of affected nonchalance. "She is certainly not in love with me, and never has been. She has made that plain." He looked again toward Constance with contempt. "No, I have no false illusions about Miss Jameson's regard for me. She has never reciprocated my attentions toward her—," a sneer formed upon Merrill's countenance, "unlike her witless sister, who succumbs with the ease of a harlot."

Ethan, whose watchful eye was ever upon Merrill's captive, saw plainly in Constance's visage that her harrowing plight had just been immeasurably compounded by the pain of this revelation.

Ethan scowled at Merrill.

Merrill merely smiled, unperturbed. "Now, now, Mr. Shaye," Merrill taunted, "let us not be rankled. I am sure we can work something out to our mutual satisfaction. You have something that belongs to me . . . I have something that belongs to you. I think a fair exchange is in order."

Ethan maintained his steadfast stance. Indeed, he knew he must remain outwardly composed . . . Constance's life depended upon it. He chose his words with care:

"I have what you want. I have, on my person, your document from the king." Ethan perceived a gleam light Merrill's eye, and Ethan went on: "Release the girl to my custody, and I will return it to you."

Zachary Merrill chuckled disdainfully. "Come now, Mr. Shaye. I am not such a fool as that. Nay, I am afraid you must first surrender the document. *Then* I will release her."

But Ethan was not about to give up the king's letter while Constance's life was yet in danger. He knew that once Merrill had the letter, Merrill would have no incentive to free Constance nor even to keep her alive.

Ethan glanced again at Constance. Her face was ashen, her eyes — wide with terror — were fixed fast upon him.

The tension of the moment was palpable, and, despite the chill of early winter, Ethan felt the dampness of perspiration upon his brow. Though he maintained his outward display of calm, his mind yet raced — desperate to conceive of a plan which would set Constance free. He knew he could easily best Merrill in any physical contest or in the use of weaponry; but Merrill was clever enough to have purposefully circumvented the possibility of such a challenge.

Merrill had very deliberately orchestrated a confrontation which relied upon his own strengths — rhetoric and manipulation. The judge's grandson was eminently sure of himself in this situation, and so he stood there, waiting with an air of cool, confident indifference, nonchalantly dallying with the innocent life whose fate was in his grasp.

But Ethan's mind was fast at work, recalculating each party's advantages. Merrill was in possession of at least two weapons — for in addition to the pistol he assuredly had on his person a blade of some sort, as evidenced by Constance's wound. But so, too, did Merrill have one severe liability: So long as he held Constance in his grasp, he had but one free hand — and that hand currently wielded a pistol, leaving no hands free. Ethan must utilize that limitation to his own advantage.

Merrill, meanwhile, grew increasingly impatient at the prolonged silence. "This must be somewhat disheartening for this girl," he intoned callously, "—to see that the man she loves would thus hesitate to save her life."

Ethan scowled. He knew well enough what anguish must be compounding Constance's distress, and the thought of it tortured him. He longed to speak to her — to reassure her of the depth of his love; to convey that he would readily forfeit his own life to spare hers. But he could not impart to her even one word; indeed, he knew that Constance's life depended upon the fact that Merrill could not be certain of the extent of his own advantage; and Ethan must not thus empower him.

So it was that, despite his internal angst, Ethan maintained his outward stance of composure, sustaining level eye contact with Zachary Merrill.

"I have no reason to believe you would free her upon receipt of the king's letter," Ethan said evenly.

Merrill chuckled softly. "What? Is this an insult? Would you doubt my word, Mr. Shaye?" Merrill's blue eyes gleamed scornfully. "You are going to have to trust that I am yet a man of honor. I do not see where you have any choice."

Ethan paid no heed to this derisive provocation. His thoughts were yet unrelentingly engaged in strategizing a means of securing Constance's safety. He must draw Merrill away from the cliff's edge.

"How shall I convey the letter to you?" Ethan asked. "You will not allow me to approach you."

Merrill's eyes narrowed. "Let me see the letter," he demanded.

Ethan started to move his hand toward the pocket of his coat.

"Slowly!" Merrill barked. "Do not make any sudden movement, or this girl's life will be forfeit!"

Ethan, who had stayed his hand, gave a nod and slowly reached into the pocket of his coat, keeping his eye fixed upon Merrill, whose own eye was trained intently upon the movement of Ethan's hand.

Inside his pocket, Ethan's fingers touched upon a loosely rolled parchment. But he did not grasp it and instead continued moving his hand along the pocket's lining, for there was yet another roll of paper therein — one tightly bound with sealing wax — and it was around that document that Ethan's fingers tightened. He pulled it slowly from his pocket and held it aloft, taking care that the sealed edge did not face outward. He said nothing, but studied Merrill's face intently.

Though Merrill's visage retained its cold edifice of contempt, his eyes once again lit up with heightened intensity when he saw the document . . . and in that moment Ethan knew for certain what a weighty bargaining tool he held in his grasp.

After staring at the rolled document for a few seconds, Merrill diverted his gaze, quickly scanning the vicinity. His eye came to rest upon a rather large, flat rock near the center of the clearing.

"There," he inclined his head toward the rock. "Put it there."

Ethan did not move at once, but stood for a moment, steadfast and self-possessed, as if issuing a silent challenge as he held the paper aloft before Merrill. Indeed, he had seen and comprehended the momentary glint in Merrill's eye, and he knew that for Merrill the document held the key to the realization of a future endowed with immeasurable wealth, power, and influence; a future which had nearly slipped from Merrill's grasp and had driven him to the desperate measure of abduction but was now on the brink of being recovered.

Nevertheless — though Ethan could see how desperate Merrill was to regain possession of the letter — Merrill yet held the stronger bargaining tool.

Ethan at last moved toward the flat rock, ever keeping Merrill and Constance in his sight, even as he bent to lay the rolled document upon the rock's surface, once again taking care that the seal was not in Merrill's view.

"Now step away!" Merrill ordered. "Far away!"

Ethan acquiesced, backing slowly away from the rock. He did not return to the exact spot in which he had previously stood, though, but rather moved subtly to his left, staying parallel to Merrill, yet placing himself nearer the rim of the ravine than he had previously been.

Merrill showed no concern over this slight discrepancy of position; indeed, he seemed much preoccupied, his eyes fixed upon the document, undoubtedly ruminating over how he might maneuver in order to procure it.

There followed an extended, tense silence, but when Merrill at last moved, he did so quickly. From his position at the edge of the ravine, Merrill suddenly pulled away, bringing Constance with him, and as he did so, simultaneously turning his pistol's direction, pressing the barrel against Constance's side.

His movement was so sudden that Constance could do no more than emit an audible gasp, and it was not until Merrill brought her to a halt beside the flat rock that she became aware of the firearm pressing against her side. A renewed terror was reflected in her eyes.

She did not know that her peril had actually been somewhat mitigated, for as swiftly as Merrill had dragged her toward the rock, so had Ethan made swift movement of his own, edging quickly in a semi-circular path to the rim of the cliff, coming to a halt at the very spot Merrill had just vacated.

Merrill would not be able to take Constance back to the ravine's edge.

What's more, Merrill now faced a dilemma, for in standing beside the rock, mere inches from the document he so longed to obtain, he was yet constrained from its procurement. He could not retrieve the document without surrendering his hold upon either the pistol or the girl.

Merrill paused for but the briefest interval, a calculating frown etched upon his countenance, before arriving at a swift resolution. Loosing his hold about Constance's neck, he rapidly grasped her by the arm, roughly pushing her downward.

"Get down!" he ordered, though such a command was unnecessary, as Constance, being helpless to resist, fell to the ground — first upon her knees, then nearly upon her side, for her hands were yet fast bound behind her, giving her no means by which to stabilize herself. Only Merrill's hand pressing down upon her shoulder allowed her to maintain a precarious balance upon her knees.

The sudden violence of Merrill's movement set Ethan instinctively to action, and he started forward toward Constance.

Merrill reacted at once, though, with a threatening flash of his icy blue eyes and a renewed jab of his pistol's barrel against Constance's head.

Ethan came to an immediate halt, his chest heaving.

"I do not yet have what I want," Merrill intoned sharply, then added with a menacing sneer, "and even when I do . . . well, there are no guarantees, are there?"

Ethan glared but made no further movement.

Merrill turned his attention back to Constance. Pulling the pistol back, he moved his other hand from her shoulder to the top of her head.

"Put your head to the ground," Merrill hissed.

Constance, frozen with fear, did not move.

"Put your head down!" Merrill repeated forcefully.

Constance instead turned her head slightly. Terrified and imploring, she looked toward Ethan.

Ethan looked into Constance's eyes, desperately wishing he could say aloud what he knew to be true — that Merrill would not readily discharge the pistol, for it was now his only defense against Ethan. But Ethan could say nothing, for as long as Merrill's hand remained upon Constance, Merrill could yet utilize physical means to harm her, and Ethan must do whatever it took to protect her, though it meant that her present anguish must be prolonged by his silence.

Ethan gave a slight nod, indicating to Constance that she must obey.

So it was that, with a last look of heart-wrenching despair, Constance turned her head away, and, casting her eyes downward, lowered her body until her head came to rest upon the ground. Though her eyes remained closed, her visibly throbbing breast gave testament to her protracted fear.

Satisfied that his captive would not be making a hasty escape, Merrill glanced at Ethan then proceeded to reach for the document on the rock before him.

Ethan's voice breached the silence. "It is sealed."

Merrill paused at this unexpected statement. Still bending forward over the rock, he turned his head toward Ethan.

Ethan, self-possessed and audacious as ever, looked Merrill squarely in the eye. "It is bound with my seal," Ethan elaborated. "I was going to deliver it to my commanding officer."

Merrill frowned suspiciously.

Ethan's eye gleamed with a defiant challenge.

Both men knew that in order to verify that the document was indeed the king's letter, Merrill would need to break the seal. It would require both hands, one of which was yet clutching the pistol.

Still frowning contemplatively, Merrill slowly reached for the document.

As Merrill reached for it, however, Ethan was suddenly distracted by an unexpected movement glimpsed out of the corner of his eye.

Quickly shifting his gaze toward the wood, Ethan very nearly gave a start, for there he beheld, emerging from the shadow of the trees, a figure. It was with great astonishment — even disbelief — that Ethan not only beheld the figure's approach, but recognized at once the individual's identity. Indeed, it was the second time that day he had discerned from a distance . . . Jenny.

Ethan's mind immediately flashed back to his previous sighting of her upon the road, back to the moment Jenny had paused in her step when she had simultaneously sighted him . . . when she had assuredly watched him ride swiftly away toward the foothills.

It seemed incomprehensible that she would have thus altered her own course and followed him on foot across such a distance. And yet— who could say of what Jenny was capable or to what length she would exert herself when the life of her mistress was at stake?

At present, though, Jenny did not see Ethan, for he was far to the periphery of her field of vision. It was upon Zachary Merrill that Jenny's eyes were fixed — eyes round with bewilderment and fright, for she saw, too, the form of her mistress upon the ground beside Merrill.

Ethan did not call out to Jenny; indeed, he had realized nearly at once that her unexpected presence could prove to be of inestimable benefit, but he knew that if he called out to her, she would likely halt in her tracks . . . and he needed her to come a measure nearer.

Though Jenny had immediately slowed her step upon perceiving Merrill in the clearing, she was not practiced in treading with caution, and Merrill was alerted to her approach as a dried twig snapped beneath her feet.

Merrill instantly straightened, leaving the document yet upon the rock, the barrel of his pistol directed toward the intruder.

"Halt where you are!" he called out gruffly.

Jenny obeyed, perplexed and fearful.

"Well," Merrill went on, his eyes narrowing with scorn as he recognized the swarthy slave woman, "'tis Miss Jameson's loyal servant. What the devil are you doing here?"

"Jenny!" Ethan interjected sharply, so that Jenny, caught off-guard by Ethan's voice and presence, turned her head in his direction. "Do exactly as I bid you," Ethan commanded her, speaking hurriedly. "You can be of great help here—"

But Merrill cut him off. "Not another word out of you!" he charged Ethan, then turned his attention back to Jenny. "Do not pay him any heed, or I shall not hesitate to discharge this upon you," and he brandished the pistol once more in Jenny's direction.

Jenny regarded Merrill and the weapon with trepidation before glancing uncertainly toward Ethan once more.

Ethan met her eye steadfastly — and proceeded to direct her, though unbeknownst to Merrill.

Ethan looked downward toward the ground in front of Jenny, inclining his head purposefully, then looked back up at her, his gaze piercing and deliberate.

Jenny lowered her eyes and beheld what it was Ethan had silently bid her to perceive: his rifle on the ground, not four feet from where she stood.

Jenny glanced up toward Ethan once more, then slowly raised her hand toward her head until her fingers closed around the oblong bit of gold dangling from her ear. She gave a slight tug upon the earring, and Ethan knew that she had understood.

Zachary Merrill, however, knew nothing of what had been communicated across the silence, though he frowned in consternation when Jenny slowly began to advance.

"Stay where you are!" Merrill ordered angrily, extending his arm so that his pistol, still aimed at Jenny, was parallel with his line of sight.

But Ethan countered Merrill's command, addressing Jenny calmly. "Just two more steps, Jenny," Ethan directed, his tone level and assured. "I promise you, you are well outside the range of his pistol."

For her part, Jenny kept her eyes fixed downward as she continued her slow advance . . . two paces more; then she bent — her sizable frame shifting forward.

"What are you about?" Merrill demanded sharply, his tone brusque with agitation. "Do not move, I say!"

But Jenny did not pause, and Ethan saw that her large hands were shaking as she reached for the rifle.

When Merrill realized what she was doing, his fury boiled over. "Put that down, I say!" he shouted, even as Jenny stood upright once more and maneuvered the rifle — crudely and without dexterity — so that it was aimed toward Merrill.

There was a long silence.

Merrill's chest heaved visibly, and droplets of perspiration appeared upon his face. Nevertheless, he emitted a gruff, scornful laugh. "Is this meant to intimidate me?" he sneered. "Shall I feel threatened by a firearm in the hands of a simple-minded slave woman who can barely hold it aright?"

But Ethan again countered. "Steady, Jenny," he intoned quietly. "I assure you, a child could fire that rifle with accuracy at a greater distance than you are from Mr. Merrill."

It was something of an overstatement, to be sure, but Ethan could see at once from Merrill's scowl that he was well-aware of the rifle's superior range and accuracy compared with the pistol.

What's more, Ethan's words gave Jenny the courage to maintain her stance, for she knew nothing of weaponry. And though Ethan had no expectation of Jenny actually firing the rifle with any accuracy, her presence and her stance were yet crucial to Ethan's efforts to free Constance.

Merrill, in spite of his overtly derisive tone, was plainly disconcerted by the situation, and for a long moment he made no movement nor uttered any word, but only glanced from face to face, his own countenance twisted into a contemplative glower. But he finally settled his cold, calculating eye upon Jenny.

"It is true that this pistol's aim may not be precise at such a distance," he conceded, his tone even and edged with scorn. "Better I should discharge it upon a target that cannot be missed!" And he suddenly and swiftly thrust the pistol downward, levelling it toward his captive, the end of the barrel mere inches from Constance's head.

Jenny's reaction was immediate. She emitted a hoarse, throaty cry and lowered the rifle, faltering.

But Ethan, whose own senses had been jarred by Merrill's sudden action, quickly regained his self-possession, knowing instinctively that he must maintain an air of composure if he was to rescue Constance. "No," he countered steadfastly.

Merrill turned his head, and Ethan looked him fixedly in the eye.

Ethan went on, his words deliberate, his tone low and dangerous. "Mr. Merrill will not discharge his weapon upon the girl . . . because he knows that if he does, I will kill him."

It was a formidable threat. The pistol was good for but a single shot, and Merrill's defense relied entirely on keeping Ethan at a distance.

Keeping his eye fixed purposefully upon Merrill, Ethan began to walk slowly toward him, and as he walked, Ethan continued speaking in an even, deliberate tone. "Mr. Merrill knows that if he fires that pistol, I must be the target . . . if he hopes to escape with his life."

Merrill was visibly agitated at the unexpected change of the dynamics he had so carefully orchestrated. He abruptly raised his pistol, aiming it at Ethan, who yet approached with measured step.

"I will be only too happy to oblige," Merrill hissed venomously. "If you take one step closer, you will die with the knowledge that you delivered these two women squarely into my hands."

Ethan glanced down at Constance. Although she could not see him, he prayed that she trusted him, for what she heard must assuredly frighten her.

Then, looking Zachary Merrill in the eye once again, Ethan's own eyes gleamed with defiance.

Merrill's state of agitation was apparent. "Do not provoke me, Shaye," he warned. "One more step and I will fire."

Ethan said nothing, but kept his eye fixed steadfastly upon Merrill and took another step forward. He was but thirty feet from the pistol's barrel.

Zachary Merrill, incensed and antagonized, pulled upon the trigger.

The pistol's shot rang out deafeningly across the clearing.

Terrified, Constance raised her head. But what she beheld was not the realization of the nightmare she had anticipated.

Indeed, Ethan had known that, at such a range, the pistol's ball would curve long before it reached him, and so he had stood motionless as the weapon was discharged. But the moment the shot rang out, he darted forward toward Constance.

Zachary Merrill, realizing at once that his shot had missed, also took instantaneous action. Dropping the pistol, he snatched up the document and sped across the clearing toward the spot where Jenny yet stood.

Ethan, pulling from his waist the weapon he had heretofore concealed from Merrill — the brass-hilted blade that had been Henry Dowling's — bent swiftly down as he reached Constance, and, taking hold of her arm, severed with one twist of the dagger's blade the rope that bound her wrists.

"Stay low," Ethan ordered her sharply. "Take cover in the wood."

And before Constance could even grasp what was happening, Ethan raced away again, for as dearly as he would have wished to remain with her and take her in his arms, her life — and Jenny's — yet remained in grave danger.

Jenny, indeed, had stood momentarily frozen in fear when she saw Zachary Merrill fire at Ethan then run toward her. But as Merrill neared, she regained her senses and attempted to level the rifle in her large, unsteady hands, fumbling with it awkwardly, so that when Merrill reached her he easily took hold of the rifle's barrel, turning it upward as he did so. He could not wrench it from her grasp, though, and the two struggled to gain control of the deadly firearm — Merrill spewing insults at the slave woman as he moved his hands along the barrel, forcibly pulling Jenny nearer, until he was able to grasp her hand. Try as he might, though, he could not pry her hand away, for her hand was large and solidly encircled the weapon. Although Jenny was not adept at physical defense nor combat, Merrill had underestimated her strength, and the two of them struggled mightily as Jenny desperately sought to retain her grip upon the narrow stock end of the rifle.

Suddenly, though, an unseen force pulled laterally upon the weapon.

"Drop it, Jenny!" Ethan commanded — for indeed, it was he who had grasped the weapon unforeseen and who now easily and forcefully replaced Jenny in the struggle, moving fast as lightning, superior to his adversary from the start.

With swift motion, Ethan took control of the rifle, first pulling it from Zachary Merrill's grasp, then, wielding it like a staff, striking

Merrill forcefully across the abdomen, delivering a powerful blow that sent Merrill reeling backward. As Merrill turned, Ethan lunged forward, delivering a second blow as he rammed the rifle across Merrill's lower back, causing Merrill to fall to the ground, twisting and gasping in pain. Ethan was instantly upon him, the heel of his boot pressing down upon Merrill's chest, the barrel of the rifle — now wielded according to its purpose — mere inches from Merrill's face.

"Jenny!" Ethan uttered sharply. "Bring me that rope!"

Jenny, though shaken by all that had passed, quickly obeyed, scurrying to the spot beside the flat rock where Constance had earlier been forced to the ground and where the cord that had bound her wrists yet remained, now in two segments where Ethan had severed it.

Taking up the segments of rope, Jenny hurried back to Ethan, who yet held the rifle's barrel to Zachary Merrill's brow.

"Bind his legs," Ethan ordered Jenny, and once again the slave woman obeyed, though her hands shook as she looped the rope about Merrill's legs, just above the top of his boots. It was not an expert binding job, but it sufficed.

Ethan himself undertook the remaining measures involved in securing the captive. Casting the rifle aside, he bent and grasped Merrill roughly by one arm, pulling him slightly upward. There was a brief struggle as Merrill resisted surrendering his other arm, and he managed to maneuver his hand toward his coat, from which he withdrew an object. It was the rolled document he had confiscated from the rock. Before Ethan could grip Merrill's free arm, Merrill twisted his elbow away and, with a flick of his wrist, flung the roll of parchment sideways, sending it clear over the side of the cliff and into the chasm of the ravine.

Ethan did not pause to censure or comment upon this action, but only moved swiftly to secure Merrill's free arm and twist it behind.

"Jenny!" Ethan again summoned the slave woman, who comprehended what was desired and brought forth the second segment of the rope that had once bound Constance and would now be used to restrain her captor.

Merrill yet put up a struggle as Ethan slipped one arm behind both of Merrill's (that he might have a free hand to take the rope from Jenny), but Merrill's struggle proved futile, for Ethan was stronger and in a far more advantageous position to maintain his stance.

"What are you going to do?" Merrill growled as Ethan secured the cord about his wrists.

Ethan did not respond at once, but instead continued directing his focus to the task at hand — pulling the rope's loop into a knot and setting it into place. As he pulled it tight and began a second knot, he gruffly gave answer to Merrill's query:

"You can thank that gentle lady, whom you so grievously injured," Ethan began, inclining his head toward Constance, who was yet in sight across the clearing, "that I am sparing your life this day. I assure you, it is nothing but her presence that is preventing me from killing you for the harm you have done her. As it is," Ethan continued, pulling Merrill upright to a sitting position, "the tribunal will determine your fate. I do not think they take kindly to treason."

Merrill's eyes gleamed scornfully. "They will have no basis for any conviction," he asserted heatedly. "The tribunal cannot accept the testimony of a slave — if Thaddeus is yet alive — and there is no evidence on this earth, save that letter . . . which now lies at the bottom of the ravine."

"Do not be so sure," Ethan countered with such calm assurance that Merrill looked sharply up at him.

Taking a step back, Ethan reached into his pocket and withdrew from it a rolled document — nearly identical to the one that Merrill had moments before cast over the edge of the ravine.

Merrill's eyes inadvertently widened as Ethan turned the document sideways, that Merrill might see affixed to it a seal, broken, and unmistakably inscribed with the mark of the king.

Ethan did not tarry further nor pause to observe Merrill's incredulous grimace, but again bent and took hold of the captive's arm, addressing Jenny as he did so:

"Jenny— here! Take his other arm," Ethan directed.

Jenny, coming around to Merrill's opposite side, took hold of his other arm.

Ethan and Jenny then dragged the dead weight of Merrill's inert frame a few yards backward to the foot of a sturdy chestnut oak.

Merrill frowned. "What are you doing?" he demanded, but Ethan made him no reply.

Instead, kneeling beside Merrill, Ethan swiftly untied the loose knot of the cord with which Jenny had bound Merrill's legs, and, while Jenny yet retained her firm grasp upon Merrill's arm, Ethan wound the cord first about the rope which bound Merrill's wrists then about the sturdy trunk of the tree, encircling it twice before fastening the rope into a secure knot, ensuring that the captive would remain thus anchored.

"You cannot leave me here," Merrill protested. "The sun is setting even now."

"Aye," Ethan nodded, unrelenting in his purpose. "All the more reason I must depart. A contingent from the militia camp will be coming to take you into custody. Pray they arrive before night falls."

And rising to his feet, Ethan turned away and said no more.

Indeed, Ethan had but one thought in his mind, one sight upon which his gaze was fixed, and he did not pause to rest from his exertions, but instead moved yet swiftly, hastening at a run toward that objective — toward the girl who yet remained at the opposite end of the clearing.

Constance had not heeded his command to flee into the wood; she had only been able to summon the resolve to crawl a few yards to the edge of the clearing, where she now lay huddled at the base of a tree.

Ethan could think of nothing except reaching her side, and it could not be soon enough for him; he slowed his step only slightly as he neared the spot where she lay, and, with chest heaving, he dropped to his knees beside her and gathered her into his arms.

"Constance—"

His voice was husky with emotion and exertion as he pressed her to his chest. The intensity of his fervor as he enfolded her in his strong arms bespoke of one who had nearly lost that which was dearest to him in all the world.

As for Constance — throughout her peril she had not shed a tear, so overcome with fright had she been. But now, from the depths of Ethan's embrace, she let out a great, gasping sob, and she began to tremble as her body succumbed to the distress that her mind had hardly dared to process during her ordeal.

Ethan yet held her close throughout. "Hush, my dearest girl," he whispered, pressing his lips against the top of her head. "You are safe. You are safe now. All is well."

Constance remained thus in his protective embrace until the trembling subsided.

Even then, Ethan did not fully release her, but — shifting slightly back, that he might look upon her face — he placed his hands about her shoulders, and, gently brushing her hair aside, he examined the wound below her neck.

The blood had already dried to a deep rust color, and though the incision was but small and narrow, Ethan yet frowned as he traced his finger lightly beneath it, for the incision was so precariously near to Constance's throat that it could have served but one purpose — to inflict upon her a mortal fear for her life. It was evidence of Zachary Merrill's callous indifference to innocence or honor.

Suddenly aware of the coldness of the ground beneath them, Ethan removed his coat, and, placing it about Constance's shoulders, he rose, lifting her to her feet as he did so.

With his arm about her, he began to lead her across the clearing toward the forest's descending gradient.

For Constance, though, the trauma she had experienced yet overwhelmed her, and after only a few paces, she faltered in her step; what little strength she had summoned faded.

Immediately perceptive of Constance's weakened state, Ethan swiftly and effortlessly scooped her up in his strong arms and carried her across the uneven ground toward the ridge's descent.

But even thus bearing Constance in his arms, Ethan yet paused at the far end of the clearing where Jenny stood waiting — her round eyes fixed uncertainly and expectantly upon him.

In spite of her own harrowing ordeal, Jenny had had the presence of mind to collect Ethan's rifle and pistol, and now, as she stood there beneath the trees, she looked to him for guidance, her countenance troubled and even timid; it was an acute change from the dark glower she had once cast upon him beneath the garret's rafters.

As Ethan paused before her now, he did not speak lightly nor hastily, but looked steadfastly into Jenny's eyes, and though there was a certain gruffness to his tone when he spoke, so too was there unmistakable conviction. "I thank you, Jenny. I . . . have never properly thanked you for what you did long ago. And now— now you have again rendered aid and helped to save a life." He glanced down at Constance, who lay insensible yet safe within his arms. "'Tis a life I count dearer than—," his words trailed off, yet what eloquence of meaning was conveyed in the silence of the unfinished sentence. When he once more looked at Jenny and addressed her again, his tone was purposeful, his words deliberate. "You have done well. No man — master nor slave — can claim to be your better."

His words were not insignificant. They were an affirmation, and Jenny's eyes glistened with tears.

Nevertheless, it was upon Constance that Jenny's gaze ultimately fell, and Ethan understood.

"She has endured a great deal, and her strength has given out," Ethan put forth evenly. "But she is not harmed, and she will soon recover. We must get her back to shelter, though, and to the warmth of the fireside. Come."

And he set forth upon the ridge's descent, with Jenny following after him, neither one paying heed to the voice of Zachary Merrill, who was flinging vehement protests at their backs as they disappeared from his sight.

Though the descent from the summit was long and winding, and though their arms were laden — for Jenny yet carried Ethan's weapons — a downhill trek is always more expeditious than an ascent, and they progressed at a measured pace until the trees thinned and they came to the spot where Ethan's horse was tethered.

Constance's eyes fluttered open as Ethan set her atop the horse's back. As Ethan proceeded to unfasten the rein, he paused, then turned to Jenny.

"Would you ride with her?" he asked the slave woman. "She cannot ride unattended in her state. I . . . would have you ride with her, if it suits you, and I will lead the horse."

It was a gallant offer, but Jenny refuted it, shaking her head emphatically, her round eyes wide with trepidation. Ethan did not press the matter; Jenny had assuredly never been seated upon a horse in her life.

Ethan merely gave a nod as he took the rifle and pistol.

Once the weapons were secured in place, Ethan climbed up behind Constance, pulling her close so that her body rested against his. As he took the rein in hand, he turned his head and glanced down at Jenny, who yet stood beside the horse. She was looking up at him — her large eyes suddenly apprehensive. Ethan did not need words to comprehend her anxiety.

"Have no fear," he assured her. "I will see that no harm nor punishment befalls you. Come now, let us be on our way while we yet have daylight to guide us."

So it was that, with one arm about Constance and the other commanding the rein, Ethan set his mount upon the course toward the high road. He kept the animal to an easy gait, that Jenny might keep pace.

As they emerged from the cover of the trees onto level ground, Ethan felt Constance's body go limp as she succumbed entirely to the fatigue which now overpowered her senses. Ethan shifted her slightly upward, repositioning her more securely in the fold of his arm.

For Constance, the long day was over at last, and her wearied mind and body found refuge in the dreamless darkness that enveloped her consciousness.

FOR THE SECOND TIME THAT day, Ethan entered the Porters' house unbidden, this time the door giving way forcefully beneath the heel of his boot. He paused for nothing, but moved swiftly through the central hall, his countenance dark as thunder.

The sudden, jarringly violent sound of the forceful entrance immediately caught the attention of the occupants of the parlor, who turned their heads toward the hall in astonishment but had no time to set foot in that direction before Ethan Shaye strode into their midst.

Polly Jameson gasped, for it was not only Ethan's abrupt entrance that startled her, but the sight of that which he bore in his arms.

"Constance!" Polly cried, rushing forward.

"Good God!" exclaimed Joshua Porter, the room's only other occupant, likewise hurrying forth.

Ethan paid no heed to either of them, but hastened with unyielding, decisive step to the fireplace, before which was situated a roll-arm bench. He lowered Constance onto the bench, while Joshua Porter hastily plucked from a sofa a small pillow, which he placed beneath Constance's head.

Polly, rushing to Constance's side, hovered over her, taking her hand. "Constance!" Polly uttered again in great distress, for her sister was yet insensible. "Oh, what has happened? Is she killed?"

Joshua Porter, meanwhile, had rushed to the hall door. "Betsy!" he called out to the housegirl, who was scurrying forth from the rear of the house. "Fetch Dr. Harwood — quickly! He is upstairs looking in on Mrs. Porter. Quickly now!"

"She will be all right," Ethan assured Polly briskly, his chest yet heaving, his brow yet furrowed intently. "She has been badly frightened and will need time to recover, but she is not harmed."

While his words were true, his brusque, frowning demeanor set no one at ease. Though Constance was safe, it was plain that there were other matters yet unsettled. Before Ethan could speak further, though,

Dr. Harwood entered from the hall with Anne Porter and Betsy bustling in behind him.

The doctor's eye immediately fell upon Constance, and he hurried to the bench where she lay.

"What has happened here?" the doctor queried, as Polly gave orders to the housegirl:

"Betsy, get a quilt from one of the bedchambers."

"Why, Constance!" Mrs. Porter exclaimed, starting across the room on the heels of the doctor.

But Anne Porter was at once impeded from reaching her sister's side, as Ethan stepped forcibly in her path, his visage sternly forbidding.

"*Do not touch her.*"

Anne Porter gasped, startled at the sudden obstruction and at the severity of Ethan's tone and manner.

"Wh—what?" she stammered incredulously.

"Do not even go near her," Ethan went on, his tone ominously firm, his eye flashing a dark warning. "I will not have her look upon you when she wakes."

The others present looked on wide-eyed and silent as the mistress of the household stood speechless and aghast.

Mrs. Porter turned her eyes appealingly toward her husband.

Joshua Porter was frowning in consternation and bewilderment, but Ethan addressed him directly, his tone losing none of its firmness:

"I would have words with you, Porter."

Before Joshua Porter could make response, his wife's voice interposed shrilly:

"Why?" Her face was blanched, and her tone continued to rise unnaturally as she spoke. "What words would you have? What words?" she persisted, her demeanor suddenly verging on hysteria as she rushed to her husband and clutched desperately at his arm. "There can be nothing to discuss with Mr. Shaye! You heard how he spoke to me!"

Joshua Porter stared at his wife in astonishment, confounded by her sudden change in demeanor.

Ethan, however, was impatient. "We have but little time," he contended. "The militia will soon be in Merrilltown."

Joshua Porter understood none of this, and he yet frowned as he glanced from Ethan's stern visage to Mrs. Porter's peaked face.

Finally— "Go upstairs, Anne," Mr. Porter directed his wife, who began to protest, but her husband continued, "I will sort things out with Mr. Shaye." And he motioned Ethan toward the study door, as Dr. Harwood resumed tending to Constance.

The two men remained sequestered in the study for a long while, nearly three-quarters of an hour, and when they finally emerged, it was with hurried step and an air of urgency.

Joshua Porter directly hastened up the stairs, his jaw clenched with grim resolve.

Ethan was met outside the parlor by Polly, who seemed not to notice his purposeful gait as she handed him his coat. She was smiling reassuringly.

"You were right, Mr. Shaye . . . Dr. Harwood said Constance will soon recover. We're to give her some warm broth when she awakes."

Ethan nodded as he donned his coat, and in spite of his hurried state, he paused at the parlor door.

The room was now deserted, save for Constance, who appeared to be sleeping peacefully upon the bench before the fire, covered with a warm quilt.

"Get her back to her father as soon as she is well enough to travel," Ethan instructed Polly, even as his gaze lingered upon Constance. "She must not bide longer in this place."

Polly comprehended the gravity of this directive, and she nodded, solemn and obedient.

Before she could make reply, though, both were distracted by the sudden clatter of a door slamming shut in the upstairs corridor. The sound had been preceded by a momentary wail of protest — unmistakably the voice of Anne Porter — which was immediately muffled upon the door's closing. The noisy and impatient jangling of keys could be discerned, and then the distinctive sound of a key turning in a lock, followed by rapid footsteps.

Joshua Porter appeared at the top of the stairway and made his way swiftly down — the key-ring yet jangling in his hand — bellowing orders as he descended. "Betsy!" he called out brusquely. "Have Marcus bring my horse and two lanterns round to the front. Tell him to make haste! Then fetch the slave woman Jenny. Move her into the house at once."

Betsy, who had appeared at the rear of the lower hall upon her master's summons, nodded wide-eyed, and with a murmured "Yes sir!" quickly scurried out the side-door.

"Jenny!" Polly exclaimed in bewilderment as Joshua Porter reached the foot of the stairs. "But I thought she—"

"She has returned," was all that Joshua Porter related, his tone yet firm, his manner yet hurried. "She can help you attend to Constance." He continued addressing Polly, his words pouring out rapidly as he donned his hat and coat. "When Betsy returns, send her upstairs to assist Rachel in packing Caleb's things. I'm sending him to stay with my sister in Richmond. See that he is dressed and ready for the journey in the morning. I cannot say when I will return — likely not until the morrow. I shall entrust these to you—", and he pressed the key-ring into Polly's hand, adding sternly, "Do not, under any circumstances, unfasten the lock to my wife's bedchamber, however much she may entreat."

Polly, quite overwhelmed by all that was unfolding, nodded silently, though Joshua Porter did not wait to see her acknowledgement, for, having settled such domestic details, his thoughts reverted back to the more critical matters at hand.

He turned to Ethan, his manner of urgency unabated. "Let us be off then."

"I will ride out with you to meet the militia," Ethan said briskly, as both men strode toward the door, "and accompany you as far as the foothills' perimeter, but then I must head north upon the high road. I must ride through the night to reach the regiment camp by dawn. I shall not be returning to Merrilltown."

Joshua Porter nodded as he quickly unlatched the door. "I will have my man collect your things from Lethbridge's tomorrow. Send word of your regiment's whereabouts, and I will dispatch your belongings to you."

That was the last of their exchange that Polly heard before both men hastened out the door into the burgeoning darkness outside. As she watched them depart, though, she noted that Ethan, as he turned to pull the door closed behind him, tarried upon the threshold with his hand upon the latch. It was only the briefest of pauses, but in that moment Polly saw him cast his eye once more toward the parlor door, and in that moment Polly began to understand what she had not before.

But the urgency of matters at hand necessitated Ethan's swift departure, and so he turned away and rode off into the night, taking leave of the Porter house — and of Merrilltown — for the last time.

PART V
The Colonel's Headquarters

January 1777

COLONEL NAISMITH ROSE FROM HIS seat at his makeshift desk, in his hand a paper marked with an official military seal.

"I've received word from General Washington," the colonel began. "Your request has been approved, and I have here your new orders, Captain." The colonel's mouth betrayed the hint of a smile as he uttered that last word, for the captain's rank was yet newly-bestowed, and the sound of it well-satisfied the colonel.

Though Ethan gave but a nod in response, the gleam that lit his eye made it plain that the colonel's news pleased him greatly.

Colonel Naismith continued, "I need not tell you how happy the general is with your accomplishments. He wrote extensively in praise of your deeds." The colonel regarded Ethan warmly. "You have done fine work indeed, my boy . . . opening up once more our supply lines to the north and putting an end to the treachery that had claimed too many lives. Your testimony before the tribunal was definitive, and the tribunal's decision to convict Merrill upon the grounds of treason was the swiftest conviction I've ever seen." The colonel paused and glanced down at the paper in his hand. "Your new orders have been put into writing," he said, extending the paper to Ethan.

As Ethan examined the document, the colonel fell silent and reflective, contemplating the younger officer. A pensive crease formed across the colonel's brow.

"Are you sure it's what you want?" the colonel put forth. "The general would have you in his own service if you were agreeable to it."

Ethan did not hesitate in his response. "I appreciate the honor, but I am certain."

Colonel Naismith nodded. "'Twas your own wish to have this new assignment, and I confess, there was a time I'd have been as astonished as the general at your request, but now—," he eyed Ethan thoughtfully, "now I think it is perhaps well that you should undertake such a command."

The colonel did not elaborate on his reasoning — and neither did Ethan question the colonel's conclusion — so, after a pause, the colonel moved on to another topic. He picked up a small burlap sack that had been sitting upon the desk.

"You left the tribunal before I could return this to you," he said, sliding the sack across the desktop toward Ethan. "It provided damning evidence against Merrill, but now — I think it belongs with you."

Ethan well-knew what the sack contained, but he nevertheless reached inside and laid his hand upon Henry Dowling's scabbard and blade. He did not entirely extract the items from the sack, but he pulled the scabbard out far enough that the dazzling blue of its stone glimmered in the light.

"Sergeant Dowling had no family to speak of," the colonel continued, as Ethan fingered the scabbard respectfully, "but I think he regarded you as near to a brother as he was ever to have, and there can be no doubt that he would wish his most prized possession to be entrusted to you."

Ethan, yet contemplating the weapon and the friend who had carried it so proudly, made no reply, but gave a nod of acknowledgement, his reflective silence conveying the gift's significance.

He slid it noiselessly back into its casing.

The colonel alleviated the somber mood with a lightened tone. "Well, Captain Shaye — have you any other requests? The general will likely grant whatever you ask; he is that pleased with you and would reward you beyond your promotion. Is there anything — anything at all — you would request of us before you depart upon your new command?"

The colonel may well have been surprised at how readily Ethan nodded in affirmation; but indeed, Ethan had anticipated this question.

"Aye," he responded earnestly. "I have yet one request . . ."

PART VI
The Fireside

Late January, 1777

FLURRIES OF SNOW FILLED THE air, obstructing the sun and turning the afternoon grey. The rooftops were dusted with a soft layer of white, and beneath them the windows of shops and taverns glowed with the warmth of lantern-light, for even amidst the falling snow it was not long past mid-day, and the activities of daily commerce yet continued with the usual bustle along the harbor of New York.

Away from the main thoroughfares, however, the side streets were quiet, for those residents who had no immediate need to venture out were content to remain inside their houses upon such a frosty day.

It was before one such abode — a plain and modest house — that Ethan Shaye drew his horse to a halt, the soft crunch of snow beneath the animal's hooves the only sound heralding their arrival. Ethan dismounted and tethered his horse, but, as the area was unfamiliar to him, he surveyed both the surroundings and the house with cautious interest as he ascended the front steps.

His knock upon the door was met with the sound of scurrying footsteps within the house — testament to an occupant who was undoubtedly happy to have the monotony of a snowbound day alleviated by an unanticipated visitor.

So it was that the door was opened eagerly . . . and by a young lady who gasped in surprise upon beholding the visitor, for she recognized him at once, though his presence was entirely unexpected.

"Why— Mr. Shaye!" Polly Jameson exclaimed in astonishment. "I— I mean . . . *Lieutenant* Shaye," she corrected herself, reddening a bit self-consciously.

Ethan gave her a nod. "'Tis Captain now," he acknowledged with a smile.

"Oh!" Polly's eyes widened at this news. "I— I did not know that you . . . that is, how did you . . . I mean—", she faltered, not yet recovered from her astonishment at seeing him, though she finally collected herself and opened the door wider. "I mean to say, do come in."

Ethan stomped the snow from his boots and removed his hat before entering the house.

Once inside, he found himself in a small, rectangular hall, simply furnished, with a narrow staircase upon one wall and a fire crackling upon the hearth-wall opposite. A book lay open upon the chair before the fire, where Polly had undoubtedly left it in haste in her eagerness to respond to the knock upon the door.

"'Tis not our house, you know," she explained as she closed the door behind Ethan. "Our father leases it from his acquaintance. He means for us to stay here until the war is over."

"Is your father at home?" Ethan asked.

Polly shook her head. "No, though I expect he shall return shortly." A thoughtful frown creased Polly's brow as she studied Ethan for a long moment. "Is— is it my father you have come to see?" she asked hesitantly, as if she did not think that to be the case.

Ethan gave a slight shake of his head. He paused, then put forth, "I . . . would speak with Constance, if she would see me."

"If she would see you?" Polly repeated. She stared at Ethan incredulously. "Do you think she would not see you?"

Ethan made no immediate response, and Polly shook her head again. "There are a great many things I do not know or understand, Captain Shaye, and I am sure that I cannot speak on Constance's behalf. We must let her decide whether or not she will speak with you. Come, I will take you to her."

And taking up a chamberstick from beside the door, Polly beckoned Ethan to follow her up the narrow staircase.

As Ethan mounted the steps, however, he chanced to glance back down into the hall below, and what he saw there gave him pause, for though the room was deserted of occupants, he caught a glimpse of a figure in a doorway beside the fireplace. The figure was silent and still and half-hidden by shadows, but neither did it scurry away upon being sighted. Indeed, it was a figure Ethan recognized, even amidst the obscurity of the darkened doorway, and he tarried a moment upon the stair.

"Jenny."

As Ethan spoke her name, Jenny took a step forward through the doorway into the hall. Though she must remain silent, her eyes were bright and her mouth curved upward into a smile as she nodded to Ethan. He smiled back at her and gave her a nod in return — a wordless exchange that nevertheless conveyed a message of respect and understanding between them.

CONSTANCE SAT ALONE BEFORE THE fire in the little upstairs room that she and her sister had fashioned into a sitting room for themselves. She had some sewing in hand, though in truth her needlework was progressing slowly, for she had been at it a while, and her thoughts kept straying to daydreams and reveries, as is apt to happen upon a winter day. She gave a start, therefore, when her sister's voice abruptly called her out of her meditation.

"Constance!"

The door opened and Polly entered the room, keeping one hand upon the latch as she closed the door behind her. Her eyes were bright with excitement, though she kept her tone deliberately even as she addressed her sister:

"Constance— there is a gentleman here to see you. A captain."

Constance stared at her sister, caught entirely off-guard, both by Polly's entrance and by her announcement.

"A — a captain?" Constance ventured, bewildered and flustered. "Is it one of our father's acquaintances? I — I do not— oh!" she drew in a sharp breath, for Polly had quietly loosed the door latch, allowing the door to open upon the unanticipated visitor without.

Constance's sewing slid from her knee as she slowly rose to her feet. "Ethan," she whispered, quite overcome.

As Ethan stepped forth into the room, Polly slipped out the door, pulling it closed behind her.

A stillness enveloped the room as Ethan and Constance beheld one another, each unconscious of anything except the other's presence. Neither one spoke for a long moment; indeed, words would have been inadequate.

When at last Ethan did speak, his tone was low and conveyed a depth of meaning beyond the words he uttered. "Constance . . . I am pleased to see that you are faring well."

Constance's gaze turned thoughtful, and she tilted her head slightly to one side in the manner that was so familiar to Ethan, which he had first observed in the garret, long ago.

"You . . . you have been made a captain?" Constance ventured. She smiled softly. "I am very glad of it. 'Tis well-deserved, truly."

Ethan acknowledged this commendation with a nod, as Constance went on:

"But how did you— I mean— this city is under British authority — how did you . . .?"

There was a hint of a twinkle in Ethan's eye as he related, "I . . . obtained a pass."

"Oh." A wisp of a knowing smile played about Constance's lips. "Well . . . do not tell me how you 'obtained' it. I would rather not know."

The warmth of their smiles made plain their happiness at this familiar exchange.

"I must leave the city by sunset," Ethan imparted, setting his hat upon a chair near the door, "but . . . I wanted to bring these to you." And he stepped forward, reaching into his coat pocket, from which he withdrew a small packet of folded papers. He extended them to Constance.

Constance glanced down at the papers then back at Ethan again, her expression puzzled.

But Ethan made no explanation, only gave a nod toward the papers, indicating to Constance that she was to take them.

Reaching slowly forward, Constance took the folded papers from his hand. She looked at them curiously, for she truly had not an idea of what they could be. There were two pages, each folded into a quartered rectangle, neither bearing any distinguishable exterior markings, though one was discernibly wrinkled and worn.

As there was no directive as to which she was to open first, Constance set the worn page upon the bench behind her and, turning her attention to the other paper, glanced once more at Ethan before she set about unfolding it, her movements tentative and uncertain. In holding the page open before her, she did not immediately comprehend what it was, though she could see that it was a document of some kind, for her eye was immediately drawn to a signature and seal near the bottom. Most of the page was covered in writing, though there was a simple, hand-drawn diagram at the bottom, flanked by coordinates. As Constance began to read the words upon the page, however, she came to perceive what it was she was holding, and she gave a sudden gasp of disbelief.

"Why— why—," she stammered, "'tis a deed. 'Tis the deed to my father's house and land in Pennsylvania." She looked up at Ethan searchingly, struggling to comprehend. "It . . . it bears my father's name."

Ethan nodded. "Aye," he affirmed quietly.

Constance stared at him, speechless and quite overwhelmed. She shook her head, unable to fully grasp the situation. "I . . . I don't understand. How did you — the rebels seized the land, took possession of my father's house — how could you have come into possession of—?"

Ethan gave her a rueful smile. "Do not worry," he assured her, "'twas legitimately obtained. My commanding officers were in a generous frame of mind after—," his words trailed off into silence, for he did not wish to bring up a subject which was sure to be painful for the young lady standing before him. "At any rate," he continued, "'tis rightfully your father's property, regardless of the war's progression."

Constance was yet overcome. "I . . . I do not know what to say."

"Do not say anything!" Ethan's tone was suddenly gruff, and his brow furrowed into a sullen scowl as he turned away. "I am not seeking your gratitude. If this brings you any measure of happiness . . . that is enough. I am . . . merely returning to your family what is rightfully theirs."

Ethan fell into a brooding silence, but Constance's eyes were shining with warmth as she looked at him.

"Ethan," she ventured softly after a moment.

He turned.

Constance continued, "You . . . you did not turn Anne over to the authorities."

There followed another silence before Ethan finally gave a shake of his head. "No," he conceded. "Her husband knows what she has done. It is enough."

"I think that . . . her husband does not know of *all* that she has done," Constance pressed him gently. "You did not tell him everything."

There was a pause. Then— "No," Ethan accorded. "Joshua Porter is a good man. He has endured enough. As for his wife— she will not stray again."

Constance said no more upon the subject, but though she knew that Ethan did not wish her to express her gratitude, the way she looked upon him assuredly imparted far more than that sentiment.

Indeed, their gazes lingered again across the silence. So many words unspoken.

It was only after some moments that Constance came to recall the other paper, sitting folded upon the bench behind her. Turning slightly toward the bench, she exchanged one page for the other and took the worn paper in hand. She had not examined it closely before, but now, as she looked at it, something stirred within her. And as she began unfolding the paper, a change came over her . . . her face paled and her fingers began to tremble. For indeed, this page was suddenly familiar in her hand, and even before she had fully laid eyes upon its contents, Constance uttered a faint cry, a stifled sob.

So altered was her state that Ethan became alarmed and hastened to her. When Constance looked up into his face, he saw that her eyes had filled with tears.

"'Tis your letter," Constance whispered, "from the garret." Ashamed of her tears, she lowered her eyes, glancing down again at the letter in her hand. And though she had not held it nor looked upon its familiar, fading words for months, her eye fell instinctively upon one line near the bottom of the page.

Ethan did not need to look to see which line it was that drew Constance's eye. He had seen her gazing upon it before. He bent his head to hers. "Constance," he whispered, and Constance's heart began to throb, sending her blood coursing through her veins, for she felt Ethan's hand soft upon her cheek.

"You know why I had to leave the garret before you awoke," Ethan murmured. "If I had waited — if I had seen you again — I could not have left. We both knew that I could not stay longer."

Constance's eyes remained yet averted, but though she remained silent, her mind was awash in undimmed memories and the acute awareness of Ethan's touch.

She felt his hand slide gently from her cheek and alight upon her shoulder.

Constance lifted her eyes as Ethan's fingers continued to move softly, coming to rest just below her neck. Ethan frowned darkly as he looked upon the small scar etched there upon Constance's skin.

"I shall never forgive myself . . . for that," Ethan murmured, ". . . for what you have endured."

But Constance gave a slight shake of her head. "'Twas not your doing," she avowed with conviction. "Besides," she added with a soft smile, "'tis no more than the scar you bear." And she allowed her eye to fall upon the spot where, beneath the layers of Ethan's outer garments, she knew him to bear a scar more substantial than her own.

Ethan made no reply, only continued frowning absently and turned away. It was evident his mind was preoccupied. He began to pace the room. "Your father must wait until the war is over, before he takes possession of the house and land again. 'Twould not be wise to do so beforehand. But then—," Ethan yet would not meet Constance's eye, "then you can go back there . . . back to the home you love . . . to all the places that are dear to you. Of course—," he paused in his step and turned to face Constance, "I myself have a nice piece of land in North Carolina, left me by my father. 'Tis vast acreage — on a river, with rolling hills and green pastures and a very pretty house of red brick. You may well take a fancy to it . . . should you ever be inclined to leave your father's house and take the name of Shaye."

A vast silence fell over the room.

For Constance, breath and time were at once suspended. It was as if her heart both stopped and soared in the same moment. The room about her became enveloped in a dizzying haze. She could not speak; she could not think. She could not avert her eyes from Ethan's.

"But I— I— you—," Constance faltered piteously when she at last attempted to make reply. "You— you said that you . . . would never take a wife. You said that . . . a soldier ought not to marry . . ."

Her voice trailed off, for even as she spoke, Ethan crossed to her and stood before her — his nearness and the tenderness with which he looked upon her rendering her again speechless.

"I hope that you will forgive such foolish words," Ethan said, "spoken long ago by one who regrets that ever he uttered them. However—," he continued, smiling at her very affectionately, even as a twinkle lit his eye, "I seem to recall that a certain young lady likewise expressed dismay at the lot of a woman who finds herself so unfortunate as to be bound to a soldier."

Constance did not sever her soft, ardent gaze. "I . . . I shouldn't mind if—," tears welled again in her eyes, "—if it was you." Her voice broke with a sob as the tears streamed down her face. She shook her head helplessly. "I . . . I cannot seem to stop loving you . . . even when we were parted . . . even when I had no hope of seeing you again."

And she said no more, for Ethan drew her into his arms.

"I want you at my side every day," Ethan murmured, ". . . in my arms every night."

Constance closed her eyes, savoring every word, every sensation. "Do not leave me . . . not for one moment," she whispered fervently.

"Have no fear," Ethan reassured her. "I shall not leave this house without you." He shifted slightly back, that he might look into her face. "And I promise you . . . we shall not be parted more. Neither shall you suffer the grief and uncertainty of being the wife of a spy."

Constance stared at him, trying to comprehend what he might mean. She shook her head. "You must not give up your cause," she declared. "It is dear to you. I will not let you do so!"

Ethan smiled at her. "I am not giving up the Patriots' cause. I am merely taking on a new role in support of it. I am a captain now — I shall take charge of a company of men. General Washington has approved my request . . . to be transferred to North Carolina."

Constance's eyes widened.

"The war has not reached North Carolina as of yet," Ethan continued. "There is no standing army there. I will be responsible for assembling a provisional company and enlisting recruits. My commission shall allow me to reside upon my own land, in my own house . . . in *our* house."

Upon hearing his words, Constance's eyes shone, her countenance was radiant. Indeed, her whole world was aglow.

Ethan smiled upon her fondly. "I saw Jenny downstairs," he mused. "She will undoubtedly be grieved that I am taking you so far away. She will miss you greatly."

Constance nodded. "'Tis true," she acknowledged wistfully. "And how I shall miss her! We have never really been apart. But . . . she is needed here. She must stay and look after Polly." She smiled absently as she added, "Polly does need some looking-after, I daresay." And she lapsed into silence, undoubtedly thinking upon her spirited young sister.

"Constance—," Ethan gently summoned her from her reverie, his countenance reflecting some concern. "I fear it will be difficult for you — to leave your family and your home . . . your mother's grave. But if you do . . . if you come with me . . . I swear I will love you, protect you, care for you all the days of my life."

And Constance did not waver at his words, but smiled up at him, her soft eyes filled with warmth and tenderness. "Ethan . . . I give myself to you with my whole heart. All of those things — my home, my family, my memories of my mother — I shall not be leaving them behind, for they are here," and she placed her hand gently over her heart. "But . . . wherever *you* are on this earth — and forever after — that is where I ever wish to be."

"It appears the snow is abating," Matthew Jameson announced as he removed his snow-dusted cloak and bent to receive the greeting kiss his youngest daughter bestowed upon his weathered cheek. "The sky will be clear within an hour," he predicted, crossing to the fire, "though it is un- likely the sun will break through yet today." He glanced about the small room, as if he expected to see someone other than his daughter upon the premises. "There is a horse tethered outside," he put to her as he stretched his hand toward the fire's warmth.

"Aye," Polly affirmed quietly.

Dr. Jameson glanced at her, sensing that she had further knowledge of the situation. "Whose is it?" he pressed, puzzled at her reticence.

Polly hesitated. "It . . . it belongs to Captain Shaye. He has come to see Constance. He is upstairs with her now."

Matthew Jameson's brow knit in cogitation as he glanced at the stairs. "Captain Shaye?" he pondered aloud, then shook his head. "I do not recall any acquaintance with a Captain Shaye."

"Sit down before the fire, Father," Polly gently bade him, removing her book from the seat of the chair. "Your boots are wet with snow. Sit here . . . and I will tell you about Captain Shaye."

Dr. Jameson stared a moment at his daughter, for her manner — quiet and deliberate — was out of the ordinary and bespoke of a gravity to that which she would impart. Nevertheless, he took his seat before the fire as he had been bidden.

Polly knelt before him and began to pull his boots off. She worked methodically, as if her mind was upon other matters, and when she spoke, it was yet with steadfast calmness, keeping her eye fixed upon her task.

"We met Captain Shaye at our sister's house in Virginia. He is an acquaintance of Mr. Porter's." She paused. "He is an officer in the Continental Army."

Matthew Jameson's eyes flashed. "Indeed?"

Polly lifted her eyes to meet her father's. "'Twas he who saved Constance's life."

There followed a silence, as Dr. Jameson internalized this circumstance.

"Well," he said at last, his tone resolved, "I had best present myself to him, then, and express my gratitude."

He started to rise from his chair, but Polly hastily grasped his arm, rising to her feet as well.

"Nay, Father, do not go up there; not yet."

Dr. Jameson gave his daughter a questioning look, plainly unsettled by the situation.

The color rose in Polly's cheeks. "I— I have not yet told you all that you need to know," she stammered.

Her father frowned and sank back into his chair.

Polly took in a deep breath; then, bending, she collected her father's boots and set them upon the hearth.

Her father waited in expectant silence.

Polly lingered before the fire, and when she spoke again, she did not turn to meet her father's eye. "I . . . I think that Constance is in love with

Captain Shaye. I . . . think that he came here to . . . that is . . . I think that . . . Constance is going to go away with him," Polly summoned the courage to turn and face her father as she concluded, "—and would be his wife."

It was with some apprehension that Polly regarded her father's countenance, for she knew what she imparted would not be met with indifference. Indeed, Matthew Jameson's visage well-reflected his change of demeanor, and his eyes flamed with indignation.

"It is inconceivable," he admonished, his greying brow furrowed darkly. "That she should— it is out of the question that I would permit such a—," he broke off and glanced warningly at his youngest daughter. "Take care, young lady, that you are not raising unfounded conjectures which are bound to create discord."

Polly shook her head in some dismay. Kneeling again before her father's chair, she took his hand. "Father, I beg you not to be hasty in your judgement. I love my sister dearly — you know that I do — and as much as it pains me to think that we would be separated from her, I would yet defend her choice. I would appeal most fervently to your sensibilities, as well as to your sympathy. For surely you cannot judge a man's worth merely by his political loyalties. After all . . . would you have consented to give Constance to a Loyalist— a Loyalist who would have done her harm?"

It was a question of great substance and great consequence, and Matthew Jameson's silence bespoke of its significance.

Polly continued, her tone gently appealing. "Constance is of age . . . she does not need your consent to marry. But she would assuredly seek your blessing."

Matthew Jameson yet frowned obstinately. "It is out of the question. What man would sanction the marriage of his daughter to a complete stranger? I know nothing of this Captain Shaye."

Polly's eyes flashed with sudden indignation. "Indeed, how should you know of him?" she demanded. "How should it be Constance's fault that you do not know him? You were not there! You sent us away those many months!"

Dr. Jameson was not unmoved by this emotional declamation, and though he gave no indication of relenting, Polly detected a slight mitigation in the gruffness of her father's tone when he put to her a question:

"And what do *you* know of this Captain Shaye?"

Polly did not answer at once, and when she did so, it was quietly: "In truth, I know him not well at all," she admitted. "I have had but little discourse with him while we were in Virginia. But he is well-bred by his manner and speech, and able-bodied — for indeed, he not only saved Constance's life, but once, upon the river, he saved mine, too . . . and Anne's. Truly, we are indebted to him." And here she paused, shifting her gaze away from her father's face, staring into the distance, into the depth of her memory. "What do I know of him? I know that . . . that I might never have seen Constance again if he hadn't rescued her on that last day — the last day I saw him in Virginia — that terrible day when we nearly lost Constance forever. And I know that when he brought her into the house afterward, he carried her in his arms, and . . . before he left, he looked back in such a way . . . And I know that when Constance at last awoke, the first words she uttered were his name. And I know that when we told her he was gone, her eyes filled with tears of such anguish as I have never seen . . ." Polly's voice trailed off, but when she looked up at her father, her tone took on a new warmth. "I know, too, that my sister Constance is a person of virtue and goodness, and that the man upon whom she chooses to bestow her love must be worthy indeed."

And as Polly looked earnestly into her father's face, her father turned his own head away; indeed, he was quite overcome, not only by the eloquence of his daughter's words, but also by her outward appearance. For in Polly's earnest appeal, her father had seen something in her countenance that he had never seen there before; it was something in her expression, perhaps a certain gentle curve of her mouth or a light in her eye that was so very like her mother's . . . her mother whom he had loved and whom Polly had never known.

There was a very long silence, and when Matthew Jameson looked again upon his youngest daughter, Polly saw that there were tears brimming in his eyes, and her own eyes filled with tears, for she knew then that he would give her sister his blessing.

"Dearest Father—," Polly rose, and, perching upon her father's knee as she had done when she was a child, she put her arms about him as they smiled at one another through their tears. "You must accustom yourself to having only one daughter at home. I think that from this night forward, 'twill be only me for you and Jenny to look after. But do not worry, Father," and her smile conveyed as much affection as her tone. "When the time comes for me to marry . . . then 'twill be I who shall look after Jenny and you."